PRAISE FOR
CYNTHIA VOIGT'S
JACKAROO:

"Gwyn, an innkeeper's daughter, pities the desperately poor and understands their need to believe in the legendary Jackaroo, righter of wrongs. The girl dismisses the stories of the highwayman giving to the needy, enraging the nobles, as myths. But when the innkeeper sends Gwyn and his bondsman, Burl, on a journey to serve a lord and his son, the experience convinces her that Jackaroo had been real if he is no longer. . . . Burl and the other characters play intriguing parts in the swift, many-layered, tense story."
—*Publishers Weekly*

"An intense and elegantly written historical adventure-romance set in 'a distant time and place.' . . . *Jackaroo* will stimulate the imagination and make readers marvel at Voigt's creative genius. She presents a carefully designed, mystery-filled plot which once again illustrates her abilities as a master storyteller. Characters are somewhat reluctant to reveal themselves—but this is a most appropriate style for a tale of dangerous and uncertain times."
—*School Library Journal*

"... a moving and engrossing story.... As in all of Cynthia Voigt's books, the style is fluid and consistent with the personalities of her characters; the setting is evoked through skillfully crafted description; the situations speak directly to the human condition.... This is a fully realized country—so convincingly delineated that it seems as if it had once existed only to be rediscovered by a master storyteller."

—*The Horn Book Magazine*

"Cynthia Voigt moves into the romantic/medieval milieu in a tale that uses the theme of a defender of the poor, and she does it with great success."

—*BCCB*

"... a fine strong fantasy.... The story of how [Gwyn] uses wit and courage to save herself and her people makes an adventure as deeply satisfying as a timeworn fairy tale."

—*Wilson Library Bulletin*

"Readers can't help but tune in to Voigt's slices of wisdom, so deftly worn into the story fabric.... Voigt lets her readers know that love must carry the seal of loyalty, otherwise it's love that's hollow."

—*The Christian Science Monitor*

A Kingdom Book

Jackaroo

Other POINT SIGNATURE
paperbacks you will enjoy:

Local News
by Gary Soto

Make Lemonade
by Virginia Euwer Wolff

Orfe
by Cynthia Voigt

Plain City
by Virginia Hamilton

Toning the Sweep
by Angela Johnson

POINT • SIGNATURE

Jackaroo

Cynthia Voigt

SCHOLASTIC INC.
New York Toronto London Auckland Sydney

ISBN 0-590-48595-4

Copyright © 1985 by Cynthia Voigt. Map copyright © 1985 by Walter Voigt. All rights reserved. Published by Scholastic Inc., 555 Broadway, New York, NY 10012, by arrangement with Atheneum, an imprint of Macmillan Publishing Company. POINT is a registered trademark of Scholastic Inc.

12 11 10 9 8 7 6 5 4 3   6 7 8 9/9 0/0

Printed in U.S.A.   01

First Scholastic printing, April 1995

FOR PENNY AND SUSAN
and Good Times Remembered

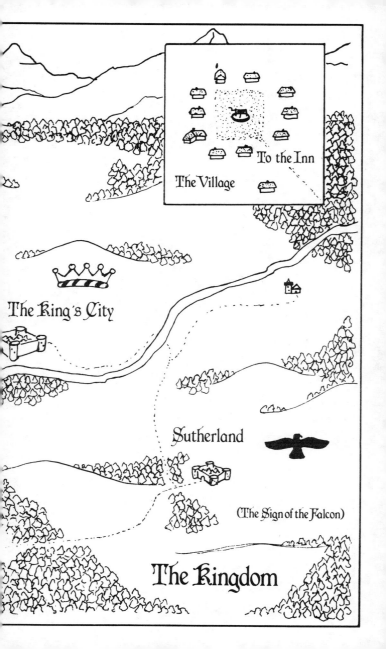

The Village

To the Inn

The King's City

Sutherland

(The Sign of the Falcon)

The Kingdom

 Contents

Part One

The Innkeeper's Daughter

One

GWYN STOOD crowded in among the women. She held the hood of her cloak close around her head, covering her hair, shadowing her face. The basket she kept at her feet. Like the others, she kept her long dark cloak close around her, as if she too were cold.

Tad moved restlessly at her side, and she placed a hand on his shoulder, warning him without a word. She wished he had been willing to stay outside and play with the other children. But he stuck close to her.

They had been standing so for over an hour now. Gwyn's eyes smarted. The long, low-ceilinged room was stuffy. While the heat from the fireplace, back behind the polished wooden table, did not penetrate the length of the room, its smoke did. The door beside the fireplace was closed. Closed also was the door behind them, through which they had entered. The little windows up high on the walls were shuttered. The air in the room smelled of wood smoke and wet woollen cloaks drying out, of bodies gone long without washing, of damp hay spread over the dirt floor.

Low conversations flowed all around her, swirling like gusts of snow. The air in the room grew warmer, which increased the odors of smoke and bodies. Tad put his face in against her arm, burying his nose. Gwyn employed an old trick: she closed off her nose from inside, as if it were stuffed up with a cold, and breathed through her mouth. With her nose closed off she could not taste the stench.

Men didn't come to the Doling Room. The shame would be too great for a man to carry. So the women carried it, Gwyn thought. It was a hard thing to be a woman, her mother had often told her. Looking around her, Gwyn could agree. Why then should she marry? Because, her mother would say, there was nothing else for her. "Would you live always at the Inn, serving in another woman's house? Would you go with a widower and raise another woman's children and your own disinherited? Or live alone, like Old Megg? Or maybe you'll go to serve a Lord, perhaps, you with your proud tongue." Her mother, Gwyn knew, gave practical advice. When winter broke, her parents would look about to see who had a good holding, good enough to last out the lean years. They would announce her dowry of four gold coins and wait to choose among those who might come forward. Cam, she knew, would not come forward.

In the spring, then, she would have to say yes to some man, or let Da announce her intention never to marry. One or the other, because service in a Lord's house was unimaginable. One or the other was her choice, and she liked neither; but she could do nothing about the hardness of that.

Gwyn kept her eyes on her basket; she didn't want to catch anyone's attention. There was no one here to recognize her, the Innkeeper's daughter from the Ram's Head, but between the bitter envy of those whom hunger held close and the danger of traveling without a man's protection, she preferred to be unknown.

Women of all ages had gathered in the low room, each

bringing her basket to be filled. Some were young and straight, some older and beginning to be bent under the years, a few held infants, a few were swollen with unborn children. All—young or old, fair or plain—had hungry faces: eyes dull, skin stretched pale over hollow cheeks. All clutched their cloaks close and pushed as near as they dared toward the fire. And well might they seek warmth, Gwyn thought to herself, for hunger adds teeth to the bite of winter. She hung back, keeping Tad with her, for their cloaks concealed warm sheepskin jackets and heavy boots, under which they each wore two pairs of thick woollen stockings. In the same way, their hoods hid round cheeks made rosy by the long walk and their lowered lids covered bright eyes. It was not their fault that their family's luck held good; but this was not the place to display good fortunes. With nothing else to do, Gwyn eavesdropped on the conversations around her.

"Steward's late."

"And would you hurry out of a warm bed on this day?"

"Osh aye, and didn't I just do that, with the mouths to feed."

"Steward'll have servants to make him his porridge. Or bread more likely. Steward'll have fine bread and rich cheeses."

"And soft blankets to pull up close around his chin while the servants stoke the fire."

"The Earl keeps his men well, they say."

"Well, but not too well, is what I hear. It'll be down comforters."

"—Could the Earl's storerooms still be full? There's more come each Doling Day."

"—More soldiers out on the King's Ways, think you?"

"Because there are more thieves out. Come hunger, come thieves."

"—One to be hung, as I hear, a young man—a highwayman, they say, with a way of taking the purses off of wealthy travelers."

A quick attentive quiet all around greeted those words. Then:

"Young, was he? And handsome?"

"As I heard at market."

"In the south, he was, and he rode the River Way. It's Earl Sutherland's men who took him."

The name no voice would speak rang loud in the thick air.

"Are things so bad in the south, then?"

"Osh aye, things are bad everywhere."

"Worse in the south, as I hear. So long as the troubles stay south, I'll sleep contented."

"The old Earl Sutherland had too many sons—"

"—The sons have too many soldiers—"

"Is he dark or fair, this young highwayman?"

"Hair dark as night."

"Gold as the sun, I heard."

"—The new Earl's a greedy man, as I hear—"

"A greedy man should not have brothers." Somebody laughed, without humor.

"And likes his wine more than he should."

"He'll die before his time then."

"And leave a son too young."

"The king'll have to name a regent then, unless the new Earl's wife—?"

"As vain and greedy as her husband."

"Such Lords have a way of dying before their times, while their Stewards get fat."

"And the brother takes the title—"

"If there's no son—"

"The sons of such men die in their cradles—"

"Osh aye, I'd never dare to take a meal in a castle. Better my own cabbage soup without fear."

"Such things don't happen among the people," someone agreed.

"The Lords and the law don't permit it. A man must name his heir before the given time. You'd think the Lords would govern themselves as wisely."

"Whoever said the Lords were wise?"

"That same man who claimed that pigs would fly."

"One of the Lords that was, wasn't it?" a bitter voice asked.

That was a dangerous envy to be spoken aloud, that envy of the Lords, warm and safe in their castles, well fed, with soldiers to protect them. Any one of the cloaked women in the room might be Steward's spy. Somebody spoke loud into the silence: "They'll be journeying him around then, this highwayman."

"They'll wait until the weather breaks. They wouldn't want him to take a chill and die before his time. We'll not see him until spring."

"Some men they never do hang, you know." A voice creaking with age spoke. "Some have friends to rescue them—"

"He rode alone, they say."

"And no sign of his booty about him?"

"No sign. No sign about him."

They all wondered, silently.

"In my grandmother's mother's time . . ."

"Osh aye, now, those were bad times. Needy times."

"When the King as then was began the Doling Rooms—"

"Men with hope of food don't follow a highwayman into the forest—"

"They hanged enough, then."

"But never *him*, not as I heard."

This caused another uneasy silence, a fretful quiet that pooled out. They all looked toward the door by the fireplace, as if expecting it to—at that precise guilty moment—swing open and fill with men.

"Where would we be without the old tales." The creaking voice behind Gwyn spoke again. She turned to look at the speaker, a bent old woman whose white hair coiled in thin braids over her ears, whose cloak hung in folds over her body. "Tales of elvish folk, flying through the air—"

"Aye, and dwarves mining under the mountains for stones as big as my fist." A voice answered laughing, from the front of the room.

"As if there ever were a man could do such things."

"Or even want to."

"And never grow any older, not in the hundred years."

There was none not of their kind to hear them, but still, newly hasty, they spun the room round with stories of disbelief. Gwyn knew, thus, that they must believe, or maybe merely hope, and she couldn't blame them. There was so little else in their lives to hope for.

Beside her, Tad tried to burrow his nose in under her arm and she elbowed him in protest. "It smells in here," he complained up at her. Gwyn felt the rustle of interest among their nearest neighbors. She could have smacked him.

"Hold your tongue," she whispered. His expression turned sullen. He was nine now, too old to whine the way he did. But Tad was the baby of the family, and spoiled.

The damage had been done; she felt hostility around her. "The Innkeeper's daughter, from the Ram's Head." She heard herself identified. "The unmarried daughter."

"That's the only son."

"Too good to play with ours then, is he?"

"Too weak and mollycoddled to stand the cold, more likely."

Tad's cheeks burned red, with temper probably.

"Do even the inns lack for food then?"

"No, no. Rest easy, they feed Old Megg. The Innkeeper at the Ram's Head lives like a Lord, fattening on the lean years. He knows no lack."

"It's the youngest daughter came before. She's to marry her blacksmith."

"Unless she's taken sick. And she has a burning not a wedding." The voice didn't sound displeased by this possibiltiy.

They could say what they wanted, Gwyn decided. She brushed back the heavy hood and looked boldly around her at curious eyes. Besides, they'd say it anyway. And she didn't blame them, she thought, as pity closed its hand around her heart.

The crone behind her spoke up again. "Osh aye, it's never the child to blame for who her father is."

Gwyn's head turned. Murmurs of agreement met that statement, but she would not hear people suggest such things about her father.

Little dark eyes met hers and one eyelid lowered slowly: Why should the woman wink at her, Gwyn thought furiously. The crone added then, "For good or ill, it's not the child's doing."

Gwyn stared at the aged face, the mouth sunken into folds of skin, the hooked nose, the body bent so badly that the old woman had to tilt her face sideways to look at Gwyn while the voices around took up the idea and carried it away.

"Nor a woman to blame for her man."

"She's in the right about that, no woman to blame for the good or ill of her man."

"More ill than good is what I've seen."

Gwyn thanked the old woman with a smile. Then she whispered to Tad, "Ask if she'd like you to hold her basket while we wait."

He shook his head.

"Do as I say."

He shook his head more vehemently. His hood fell off and his bright red curls, looking as warm as fire, ruffled as if a wind had blown over them.

"Or I'll tell Da you wouldn't play with the others," she threatened. That wasn't fair, she knew. The boys would have pummeled him, if their mother's feelings gave any hint of how the rumors ran. Still, if she'd been Tad, she'd have stayed outside—and given as good as she got.

Sulky, he moved over to speak to the old woman. She shook her head, holding the handle tight in gnarled and knitted hands. But she pushed over to stand behind Gwyn, following Tad's path through the crowd of bodies. "Steward was late last fortnight too," she said, to nobody in particular.

"Because he doesn't have the long walk back to his own fire."

"—Women who live in the city should let the others go first—"

"Until the Lords say it has to be done that way I'll not—"

"What brings you to the Earl's Doling Room, Innkeeper's daughter?" the crone asked.

"Da told us to," Tad answered her shortly.

Gwyn resisted the urge to kick her brother. Instead, she explained more politely, "Lord Hildebrand's messenger came around at the start of winter. He told us his master's store-rooms were not over full. There are many of us at the Inn to share out the journey, so Da decided we should come to the Earl, who has more."

She kept her voice low but the ears around her listened to her words.

"You'll have a long journey back," the crone observed.

"Yes," Gwyn agreed, because it was the truth.

She looked again to the door behind the table, at last becoming impatient. She knew that many of the women in the room were also thinking of the long walk home, to get back to their families before dark fell. Even to the poor and especially for women, there were dangers—from thieves, and after dark, from the soldiers too. They were right. The women from the city, which lay within circling stone walls just beyond the Doling Room, ought to let those with longer journeys go first when the Steward came. They would not, she knew, even though they ought. Three hungry winters made everybody less willing to look to her neighbor. And the dangers of city streets were worse, she'd heard. A man might die between his own house and his neighbor's, killed for the clothing he wore. The people of the cities suffered worse in lean years, when fevers came, when the land was uneasy. If she were a man, and a Lord, she thought angrily, she'd find a way to keep the people safe. But there was no way to change the way things were, any more than you could change the weather. All she could do was get home safely and advise Da that they shouldn't send again to the Doling Room, even for Old Megg. That was all she could do, just see that the people of the Ram's Head kept safe.

"They say the Innkeeper at the Ram's Head pours a fair measure," the crone said to her.

"He does," Gwyn agreed, thinking of her father's heavy voice and the stolid temper that belied his red hair.

"Your sister is dark."

"Like my mother. Only my brother and I have Da's hair," Gwyn said. Her hand went to the braids coiled over her ears, in the fashion identical to every other woman in the room. "And mine is growing darker. But do you know our father?"

"I knew him," the old woman answered. "Long ago."

Gwyn was about to ask her about that, but the door at the front of the room clanged open, giving them a glimpse of low gray skies before it filled with men. The entire long room fell silent. Every eye in the room watched the Steward enter, peel off his heavy gloves, take off his cloak and hang it over the back of the chair. He turned to the fire and rubbed his hands before its warmth. He stood there with his back to them, in leather leggings and a blue woollen overshirt belted about the waist. Three soldiers entered after him, in shorter cloaks and high boots, their swords sheathed at their sides. They lined up behind him as he sat at the table and opened up his long book.

The open door let a blast of icy air blow down the length of the room, while servants in sheepskin wraps hauled in the great baskets of turnips and the barrows of grain. There was no sound in the room now except the scrape of feet and the drag of baskets. A baby fussed somewhere ahead of Gwyn and was quickly put to its mother's breast to quiet it. The silence held itself tense while the Steward, without looking up at the crowd of women, slowly turned the pages of his book. He lifted his head once, to call for a cup of hot wine, which one of the servants scurried away to fetch to him. Slowly, the Steward sharpened his quills with a little silver knife, laying them out in a row before him, ready to hand. He uncapped the jug of black ink. He put beside this two thin sticks of charcoal. The soldiers stood motionless behind him, their eyes fixed above the heads of the women, their hands ready at sword hilts.

As if, Gwyn thought angrily, anyone in this room would be a danger, all women and weak from long hunger, all standing in patient and humble obedience until they could step forward to be given the food that would keep their families alive for the next two weeks. She was shamed to be here, standing so. She would rather be home in the kitchen, under the lash of her mother's voice. Even knowing it was for Old Megg, not for themselves that they came, she was shamed.

Gwyn and Tad waited, as silent as everyone else. The men at the front of the room might as well have been alone from human company. They could have been standing before a herd of cows, preparing to pour fodder into the troughs. Gwyn felt her throat close up in pity for these women, who had worked —she knew it and their hands and backs showed it—worked so hard for such poor crops, for such long hours, and who were now come hand in hand with hunger and shame because the rains in the spring had been too hard and the summer too hot and dry. Gwyn knew that without the Lords' food, many would die, even more than winter claimed by right. She thought, then, that the women had reason to be grateful.

At last the Steward allowed the women to come forward, one at a time. The servants put into their baskets the measures of grain and the turnips, while the Steward wrote the record into his book. The crowd shuffled forward, in that unquiet silence.

Gwyn move steadily with the crowd and at last stood before the Steward. She identified herself and watched his hands turn the long pages over. Each page was ruled into columns, each column headed with the lines and circles that those who knew could interpret. When he found the column he wanted, his slow quill scratched marks in black ink. Gwyn gave her basket to be filled. Tad stood behind her.

The Steward never looked up once at her, and while she stood there before him she studied the top of his head, where a pink scalp showed through thin blond hair. The firelogs crackled behind him. His pen ceased moving. He reached to dip it into the inkpot. His hands were white, the nails smooth and clean. The Earl's signet was on his finger, the sign of the bear cut deep into the gold. Gwyn's basket was returned to her, heavy now. She and Tad moved out of the room.

She pulled Tad aside by the doorway. For a while he was content to breathe deeply of the clean cold air. Ahead of them, women called their children out of the group now huddled together for warmth, then moved quickly off, looking at the low sky with worried faces. Gwyn too hoped the snow would hold off. The King's Ways were all bordered by rail fences, so you wouldn't get lost in a snow, but they had ten miles to walk, long enough in good weather.

These women had wrapped their felt shoes around with woollen rags and probably lined the inside with straw as well, uncomfortable to walk on, but it gave protection against the cold ground. Unfortunately, when the felt footwear got wet, as theirs had with melting snow while they waited the long time in the Doling Room, their feet would be colder still on the journey home. Gwyn looked down to where her own feet were covered by the cloak, glad her heavy leather boots were hidden.

But why should she feel badly to have warm, dry feet? Or guilty—because she felt guilty too—that she had good fortune and did nothing to share it. Even if she did give her boots away, that would be only one pair of feet, out of the many, kept dry and warm. Only one pair of feet out the many. Still, she half wished she had the heart to give them, even though it would do only a little good.

What her mother would say, though, and her father too if he were told, if she did that!

"Gwyn, let's *go*." Tad pulled at her arm.

Gwyn saw the old woman. The door slammed quickly shut behind her, and she hesitated in the pathway, her basket pulling her body lower, like an aged apple tree over-laden with fruit. "Which way do you take, Granny?" Gwyn asked. The face did not look surprised to see her. "We're going east and could carry your basket."

She smiled up at Gwyn, showing a mouth where few teeth remained. "Osh aye, I'd be glad of the help and of the company," she said. "It's not so far."

"Tad"—Gwyn fixed him with her sternest expression— "you can carry our basket. It's lighter," she added quickly, as he opened his mouth to object

"Let's just get going," he muttered.

Behind them the city walls rose up into the sky, the stone as gray as the clouds. Women and children moved between the oval gatehouses to enter the city through the narrow gate. Thinking of what might lie waiting for them in the narrow, empty streets, Gwyn didn't envy them their briefer journey home.

Two

EARL NORTHGATE'S CITY lay back in the foothills, against the mountains that ringed the northern border of the kingdom. The King's Way went off to the east, down hillsides, then up. Dark figures moved along it. Close to the city, the snow had been packed down by feet and the hooves of horses. It was firm underfoot, but often slippery. Their companion moved with stiff, shuffling steps, her hand on the fence rail, her head weaving from side to side. They walked abreast, Gwyn in the middle, Tad shifting his basket from hand to hand every few steps, glaring up at Gwyn every time he did so. The old woman's basket pulled at Gwyn's shoulders, but she ignored that. The work of the Inn, from currying the horses at the stables to hefting bags of flour up from the cellars, from helping to turn the straw mattresses on the beds to stirring the vats of ale as they brewed, had made her strong and had taught her how to use her strength.

The crone did not speak while she was pulling herself up a slope or creeping cautiously down one. When the ground was level, she talked to them.

"I don't know your name," she asked.

"Gwyn, and this is my brother Tad."

"You'll be eight?" the old woman asked Tad.

"Almost ten," he told her, angry that she had thought him younger than he was.

Gwyn sighed at his rudeness and at his way of resenting truths he did not like. "I'm sixteen."

"Osh aye, you'd better marry soon. With your rich dowry, you'll marry well. Have you been spoken for?"

Gwyn's cheeks flushed. She shook her head. Before Tad could say anything, she asked, "Have you a husband waiting?"

The crone nodded but did not answer, because the Way rose up under their feet again. When she saw how much their companion's steps pained her, Gwyn couldn't be sorry that they were with her, however much time was added to their journey. Sparse trees, bare in winter, marked the hillsides between which they walked. Their branches were mounded with snow, while the pines and spruces held out their white burden, as if offering it from dark, feathery arms. Occasionally, rising smoke showed where a house lay under its heavy snow mantle, or little clusters of houses. The few women still moving along the Way passed them, at a hasty, uneasy pace, looking back, peering ahead.

"Hap was one of the Earl's gamekeepers," the crone told her as the Way leveled. "Before his accident. Now we watch the southern pathway into the Earl's forests, and Hap has permission to set snares so we can live. Come winter, Hap stays abed."

"Granny," Gwyn said, "my father had a brother had a friend . . ."

"That's Hap. Aye, that's my Hap."

"They say—my mother says—he could dance the legs off a rabbit."

"And he could," the old woman said. "Not any more, not for years now, longer than you've been alive."

"There was an accident?"

"He was beating out the birds during one of the hunts and a horse rode over him—they say the beast panicked. They brought him home to me, over their shoulders, as soon as they could, but his knee would never mend right again. Winters, the cold pains him."

The Way went down, then, into a little dell where the forest edge made a dark smudge on the smooth white landscape. At the bottom of the slope the old woman stopped. "I go off here."

Following the trail with her eyes, Gwyn could see a low hut backed up under the first of the trees. "Let us come with you," she offered.

"Gwyn!" Tad exploded.

"You can wait here if you like," she snapped at him. If he couldn't see how tired the old woman was, she could. "I don't think there's much danger of wolves this close to the city," she added, as if she were seriously considering that question.

"There's no need. You've helped me along the worst of it." The old woman tried to make peace.

"It's cold," Tad added.

Gwyn just started to move onto the track. "Granny? You had better hold onto my arm," she said.

"Can't we even rest?" Tad demanded.

If it had been just the two of them, Gwyn would have ignored him. But the old woman was breathing hard and looked near the end of her strength. It was probably a quarter mile through deep snow ahead of them. So they dusted the snow off some large rocks and sat down. Tad huddled close to Gwyn, for warmth not affection.

The old woman looked toward the dark forest, spreading like a cloak up over the hills. "We have two apple trees," she said, "and that's good fortune. And a little nanny who gives us milk. Old people"—she smiled at Tad—"are like babies when it comes to milk. So we keep alive through the winter, and it's easier the rest of the year."

"You have no neighbors?"

She shook her head, quickly pulling her hood close again against a rising wind. "Nor children living. Just Hap and me and the dog."

"What do you watch the forest path for?" Gwyn wondered.

"We watch the deer, if they start to come out foraging, rabbits and foxes, grouse and duck. We listen for the wolves, should they start moving down into the forest. We give shelter to soldiers, should need arise, and we know the travelers and hunters who come out and we watch for—anyone who should not be in the forest." She hesitated and looked at the Innkeeper's children and then lowered her voice even though they were alone in the white landscape: "Will he be Jackaroo then, think you?"

"That's a story," Tad told her. "Just an old story."

The old woman didn't argue with him. She looked quickly at Gwyn, whose only thought was of pity for those whose lives were so hard they needed such stories for hope.

"There's no one then, bold enough, brave enough, to stand for the poor when the Lords get greedy, or when times are bad?" the old woman asked them.

Gwyn shrugged.

"And if I told you I had seen him once?"

Gwyn didn't know what to say. She didn't want to hurt the old woman's feelings.

"Osh aye, then, and maybe I didn't; it was so long ago I wasn't even as old as yourself. I never know what's memory and what's dreams, not any more."

"We'd best be on, or it'll be dark before we get back." Gwyn changed the subject. "My mother worries," she explained.

"She always was a worrier, that I remember clearly," the crone said. "And you'll have eight more miles along the

Way for her to worry about, and she'll be right to worry, these days."

They trudged through the snow, Tad behind and the old woman on Gwyn's arm. "You'll have a mug of nanny's warm milk before you go on again," the old woman said to Gwyn. "You'll warm your hands at our fire. And I could find an apple for a boy, even in this winter." She turned to look at Tad, sulking along behind them.

He opened his mouth to tell her that they had baskets of apples in their cellar and bins filled with potatoes and onions, but Gwyn glared at him. He snapped his mouth shut, but he might as well have spoken, Gwyn saw, looking down at the old lady's wrinkled face.

She didn't know what had happened to Tad, to make him the way he was. He was as bad as a Lord, the way he acted. He hadn't been whipped enough, he hadn't been given enough work—but her mother had been so afraid to lose him and Da had given way to her in everything concerning Tad. Well, her father had waited so long for a son and had suffered the loss of two before Tad had been born. Her mother too, although neither of them spoke of it, had watched anxiously over Tad during his first years, keeping him in during bad weather, keeping him away from other children when there was contagion nearby, nursing him night after night when his little body was wracked with the cough that brought up any food he could get down. And Tad, unlike his two brothers, had turned three, then four, and on. Gwyn's hand often itched to smack him as he rested beside a fire while others worked, but she knew why her parents cherished him so. She had lain awake for the three nights her mother keened over the last, dead within a week of being born, dead in the morning who had been alive the night before. She had seen Da's helplessness before her mother's grief, and his own grief, too, with no son to inherit the Inn.

As they came nearer to the little house, Gwyn heard the old woman take in a sharp breath and felt her stumble as she tried to rush forward. Gwyn looked up from the snow underfoot to see a dark shape flat on the snow, motionless. The door of the hut stood open. Smoke rose in a scrawny curl from the chimney. They hurried forward, ignoring Tad's protests.

The dark shape was a dog, a brown and black dog with bones jutting out under his coat and his blood dried on the snow around him. The snow near the door was trampled with footprints. The old woman didn't look twice at the dog, but stumbled up to the door and through it. Gwyn hesitated, looking down at the dead animal while Tad caught up to her.

"Let's go home, Gwyn," he asked, pleading.

Gwyn just stood there. It was a skinny, scruffy dog, and it was hungry before it died.

"Something bad has happened, Gwyn," Tad whispered at her. "We can't go in there."

Gwyn nodded her head, then followed the old woman into the house. She didn't know, really, why she did that. She could have put the basket down on the doorstep and fled. Whatever had happened, there was nothing she could do now.

Inside, the air was chilly. Gwyn saw, in the one room, a fire burned down to bright ashes, a rough table with two stools beside it, a shelf for dishes and mugs, a shelf for food, a ladder leading up to the narrow loft, and a bed beside one wall on which two old people huddled together like children.

Gwyn went to the door and grabbed Tad's arm, pulling him inside. "Just be quiet," she told him. He knew better than to argue with her.

Without looking at the couple on the bed, the old man mumbling into his beard and the old woman rubbing helplessly at his shoulder, Gwyn took some wood from the box and put it over the coals. Calling Tad to help, she blew on it, gently at first and then, when the little flames licked upwards around the logs, more strongly. "You watch that," she told her brother. He didn't answer, but he obeyed her.

Gwyn unpacked the old woman's basket onto the table. As she took out the last turnip, the old woman called her name. She went to stand by the bed.

"Hap?" the old woman croaked.

Gwyn looked into an aged face. The man's hair was whitened, like snow-bearing clouds, and his beard was as tangled as the hair on his head. His eyes were red with weeping and his lips rolled into his mouth the way lips did on the toothless old. He sat hunched forward on the bed, covered by a worn quilt that was as dirty as his hair. His head swung back and forth.

"Gwyn, the Innkeeper's daughter, at the Ram's Head," the old woman said.

The eyes focused on her.

"She walked me home."

The man coughed and wiped his sleeve across his eyes and nose.

"I thank you," he said. He started to move on the bed, to sit up straighter.

"But what happened?" Gwyn asked.

"They came, three of them, and took our nanny—it was just after you had gone." He coughed again. "And the dog followed them out, but he hasn't come back yet. I couldn't close the door against the dog, could I?"

"No, of course not," his wife soothed him.

Gwyn asked, "The soldiers came?"

"I didn't know them," the old man said to his wife. His withered hand moved up to indicate the bottom half of his face, "but they were bearded." They spoke to one another, ignoring Gwyn. "I'm worried about the dog." His voice was rough, like unplaned wood, and he coughed as if his words irritated his throat.

The crone's eyes met Gwyn's and the old head gave a shake. She didn't want him to know yet.

"And how will we live, without the milk nanny gave," he asked, his voice shaking.

"Osh aye," the old woman crooned, nodding her head and getting up, as if that question told her what she waited to hear. "We'll live on the Earl's Dole and apples, and when the thaws come the snares will fill."

"We'll never be able to buy another goat," he reminded her.

"No, we won't. So maybe we'll die, this winter or next, and that'll be together like everything else we've had from life, good or ill." She moved clumsily around the room, hanging up her cloak on a hook behind the door. "They'll try to eat her, as I think, and they'll find her tough. They'll lose teeth on our nanny. She'll have her revenge," she told him, her laughter creaking like an ill-hung door.

"You're a terrible old woman," he said to her, but a smile washed over his face.

"These children have built up the fire again. Isn't that nice?"

"We have to be going on now," Gwyn said. "But I wanted to ask you where—" She came close to the old woman who stood at the table, her hands moving among the turnips. Gwyn lowered her voice and picked up a turnip, standing with her back to the bed so that her low words would be muffled. "—I could move the dog?" she asked softly.

"Yes, I do see." The old woman nodded her head, and her eyes filled with tears which she blinked back. "I won't try to keep this one long. You've a sharp eye as well as a good heart, Innkeeper's daughter."

"Tad, come along," Gwyn said. They left abruptly, pulling the door sharply closed behind them. Gwyn shoved their basket into Tad's hands again, with an expression so fierce he didn't dare question. She picked up the dog's hind legs and pulled it around the side of the hut, dragging it into the trees that crowded close to the little building. Only a patch of blood marked the snow where he had lain. This she kicked snow over, to conceal it, knowing that the wind—which had blown her hood back from her face—would finish the work.

From inside the house they heard the old man's rough voice rise up again. "But who could it have been to do such a thing to us?" His coughing drowned out whatever answer his wife gave.

Gwyn took the basket from Tad and they hurried away along the path. She didn't speak and neither did he. Their footsteps scrunched in the snow and the field flowed white up at them. They moved quickly, side by side. As they reached the Way, Gwyn realized that Tad was practically jumping beside her, and she shoved aside the heavy feeling that seemed to be pushing against her chest to look curiously at him.

Words burst out of him: "I bet I know who did it. Gwyn, listen. Gwyn?" He broke into wild laughter. "Jackaroo!" He doubled over slapping at his knees. "It must have been Jackaroo!"

Gwyn pushed him—hard, harder than necessary—to get him moving. Sometimes she hated him. It was such a cruel thought, that he would do such a thing to those the stories said he protected. "That's not funny at all."

"Oh, yes, it is," he told her. Her hands were occupied with the heavy basket, and if she kicked at him she would likely slip and fall, even though kicking him would make her feel better. "It's very funny," he told her, unable to stop laughing.

Then he burst into tears. "I'm going home," his voice wailed over his shoulder as he ran off ahead, the hood dropping back from his head.

Tad was managing not to carry the basket, Gwyn noticed, watching him run ahead. She hefted its weight and began to move along at a steady pace. The heaviness pushed out at her chest, and Tad's reaction just made her feel more helpless. Tad had no sympathy for the troubles of others. Gwyn almost wished she had his cold heart, as she tried not to remember, trying to think ahead to the safety of home. But how could Tad have such a terrible thought and laugh? As if he would ever do something like that, even if he were real, Jackaroo.

~~⊗~~ Three

JACKAROO it was who slit the bag of the greedy Bailiff, so that every coin the Bailiff put into it slipped out as he rode away, his leather bag bouncing on his saddle. That was an old story, from the times before the Earls swore fealty to the King, times when the people served only the Lord and the Lord served only himself. As the story told, there was a greedy Bailiff who put the coins for his Lord into one hand and the coins for himself into the other. Jackaroo emptied the bailiff's bag, returning to each man just that which he had unjustly paid, no more nor less. At the last, the Bailiff's greed was his own undoing, for he put his hand into his Lord's gold to make up for himself what he had lost. That was a hanging day where the sun shone bright, as the story told.

Gwyn walked along, the snow crisp under her feet, a few flakes now blown down from the sky. She should, perhaps, hurry to catch Tad; anybody else would have, to ask what the matter was, to keep him safe in sight. But Tad was old enough to follow the roadway home, if he was too silly to know that two traveling together were safer than one traveling alone. And she already knew what the matter was: He had no stomach for poverty, he feared the ugly hunger and the dead animal outside the door.

Her brother could do as he wanted, but she would go along at her own pace, thinking her own thoughts. What trouble would greet her at her own door when Tad had arrived alone, she could predict. What trouble lay behind her she had seen. But for now, she had only her own company, and the snow falling sparsely over the frozen hills.

Jackaroo it was who cut the hangman's rope from the neck of the man falsely convicted and pulled the man onto the saddle behind him, where he bounced and clung on the unaccustomed mount, and he was never seen again. The Lord's verdict was on him, even though the people knew it was his jealous brother who had done the murder. That time, especially, the story told, the Lords had sought Jackaroo and tried to take him. But they never could. They named him outlaw, but he was too quick and clever for them.

Jackaroo it was who put beside a poor man's fire the coins that would pay his tithes, or the grain that would feed his family in the days before the Doling Rooms, or sometimes just the bitter drink that would ease the pains of dying. And Jackaroo it was who wove for the poor girl a wedding skirt, delicate green vines twisted together and their flowers scattered over it like stars scattering the sky, so that she could marry her love proudly, even though she had no dowry to bring to him.

It was all old stories, Gwyn knew. She didn't mind old stories. When she was a child, and listening to the other children tell one another the tales, she believed they were true. She even dreamed once or twice of Jackaroo. In her dreams, as in the stories, he wore a short cape, like a soldier's, only his was red as cherries. His tunic, over the fine cambric shirt he wore, glowed blue as a midsummer sky and fastened ıth silver buckles all down the front. His high boots folded over at the thighs, the leather soft and silent as a Lady's gloves. His face was hidden by a silken mask that fitted down over his nose, concealed his chin, and muffled his voice. Only his eyes could be seen under the plumed hat. Even in her dreams, Jackaroo had no face.

The wind rose up strong from the west, behind her. It was a wind that blew her homeward, making it easy to walk ahead. Snowflakes fell more thickly, and Gwyn spared a thought for Tad, telling herself that the Way was clear, that if at nine years he didn't have the sense to keep a hand on the rail fence he would be a poor dunce.

They had told themselves the old tales, the children, because at the sound of the name their parents' faces grew hard and forbidding. The children told themselves the tales of how Jackaroo was once a poor man, his family lost to famine and fever, gone mad with grief; and he had been found by the elves in the forest, who took pity on him, even though he was a mortal man, and gave him power. They told the tales of a Prince, kidnapped for ransom, who was taken out through the land and saw how things were for his people; and some said the kidnappers were his own Lords who wanted his rich lands for themselves, but proved their own undoing because the Prince rode out at night as Jackaroo, to right the wrongs done upon the people. The story Gwyn liked best was the one that told how Jackaroo was a mighty king who could not rest after his lawless and cruel life, but must ride the land he had tyrannized until the weight of his good deeds measured equal with the heaviness of his evil deeds.

Behind the mask Jackaroo wore, there could be a face of bone, its flesh long since eaten away. Jackaroo could fight as a trained soldier, with swords and shield; he could ride a horse like a Lord; and he had the knowledge of letters which only the Lords held. For hadn't he once posted at the gates of every castle, sending each of the three Lords that served each Earl, each of the two Earls, and even the King himself in his high city, the same message, bravely written and cunningly argued as the story told, to show the Lords the profit they could make if the people walked without hunger and slept without fear for their holdings. Or so the story told.

False, they were all of them false, the stories; as false as the stories of fairies dancing in moonlight glades on Midsummer Night. But they were stories to warm the heart by, to give hope where no other hope existed, and so they had their use. They had also their believers, but that did not concern her.

Falling snow whispered down. It coated the bags of grain and the turnips in her basket and made a cold ridge along her shoulders. She shrugged that off. Unbidden, from behind the Jackaroo stories she had been whispering down into her head, came the picture of the two old people in the hut beside the forest, huddled together on the bed. Tomorrow, the old woman would probably drag the dog into the forest, and then there would be the waiting time while the old man came to understand that the dog would not return. Better, Gwyn knew, than knowing that whoever had broken in and taken the goat had also killed the dog. If the people would do that to one another, she thought, then times were worse than any she had known— if the poor were not safe from one another. How long had it been that each year was harder than the one before? Since she was Tad's age, she thought.

At last Gwyn saw through the veil of snow the dark shape of the hills that marked the last mile before home. One more long rise to go, then she would see the Inn and, beyond the trees stretching off along the rise behind the Inn, the smoke from the few houses that made their village. Tad would be safe home by now, she thought, and soon she herself would be kicking snow from her boots at the kitchen door and stepping into the bright warmth. Her feet were cold, and she would welcome the fire on her toes, let her mother say what she would.

But Tad moved forward to greet her from the top of the rise, where he sat waiting on top of the fence. He had let his hood be blown back so his hair was dusted with snow. He stamped his feet on the ground to keep them warm. Gwyn's temper rose. "You should be in the house by now," she told him. She increased her speed. "It's almost dark. Mother'll be wondering."

Tad fell into step with her, unconcerned. He had no sense at all. "You should have gone in," she repeated. Just like him not to offer to take the basket from her. "At least put your hood up." Or was he trying to get her a scolding? "Mother'll have my skin if you come down with a chill."

Maybe he was just slow-witted. Maybe he'd forgotten the way a cough racked his body. It had been two winters now since he'd been kept to bed, coughing through the night while they fed him hot watered wine to give him rest. Maybe he thought it couldn't happen again. "Honestly Tad," she scolded.

"They'd have asked me where you were," he muttered. At least he had the sense to pull his hood up, but nothing would disguise his wet hair.

"So?"

"You'd have told them I ran off."

"It's the truth."

"I'm supposed to—we're supposed to stick together —in case . . ."

Gwyn laughed aloud. "You'd protect me?"

"I wouldn't even want to," Tad told her, angry. "But Da would tell me I should; you know what he'd say."

Gwyn remembered the quarrel that morning. Da and Burl were going out to find trees, to replenish the woodpile, and Mother would not let Tad go with them, because the work was too hard. Rose was at her time of the month so couldn't be sent to the Doling Room, which was why Gwyn was going. Tad had to walk with Gwyn, when what he really wanted was to stay inside watching the loaves of bread rise or the stew bubble. But at the thought of Tad protecting her from whatever danger might arise on the road, Gwyn laughed again. She carried a dagger and knew how to use it.

The thought of how he had stayed out in the snow, with dark and the temperature both falling, just to keep himself from a scolding, cut her laughter off short, and she hurried the last distance to home, feeling no pity for her brother who, with his shorter legs, had to half-run to keep up with her.

The sign that marked the Inn clanked in the wind, a dark shape in the snowy dusk. Tad and Gwyn hurried into the protection of the Inn yard.

From the yard the Inn looked empty. The main section, two stories at its center, two wings built off the ends, was shuttered against the weather. Only the three big chimneys, their smoke barely rising above the high central roof before low clouds forced it downward again, gave signs of life within. Seeing smoke rising from the third chimney, on the west wing, which held the parlor and the two bedrooms that were almost never occupied in winter, Gwyn wondered if one of the Messengers was abroad, and if so, why.

Tad ran ahead of her to the kitchen doorway, ignoring Burl who was hauling up water from the well. Gwyn stopped to greet him. "Not frozen?" she asked.

"It'll freeze over in the night," he promised her, without breaking the rhythm of his work, lowering the bucket down on its rope, hauling it up and emptying it into the four wooden buckets at his feet. He wore no mittens, and his dark hair was layered with snow. "Once the wind blows these clouds away, it'll freeze."

She left Burl to the job and pushed open the door to follow Tad into the kitchen. There, her mother fussed over Tad, pushing him into a seat at the table. ". . . so late, I don't know what kept you so long. Take off those boots before you step onto my floor, Gwyn." Gwyn obeyed, removing the heavy boots and slipping her feet into the felt shoes waiting there, while her mother talked on. "We've long since eaten and I don't know why you couldn't get back before dark. And you with your head wet—How did your hair get so wet and will you get him a spoon, Gwyn? We have to feed him and get him to bed, and with this extra work to do—don't sit down, Gwyn, there's a tray to carry into the parlor. Don't just stand there, bring down a loaf and slice it."

A tray with two wooden bowls on it lay on the table. Two

pewter mugs stood filled with wine. Gwyn added a platter of bread, some cut into thick slices and the rest waiting with a knife beside it, then a cup of butter. Impatiently, her mother took two of the cut slices to put in front of Tad, to whom she served a bowl of stew before she ladled helpings into the bowls on the tray.

"Guests?" Gwyn asked. She took a fresh apron from the pile on the shelf and wrapped it around her.

"Take the tray to Da, he'll serve them, and you get on back here before all this food in your basket gets wet with melted snow." As Gwyn left the kitchen, she saw her mother start hanging out cotton sheets on the line before the fire. The guests were staying the night then, and the rooms would have to be got ready. The aroma of stew filled her mouth, making her aware of how hungry she was.

Her father waited in the barroom, where six trestle tables ran the length of the empty room. "You're back now," he greeted her, then turned to serve the men in the parlor while Gwyn went back to the kitchen where her mother told her to dry Old Megg's food, build up the fires for the guests, and see that Burl had the wood box filled. "I'll make up the beds," she told Gwyn. "You fetch logs for the night, then help Burl with their horses."

"Who are—" Gwyn started to ask.

"No chatter." Her mother cut her off before turning to Tad to say, "Out to the privy, then off to bed with you. Like as not you've given yourself a chill and why"—she turned back to Gwyn—"you couldn't see that he kept his hood up is—" Gwyn quickly unpacked the basket, then picked up four thick logs from the stack by the fire and shouldered open the door into the barroom.

The two bedrooms still had a chill in the air, although fires burned there and the stones of the fireplace were warm. Gwyn set logs down carefully on the fires. They would burn all night. By the time the men had finished their meal, the rooms would be warm enough. The beds were covered by thin blankets, to keep dust off. Gwyn removed those and folded them into the cupboards. The feather pillows smelled slightly dank, so she shook them out and lay them on the hearthstone. She shook out the comforters. In the kitchen, she changed back into her boots. She needed no cloak to cross the corner of the yard and enter the stable. The snow was already ceasing.

The stable was a long building, half the size of the Doling Room, with four stalls at the far end. The end that shared a wall with the kitchen backed up to the stones of the kitchen fireplace, which kept it warm in winter and over-hot in summer. Two rooms occupied that end, a large tack room and the closet where Burl slept. Gwyn followed the light of a lantern and found Burl rubbing down a chestnut mare in one of the stalls.

"Glad to see you," he told her. Gwyn picked up a soft cloth from the pile he'd left and entered the next stall. When she saw the horse in there she grinned. It was a leggy stallion, his shaggy winter coat a dull dappled gray, his head moving nervously as he watched her. Burl would be glad indeed to see her in time to curry this animal. The stallion moved back away from her, his feet stirring the hay. "Osh aye," she spoke to him, watching his ears, "it's never me you need fear." Talking steadily, she held the halter and rubbed the stallion's nose until he quieted. Then she started rubbing him down, her hands calm on his coat, tracing the broad muscles over his shoulders and down his legs. Burl could handle horses but, like most, he didn't trust them. Sheep, goats, cows, even pigs, he enjoyed, but horses were too large and nervous. Gwyn didn't mind them and didn't mind exercising them when they had been standing too long in the stable. She even sometimes walked them out away from the Inn and village and then climbed up to ride. This happened rarely, because the chance rarely came her way, but she liked sitting so high, with her legs clamped around the horse's ribcage and the animal moving slowly underneath her. She had never dared go faster than a trot, not knowing if she could stick on at a faster gait, not sure the horse would still be obedient to the reins at that speed. Nobody knew she did this. Nobody even suspected.

Nobody could imagine wanting to, she thought. "Great brutes," Burl called horses. Even the little mare he curried would be a great brute to him.

Gwyn got the brush and comb and began on the stallion's mane, pulling through the thick hair, thinking about Burl. He was nineteen, and his heart, which broke for Rose, seemed to be healing. Burl could never have spoken for Rose. He was a servant bought from the Priests at the Hiring Fair, his price the cost of seven year's labor. He'd been seven when his family died in a fever that swept through Lord Hildebrand's City. Gwyn could just remember the thin, silent boy with sad, dark eyes Da had come home with. He'd been frightened, too, not knowing what waited for him at the Inn, knowing that most bought servants were worked or whipped to death long before their years were up and they could earn wages. Burl had been treated fairly, because that was Da's way. He had stayed in their service. It would be good for the Inn to have a steady head like Burl's under Tad when their father stepped aside. When he had saved enough, he could go to a Hiring Fair himself and find a girl who would be his wife when she grew old enough. With nothing but the work of his hands to offer, he couldn't speak for Rose. Rose would marry Wes, the Blacksmith's named heir, at the Spring Fair. Burl never said anything to indicate how he felt, and his work never faltered, but Gwyn had seen the way his eyes lingered on Rose's face, and how a kind word from her could bring a smile.

The stallion had the King's mark in his ear, she saw, a lion rampant. Calling over to the sounds in the next stall, she asked, "Who are the guests?"

"A man and a boy," he answered. Gwyn waited, but he didn't add anything.

"Burl," she protested.

"His son. From the High City." His voice in the darkness brought to Gwyn's mind the fields in summer, it was so deep and slow. "That's all I know."

Gwyn brushed down the long legs, stroking hard, the way

the horse liked it. His muscles rippled in pleasure under the bristles.

"How long do they stay?"

Burl didn't answer.

"Why are they traveling in winter?"

No answer again. That was reasonable, since he probably didn't know. Gwyn would ask Da, later. She picked up the stallion's feet, to check his iron shoes, poured water into the drinking bucket, mounded up hay at the far side of the stall, and stepped out, latching the half door behind him.

Burl waited beside the lantern, lit by its yellow light. He took up the soiled cloths, then held his hand out for the brush and comb.

Burl knew all the business of the Inn. He knew how to herd goats as well, but nothing of the fields or vineyards. Gwyn followed him to the storage room, carrying the lantern. She knew Burl's value to the Inn, because she knew the Inn's business even better than he, and she could live usefully on any one of her father's holdings. When Tad married, his wife would take over the kitchen and closets and Gwyn would be in the way. She could go to live in Old Magg's house, then, to herd the goats and guard the vineyard. Gwyn sighed, but half in longing, to have it all behind her and the talk finished.

~~⌐❦~~ Four

T HE CLOUDS were already blowing away as she crossed
back to the kitchen. There she considered taking
more large logs to the guest rooms and decided to. The Inn
was built of stone, and it tended to be cold in winter. Should
the guests need more heat, it was the business of the Inn to
provide it. She piled the logs beside the hearthstones and
looked around each bedroom. The comforters were mounded
high on the beds, the pillows covered now and fluffed up to
look soft. The fires burned hot, and the rooms were warm
enough for comfort. A jug of water stood on each table, the
bowls ready beside, and beside those the cloths for drying.
Gwyn pulled the doors shut behind her, resisting the tempta-
tion to open the door into the parlor and glimpse their guests.

She was thoroughly hungry, she realized, as the pangs of
her stomach finally claimed her attention. Her mother kneaded
bread dough at the table, but she didn't protest when Gwyn
served herself a wooden bowl of the stew from the fire, poured

herself a mug of cider from the jug on the shelf, and cut a thick slice of bread.

Gwyn sat on the bench with her back to the fire, letting the heat toast her shoulders while she ate. Her mother stood across from her, working the dough with her strong hands.

The stew was hot and filling. Gwyn wolfed down several spoonsful before her hunger became less desperate. Chunks of meat, onions and carrots, pieces of fowl, and the inevitable turnips, all flavored the thick gravy. The stew pot was kept warm at the side of the fire and her mother added into it anything left over from other meals. Sometimes the stew was dominated by the flavor of smoked meat, sometimes by the gamy taste of deer, sometimes by the acrid flavor of turnips or the bland flavorlessness of potatoes. That evening the taste of gravy dominated, which was the way Gwyn liked it best. She dipped her chunk of bread into the bowl, soaking it with gravy, then chewed off a large bite. Her mother titched at her manners, so Gwyn picked up her spoon again.

Her mother's gray braids ringed her ears, and the lines on her face were becoming deeply dug, especially the frown lines from her nose down to the corners of her mouth. "How's Rose?" Gwyn asked.

Her mother shrugged, turning the dough over. "She took some wine in the afternoon. She'll live. After she marries it'll be Wes's problem, and once she has her first child it'll pass."

Gwyn watched the hands work the dough.

"She'll birth hard," her mother continued, "with her first. Not you"—she looked quickly up at Gwyn—"when your time comes."

"If I marry," Gwyn said.

Her mother shrugged. "And what else would you do?" she asked, not expecting any answer.

Burl entered the room and served himself stew, sitting down at the far end of the table to eat. Gwyn pushed the round loaf down to him. He nodded his head but didn't speak. He looked tired, as they all did at the end of the day. Guests at the Inn meant extra work for everyone, extra meals and extra washings, extra buckets of water hauled up from the well, extra butter to be churned and the rich food Lords were accustomed to, which was why her mother was starting bread so late. It would rise by the ashes overnight, and she would form fresh loaves in the morning, to have them ready when the guests were hungry for their morning meal.

"Where's Da?" Gwyn asked.

"Seeing to Granda. He's slept all day and your Da wanted to take him some wine, if he could wake him." Granda would not live this winter through, they all knew it. He was old, and his life had been longer than most. He had left his son's family well provided, so they did not grudge him the care he gave nor would they weep his passing. "Guests mean payment in gold," her mother said. "That's something."

"Why does anyone travel in winter?" Gwyn wondered.

"You'll have to ask Da. I have too much to do to chatter." Her mother always spoke short and impatient, as if talk were just another trouble among many. Her voice sounded like wind down the chimney, mournful.

Burl stood up to refill his bowl. Gwyn was content to sit still, sipping at cider and letting her body rest. It felt good to be doing nothing, for however short a time, with sleep just ahead of her. She watched Burl bend over the pot and ladle out stew. He was tall, but he seemed shorter than he was because he was thickly built. He looked even stockier than he was in heavy winter clothes: the skins wrapped up around his legs for warmth, the heavy woollen overshirt. His hair was dark, almost black, and straight; his face square with a broad forehead and broad jawbone. His beard had grown in as dark as his head, she noticed. He was a dark man, olive in his complexion and his brown eyes dark under heavy eyebrows.

She heard her father's steps on the stairs in the barroom, and then, a few minutes later, he entered the kitchen, carrying the tray from the parlor. Da's hair was fading into grayness, but his beard was still red, a dark red like the chestnut mare, like Gwyn's own braids. He was a neat man, Da, and kept his beard trimmed short, his overshirt freshly washed, and his boots scraped clean. He was getting heavy, she noticed, a little more added to his girth each season. Mother still had her straight figure, was still a fine-looking woman.

Da drew himself a mug of ale and sat down facing Burl.

"They were late back," Gwyn's mother said. "She's never said why."

"Are the horses cared for?" Da asked Burl, settling first things first.

"And if the boy takes a cold, we'll know who to blame," Gwyn's mother said, but then let the subject drop.

"Why are they traveling? Burl said it's a man and his son," Gwyn asked, then before he could speak, knowing he would take his time answering, she added, "The stallion has the King's mark on him."

"He's a mapmaker," Da told her.

"That's what he says," Mother added.

Da didn't say anything, so Mother went on. "More likely he's from the King to overlook Lord Hildebrand's revenues, or the Earl's. Because why would anyone make a map in winter?"

"A map of what?" Gwyn asked, to distract her mother and because she was curious.

"Of the holdings and their value," her mother snapped.

"Of the Northern Kingdom, as he told me," Da said.

"Well, he had that box; it could hold books and ink," Gwyn's mother said. "But what he'll be writing down on that paper I wouldn't like to swear to. Not on a Lord's sayso. And dragging a boy around with him; he can't be more than ten or eleven."

"You were late returning, daughter," Da said. It was a question.

Gwyn nodded and finished her cider. "We walked an old woman home, to help her with her basket. It took us out of our way, and the Steward was late, before that."

"You were late from the Doling Room and still took

that time? In the snow? Didn't you think of your brother? What we'll do if he takes cold, and guests in the house—honestly Gwyn, and here I was fearing you'd met trouble on the road."

"I'm sorry," Gwyn said. She meant it. She didn't like her mother to worry more than usual. But she made no more apology, and they required no more of her. They knew her. They respected her as she respected them. And she knew her own value to the Inn.

"That's explained then," Da said. He looked at his wife. "It may be one day you'll be an old woman at the Doling Room and glad of a young arm to carry your basket."

"I wouldn't go there, as you well know, Innkeeper, or you should."

"Aye, I think I do," he answered with laughter buried in his words. "So why don't you pour me another mug of ale, and one for yourself, too, and I think we could put the cider jug on the table." Gwyn's mother did as he asked; the pouring and serving calmed her temper.

When they were all seated together, and the long day at its end, Burl took out his pipe and played quietly on it, music as soft as the last flakes of snow drifting down.

"The old woman was married to Hap," Gwyn told her mother, remembering.

"It was Nell then," her mother said, looking up with interest at the first of the news from the Doling Room. "It's as well you helped her then, as long as Tad doesn't take cold."

"I don't know how she makes that trek, she's so old. Her husband is kept to his bed all winter—"

"I'd heard," her mother nodded.

"They'd been robbed, when we got there." She turned to her father with this troubling news. "Bearded men had come and taken the goat. And killed the dog, too. He couldn't stop them."

"He wasn't ever a fighter, Hap," her father said.

"It was Win who did the fighting for them," her mother remarked. Gwyn waited to hear more of her Uncle Win, Da's brother, who died before her parents were married. "And Hap who did the dancing for them."

Gwyn gave them time, but they said no more. "Did you dance with him?" she asked.

"Aye, once or twice, but I was just a girl, a little younger than you are."

"But they were so old," Gwyn said.

For a long time the only sounds in the room were the notes from Burl's pipe and the rumble of the logs in the fireplace.

"He was older than we were; he was Win's age," her mother said.

"They've had ill luck, more than a fair measure," her father said.

"Can't you play something cheerful?" Gwyn's mother asked Burl. He nodded and switched to a melody that tumbled along, like the brooks filled with water in the spring, as the snows in the mountains melted.

"They were speaking of trouble in the south," Gwyn reported. "They didn't know that there was another new Earl in the castle."

"You never told them, did you?" her mother demanded.

Gwyn shook her head. "And there's a man to be hanged, a highwayman. A young man, they said. He'll be journeyed in the spring."

"I don't know why this journeying," her mother complained. "I've no need to look upon the faces of the poor wretches. Nor do I know why they must wait for their hanging. We'll send Tad to Old Megg when he comes, won't we, husband?"

"If you like," Da agreed.

"He won't be pleased," Gwyn told her mother.

Her mother snorted. "Then he'll have to be displeased, won't he?" When she wanted to protect Tad she could be stern enough with him. "It's not folk like us that need to be frightened into obeying the Lords."

"They don't journey all those they hang," Da said.

Gwyn thought about that, with Burl's melody in the back of her mind. "I'd be glad of any time they'd give me, before my hanging," she said.

"What would you know of how such a man would feel?" her mother demanded. "You let your imagination run away with you. Glad to wait, indeed. What would you know?"

"Do the women think it's Jackaroo?" Burl asked, raising his eyes to Gwyn's face. He spoke seldom and even more rarely did he ask a question.

"They think of it, as you'd expect," she told him. "And I can't blame them."

"If it's not your imagination that gets you into trouble it'll be your soft heart," her mother predicted.

But Da had been thinking along other lines. "Tad will go with you to Old Megg's tomorrow," he told Gwyn.

"Tad'll spend the day inside tomorrow," her mother answered. "He'll not walk through the cold two days together. I'll not have the nursing of him as well as the rest."

"Then we'll send Burl with you," Da said.

"That's not necessary," Gwyn protested.

"I'm afraid it may be. Two are safer than one."

"I can take care of myself." She was insulted. He had taught her to use a staff, as well as where a knife would cripple a man, or kill him.

"Then you can protect me," Burl said.

It would do no good to argue. For a minute she imagined herself fighting off men, while Burl cowered behind her. She heard the thud of the heavy staff as it knocked against a man's skull and smiled at the vision of Burl's face lit with timid gratitude as the attackers ran off over the snow. She was amused at her own imagination—should need arise, Burl would fight beside her. "Burl could sooth them with his music," she suggested.

"I might try that first," he answered her. "It would distract them while you made ready for the fray." His eyes smiled at her. Burl wasn't afraid of her sharp tongue, and he was never too proud to take her help. He never had been. Tad would do well to keep Burl on at the Inn.

"I'm to bed," she announced. She put on her cloak and went out into the garden. Behind her, her mother's voice reminded her to look in on Granda, to say goodnight to the old man, but not to wake him. Gwyn nodded but did not answer as she slipped out into the night.

Before she entered the privy she stood to drink in the darkness and the air fallen still after a snowfall. The clouds had all blown away. Faint moonlight silvered the fresh snow. Stars shone in a black sky, like jewels on a Lady's cloak. The garden lay shrouded in silver white silence, all its roughness made smooth. Such snow, Gwyn thought, had a way of turning the world into what it was not and making it seem safe. Such snow masked the true face of the world.

 Five

ARLY MORNING SUNLIGHT washed over the snowy hillside with light the color of new peaches. The air
tasted as freshly blue as the sky. Gwyn's head was bare in the
weak sunlight. She wore a sheepskin jacket. It was enough
trouble moving through deep snow in her long skirt, without
adding to that the weight of a cloak.

It had been days since anybody walked the path leading
from the Inn to the village. Burl stayed behind her, so she had
the sense of being the first and only as she moved steadily uphill and downhill through the woods, the basket for Old Megg
on one arm, her staff in the other hand—as if in the whole
white world, nobody had preceded her.

Thin spires of smoke rose up from the village, which was
hidden in a tiny valley. Old Megg's hut lay a mile to the north
of the village, near to Da's vineyard. Da was lucky to have
bought the vineyard. It was rare that a vineyard came up for

purchase, because Lords and Innkeepers would always purchase a man's wine so that he always had coins to pay his tithes, spring and fall. But this vineyard had been mismanaged—between poor crops and careless wine-making. Then the vineyarder had taken a chill that moved into his chest, and he died. He left no one to manage the holding, so it had come into Da's hands, the widow acting for her young children. Da had built the goat pens near to the little house. Old Megg cared for the goats and watched over the vineyard. Thus the Inn could make its own cheeses as well as have the smoked meat of those animals they could not feed over a winter.

Their path that morning lay above the village, along the crest of a hill. Gwyn waited for Burl at the top of the rise overlooking the cluster of houses. The well, with the big iron bell hanging above it, was at the center of the village. Around the well was a flat, open space, the snow crisscrossed with many paths. Of the several houses, the Blacksmith's was by far the grandest, made of stone, and the workshop built off one end. Those who lived in the villages were those who worked for others, as field hands, weavers, smiths, cobblers. Their holdings were small, enough land for a kitchen garden and a few fruit trees, no more. The money earned by their labor bought necessities and paid the tithes.

Gwyn's eyes went to the north, beyond the village, beyond the hills rising steep and steeper, to the mountains. On this clear morning the mountains rose up deceptively close, tall ragged peaks gilded with snow. They bit into the sky.

From the north the Kingdom was like a walled city, with the mountains preventing entrance. Travelers into the kingdom came through the broad forests to the south, along the river. Nobody knew anything of the lands beyond the mountains. They knew little of the lands to the south, and that news came only from the rare travelers, mostly merchants, who made the long journey for the Spring Fair or the Harvest Fair. The Kingdom was protected by mountains to the north and forest to the south. Gwyn had never seen the endless forests, but she had lived all of her life beneath the mountains, and she let her eyes linger over them while Burl caught up with her.

When he stood beside her, they waited a time, looking down at the village. The dark shapes of the houses stood out sharply against the snow. The bare branches of the trees showed black. Smoke curled upwards. The only person visible, on this cold day in this hungry winter, stood leaning against the stones of the Blacksmith's shop, a long, slim body wearing no protection against the weather. Gwyn stared down at him, wondering if he was, as it seemed to her, staring up at the two figures on the hill. Burl took his pipe out of his belt and started to play. The ribbon of melody slid down the hillside, then floated up into the sky. The figure raised its hand and then, looking tiny from the hilltop, went inside. Another figure came out from the shop, bigger than the first, pulling on a cloak and hurrying, with a wave of the hand over the head, to meet their path above the village. The original figure returned, to watch them, Gwyn was almost sure, just as she was almost sure she could see sunlight glinting off of the silky hair that turned gold during the summer but changed to the color of dried grass during the long winter months.

"Is that Cam, do you think?" she asked Burl, just to say the name. He finished out the line of melody and put his pipe away. Gwyn moved on, now, as the figure from the village clambered up the slope ahead. "Wes'll think it's Rose."

"No, he won't," Burl said. Gwyn looked questioningly at him, but he said no more.

"Why not? From the distance how could he tell?"

"You don't walk in the same way," Burl answered. "Besides, Rose would be wearing a cloak, with the hood up."

"What do you mean we don't walk in the same way? There's only one way to walk, you put one foot ahead of the other." But she didn't expect an answer because she did know what he meant. Whatever Rose did, whatever gesture she used, there was something dainty to it. Gwyn had never seen herself, but she felt inside herself a strength that flowed down her arms and legs, she could feel it especially in her shoulders. Gwyn was more like their oldest sister, Blithe, married two years this spring, and her first child died last winter.

Cam had spoken for Blithe, even though he had no holding of his own. It was his mother who had sold Da the vineyard and used the purchase money to buy a weaver's holding in the village, from Lord Hildebrand's Steward, when the Weaver and his only remaining daughter had died of a fever and the holding was empty. Cam's mother wove cloths, all the year round, on the loom set up in their main room; his two sisters wove also and their hands would be their dowries; but Cam didn't like sitting down to work. He said he had no need of roots chaining him to any single place. When Cam asked for Blithe, Da had answered with scorn in his voice. "I wouldn't give a field into your hands, much less my daughter." Cam turned it into a joke: "I take it then your answer is no," he had mocked, but Gwyn had heard the humiliation beneath his laughter and wished him better luck in his life.

Wes moved heavily through the snow. Gwyn put down her basket while they waited for him to regain his breath. She planted the thick staff in the snow and leaned on it, hearing Wes's heavy breathing and the echo of Burl's melody against the silence of the snowy hills and the overlooking mountains. The sun shone warm on her head.

Wes she liked and thought Rose had done well to say yes to him. He was big and slow, and work at the forge put thick muscles onto his shoulders and legs. Like Da, he trimmed his beard short. His head was large, his hair brown and curly, his broad face frank and open—a face that concealed nothing.

"You didn't have to rush, we'd have waited for you," Gwyn told him. He had taken time to put on a wrap, and a scarf to keep his neck from cold.

"Good day to you," he said, greeting them both. His voice was as deep and rich as Mother's stew, and his words came out as slowly as thick gravy boiling upwards over the fire. "Gwyn. Burl."

Gwyn grinned at him. Wes's way of doing things was slow and deliberate. He had been so slow and deliberate in his courting of Rose that sometimes—she told Gwyn later—she had felt like taking him by his shoulders and shaking him. She would have had to climb up onto a stool to do that, and even so Gwyn doubted the tiny Rose could budge Wes in the slightest. "Good day," she greeted him. He had come up to say something. He would say what he intended to say in his own time.

"It's a pleasant morning," he said.

"But cold," she reminded him. She waited. "Especially standing still," she hinted.

"Aye, it's that," he agreed. "I was thinking of coming to the Inn to see Rose, some afternoon. Do you think she would welcome a call?"

Gwyn shook her head solemnly at him. "I don't know." His face fell. "Rose was saying just the other night that she thought there was something—or someone—she ought to be remembering. Isn't that so, Burl?" She turned to draw him into the joke but he didn't follow her lead. "There was someone, and Rose knew she ought to know who it was, but she couldn't for the life of her remember who. Something to do," Gwyn improvised, "with horseshoes, but she wasn't sure if it was good luck or bad luck—"

Wes finally caught on. He clapped her on the shoulder. "Get away with you," he said.

"I could take a message," Gwyn offered.

"What I have to say I'll say myself, not trust to your quick tongue. Just tell her that I asked after her."

"Not that you'll be calling?"

Wes refused to be drawn in. "That too. But no more."

"Not a word more," Gwyn promised. "I won't tell her how you looked, or that the forge was working, or whether or not you seemed eager to hear news of her."

"Aye, and if I know you you'll tell her whatever you've a mind to," Wes answered. "Does the girl keep you good company, Burl?"

"Da sent Burl to protect me," Gwyn said quickly.

"That's a good thought," Wes said, serious again. "So the Innkeeper thinks there's danger."

Gwyn shrugged.

"It's a bad winter," Burl said then. He stated this quietly, as was his way, but his very quietness gave his words more meaning.

"It's been five days since we had need to light the forge," Wes agreed. "There was scant to be had at Lord Hildebrand's Doling Room yesterday. My mother went with the Weaver's daughter, and they say the Steward questioned them closely before he gave anything. They were gone all day. You'll be safe enough between here and Old Megg's though, I should think."

Gwyn agreed with him. In this village, with the Inn to give the Weaver work, and the Blacksmith's shop, and Da's holdings to employ the people, hunger didn't gnaw so hard.

"I must go back," Wes said. "You'll tell Rose?"

"Rose would welcome a visit." Gwyn answered him at last what he wanted to hear.

"Would she then? It'll be good to set eyes on her." At this embarrassing declaration, he turned away quickly and hurried down the hill. Gwyn and Burl walked on, their heavy leather boots making deep footprints into the snow.

Burl had never before spoken of the hardness of times; he never seemed uneasy. "Are times worse than ever before, think you?" Gwyn asked him. She wanted him to deny it.

"The worst I've seen. The men who come to the barroom are troubled," he told her. "Afraid. When men are afraid, they're dangerous, that's what I've found."

"Are you afraid?"

"The Inn's safer than most, lass," he comforted her. "The Innkeeper has stores, and the Lords need to keep the Inns safe for the Messengers and the soldiers."

"Do you think there's trouble coming?"

"Trouble's here, Innkeeper's daughter."

That wasn't what she wanted to hear, but oddly enough he had comforted her. "Do you never wonder? Burl, why should we have so much when others have so little."

He laughed then. "And if I could answer that question, I'd be a wise man."

"Just because you can't answer a question doesn't mean you shouldn't ask it," she snapped. She didn't like being laughed at.

"No, it doesn't. I won't quarrel with that," he told her in his calm voice.

Gwyn moved ahead, to walk alone again.

In the land around the village there were few trees. This land had been cleared for fields of turnips, potatoes, onions. As they went higher, the hillsides grew steeper, difficult to plow and plant, better for grazing. Old Megg's hut was beyond the vineyard, over the crest of the hill, invisible until you came upon it. The snow had blown up against the low fences over which they trained the vines in the growing season, so that the hillside was crossed along with dark lines, like charcoal marks across the snow paper. Once again, Burl piped their arrival.

There were only a dozen goats in the herd at this time of year. The goats had a long open shed and fenced pen to keep them safe and give them some shelter. The one-room house sat close beside this. But the pen held only three goats and one kid. The gate to the pen hung open. Gwyn didn't hesitate— she ran through the trampled snow as fast as her long skirts would permit.

Burl was there before her, and she saw immediately the figure of Old Megg, sitting with her back to the stones of the fireplace, where a small fire burned steadily. Old Megg sat stiff, her legs covered over with blankets. Her white hair, the coiled braids slicked into place with grease, looked tidy, but her face was gray and exhausted. When she spoke, her voice had none of its usual energy. Gwyn had heard that voice all of her life, telling stories, telling her briskly to build a fire, instructing her in how to mix pastry dough or gut a chicken while Old Megg's hands acted out the instructions. Now that voice spoke in broken phrases, as if each phrase had to be squeezed out of her throat.

"Thought someone'd come. Sometime soon. Goats are out." Her eyelids closed.

"I'll shut the gate to keep in whatever's left," Burl told Gwyn.

"I'll put on porridge. Can you bring wood?"

Old Megg seemed to be breathing all right, so Gwyn assumed she was asleep and set about stirring up the fire and putting on a spot of watery meal, made from the grain kept on the shelf by the fire. She looked around at the tidy room, where nothing seemed out of place. Half a dozen cheeses, each covered, with thick wax, waited on the shelf. Opening the cupboards built into the walls of the house, Gwyn saw shawls and blankets in folded piles. The bedclothes hadn't been straightened.

"Four of them," the unfamiliar voice said from behind her.

Gwyn crouched by the fire, stirring the pot. "Don't try to talk. I'll have food for you soon."

"Hungry."

"Are you warm enough?"

The eyelids fell and rose, assenting. Old Megg sat so still under the blankets that Gwyn wondered if she *could* move. There was a pot of honey on the shelf and she dribbled some of that over the thin gruel, stirring it in before offering Old Megg a spoonful.

"Feed myself," the old woman protested, but Gwyn shook her head. Burl brought an armload of logs into the room. He put two onto the fire, then sat at the stool by the table, letting Gwyn do and say what she thought best.

By the time the bowl of gruel was emptied, some color had come back into Old Megg's cheeks. Gwyn took another bowl and went outside the door to scoop it full of fresh snow. This she melted by the fire. When it was liquid, she spooned that into Old Megg's mouth, ignoring protests that were becoming more vigorous. At last, the old woman pulled her arms impatiently free from the blankets and took the bowl from Gwyn, drinking the water down. "And that's enough coddling," she declared.

Gwyn sat back.

"My ankle's twisted. That's why I'm sitting here."

"What happened?"

"Four men came, thieves, to take the goats."

Somehow, Gwyn wasn't surprised.

"I knew I couldn't fight them off, so I opened the gate. Shooed the creatures out."

"Were they bearded?" Gwyn asked.

"They didn't like that, they didn't like that one little bit. They shoved me aside—and then set off chasing the goats." Old Meg smiled then, remembering. "I don't think they'll have caught many."

"You fell," Gwyn said.

"Are many returned?"

"When was this?" Gwyn asked.

"I thought sure the ones with milk would come back, when it was time for milking. How many are in the pen, lad?"

"Three," Burl told her, his voice unworried.

"I wouldn't close that gate, there's more. The others—" She turned to look at Gwyn again. "I don't know where they'll have got to."

"Unless those men were total fools, there'll be some in their pot."

"Tell your Da I'm sorry."

"He'll know."

"It was the night before last, unless my mind wandered. I could swallow down some cheese."

Gwyn cut her off a chunk. Old Megg gnawed at it. "I didn't like to stand on the ankle. The cold has done me no good."

"What do we do now?" Burl asked Gwyn. She cut them each a chunk of cheese while she thought.

"She can stay with the Weaver. Da will see to that."

"We'll bring the goats down to the Inn," he said.

"This house will need to be closed up."

"I've my own blankets, and food to take," Old Megg said. "That'll ease the pain of her hospitality. But I'll need your shoulder, lad."

"Both our shoulders," Gwyn said. "And then we'll return to see what's to be done here. Things'll be safe enough, I think, for a time."

"Not bearded," Old Meg said. "They weren't our people, they were soldiers. Their hair—"

Gwyn understood. The soldiers had shorter hair than the people or the Lords, cut into a round circle over their ears. Probably so it couldn't be pulled when they fought, she thought, although it might have been to prevent them from becoming vain. "Whose soldiers?" she asked.

"They wore shirts and wraps, not the uniforms. I don't know whose they were, Hildebrand's or Northgate's, or maybe even up from the south. It made no matter to me whose they were. They didn't speak—except to curse me," Old Megg added, "and that was like music to my ears."

"We'd best be going on, if you've the strength," Burl said.

"I've the strength, lad," Old Megg sighed. "It's the bones for it I haven't got. All I ask is that I don't take a long time dying."

By the time they arrived back at the village, the sun was high in the sky and Old Megg's breathing was ragged. She kept her eyes closed and didn't respond while the Weaver made up the bed in her spare room and complained. One of the daughters built up a fire while the other put away the food and clothing Gwyn had carried down, and the Weaver complained.

Cam sat by the kitchen fire, watching the activity, a lazy smile greeting his mother's more petulant observations.

"—why she couldn't go to the Inn as I'm no nurse, and my own living to get," the Weaver muttered.

"We have guests," Gwyn explained again.

"Bringing her here to die. You have a stable too, unless I'm mistaken."

"It's not warm enough for an old woman," Gwyn repeated. "I'm sure Da will—"

"Of course he will and he ought to, but you know as well as I do it won't repay us for the time lost at the loom."

"I'll fetch down the extra food," Gwyn said, trying to appease her. "You'll have use for some cheeses."

"Osh aye, and if we're so generous, couldn't it have come sooner," the Weaver answered. She was thinking, Gwyn knew, of old bitterness; of the time when her husband had sickened and she had been left with the three children to raise.

There was nothing Gwyn could say so she gave up trying. She looked up to meet Cam's eyes, smoky blue, flecked with yellow.

"It's a hard life my mother has," he said. As always, his voice sounded as if it had laughter just barely held back behind it, however serious his words.

"And you, good-for-nothing"—the Weaver turned on him —"sitting by the fire spinning tales all day, telling us what a great man you would be, given a chance." But her voice softened as she looked at her son, who went over to put an arm around her and ask her, "Would you have me desert my home, then? And my poor weak and helpless mother who cannot stand up for herself? In times like these?" The Weaver shoved him away, but her eyes watched him move back to the fire, and she didn't look displeased.

The Weaver put water on the fire to heat, for compresses to wrap around Old Megg's ankle. "—and she shouldn't have been walking on it all the way down here, if anyone had any sense—" Cam grinned at Gwyn behind his mother's back.

Gwyn wanted to close up Old Megg's house. Burl insisted on staying with her. "They'll have expected us back at the Inn by now," she told him.

"You shouldn't go alone," Burl said, his voice firm.

Gwyn felt her temper rising. It was, after all, her decision to make. She caught Cam's eye.

"Not me, Innkeeper's daughter." Cam shook his head. "It's bitter cold." She knew his real reason. He wouldn't go near the vineyard that once had been his father's holding, and he wouldn't stir to help the Innkeeper in any way.

"But the goats," Gwyn said. They had to do something about securing the goats that were left and trying to recapture any that were wandering about.

"I'll see to them," Burl told her, "and put the fire to bed. Let Cam walk you back home."

"Oh no," Cam said, stretching his feet toward the fire.

"I'll be all right," Gwyn told Burl. "We're wasting time arguing," she pointed out.

Burl was studying Cam.

"The Innkeeper doesn't like me keeping his daughter company," Cam said easily, laughter rippling behind his words. Gwyn felt so sorry for him with his queer pride. . . . She turned around abruptly.

"I've the staff, which I know how to use. It's not far and I'd hear them coming. Da won't blame you," she promised Burl.

"That's not what my concern is."

"Then let's get going," Gwyn said roughly. Without looking back, she left the house and turned south. No, she told Burl, she wouldn't wait for Wes, and no she wouldn't wait for him to get back with the goats. Her mother would be making everybody miserable with her worrying. Gwyn thought, for a moment, Burl would insist on coming with her. She drew herself up tall and told him to "See to those goats." It was an order. Burl obeyed it.

It didn't take Gwyn long to walk off her crossness, but there was a confusion inside her that neither the white woods nor silent sky could soothe. What kind of men would attack an old woman? Or an old man, for that matter, she thought, remembering the day before, and slaughter a dog, too. And if, in these two days—

She thought she heard something . . . behind her? She turned to catch a glimpse, but the sound had ceased.

If, in these two days, she had heard of two different bands of men . . .

She heard it again. Stopped again and the sound stopped. Her heart beat loudly. Then she realized that it was only an echo of her own footsteps she heard and she relaxed her grip on the staff.

The Innkeeper's goats didn't distress her as much, some-how, as that old couple's one goat, which gave them milk. Gwyn strode along, thinking. She would like to take them a goat to replace their lost nanny, but Da would never permit that. But if his herd was all wandering around loose, who would know about those that didn't return? She could take one goat for the old couple, and nobody would know. But that would be stealing from Da. Except that, in a sense, some of his wealth was hers, for dowry. So it wasn't really stealing from Da but from herself. No, she admitted, it wasn't stealing from Da, it was stealing from Tad, who would inherit. She didn't much mind taking from Tad, who managed to give so little. If she wanted to talk her father into it, she would have no trouble doing that, but it would take weeks and weeks, and the old couple would likely starve by then. It was the right thing to do, she thought, to give them a goat, just one goat out of the Inn's whole herd.

The difficulty would be in having a day to make the jour-ney there and back, when nobody would notice that she was gone. It would take a day to clean out Old Megg's house. If Rose were the one to come with her, and Rose stayed the day with Wes's family in the village, then Gwyn would have her day.

The idea unrolled itself in Gwyn's mind, and her spirits lifted. If Gwyn could manage to take the old couple a goat, then she wasn't entirely helpless and they weren't merely vic-tims, and a good could be done, somehow, to counteract the evil that had fallen upon them. Evil would be done, that was the nature of the world; that was bearable if good could also be done.

Six

DAY AFTER DAY went by, however, before Gwyn could get away from the Inn. Da's anger and unease at the robbery was fueled by the men who came to the barroom in the evening. The men drank little but talked much, as word spread, and rumors of attacks on isolated holdings and along the King's Way spread. The men, speaking in low voices so as not to be heard by the two Lords in the rooms next door, spoke of dangers and wondered how they would protect their families and their holdings. As she served the tables, Gwyn heard their anger and unhappiness. These were bands of soldiers, rumor said, and the Lords did not care to rule them. The Lords must know of it, some men said. Others argued that the Lords didn't know and ought to be told, but there was no way to approach the Lords in their castles. Over and again Gwyn heard the same words uttered, that the people would be better off without the Lords, who rode the people just as they rode their horses. The Bailiff came for tithe money, at spring and fall, and he cared nothing for anything but that. The Steward sat in the Doling Room, and if you questioned him there he would refuse you food. Soldiers there were, but the soldiers weren't there to protect the people. When soldiers were quartered in the village they appeared unannounced, at the Lord's orders, for the Lord's purposes. The soldiers had nothing to do with the people, except to eat up scant stores of food and speak rudely to the women. Aye, men agreed, what little these bad times left to the people, the Lords took for themselves.

Gwyn's mother worked furiously during that time, keeping Gwyn hard at it, washing sheets and hanging them by the fire to dry, baking bread and the apple pastry of which she was so proud. The two horses in the stable must be walked around the Inn yard, lest they suffer from lack of exercise. More snow fell, keeping them locked inside the Inn while the air outside filled with falling flakes. Da asked Gwyn to show Tad how to use a staff to defend himself, so she spent hours with her unwilling brother in the Inn yard, trying to get him to hold the weapon properly, showing him how to ward off blows, while a pale face watched them out of the guests' rooms. The guests ate and drank, slept and washed, but what they did during the short winter days Gwyn didn't know; except that the Lordling peered out of the bedroom window at whatever activity took place in the yard.

At last a warm day came, and Gwyn asked Da for permission to close up old Megg's hut and bring down whatever goats had wandered back. He would have said yes, she thought, but then Blithe appeared with her husband, Guy, who left her at the Inn for a day's visit while he took a broken plow to the Blacksmith's. So Gwyn had to stay nearby and try to talk to Blithe, who sat hunched on a stool by the fire, resisting all of their mother's efforts to draw her out. "It's as if," Gwyn's mother said to Gwyn, watching Blithe walk away in the afternoon, drooping on Guy's arm, "she's the only woman ever to lose a child. She's stubborn in her grief, your sister."

"That's her way, Mother," Gwyn pointed out. Whatever Blithe wanted, she wanted absolutely and immediately. There was no budging Blithe. First she did not want to marry, and no man could come courting her, whatever her parents advised. Then Guy asked for her and she wanted to marry him right away. Nothing would stand in her way, not the bad weather nor the silver coin it would cost. So they went into Hildebrand's City and were married by the priest there, instead of waiting until the Spring Fair when the priest would come out to perform marriages for all who asked, at no cost. Now it was this child—nothing but the one child, dead now over a year, would ease her heart. Until that child was returned to her, she would grieve. "I don't know how Guy is so patient with her," Gwyn said.

Her mother closed the door. "If she'd just have another. Or die from grief and let him take a woman who—if she could not be his wife—could give him children."

"It must be hard to lose a child, and him her first."

"Life is hard," her mother said, crossly. "It's only death that'll be easy for us."

And then Granda slipped into a sleep from which he didn't wake even to eat. Someone sat with him, all the hours of the day or night, waiting for his thick breathing to cease. Miraculously, he opened his eyes one morning and Rose came running downstairs to tell Da that Granda wanted a bowl of broth.

The next day, Gwyn and Rose set off for the village, and Old Megg's house. It was the midwinter thaw underfoot, the snow moist and almost as soft as earth, the wind from the south bringing a gentle warmth, smelling of sunlight. They stopped at the Weaver's house to give the Weaver a silver coin for her trouble, for which she did not send thanks to Da. Cam walked with Rose across to the forge and Gwyn was at last free.

With luck, she thought, some of the goats would have returned; whether any of them would be giving milk, she didn't know. She couldn't remember how many nursing nannies there were in the flock when last she'd heard. One of the creatures Burl had brought down that first day had a kid.

If there was one, there might be more; if there were more, one might have returned to the pen. If, if . . . She hurried forward.

Four goats stood inside the rail fence, and one had a kid sucking at its teats. Gwyn waited until it had finished, then tied a rope around the nanny's neck, and latched the gate behind them. The kid bleated pitifully.

Walking as fast as she could, pulling the goat along behind her, Gwyn skirted the village and headed southwest until she came to the King's Way. There she increased her pace. The goat trotted along beside her on dainty feet. Gwyn remembered the turnoff, but once there she skirted the field, not sure what she would find and suddenly aware that she had, in her haste, left her staff behind at Old Megg's, and that she carried no knife. She approached the hut from the cover of the forest. Smoke rose from the chimney. She came close, to listen. There were two voices within, speaking. One she recognized confidently, its cracked sound familiar to her even though she couldn't pick out the words it was speaking. Another voice responded, the words interrupted by spells of coughing, and Granny's voice creaked answers to its questions. They talked together like old friends, who would never run out of words to say to one another.

Gwyn had no time for a visit, and she had no wish for word to come back to Da that his daughter had given away a goat. She tethered the goat as close to the hut as she dared. "All you have to do," she said softly, scratching the nanny behind the ears, "is make a little noise. They'll come out to you. They'll give you good care, you'll see." By evening, the goat's udders would have swollen again with milk, so she would be sure to complain. By evening, then, the goat would be sure to be found. Gwyn slipped back into the cover of the trees, glad of the snow to silence her steps. As she left it, the goat bleated after her. She hid herself behind a broad trunk. She heard sounds behind her, but didn't dare to look. Not that she wouldn't have liked to, but if Da found out what she had done—not just taking the goat, but making the journey alone—he'd be angry. And with a right.

After what seemed to her a long time, she looked around. The goat was gone, the door to the hut closed. Gwyn moved cautiously back into the trees and didn't start walking naturally until a slope hid her from the house.

She trotted along the King's Way until a stitch in her side made her slow to a walk. It surprised her that the Way was deserted. There was nobody with goods to take to the Earl's city, there was no Messenger abroad, and no soldiers stayed. In winter, the roads were often empty, she told herself. Besides, the real danger came at night, when darkness hid men's deeds. Besides, anybody she met, if she met anyone, would likely be out and about on no good business.

That thought frightened her, alone and without weapon as she was. She increased her pace, but did not try to run. If she ran she would never hear anyone approaching. Besides, they seemed to attack isolated holdings and avoid the villages, whoever *they* were. If the rumors had any substance to them, there might be several bands of men roaming the countryside. But you couldn't believe rumor, Gwyn told herself.

It wasn't until she had stepped off the King's Way, circled the village again, and was walking across the vineyard, that Gwyn breathed easy. There was nobody at the hut. The three goats she had left waited in the pen, their heads lowered patiently. The kid nuzzled at one of the others, who butted it away. The sun had crossed the center of the sky and the shadows fell away to the east. Rose would be expecting her at the Blacksmith's by now.

Even knowing she should hurry, Gwyn stopped and looked around her. She breathed in the sweet air and remembered the way the vineyard looked in summer, with the vines grown along the fences in rows and the purple grapes beginning to swell up with juice. She turned her eyes to the mountains, tall and strong and pure white against the blue of the sky. Old Megg's hut dropped melting snow onto the ground. All was well, the scene seemed to say. But she was expected back in the village, and she knew as well as anyone that the scene was false. All was not well.

Quickly, she looked into the hut. The air inside was much colder than outside, and the one little window up under the room let in almost no light. But it was tidy enough. Gwyn didn't have time to pack up the blankets on the bed, or the pillow, or to empty the cupboards, or to gather together the few plates and cups, or the side of pork, which hung down over the narrow loft. She grabbed one of the cheeses from the shelf and a piece of the rope coiled beside them. The rest she'd have to leave and hope nobody discovered that she hadn't done what she was supposed to. She noted the pile of wood Burl had chopped, stacked beside the wall of the hut near the path that led to the privy, to replenish the little left in the woodbox, but lacked time to carry any inside. In fact, she did nothing at Old Megg's except latch the door carefully behind her and loop the rope around the neck of one of the goats so that the others would follow. She left the gate open and spread some hay at the back of the shed, in case more goats might return.

Gwyn stepped out strong. She wasn't tired in the least. She imagined the surprise those two old people would be feeling, what they would say to one another, how they would wonder where the gift had come from. They might even think it was from Jackaroo. In fact, she hoped they would, because the thought would give them pleasure. It was a false pleasure, but better than none.

Aye, if the Lords would not look after the people, to keep them safe, if the Lords gave the people only enough to keep the tithes coming in. . . . Gwyn despised the Lords. They knew nothing of work, they cared nothing for those whose work fed them. Hap—crippled as he had been in the Earl's service—should have been fed and housed, not put to another job. And if someone stole Hap's goat, it was to the Earl he should be able to turn for help. But the Lords no more listened to the people than they listened to their horses. The Lords used horses to carry them and save them the work of walking. And the people were as helpless as horses, under the Lords.

There was so much Gwyn could do nothing about. She could no more bring Blythe's Joss back to life than she could wipe hunger from the land, but she had done one small something about one small wrong, and that thought eased her heart.

"What's got into you?" Wes asked her. Gwyn just smiled and shook her head, passing the cheese over to Cam. "You must thrive on hard work," Wes remarked.

"She looks to me like she's been meeting someone," Cam said. "Have you a secret lover, Innkeeper's daughter?"

Gwyn didn't answer.

"I'm not sure I like the idea of my girl meeting someone secretly."

"I'm not your girl," Gwyn pointed out.

"That's because your father plays at being lord of the manor," Cam answered. The laughter in his voice mocked the bitterness of his words.

"He only acts the master over those who act the slave," she snapped back. She was immediately sorry she'd said it, but it was too late because Wes burst into rich, slow laughter, and Rose joined in.

"She's pinned your ears, Cam," Wes said. "Answer back and she'll slice you to ribbons with that tongue of hers."

"Answer back? And me a beaten, broken man?" Cam said. "Life's too short to cross words with a shrew."

"Gwyn's not a shrew," Rose defended her sister.

Gwyn could defend herself. "You're beaten?" she asked him, looking up into his face and laughing. "That's broken?" Shave his face and let his hair hang shoulder length, dress him in a tunic and tall boots, and he would be a Lord. He looked like a man whom life could never trouble. "You don't know the first thing about yourself."

"Osh aye, and you do?"

"I might," Gwyn said. "Or I might not."

"Do I have to marry you to find out?" he answered in mock horror.

"Marry me and you'll regret it every day of your life," she answered before she thought. Well and he would; she'd teach him how to work and he'd not like being made to learn that.

"And what about you, Innkeeper's daughter, would you

regret it?" His eyes held hers, teasing, as if he knew her heart's secret.

Gwyn didn't know what to say. Cam didn't give her a chance, either. He bowed low to her in mockery and turned on his heel, taking the cheese to his mother.

Rose and Gwyn walked slowly back to the Inn, with the goats trailing behind them. "Only three goats." Rose finally spoke.

"It's twice what we had this morning," Gwyn pointed out, ignoring a twinge of guilt.

Burl did not make her feel any better, when she gave the goats over to him. "The kid would not have left its mother," he said.

"Do you expect me to know what happened?"

He didn't answer, just looked at her.

"Maybe Jackaroo had use for the mother," she lightly offered into the silence.

"Aye, Gwyn, you've no cause to lie to me," he said quietly.

What did he mean by that? "I know that," she answered, "I haven't." She hadn't lied, not exactly—and she didn't want to talk about it any more. It was only one goat.

"Nor scorn me," he said, as quietly. He turned away, to take the goats into the barn.

Gwyn watched him go. He should know she wouldn't do that. She reminded herself of how hard life had been to Burl, that it would be hard to be always serving another with nothing for your own, and no hope; yet she felt no pity for Burl.

That thought puzzled her. She waited where she was until he emerged from the barn. As he walked by her, she said, "I wouldn't scorn you."

His face turned to her, and he seemed to have forgotten his own words, for he answered, "There's no lie without it's note of truth, think you? Even the old stories, I think, must have some truth to them. If we knew."

"Even Jackaroo?"

"Even him, Innkeeper's daughter."

She walked beside him. "I would have thought you more practical than to believe in stories."

"Would you have," he answered, but it was not a question. "You'd have been right."

She would have questioned him what he meant by that, but they both had work to do.

Seven

THE THAW continued another two days, until the snow started to melt, and all its surfaces ran watery. The stones of the Inn yard became treacherous footing. When Tad and Gwyn drilled with staffs, they often fell, sloshing around in the puddles. Tad complained and Mother backed him up, saying they should give it up; but Da insisted. It was past time for Tad to learn to use a weapon, Da said. So they went out into the yard and fought mock battles. At last, Tad began to make progress enough so that he could defend himself. Then, however wet he became, he didn't want to quit. They drove each other back and forth across the yard, parrying blows with the heavy staffs. "You're bigger and heavier," Tad protested. "It's not fair."

Gwyn shifted her grip and lunged forward, as if the staff were a spear, to jab him in the shoulder. He brought his staff up to deflect the blow, but he was too slow and she had hit him before he forced her staff aside. "That hurt," he said, but he followed his words with a sharp downward stroke across her wrists.

"Good," she said.

He stopped, pleased. "It was, wasn't it?"

Before he got too confident, she struck his staff as hard as she could, spinning it out of his relaxed grip.

"Not fair," he said.

Gwyn stood panting. "Just go pick it up."

"What if I don't?"

She shrugged. "I'm not the one who needs to learn."

He wanted to refuse, she could see that and hear it in his sulky boy's voice. But he also wanted to see if he could get through her guard again, so he turned to fetch his staff.

"He's always there," Tad reported. "Watching. I don't like being watched."

"I don't think the Lords are much concerned with what you like," she answered. "Defend yourself."

Instead of doing as he was told, he raised his staff and moved toward her, with short, thrusting strokes. Gwyn was surprised and unready. She had to retreat a few steps, while he smiled at her discomfort, before she could make her own attack.

While the thaw held, Granda's health held. He was too weak to leave his room, but he swallowed broth and cups of warmed wine. However, when the cold flooded down over them from the north, as if the mountains blew their icy breath down over the hills, he declined again. Always, then, behind the daily work, they listened for sounds from the rooms above the barroom. Gwyn sat her turns with him, watching the rise and fall of his chest. Granda was old, fifty-eight, and had long outlived his friends. Until the autumn he had been alert and spry, saying over and over that he planned to live to sixty, and maybe even beyond. They had thought he might, but he'd taken a cold before the first snow and had been sickening ever since. The family cared for him, as he had cared for them.

They left him alone only at the end of each evening, when they gathered in the kitchen to eat. On the third night, as they sat over bowls of stew, they heard distant sounds, as if furniture were being tumbled about upstairs. They rushed into the barroom.

Granda stood on the stairs, out of his room for the first time since the snows began. He wore a white nightshirt. In the dim light of candles, his face could not be seen, but his long white hair shone wildly around his head, and his beard shone white. His voice rolled around the empty room, like the cry of a caged animal.

"Where is my son?" he cried. He held himself erect with one hand on the railing. "I want my son, where is he?"

Da stepped to the foot of the stairs, holding up a candle. "Here I am, Father." The light showed the old head shaking from side to side, the shadowed eyes searching out the dark corners of the room.

"I want my son. Where is my son? Where is Win?" Granda roared. Then, as slowly as the last flames burning out on a bed of ashes, his legs folded beneath him. Da ran up to catch him. Gwyn stood by Rose. Burl held a candle in one hand and Tad's shoulder with the other, to keep him from leaving the room. Their mother went up the stairs and murmured to Da, who nodded his head.

"He's dead," Mother announced. "Burl? You'll help carry him back to his bed. Rose, put on water for the washing."

Burl passed his candle to Gwyn, and Tad followed Rose into the kitchen. Gwyn watched the three living figures take the fourth back up the stairs. Then she sighed and turned around, not knowing what to do.

The door into the parlor was closing gently. She had only a glimpse of a man's figure standing against the light, and a long clean-shaven face, before the door closed.

The next evening they carried Granda's body out to the flat stone at the west of the village, where a pyre had been built up. Da and Burl laid the body on top. Da took up a torch to light the sticks. In the fall, the priest would come and say prayers there, for all who had died during the year.

Heavy dark clouds crept across the sky from the east and

the sun flamed over the distant mountain tops, turning them black. The smoke curled up from the pyre. Nobody spoke among the circle of those who had come to bid Granda farewell. The villagers had come, and Wes stood beside Rose, their solemn faces lit by growing flames. Cam stood apart, his eyes fixed on the fire.

Gwyn waited with her parents, Blithe and Guy, and Burl behind them. Tad had stayed at the Inn, not wanting to come. He would lay out drink and cups, and the bread and meats Mother had prepared that day. He would serve the guests if they needed anything while the family was gone. Flames licked upwards as the sky overhead darkened and lowered. Heat burned on Gwyn's face. She heard Blithe make little choking sounds; and she turned her head to see her oldest sister move to stand away, her back to the pyre, tears running down her cheeks. Guy tried to comfort her within the circle of his arms.

It was not Granda Blithe wept for, Gwyn knew. The pyre to which Blithe turned her back burned in memory only. Blithe pushed Guy away, wrapping her arms around herself as if she wrapped them around the grief she clutched so close. She should have stayed with Tad then, Gwyn thought, if she couldn't look straight at the end of things.

Afterwards, when the people had drunk and eaten and bid farewell, the family sat alone in the kitchen. Blithe and Guy had gone upstairs, where they would share Tad's room. Burl rinsed plates and cups at the basin, while Rose dried them on a cloth and put them away. Gwyn fed up the fire, leaving Da to sit with Mother. She heated a final pitcher of cider.

"He had a long life, and a good one," Mother said. "He made a quiet end."

A murmur of assent went around the kitchen, and Gwyn asked the question that had been in her mind all day. Bending over the fire to ladle cider into mugs, she asked her parents, "Did he forget Uncle Win was dead then?"

They exchanged a look as she set the drinks down before them.

"Aye, he must have," her mother said.

Gwyn served the mugs of cider. Rose and Burl sat down with them.

"Win was ever the favorite," Da explained to Gwyn. "I think that loss was always fresh in him. And his mind wandered, at the end."

"Don't you mind?" Gwyn asked her father.

"Osh and why should I mind? He was a favorite with all of us, wasn't he, wife?"

She nodded, but her face did not, as Da's had, soften at the memory.

"I wish I'd known him," Gwyn said.

"He was good with people," Da told her, "and with animals too; he had the right touch. But he had a temper—he wasn't a good man to cross. Even when he was young—"

"Especially when he was young," Mother agreed.

"He must have been handsome," Rose said.

"That he was, wasn't he, wife?"

"Aye he was that. He was a lovely lad. You," she said to Gwyn, "have a tongue like his. It often got him into trouble. Or out of it. But he was vain, always washed and combed, and dressed proud. He loved the fairs—"

"Because he wore his finest clothes?" Gwyn guessed.

"Oh, he would strut around." Da smiled. "One eye on the girls."

"Both eyes on the girls," Mother corrected.

Gwyn tried to picture him. "What color was his hair?"

"Brown, light brown. When he was a boy it was yellow," Da said.

"His eyes?"

"Brown, dark brown," her mother said. "Velvety."

"How old was he, when—" Gwyn started.

"Oh well," Da said. "We'll have a full day tomorrow, or the next, if as Tad tells us the Messenger is due. It'll mean the stabling of three horses, Burl."

"The goats can stay in the barn with the cows."

"And we'll have baking to do," Mother said to Gwyn. "When we'll get Granda's room cleared out, I don't know."

"Tad said it's only for the one night," Gwyn reminded her.

"Aye, but with guests already in the house."

"Besides, Tad sometimes gets messages wrong," Rose reminded them.

"Not any more, he's learned how. Not for a long time now," Mother said quickly. "And blankets for the soldiers, and the bed to be carried down to the parlor, places made for the soldiers in the barn. We'll earn our gold pieces. You, Burl, have you a clean shirt for serving?"

"Aye," he said. When there were soldiers staying at the Inn, the women remained in the kitchen as much as possible. No matter how a man might have been raised, after a year of soldiering he wasn't fit company for women, not women of the sort in the Innkeeper's house. The soldiers' women lived in camps and moved from camp to camp, setting up cloth tents in good weather, living like cattle in the city barracks during the winter months.

"I wonder why the Messenger is going to the Earl at this time of year," Gwyn asked.

"It has nothing to do with you," her mother said.

"I know that," Gwyn answered. "It would be bad luck for me if it did, wouldn't it."

"We're tired," Da announced, sending everybody to bed. "I'll bank the fire. Tomorrow will be long."

Overnight the weather turned bitter. When Gwyn left the kitchen the next morning, her mother warned her to watch her footing. Outside, the air seared her lungs with cold and the surface of the garden was sheeted with ice. Gwyn's boots broke through the crust of ice, so she had no trouble with falling, but it was times like these, she thought, she envied the Lords their indoor privies. Overhead, the sky hung black and heavy, with no stars showing. Only the kitchen showed any light, where her mother worked by lanterns. Narrow bars of yellow showed through the closed shutters and at the foot of the door. Gwyn was glad to return inside to the warmth of the fire.

"Don't loiter," her mother said, looking up from the chickens she gutted at the table. "You're needed in the stables.

Da wants to speak to you." Her voice was bitter, angry. Gwyn knew better than to ask questions when Mother spoke in that voice.

In the stables, Burl mucked out the stalls while Da brushed down the big gray stallion. The light turned gray, with a dawn when the sun hid itself behind clouds. "They're going out today," Da said. "He wants one to care for his son and one to serve him. You'll go with the Lordling," he told Gwyn.

"On a day like this?" Gwyn asked, currying the mare.

Da grunted. "He wants to map the land to the North."

"But who will serve the Messenger and the soldiers if they arrive today?"

"I'm sending Burl with you. Your mother will pack food. I'll give you silver to pay for your lodgings."

"Lodgings?"

"You'll be gone some few days, he says."

At last Gwyn identified the odd note in her father's voice: he was puzzled as well as uneasy. "Does he fear to meet the Messenger then, think you?" she asked.

"What and why the Lords do is nothing for us to think on," he answered sharply.

Gwyn took the warning without protest. She helped put bit and saddles on the horses and attached a long lead line to the mare. Leaving Burl holding both animals in the yard, she went inside to eat the bread and cheese her mother gave her and pack up food and blankets while she chewed. Her father gave her a purse of small coins to tie at the waist of her skirt, beneath her overshirt. "You'll pay whatever it seems worth to turn a man out of his house for the night," Da instructed her. "More if he gives you food."

They set off without a word among themselves. Both the Lord and his son were wrapped around with fur-lined cloaks, the hoods pulled up close against the bitter air. The Lord placed deep saddlebags behind his saddle. Burl helped the Lordling to mount and then gave the lead line into the Lord's hand. Shouldering their packs, Gwyn and Burl followed the two horses out of the Inn yard.

Their progress was slow, because the Lord stopped frequently to take a long book out of his saddlebag and mark on it with sticks of charcoal. He marked the village down, while the four stood together on the hillside overlooking the little gathering of houses around the stone well, with its bell hung high over the water. Gwyn and Burl stood silent as he worked. The Lordling sat silent on the mare. When the Lord closed his book and put it away, they moved on, without a word exchanged.

So the long day went. They would walk along the white landscape, among hills growing ever steeper, heading toward the mountains, which were invisible in the pale air, the sky above them low with flat white-gray clouds. As they walked, the horses would gradually pull ahead of Gwyn and Burl, so that they followed only tracks in the snow. Then they would come upon the two Lords, sitting silent and still while the father made marks. At about midday, the Lord asked for food and Gwyn put down her pack to cut off chunks of bread and cheese and serve them up to the two on horseback. She and Burl ate standing up.

Nobody spoke, neither she and Burl, nor the father to his son. When they angled off to follow a spire of smoke rising into the low sky, Gwyn had heard only those four words, "We will eat now," uttered in an oddly cold, metallic voice, as measured as the steady pace of the horses' hoofs through the snow. She had looked up only glancingly into the two faces she served, the Lordling's pale, with pale brown hair tied back at his neck, his pale blue eyes unseeing, the man's pale and hollow looking, as if he had just gotten out of bed after a wasting disease, or as if, like the land he mapped, he had long gone hungry. The man's hair was brown too, what she could see of it at his forehead, and his eyes seemed to see her—if at all—as from a great distance. He led them toward the line of smoke without a word.

The house and barns huddled close together at the foot of a hill, facing south, protected by the rise behind from northerly winds. Two chimneys rose up from the stone house. Only one chimney smoked so that, Gwyn thought with relief, there would be room for them, without putting the farmer out. As they rode into the farmyard, the wooden door was pulled open and a man stepped out.

The Lord waited for Gwyn to explain their needs. The farmer listened carefully to her, then nodded his head and stepped aside to allow them to enter. The family had gathered for a meal in the kitchen, two sons and a daughter, all three standing stiff beside the farmer's wife, who wiped her hands on her apron and fussed nervously at her hair to see that the braids lay neat. The farmer took the Lords into the next room, telling one of his sons to build up a fire. The other son was sent to show Burl where he could stable the horses.

Gwyn recognized the girl. They had met at fairs. Her name was Liss, and Gwyn remembered her thick black hair, which refused to be neatly contained by braids and forever came loose into little curls around her face. When they were alone, Gwyn greeted her. "I'm very glad to see you."

"You're the Innkeeper's daughter," Liss answered. "Gwyn. The second daughter."

"We've a stew hot"—Liss's mother got right to business—"and we've ale. It'll mean porridge for our dinner." She didn't sound upset at the prospect.

"Why are they here?" Liss asked. "And what are you doing traveling with them? What's the news from your village? From the Doling Rooms? From the King's Ways?" Words tumbled out, running like brooks in spring spate. At the same time, she moved around the room, getting out the best spoons and bowls, setting out a plate for bread. She turned her face to ask her questions, her eyes curious.

Gwyn hung her cloak on a hook and took the apron Liss handed to her. She was glad to find a friend here; it made her task easier. "The Innkeeper has given me coins to pay for our lodgings," she said.

"Aye, that'll be welcome," the farmer's wife answered. "Should I stew some apples for them? It'll take only a minute." Without waiting for an answer, she bustled into the storeroom.

"What an adventure, Gwyn," Liss said, admiration in her voice.

"Adventure? Walking all day in this weather?"

"My Da says there's real snow coming soon." Liss was easily distracted. She was Rose's age, two years younger than Gwyn. There had been girls born in the village the same year as Gwyn, but they hadn't survived childhood, so Gwyn was out of the habit of friendship.

Besides, she had no time to talk. They were busy finding a table and putting food down before the man and boy, bringing in firewood, seeing that the horses were stabled, and finally eating themselves, thick porridge with honey melted over its top and rich goat's milk poured over it.

Then, after all the chores were done, she was almost too tired to take pleasure from just sitting down in a warm room, with Burl's music in the background. Liss was openly disappointed in the lack of news. "The only thing that's happened in the world is that Rose will marry Wes?" she teased. "Osh aye, Gwyn, I've been locked up away here since the autumn fair. Any littlest thing would be exciting to me. Have you had many visitors at the Inn?"

"Not since the snows. Just these two."

Even Liss wouldn't ask questions about the doings of the Lords. "No other news at all?"

"Just bad news. There's hunger—"

"Aye, that we know," the farmer said. "We can keep ourselves out here, but we've been luckier than many this year."

"And these coins will help pay the tithes," his wife added. "It was good luck you came here."

"And hunger brings thieves, I'd wager," one of the young men asked Gwyn.

She nodded, yawning.

"Osh aye," Liss said. "I'll just have to marry a man from the villages, if I can find one to ask me."

"There'll be plenty to ask you, never fear," her father told her.

"Think you?" she wondered, pleased.

"As long as they don't ask us what you'd be like to live with," her oldest brother answered her.

"Oh, you, you great lout, all you think about is the weather. What do you know about it?"

"I know what a man likes, little sister."

"And what is that, may I ask?"

"A quiet temper and a peaceful tongue," he began the list. They all burst out laughing. Gwyn watched, smiling, and yawned again, unable to stop herself. At this, the family withdrew to their own quarters, leaving the two guests to roll up in blankets on the floor by the fire. "It's a good house, this," Gwyn thought to herself, falling asleep. She didn't realize she had spoken aloud until she heard Burl's voice answering from the darkness, "It is that." His voice was as sure and soothing as her mother's hand on her forehead when she was a child. Gwyn fell asleep.

~~~ Eight

EXCEPT that the ground grew rougher underfoot, the
second day was a duplicate of the first, as they made
their way up and down steep hillsides. The forest grew thicker
here, far from fields and pastures, and they saw few dwellings
that day. They were coming up to the mountains, whose mas-
sive bulk rose up ahead of them like a wall. Gwyn could make
out the variations on the mountains' faces now, long high,
smooth slopes, ravines cutting their way down, and the land
jutting out around them. She could see the distant peaks, too
high for any trees to grow; some of them rising up until they
buried themselves in the clouds.

They came that evening to a hovel shared by three rough
men, with a pen nearby where two scrawny goats were kept,
and an open shed for the goats to shelter in. The men wore
shapeless rags. Hair covered most of their faces. They stood
before the hut and heard Gwyn's request, their eyes when they

thought she did not watch them, searching out one another's. Finally, one of them put out his hand for the coin Gwyn offered. An old scar ran like a ravine down his cheek, starting at the corner of his eyebrow and disappearing into his mustache. "Them'll sleep inside. We'll have the shed," he said, and as they moved toward it, Gwyn saw that the youngest of them dragged his right foot as he walked.

Gwyn hid her thoughts, glad of the knife at her waist, glad she knew how to use it, glad of whatever protection traveling with Lords might afford her. She left Burl to tend to the horses while she opened the door.

Foul air swept out at her, sweat and urine, old food and smoke. It was the only shelter they had, so she stepped inside, her eyes sweeping the room: a small table, a fire within a circle of stones in the center of the dirt floor, most of its smoke going out through a hole in the thatched roof, the cracks in the windowless wooden walls stuffed with straw to keep the wind out, no shelves, no furnishings but two benches and the blankets tossed around.

The Lords had followed her inside. The Lordling huddled close to his father, who seemed to notice neither the filth nor the stench.

Well, Gwyn thought, the Lords would be safe enough for a night, and warm enough. These men wouldn't dare attack them here—not when it would be possible to track the two to this place. She herself didn't expect to sleep that night. These three were not men you closed your eyes on.

First, though, the Lords must be settled and fed. She tidied the room as best she could and set bread and cheese on the table. While the Lords ate their silent meal, she brought in and stacked by the door the wood Burl chopped. She cleared away the food left remaining and nodded at Burl, the signal that they could now leave.

"Innkeeper's daughter," the Lord spoke at her back. She turned, to hear what he wanted. "It would be better if we all slept inside tonight." His voice was clear and cold, like a sharp wind overhead. For a minute Gwyn could not find words. She hadn't known how much she was dreading the night to come.

"For all of our safeties," the Lord said, misunderstanding her hesitation. "Although I would almost welcome an open fight with an enemy I could see to put steel into." He added this last distantly, not really speaking to her, his hand at the hilt of his sword.

"Yes, my Lord," Gwyn said.

The long winter evening stretched out. She and Burl ate, hunkered down by the fire. She melted a bowl of snow to drink. The Lord sat at the table, his book open, making marks. The boy sat silent, watching his father, until he fell asleep. Gwyn moved him to the floor, covering him with one of the blankets from the Inn, which were clean. Then she went back to sit with Burl, their backs to the wall, both under the cover of cloaks. The fire burned steadfastly. At last Burl pulled out his pipe and played a few soft lines of melody. The Lord looked up and nodded to him, as a Lord would to the servant of a servant, giving permission.

The music played, the Lord worked at the table, and Gwyn closed her eyes, thinking that she was grateful to the Lord for saving her a sleepless night, thinking that she did not know where they were going, although he seemed genuinely to be a mapmaker, thinking that the boy was strangely still and silent for a boy.

At first light, they left, making no farewell to their hosts. They traveled for a long time, well into the morning, high into the hills, keeping together. Finally, the Lord pulled up his horse and took the long book and his charcoal out of the saddlebag. He worked silently, turning page after page. At last he took the lead line and moved off, more quickly now, leaving Burl and Gwyn to follow.

When they caught up, the two horses were standing tethered before a great rock face. A trickle of water fell down it, to form a small pool, its surface sheeted with ice. From this pool a little stream moved away under its own coating of ice, heading south.

Gwyn put down her load and looked up from the stream, following the course of the water backwards to the pool, then up. Her eyes went up, and up, and still up, where the rock mounted above her, taller by four times than the walls of Earl Northgate's city. Water slid down over the rocks and great icicles hung from stone outcroppings. Thick and heavy as a strong man's legs, the icicles pointed down. The only sound was the secret movement of the water.

Cold, it was entirely cold: the great gray rocks covered with ice, the icicles hanging down like giants' daggers, the snow fields rising above and the cold gray sky overhead. The air bit at Gwyn's lungs. The water moved with cold little musical sounds into the streambed. The water was black where it showed beneath the ice. Beautiful too, somehow, in the opposite way to the beauty of a field coming to crop under the farmer's hand.

"This is what we came to find." The Lord spoke. His voice suited that frozen landscape, Gwyn thought; the high wind his voice carried was a wind that would blow here among these frozen rocks, down from the high peaks of the mountains.

He took out his book and made marks on a page. Gwyn turned away from the mountains to follow the stream down the narrow ravine it had made for itself. She couldn't see far, but she could see to where it disappeared between bare hills.

The horses stamped restlessly, but neither the Lord nor his son seemed troubled by that. High over the little plateau where they stood, a fierce wind blew up. But it blew far off overhead, beyond the clouds. The Lord turned his horse and they crossed the narrow stream to follow the rock face to the east, watching it gradually descend to become part of a craggy hill. Snow blanketed all this high land, blown up around the trunks of the few trees, weighing down the arms of evergreens. "There," the Lord said, pointing with his arm, "is the eastern pass. When the snows melt, the pathway will be visible." He pulled out his book, made some marks, put it away again. "We'll eat now," he said to Gwyn. "We're going back to the

Inn, and we'll want to travel quickly, I think. There's weather behind us and"—his eyes turned to Burl—"I wouldn't be surprised if we had been followed through the morning."

"Nor I, my Lord," Burly agreed calmly.

Gwyn looked at Burl in surprise, but he had no more to say. She should have thought of it. She looked around behind them. But nothing moved on the landscape. Although, she thought, her eyes searching out the distant shapes of hills, the clusters of trees, a man—or three men—could follow their tracks, unperceived.

They all rode that day, Gwyn and Burl up behind the two Lords. Gwyn rode behind the Lordling, his father holding the long lead line. The horses moved steadily. They did not halt for the Lord to take out his book until midday, and even then he worked hastily, making few new marks on the pages, hastily folding closed the big leather book, moving them on without even time to eat.

Even with their steady haste they were not near any habitation when the light began to fail. The wind at their backs had risen and cut sharply. The horses held their heads low. They had come back to the gentler rises and thicker woods, but they had not yet come within the inhabited lands. At nightfall they stopped beneath a tall bare oak and separated immediately for a few moments to answer their bodies' needs. Burl gathered sticks to make a small fire, around which they huddled, cloaks pulled close around them. They were four dark, faceless figures beneath the dark night and the wind. Gwyn took down the food bag and cut off chunks of cold cheese, which they ate standing up. The black sky hung heavy over them. A dark wind blew through the bare trunks of trees, lifting the broad arms of evergreens.

Without warning, without preamble, snow erupted around them. The little fire hissed, and the dark air was thick with flakes. Gwyn waited for the Lord to speak, but he remained a tall, silent, dark shape. The wind gusted down, swirling snow into her face. The fire went out. Finally Gwyn said, "I'm not sure, but we're no more than a day's journey from the Inn, think you?"

Burl didn't answer. The Lord didn't speak. She had probably overstepped her bounds, Gwyn thought; but she thought this snow was coming down after them like a blizzard, and they'd not survive many hours without shelter.

"The horses will be more tired after a night in the cold, without food," she said. The wind caught her voice and carried it away, howling as if pleased with its treasure.

Nobody answered her.

"We'd be wise to travel on," Gwyn went on, stubbornly. "My Lord?"

His hooded head turned toward her, as if he had forgotten he wasn't alone. She wondered, briefly, if it pleased him to lose his life, and theirs with it. "Two grown men is a heavy burden for any beast," he said.

Gwyn swallowed, swallowing back as much anger as fear. "Burl and I can walk. The horses will know their way back to the stable." She and Burl could walk, if they had to; if they were just given permission, they could start off. What they couldn't do was stand here doing nothing.

The voice did not alter expression. The Lord spoke in slow and stately measure: "The Innkeeper would not be pleased if I returned without his daughter."

Anger took over. With a blizzard blowing thick around them, the chances were Gwyn would not be held responsible for her words. "The Lords do what they will. The Innkeeper knows that as well as any man."

If they were to go on foot, with the storm around them at night, her sense of direction would be useless, and she would not be able to see a familiar landscape even if she stumbled upon it. She took the bags of food down from the mare. They would at least keep the food with them. But the longer they stayed talking, the slighter their chances of survival. "You'd do well to tie the boy onto his mare," she advised the Lord, not bothering to disguise the scorn in her voice.

"Innkeeper's daughter," he answered her in that distant

tone, "whatever the people might think of their Lords, I would not be the man who left a girl to die while he took himself to safety."

"I stay with Burl," Gwyn told him.

"Then you'll be traveling with my son and me," he answered, still distant, but she could have sworn she heard a smile in his voice—if the high peaks of mountains could ever be said to smile. "Leave the food bags here. We'll ride as before, and we need no extra weight. The mare will have to carry this one bag." He moved to loop the bag holding the long book onto the mare's saddle. He put the Lordling up on the saddle and tied him to the horse with the lead rein. Burl gave Gwyn a foot up, and the Lord put the reins into her hands. "You need do nothing," he told her.

She nodded, looking down at him. It would be beyond her place to apologize to a Lord. They did not need the apologies of the people. "Give the mare her head. We'll try to keep together," he said. She did not think she needed to tell him that it was unlikely they would succeed in that. Gwyn sat with the Lordling's body up close to hers, her arms around him to hold the reins, her legs hanging down. The Lord mounted the stallion, who was almost invisible in the thick snow. He pulled Burl up behind him. Then the Lord turned around. "Son, you would be wise to sleep this night through, as much as you can." The slight figure in front of Gwyn did not stir. They set off.

The wind, at least, was behind them. The mare moved with her head low, her four feet steady. Gwyn bent her head too and held the reins in one hand, while with the other she held the Lordling about his waist. The long cloak, her long skirt beneath it, the heavy socks she wore and her thick boots all gave some protection to her legs. But not enough—for the cold still bit most sharply there.

She had no sense for how long they traveled thus. All she could hear was the wind at her back and the mare's breathing. She did not know when she realized that they were alone. She dozed off and woke herself—afraid she had been asleep for hours but knowing it had been only the briefest of times. The

Lordling did sleep, she thought, his body relaxed against hers, held up by her stiffening arm. Time passed, and she had no idea how much. Nothing around her altered, the dark wind roared, the thick snow blinded. The mare would make her way back to the Inn, if she could. If she couldn't, well, then, they said that freezing was an easy death. Gwyn emptied her mind and huddled closer to the Lordling, for the little warmth his body could give her. He was shivering now.

In the darkness, she almost missed the square shape. Something opened her eyes and cleared her mind, and she saw it briefly outlined there. The mare plodded on, but Gwyn pulled her up. A shelter on the hillside. It was no more than four steps away.

"Wake up, my Lord," She shook the Lordling's shoulders. His head lifted. "There's shelter. We must untie you."

Her stiff fingers worked on the ropes, hampered by heavy mittens. When he was free, she slipped down into snow that reached up to her knees. Her legs collapsed under her and she fell. Struggling up, she pulled the Lordling down into the snow beside her. He didn't resist.

The hut was abandoned, that was clear. No smoke rose, no light showed. Gwyn uncinched the saddle, holding the Lord's saddlebag high to keep it from being buried in snow. She slipped the bridle over the mare's head and struck her once on the rump. Even if they had found shelter, that was no use to the mare. The mare was heading back to the Inn, Gwyn hoped. She would move more safely without bridle and reins, more lightly without the saddle and riders. The mare's only chance was her horse's instinct for the stable.

Gwyn took the Lordling by the arm and pulled him behind her toward the hut. They had to go around to the front, where Gwyn pushed up the latch and entered, without any care for what might wait within. It was enough just to be out of the wind and snow.

The Lordling stumbled in the darkness. She pushed the door closed behind them and waited to hear if a voice would greet them from the darkness. No voice spoke. The air inside was cold, but not as cold as the air outside, which howled overhead. This hut had been sturdily built.

The Lordling lay down on the floor and Gwyn, wondering if she could find any light or build any fire in this darkness, lay down beside him. Immediately, she slept.

Nine

GWYN OPENED her eyes to darkness, and cold. Beside her the Lording twitched and kicked, mumbling incoherently under his fur-lined cloak. Gwyn's arms and legs felt stiffened, swollen. She was shivering along her whole body. The realization of what she had done shocked her entirely awake.

To just fall asleep like that . . . She was lucky she hadn't woken up dead . . . How stupid, you couldn't wake up dead. Gwyn got onto her hands and knees in the darkness. The cloak dragged at her shoulders and caught at her knees. There had to be a place for a fire, either in the center of the room or along a wall.

Her hands and feet felt like wooden blocks. Close around her, beyond the narrow walls, the wind howled and howled.

But no air blew over them. So, she thought, there was no smoke hole in the roof. So, she thought, it would be a fireplace against a wall and, with luck, a tinderbox nearby and, with luck, something to burn.

Crawling clumsily, groping with her hands, she came first to a pile of wood and then to the stones of a hearth. She clamped her teeth together to keep them from chattering and stood up, keeping one hand flat on the icy stones that formed the fireplace. Groping upwards onto unsteady legs, her hand found the mantelboard. Methodically, she sent her hand off to the right, until it reached the edge of the board, then to the left. When her fingers closed around the familiar shape of a tinderbox she was relieved, but not surprised. This house had been well made and well kept. With only her fingers to see for her, she tried to find kindling. In the fire-bed there were a few ends of logs, in the pile of wood some sticks more narrow than the rest. She set the tinderbox down close to her right knee and awkwardly, blind in the lightless air, tried to assemble a pile of kindling in the cold ashes. She made her hands move slowly, but her mind raced.

If, if . . . There might even be food stored, and certainly blankets in such a well-kept house. A cold draft came down the chimney and wound around her neck, as if the wind outside were reaching in with long fingers. She opened the tinderbox with shaking fingers and struck it. A small spark jumped out and flashed away before she could even see what her pile of kindling looked like.

Striking again, she worked her mind to keep fear at bay. If this wood did not catch, there would be a broom with straw, all she had to do was find it. Or the Lord's book, somewhere behind her in the darkness. Paper would burn. Surely he wouldn't begrudge her one sheet of paper to start the fire that would save their lives.

In the end, she did have to use the broom, which hung on a peg beside the fireplace. She used it like a torch, lighting first the stiff straw and then, with that light to see by, shoving it beneath the pile of sticks. Light leaped up from the fireplace, but Gwyn didn't dare turn around until she had fed larger sticks into the blaze and the final big logs had caught and began to smoke, as the flames curled up from underneath them. The heat licked tentatively along her face, and she shivered uncontrollably. That was odd, she thought, clenching her teeth, trying to clench her shoulders to stop them from shaking. She ought to stop shivering, now there was a fire to warm her.

She turned her back to the fire at last, unwilling to remove her cloak even thought it was wet with snow. She saw the one small room of the house, the wooden table in the middle of the floor and the bed behind it covered with blankets. Quickly, Gwyn shed her cloak and moved across the room, to take a dry blanket and wrap it around herself.

She had to strain her eyes in the weak light from the fire: shelves along one wall and the restless Lordling on the dirt floor near the door. She would have to move him closer to the warmth. There were dark, round shapes on the shelves. A side of meat hung over the loft. The fire burst into hot flames and crackled with joy at reaching its strength.

Gwyn knew where they were, as surely as if the old woman herself had opened the door to them: Old Megg's house, not an hour from home in good weather. Her shivering ceased.

The Lordling did not want to wake up, so she had to drag him over to the bed and lift him onto it. She took off his cloak, rolling him out of it, grateful that he was so light. He was not sleeping easily and his skin was cold to touch, but he did not wake as she pushed him under the blankets of the bed and then spread his cloak out over him.

Clutching her own blanket around her shoulders, Gwyn returned to the fire. She put on two more big logs. She bent to pick up the saddlebag from the floor and set it on the table. She wished the fire had been burning long enough to warm the stones surrounding it, so that she could sit with the warm stones at her back. She sat in front of the fire to unlace her stiff boots.

Light danced inside Old Megg's house. Wind swirled around it, crying out in a hollow black voice. The boy whimpered. Gwyn wrapped herself around with the blanket and lay down. She fell asleep immediately.

When next she woke it was to the chill of a dying fire

and the wailing of wind. A faint light illuminated the room. Gwyn looked up at the shuttered window and saw pale lines around it. She turned to the fire, stirring it up, adding wood to it.

Then she noticed the Lordling sitting up in the bed, staring at her. She wondered how long he had been awake.

Gwyn put her boots on and cloak, now dry. She opened the door to a wall of whirling white flakes and pulled it quickly closed behind her. The snow had piled up over her knees. She shoved through it around to the left, toward the pens and the privy; but out of the shelter of the little hut the wind tore at her and she had to turn back to the wooden wall before she should lose her way. In a blizzard, men had died between house and barn, wandering off lost, unable to see their way back to safety. They would have to use the side of the house as a privy, until the snow ceased. But the Lordling would require his privacy, she thought with a sigh, so when she made her way back to the door of the house she trudged on through the snow to the right, making a path that turned the corner to the side opposite that which she had used.

Inside again, her cloak spread to dry by the fire, her damp skirts hanging cold at her legs, she considered the problem of food. The Lordling sat motionless on the bed. He looked pale and lifeless. His hair hung tangled and his eyes looked as if they did not register what they saw. He did not move. He did not speak.

Gwyn took a large bowl outside and filled it with snow. Some of that she transferred to a cooking pot. When this had melted, she added oats and swung the heavy pot over the fire, hanging it on the iron bar fixed into the stones at the side of the fireplace. The Lordling slid out of bed and came to sit at the table. He looked younger than Tad, despite seeming to have no more strength than an aged man. Gwyn sighed again, leaving the porridge to bubble over the fire.

"Your privy area will be out the door to the right. I've made as much of a path as I can."

He left the table fast enough at that. Tad would have

been squirming and complaining, she thought, wondering how it was that this Lord's son was so different from her brother. She'd like to see Tad sitting so quiet, saying nothing; that would be a pleasant change from his usual behavior.

She trickled honey over the top of the Lordling's serving of porridge and stood behind him while he ate it hungrily. Then she removed his bowl and spoon. "I know this house," she said, as she served her own food. "It's not far from the Inn. When the snow stops we can easily go there. Until then we'll be safe enough."

He said nothing. She turned to see if he had a question before putting her spoon into the porridge. It wouldn't do to eat when a Lord had an answer he required, whether he was a child or man.

"What happened to the mare?" he asked her.

"I turned her loose last night."

He drew himself up, stiff with displeasure.

"There was nothing else to do," she told him. "She'll have made it safely to the stable, I'm thinking." His expression did not change. Why was he looking at her like that, Gwyn wondered, and he was only a boy after all.

"My Lord," he reminded her.

"My Lord," Gwyn repeated, trying not to smile. If that was all, just the proper form of address, it was nothing. "I apologize for forgetting."

The little head nodded at her, all dignity despite the sleep-tangled hair and rumpled clothing.

The day dragged by. Gwyn sat by the fire, dozing occasionally. The Lordling sat at the table. He did not speak except to announce his hunger.

At last, Gwyn roused herself to tidy the bedclothes, to feed the fire, to climb up the ladder to the loft and cut off some meat and stew it for a meal.

All day the wind curled around the little house. Every time they opened the door the snow crowded in. Most blizzards lasted a day or so, but Gwyn knew that some storms could take longer, three or even four days, until the snow piled up as high as the eaves of the houses. They had wood enough for the winter, piled up against the side of the house. She chopped a good supply and brought it inside, to set it near the fire so that it would be dry when she had burned through the present supply. After she had served the Lordling his stew, with a chunk of cheese and a cup of melted snow, he climbed back into the bed. He pulled the covers up and turned his back to her. Then she could start bread for the next day, mixing flour with starter from the jar on the shelf and kneading the dough on the table that was at last empty for her to use. When she rolled herself up in a blanket beside the fire, the wind still blew with undiminished strength. She hoped the boy would sleep late and not expect his morning's meal early.

Gwyn was awakened in the darkness of deep night. When she opened her eyes she did not at first know what had roused her. The fire burned low, but well banked. The wind howled around the house. There was a queer whimpering sound to the wind now, she thought, drifting back toward sleep before waking up again. . . .

That wasn't the wind. It wasn't outside either.

Gwyn got up and went over to the bed. It was the Lordling whimpering, his body stiff under the blankets. In the shadowy light she saw his cheeks shine and tears coursing out of his closed eyes to run down toward his ears.

He must be asleep, she thought, or else he would have turned to bury his face in the pillows. He must be dreaming, she thought, but what dreams could a Lord's son have that would cause such weeping?

His eyelids flew open and the watery eyes stared up at her, unseeing. He hunched up in the bed, his mouth working.

What must he be dreaming, Gwyn wondered as his mouth opened. He looked as if he were screaming, but no sound came from his lips. She sat down beside him. He was only a boy, after all, caught in a nightmare. She put her hands on his shoulders. He was shaking.

"Osh aye," she said, her voice gentle, as if she were talking to a nervous animal. "It's quiet you want now, my honey, my lamb. Quiet, now, quiet." She remembered from long ago her mother's voice saying those same words in that same tone into her own ears, when she was frightened.

The Lordling's eyes poured tears and stared over her shoulder, at nothing in the room. His mouth moved, making no sound.

"Quiet now, there's no harm to you, no harm here, no harm while I watch," Gwyn crooned at him. "Quiet now and wake, my honey, my lamb. Time to wake up." She put her hands against his wet ears and rubbed his cheeks with her thumbs, watching his eyes. "A bad dream," she said, "naught but a bad dream, wake up, lad, naught but a dream. Wake up, lad, so you can sleep again."

The eyes saw her. The body was stilled. He stared at her, and Gwyn removed her hands. He slid back under the covers and closed his eyes.

Gwyn returned to her place by the fire, troubled. What could a boy dream of that would sorrow him so? Tad dreamed and woke quickly, and when he woke the dream slipped away so that he could smile at you and turn back to sleep. Although this boy's eyes saw her, the dream did not slip away. She knew now, as surely as if she lay beside him, that he was awake still.

Fear for his father, she guessed. She would try to reassure him in the morning. She would tell him how close they were to the Inn, again, in case he had forgotten that. If he chose not to hear her, there was little she could do about that.

When she woke in the morning, her first thought was for the Lordling. She turned her head and saw him sitting straight up in bed, looking at her. Clumsily, she rose up. He turned his face away.

Gwyn built up the fire, then went outside to clear paths to their privy areas. The wind was down, but the snow still fell thickly. Over the night it had piled up again on the paths, as high as her hips. Using her legs and heavy skirt as a plow, she walked through it. As soon as she went back into the house, he went out.

Gwyn started a pot of porridge, her sympathy of the night faded. Young or old, child or grown, the Lords were the same. They would have just such a day as they had had the day before, long and silent. They would stay trapped here until the snow settled, or melted, perhaps until winter left the land, stay trapped as Lord and servant. That day, she decided, she would clean out the house entirely, do the job she should have done on the day she took the goat. What she would do the next day, she did not know. Many days like this and she would go mad from inactivity.

The snow outside was piled as high as her chest where the storm had blown it up against the house. They could not walk safely through it, even the short distance to the village, or the Inn. She formed a loaf of bread and had it rising beside the fire before the Lordling returned into the room.

She served him his food, watched him as he ate, then had her own. The only sound was the snow sweeping around the house. She scraped the bowls clean and went outside to refill their water bowl. He sat at the table. She set the bowl of snow by the fire, to melt.

"You woke me," he said behind her, in his high boy's voice. Gwyn stood up and faced him, careful to keep all expression from her face.

"Nobody has ever woken me before," he continued. She wondered if he expected her to apologize, but she wouldn't do that. If she had erred, it was an honest mistake. She wouldn't repeat it, but she wouldn't apologize for it either.

"I am in your debt," he said.

Gwyn lowered her eyes, trying to control her face. The dignity with which he spoke was so odd in a boy that she wanted to smile.

"I know that I am young," he told her.

It was this that opened her heart to him. She curtseyed and answered him as if he were his father. "Yes, my Lord."

"We are very near to the Inn," she told him then. "I would think the stallion could have made the journey easily."

"He was carrying two grown men," the Lordling reminded her. She couldn't gainsay that. "But the mare may well have arrived safely, don't you think?" When he asked that he looked like any little boy, seeking reassurance.

"A good chance, my Lord."

He sat down again and she busied herself with the tasks of the day. She shook out the bedclothes and replaced them neatly. She set more meat stewing in the pot and added one of the last withered turnips. She placed the risen bread within a covered iron pot among the ashes under the logs. She wiped off the shelves, which did not really need cleaning. Then she turned her attention to the cupboards built into the walls next to the fireplace.

The Lordling sat at the table, turning the pages of the long book. Gwyn took up an armload of folded cloths to lay them out on the bed while she wiped down the inside of the first cupboard. Each cupboard had one shelf in it, so there was not much to carry. Moving behind the Lordling, she glanced over her shoulder. On the top of the page was a picture of three faces. Before she thought to stop herself, she spoke: "Those are the three men. From the hut."

"Had they murdered us, this might have identified them, when they went to sell the book. My father wrote it down underneath the pictures." His fingers pointed to a line of shapes.

Underneath the faces and the shapes, other lines waved and curved. Gwyn stared at them until suddenly she saw what they were. She did this by a trick of mind, as if she were a bird seeing a flat landscape from above.

"It really is a map," she said. She could identify the hills now, and a pathway among them; when she looked down on it as if from the sky, she could see what it pictured. There was the dot where the mens' hut was, and forests spreading back over the hills. Then she realized that she shouldn't be standing so close, gawping. She moved quickly away.

"I don't mind, Innkeeper's daughter."

Curiosity brought Gwyn back to stand behind him. On the top of the map a cross was drawn, with shapes at each end. It wasn't part of the map, at least not that Gwyn could remember. "What is that?" she pointed.

"The directions of the compass. N means north, S south, E east and W west.

Gwyn stared at the signs. "The river runs to the south of us, so I can see why it's the curved shape, but that one for the west should be the north, because even if it's upside down it looks more like mountains."

It took him a minute to understand her. "No, they're letters, they're initials. I just named the letters. Listen: the letter N comes first in the word north, and E in east. Hear it? That's S for south and W for west. They're just the initial letters."

"W doesn't sound like west," Gwyn pointed out. It didn't look like west either, where the sun went down. It looked like upside-down mountains. She wondered if he was mocking her.

"Sometimes the names of the letters don't match their sounds, but mostly they do," he told her. "I have to go outside."

Gwyn turned the pages of the long book while he was gone, but was careful to have it open to the page with the faces when he returned. He hung up his cloak and brushed snow from his head before sitting down again.

"Look," he said. He took out a thin piece of charcoal, no broader than the twig of an apple tree, and made marks on the table. "North," he announced proudly.

"That's an N," Gwyn pointed.

"As I said." He wrote three other names underneath, in a line. "East, south, west."

Gwyn looked at them. "East and west have that letter, s, in the middle," she said, thinking aloud. "I have an N in my name," she said. "And a W too."

That reminded him, and he hastily rubbed out the words. "You're very quick, Innkeeper's daughter."

"Aye, that I am."

He looked uneasy, and she took pity on him. But she didn't know how to tell him she'd keep quiet, without making him feel worse. "My mother tells me my tongue wags," she said. That was the wrong thing to say. "But it doesn't wag over serious matters," she said.

"I don't know why the people must not learn to read," he answered.

"Well, my Lord, maybe the people need all their time for their labors." She couldn't see what use the knowledge would be to the people, how it could help them fill their bellies and protect themselves.

He retreated into silence, turning the pages of the book. Gwyn went back to the cupboard, carrying piles of cloth and then, with a rag dampened in the melted snow, wiping out the deep inside of the cupboard. She had to reach in the length of her arm to clean the back walls, above and below the shelf. She left it with the door open, to dry out while the Lordling ate his midday stew and she had hers, after him, crouched by the fire. Then she replaced the piles of cloth. At that, she stopped. With many days to fill, it wouldn't do not to have tasks waiting. Tomorrow she would do the other cupboard. There was no hurry. She sat beside the fire, her back to the warm stones, her mind empty. The Lordling sat at the table, turning the pages of the long book. She wondered again at his ability to spend long hours so quietly.

Gwyn was beginning to feel painfully restless. The bread was baked, and she could no longer sit quietly by the fire. She crossed to the bed and pulled the shutter aside, to see that snow still fell, straight down now but still thick. She would, she thought, go outside and clear their paths once again. At least, it would be good to get fresh air. At least, it would be something to do.

The Lord was watching her. His pale face revealed nothing. He had his hands spread on another page of the long book, another map. "We could be kept here until spring, Innkeeper's daughter."

Gwyn nodded her agreement.

"He'll think me dead," the Lordling said. "If they made their way to safety."

"The stallion is a big, strong beast," Gwyn reassured him, climbing down from the bed and straightening the blankets.

"As I think him dead," the boy said, his voice barely above a whisper.

He was a brave lad, no question of it, Gwyn thought. Uncomplaining although this misadventure was nothing like what he must be accustomed to. Tad would not have borne it so well.

"I put my faith in the stallion," she repeated.

Unexpectedly the pale face smiled at her. "And your brother, too, he is strong and big."

"Burl's not my brother." Gwyn was surprised into normal speech by the error. "He works for my father."

"He has an odd way of serving, then," the Lordling said.

Gwyn could not answer what she thought, so she answered nothing. Instead, she looked at the map under his hands. She saw the cross, with its initials. The marks that indicated mountains looked small at the top of the page. This map spread across two pages and showed dark lines at the south. "What is that?" she asked him.

"It's the Kingdom," he told her. For a minute, she thought he would be able to keep quiet against his desire to show off his knowledge, but then he gave in. He was not so very different from Tad after all, she thought, as he explained to her where the cities were and which was the King's High City, built on rich land where two rivers came together. These two rivers formed a third, which wound off across the kingdom to the west and south. This river ran along until it left the Kingdom, cutting through the forests to the southwest. Gwyn recognized the sign of the bear by a city up against the western mountains and asked, "Is that Earl Northgate's city?"

"It is."

That, then, was where she had gone to the Doling Room. "Where is the Ram's Head?" she asked.

He pointed his finger to a dark line running away to the

east from Earl Northgate's city. "This is the King's Way and this Hildebrand's city. Your father's Inn is just about here." His finger stopped about halfway between the two cities.

Gwyn pointed to a little mark just north of where the Inn would be. "That's the village then."

He nodded.

"So we're about here."

"Closer, I think," he said, studying the map.

She stared at it. The whole Kingdom lay before her. The river, which ran from the northeast to the southwest, divided the country almost in half. In the southern half, the sign of the falcon was marked in by a city nestled up against the endless forest. "Is this Earl Sutherland's city?" she asked.

"Yes." He hesitated. "The kingdom is divided between those two Earls and the King. He awards land to the Earls. The Earls give their lands into the care of three Lords, each in his own city. Only the four border cities have fortifications, one for each Earl and one held for the Earl by his most trusted Lord. The Lords serve the Earls, the Earls serve the King. The King's private lands lie between the two rivers that come down from the north. Those he keeps for his own revenues. The rest he gives to the Earls."

"So the two Earls have equal strength," Gwyn said.

"That is the way the King wants it," the Lordling said.

"To keep the kingdom from war."

He didn't answer.

"I would ask you a question, my Lord," Gwyn said, thinking of the rumors from the south.

"Yes, Innkeeper's daughter?"

"If the Lords who serve the Earl grow strong—or if the Earl's house is weakened—then who keeps the Lords from war?" The two horses had the King's mark on them, the lion. This Lordling might have heard.

"Nobody keeps the Lords from war, if they are bent on it. So the King must protect his Earls."

He closed the book, without warning. Gwyn moved away from where she had stood so close behind him.

The rest of the day and evening passed in silence. Gwyn sat with her back at the stones, listening to the whisper of the wind. Waiting. She was waiting, she knew, for the snow to cease. Then, when the snow had ceased, she would wait for it to settle enough so they could safely walk through it. All of her life was waiting, she thought crossly.

The Lordling made his last trip outside for the day and crawled into the bed. Gwyn followed his example and could have howled aloud at the flakes still falling from the thick sky. She forced herself to lie quietly by the fire, wrapped in a blanket, waiting for sleep.

The whimpering woke her again, but she recognized it immediately. She rose to comfort the boy. Once again, she spoke gently, touching his wet face with her fingers until the wide eyes focused on her. Once again, he lay back without a word. But she advised him, "If you tell the dream it will not return, my Lord."

In the flickering light, with the hair around his face wet with his own tears, he looked young, a small child. "I cannot."

He had misunderstood her. "I mean, when we return, perhaps your father."

"Him last of any," the Lordling said.

Gwyn shrugged and returned to her place by the fire. She did not return to sleep, however, and neither did the boy. She could hear him moving on the bed, weeping still. Finally, she stirred the fire and spoke toward the other side of the room. "We must do something or we will both go mad, cooped up here." Then, hearing how she had spoken, as if to one of her own people, she said, "I'm sorry, I shouldn't have said—"

"Please give me silence, Innkeeper's daughter," his voice asked. He did not sound like a boy.

Gwyn did not need his rebuke. She rebuked herself. Wrapped up in a blanket, lying on her back beside the banked fire, she took herself to task. It was childishness to let the feelings of being cooped up, and restlessness, govern her thoughts too. She could not afford childishness. The Lords were their own law. Just because they went on two legs did not mean they were the same as the people. And she herself, Gwyn, the Innkeeper's daughter, was just feeling edgy at this time of her life, because the time for choice was approaching her. That there was no choice she cared to make from among those offered her was an irritation to her. Her life did not belong to her.

But whose life did? Were she to wed, her life would belong to the man she married. Were she to say no, her labor would belong to Tad at the Inn, and she would become the Innkeeper's unmarried daughter, until she was too cumbersome or too old to work there. Then she would come out to one of these solitary holdings, and her works and her days would belong to herself. Since she could not have her heart's desire, and she knew she could not, then she would not. But it was hard for a woman.

No easier for a man, who without holding or wife must go serve as a soldier, unless he went into service to the Lords. No easier for a man with a holding, either, because his life belonged to his holding—whether that was what he wanted or not.

Gwyn knew what she did not want, and so she knew her choice. Da must be satisfied. To have two of his daughters well and gladly wed was more than most men could hope for. She would be useful to Tad, and Da would value that.

Gwyn too must be satisfied. She must also govern her tongue more closely, because it wouldn't do to dissatisfy the Lordling with her service.

Ten

WHEN GWYN stepped outside the next morning, she was nearly blinded by light. A bright blue sky hung overhead. Sunlight reflected off the expanse of snow. Her eyes hurt as she went around the side of the house to the privy. Returning, she did not return inside. By then her eyes were accustomed to the light, so instead of entering the house she pushed her way through the snow piled up on the hillside running down before her. The snow lay chest high. It was hard work to force her body through it. She leaned into it and fell rather than walked forward. It gave way reluctantly beneath her weight. She scrabbled upright again and fell forward again.

This was hard work and she made little progress. The air was icy around her. They could not leave that day, nor for many days yet. She stood at the end of the short path her body had forced from the snowfield and looked to the mountains, which nibbled at the rim of the blue sky.

Cold as it was, she had no desire to go into the dim house. She spread her arms wide to greet the mountains.

The Lordling stood at the door of the house, watching her. She reined in her feelings and made her face quiet. She went back to make him his bowl of porridge.

"It's stopped snowing," he said as they passed one another at the door.

"Yes, my Lord." She kept her eyes down. She would speak only when spoken to and sit quiet through whatever days they must spend here.

She served him without a word. He kept looking at her, but she stood back aloof. He looked more like a boy this morning and she wondered how old he was. He said, "Thank you," and, "I'm finished now," but there was no answer she needed to make to that. The Lords were always courteous to their servants. She ate beside the fire when he was done.

"I would like a bath," he said, when she had set the clean bowls back on the shelf.

Gwyn felt her temper rise, but she governed her tongue. She brought in bowls of snow, which she melted by the fire. She poured the water into an iron kettle to warm over the flames. He would not expect a tub, not here in this house. She stood behind him, holding a cloth for washing and a large cloth for drying.

"I will wash myself," he told her.

She went outside before he told her to. She made the pathway in front of the door broader while she waited, until it was like a small yard, where she could walk in a circle to take exercise. Even the slight exercise of walking felt good to her legs.

When he summoned her back into the house, it was to unwelcome news.

"Innkeeper's daughter," the Lordling said, "you must bathe. Bring in some snow to melt. I will keep my back to you."

Gwyn stood mute. Could the Lords order her even when to wash herself?

"After which," he continued, "we will open the door and let fresh air into this hut. The stench is intolerable."

"I cannot bathe if you are in the room, my Lord," Gwyn finally said, keeping her voice level.

"Then I will wait outside, if you must have it so."

Gwyn cleaned the kettle and hauled in more snow, stripped, and washed herself quickly before the fire, shivering because she had not waited to heat the melted snow enough. Then she rinsed out the cloths they had used and lay them beside the fire to dry. What her mother would say, washing in midwinter, Gwyn didn't like to think. But when they had aired out the small room, she had to agree with the Lordling that it was more pleasant, although she did not speak her agreement to him.

The day dragged along underfoot. Gwyn moved restlessly from one task to the other, unable to concentrate her attention, unable to find any enjoyment in any of the tasks her hands performed. She completed few of them: She washed a few of the mugs, then abandoned that chore; she went outside to increase the area she had flattened down, then tired of the cold and exercise; inside, she started on the second cupboard, but only got as far as emptying its contents onto the bed— a pile of cloths and rags of various weight, some cotton, some wool. The Lordling sat at the table, his body motionless but his fingers restlessly turning the pages of the long book. At last, he turned to an empty page and drew on it with one of the charcoal sticks. Gwyn had water warming by the fire for washing out the inside of the second cupboard, when he spoke to her again:

"I would learn to use the staff, Innkeeper's daughter."

She hesitated before answering, to keep herself from snapping at him. It would be easier, she thought, if she had been stranded alone, without this boy to act the Lord with her.

"I know you can teach me. I saw you, you were teaching your brother."

Gwyn sighed. "We have no staffs, my Lord. This room is not very large."

"You can make some from the firewood," he told her. "We will do this outside."

Well, without any exercise she would have trouble sleeping that night, Gwyn thought, and she thought she could avoid hurting the Lordling. "Yes, my Lord," she answered him.

The staffs she made were splintery and short, but good enough for learning. Her hands felt clumsy, holding the staff with mittens on, but she did not think that mattered. The Lordling was a slight and delicate little thing, and she would have to be careful to play gently.

To her surprise, he proved a quick student and a persistent opponent. At first she struck slowly, giving him time to get his guard up so that she wouldn't hit him. But he didn't like that.

"I cannot learn how to use it if you will not fight me hard, Innkeeper's daughter."

"The staffs can give serious injury, my Lord."

"Not as you are using it."

So she fought him a little harder, less careful not to alarm or hurt him. He was quick on his feet, seldom off balance. Gwyn, larger and more skillful, pressed him backwards until he fell into the high snow behind him. He sprang up and brushed his cloak clean. "Again," he said.

She pressed him again, moving him backwards, until he came to the edge of the flattened snow. There, he whirled around, like a dancer. At the same time, he swept with his staff at her feet, holding it at one end like a sword. She jumped backwards, and by the time she was ready to begin the attack again, which was no time at all, he had already moved around her and stood waiting, with the flattened snow at his back.

They didn't stop until the sun started to lower and the temperature fell sharply. Inside, he sat at the table, listless again. She served him stew, then—while he ate—cut up meat from the slab of pork to add to the pot after she had served herself. She would cook the meat during the evening, then

set the pot aside to cool over the night so that she could remove the fat in the morning before setting it over the fire
again to finish cooking. Pork released too much fat into the
gravy, making the stew oily and heavy. The Lordling, she
noticed, did not finish his bowl. She scraped what he left
back into the pot. Gwyn served her own bowl before adding
the fresh meat, a turnip and some more water to the pot. She
would start bread again that night, she thought, glad for
something to do. In the meantime, she thought, seeing him
drawing at the table, she had better finish cleaning that
cupboard so that his bed would be clear when he wanted to
get into it.

Gwyn took a bowl of warmed water and a cloth. She
worked as slowly as she could, spinning the job out, rubbing
over the boards with a damp cloth, rinsing the cloth, wringing
it out to rub over the area again, then taking a fresh cloth to
dry the rough wood. When she heard the Lordling stir restlessly behind her, she smiled. Let him amuse himself, that
wasn't her job. Her job was to keep him fed and to serve his
needs, as he required of her. No more. It gave Gwyn pleasure
to hear his restlessness behind her as she worked placidly at
her chore.

She reached her hand in to wash down the back of the
cupboard above the shelf, but could not reach in far enough.
That was curious. She moved her arm to the lower half and
found a board at the back there, which she patiently washed,
then washed again, then dried. That completed the job, but
she tried the back of the top shelf again, because she was in
a mood to be slow and thorough.

Her hand, holding the damp cloth, went into empty
space. She put her shoulder inside of the cupboard and reached
as far back as she could. The shelf cut against her shoulder as
she stretched her right arm out. At first her hand met a wall,
much deeper back than that of the other cupboard. That, too,
was curious. She groped downward with her hand. Her fingers
found rough cloth, a blanket. She brought the damp rag

out and dropped it into the bowl of water. Then she groped at the hidden storage place again. The blanket covered something hard, but soft at other places. She pulled the cloth aside, working her hand underneath it. She felt smooth leather, which ended on top of something silky, and then hard metal, long and sharp, too long for a razor—a sword? What would Old Megg be doing with a sword hidden away in her cupboards?

Gwyn's finger went back to the leather and she pulled it toward her. It lay loose, and she brought it slowly forward, over onto the shelf—a boot, the brown leather worn soft, a boot so long its top was folded back into a cuff, its soles well-cobbled but worn. Gwyn pushed it quickly back into its hiding place and pulled at the silky fabric. She didn't understand what these things were doing in Old Megg's hut, but if the silky thing was blue and was a vest and with silver clasps—

"Innkeeper's daughter," his voice said, right behind her. Gwyn froze. "I would have a word with you."

She did not dare to turn. "Yes, my Lord." She could see a silver buckle shining on blue cloth, smooth blue cloth. She did not dare pull it any further out, not at that moment when she was not sure how effectively her body blocked his view into the cupboard. She did not want to push it back into its hiding place until she had confirmed her guess.

"Jackaroo," she thought.

"Who?" he asked. "What?" She had spoken aloud.

Confusion tied Gwyn's tongue in knots. "Let me finish this. I must clear your Lordship's bed. If I may continue, my Lord?" She spoke humbly, to please him, as her hand shoved the tunic back and tried to replace the rough blanket. When she withdrew her head and shoulders from the cupboard, she saw him hovering close behind her.

"What did you say?"

"If I could replace the things in the cupboard, my Lord," she repeated. She kept her eyes down to hide her face and thoughts. What would Old Megg be doing with Jackaroo's clothing? From the old stories.

Gwyn took up an armload of cloths and hastily replaced them on the top shelf. She must fill that first. One thing she knew about boys was their curiosity.

"No, what you said before that." He sounded cross.

It would not do to appear to be concealing anything. Gwyn tried distracting him, starting with just enough of the truth. "Oh, Jackaroo," she kept her voice expressionless. She moved back and forth from bed to cupboard as she spoke. "It's just an old story, my Lord. I don't know why it crossed my mind at that moment, but for some reason it did. I didn't realize I'd spoken aloud."

"I've heard the stories," the Lordling said, not interested. "I said I wanted to speak with you."

Gwyn closed the wooden door and turned to face him. That was safe, now. She clasped her hands together in front of her, to conceal her nervousness, and looked him in the eye, to conceal her secrets. "Yes, my Lord?"

After he was asleep she would look again, or if she could get him out of the house during the day. She wondered if he would believe that she needed another bath tomorrow. She could think of no other way to guarantee herself the privacy to take out the contents of the secret cupboard.

The Lordling stared at her, his face pale and expressionless as he tried to appear older than he was. "I have been thinking that we must speak to one another."

"What about, my Lord?"

"I don't know," he answered her impatiently. "I don't care." His dignity fell from him. "But—I'm going crazy, and I will, with another day like this one, and the others. Trapped here. Nobody need ever know, if we just talk. Nobody ever would, would they? And if we never do get back, nobody will know anyway. You *must* have something to talk about. I just—"

He broke off speaking and walked to the fire. "This hut is so small and close, and we are kept so close together in it and—"

"If you wish it, my Lord," Gwyn said cautiously.

"That's not what I meant," his voice rose. "Not my-Lording me and everything. I just sit here—and think and—I can't just sit here and think and—"

His body was tense with frustration because he was, Gwyn reminded herself, just a boy, a boy Lord but still . . . She sat down at the table and after a minute he sat facing her.

They were silent, having nothing to say to one another. The fire crackled. The Lordling stared at Gwyn, waiting nervously. She stared back at him but didn't see him because her thoughts were still whirling about, trying to make sense of the clothing she had discovered.

He had no patience. "Oh, never mind. It's no use. I shouldn't have anyway."

"It's all right. I'm feeling—cooped up, myself," Gwyn told him. She gathered her thoughts together. "You did well today with the staff. I didn't think someone as slight as you are would do so well."

"I'm not slight."

"Compared to Tad you are," she told him.

"Who's Tad? Your brother?"

"My brother, yes."

"You could tell me about your family," he suggested. He was unwilling to ask anything of her and his words came stiffly. "No, never mind." He got up from the table and paced to the fire, then back.

"It's all right, my Lord. I wouldn't tell anybody."

"Oh, I know that, I can tell that," he assured her, looking once again as young as he was. "It's me. I might." But he came back to sit with her again.

"You might, if you say so, and I guess you'd know that." That was certainly an honest thing for him to say. "But even if you did, the worst that could happen is that my father would be reprimanded, and he would be angry at me. If you told. But I don't think you would tell, or at least, not in any way intended to harm me. Would you?"

"No, I wouldn't do that."

So she told him about the Inn and Rose's wedding and

Tad's sickly childhood. He listened eagerly, asking questions, about her chores and the making of the wines, about Tad's responsibilities, about how a man had to name his heir when he reached thirty-five years and pass on the holding before he was forty-five.

"It's not like that for us. It's the oldest son who takes the title, when his father dies," he said, then changed the subject. "I don't have nearly so much to do," he told her. "I'm tutored in my letters and numbers, and I take fencing lessons and I have to learn how to conduct myself. It's dull."

"It wouldn't be dull learning those things."

"Oh yes it is."

"I don't think so."

He told her about the priest who tutored him and described his schoolroom. He described the great hall where dinners were served and, when she asked him, what the Lords and Ladies wore there. She told him about Old Megg, who lived in this house, and how she had saved the goats from thieves.

"Does she live alone here?"

"Yes."

"Why doesn't she have a husband and children?"

"She never married. I think she had a brother, but he went for a soldier, years ago. At least, I think that's what I heard. When a man goes for a soldier he never comes home again."

"Like our servants."

"Yes," Gwyn said. She didn't add what she was thinking, that whoever went into service to the Lords in any way must leave his home and never return.

The Lordling had been following his own thoughts. "I wonder why they don't. Everybody says they don't want to because they don't have the same feelings about home that we do, but . . . do you think that's true?"

"No," Gwyn said, angry.

"I miss my home," he told her. "Even if we never do go back, I'll always miss it."

"Why wouldn't you go back?"

"I can't talk about that. Really, I promised."

Gwyn felt a rush of curiosity, but she knew she couldn't pry or cajole, as she would have with Tad, because this was a Lord. So she asked him what he learned when he was learning how to conduct himself. He described the way to eat at a table covered with an embroidered cloth, how to cut a serving from a fowl and set it on your plate while the servant held the tray for you, how to address Lords of different ranks, how to greet a Lady. Gwyn asked him about how the Lady should act, and they had a pretend conversation where she was the Lady and he the Lord, until they were both laughing. They ate together at the table that evening and spent the long dark hours discussing how the Inn was run.

"You really know how to do all those things?" he asked, lying in his bed with the covers warm over him.

"Someone besides Da must know. Tad will learn them, so that when he inherits he can manage it well. He'll be named this summer."

"What about you? How old are you, Innkeeper's daughter?"

"Sixteen. Seventeen in the fall."

She heard him rustling in the bed as he raised himself onto one elbow. "And not married?"

"No, my Lord, not married."

Because he said nothing, she knew he was considering her problem. Then he spoke. "You could come and serve us. Except, we wouldn't be able to talk like this. We're never left alone with a servant, you know."

"Besides, I'd make a terrible servant," Gwyn agreed, although she smiled at the kindness of his intention.

"You'd hate it, wouldn't you."

"Aye, I would."

At last he slept. Gwyn lay in the faint glow of the banked fire then, her mind at last free to work at the question of the hidden clothing. Old Megg had only lived in this house for five years. Before then it was empty, except during the summer when Da's hireling lived in it to watch the grapes. Before that, the Weaver's family had occupied it. So perhaps the sword and boots, tunic and—she was sure they were in there also—silk mask, plumed hat and trousers, belonged to Cam's family.

But if so, why would they have left them hidden here? Perhaps only Cam's father, the dead vineyarder, had known about them. Perhaps they had been in his family for generations and even he didn't know. It made no sense.

Except it meant, of course, that they were not just old stories, the tales of Jackaroo. It meant that there was some truth at the heart of it. And hadn't the old Granny told Gwyn she had seen Jackaroo herself? He would have been a living man then, and he would have used this isolated house as his changing place, trusting the man of the house to keep his secret. He must have really trusted that man.

Or perhaps it was a fancy he had, this Lord or this King or whoever it really was, and he simply spun stories around the fancy. He would have had the clothing to wear himself, because if it was years ago it might have been the way the clothing was made and worn then.

Or perhaps the long-ago vineyarder had come upon a body in the forests, or on the hillside, or a herder found a dead man in the mountains. Perhaps someone had stripped that body of its finery. He might have hidden his booty away, knowing that when a Lord was discovered missing there would be a search, and if a Lord was found by his men before he was found by the wolves then the men would know he had been robbed. In that case, the clothing must be hidden away or the man would be hanged for his deed. The body, Gwyn thought, might have been that of Jackaroo, wounded and fleeing to the hills for safety, or to the mountains for escape, with the hunters close behind him. That would explain why the Lords had never captured him.

However the clothing had come to be hidden here, one thing was clear: there had once been such a man, and the stories had at least a kernel of truth to them. Gwyn found that a peculiarly satisfying thought and fell asleep smiling over it.

When the Lordling started to whimper, Gwyn woke quickly. But that made no difference to the process of his nightmare. He must, it seemed, turn and whimper. The tears must flow and his mouth must open in soundless cries before he could be awakened. Gwyn spoke to him, soothing, until at last his open eyes looked with recognition at her. "Innkeeper's daughter," he said. In the restless yellow light from the banked fire, he looked as old as his father, like his father, ageless.

"Aye, it is, my Lord," she answered him in the same warm voice she had used to soothe and awaken him.

"I thank you," he said, turning to sleep again.

She watched over him for a few minutes, knowing by then his way of turning away to conceal further tears. But he seemed quiet. She returned to her blanket.

"You must have a name," he said sleepily.

"Aye, I do." She gave it to him. "Gwyn."

ᵇᵉᶻ Eleven

G WYN AWOKE the next morning to the first of many surprises, the sound of the Lordling dumping an armload of wood beside the fireplace. She sat up quickly, to protest.

"I'm glad you're awake. Gwyn," he added; he dropped the last word as clumsily as he had dropped the wood beside the fire. "I chopped it myself. It's sunny today. I never knew I could chop wood, did you?"

Gwyn looked at his work. "You could take a few lessons from Burl," she said. His face fell and she added quickly, ". . . although it's unusually good for a first try. And how did you enjoy the work, my Lord?"

His blue eyes sparkled as he smiled up at her. "At first it was fun. Then, it wasn't, it was just hard work. But I kept doing it."

Gwyn smiled back at him and went outside, to go to the bathroom and take a measure of the day. The sky hung clear blue overhead, and the few clouds floating in it were white and soft. She thought that the snows were starting to sink. They must be, because she saw the dark leather of the saddle showing through. She dug it free and carried it inside, the bit over her shoulder. She sat them beside the fire to dry. Old Megg would have no oil in the house, but if she rubbed at it with her hand the leather should come up soft again.

The Lordling fetched in a bowl of snow to melt, while she built up the fire. As their porridge cooked, he chattered at her, about the similarities between the wood-chopping axe and the axe men took into battle, then about the weapons in his grandfather's house, some of which were old and no longer used except to decorate the walls, and about his own lessons in sword-fighting and, when they sat down together to eat their bowls of porridge, about the leather vest he had to wear during his exercise with the sword and his father's emblazoned shield and—

"Hold off," Gwyn begged him. "You're like rain the way you talk. I think you haven't talked for years and now you're spending all the words you've saved up."

"Oh," he said, falling suddenly silent. For a minute, she thought she had spoiled his day with her teasing, but then he started up again. "Really, Gwyn, his shield has three metals on it, I'm not telling tales."

"I didn't think you were. And if you were, I wouldn't mind, since I'll never find you out."

"Circles of bronze in the steel, and the"—he stopped himself—"the animal in it is silver, all silver."

He was keeping his secret well, although why it should be a secret Gwyn couldn't guess. "That must be work for someone to keep shined," she remarked.

"And I *don't* have anyone to talk to," he babbled on. "I haven't any brothers, or even any sisters. I had a brother, an older brother."

Gwyn knew how that was. "I had two others myself, who died."

"Why should they die?"

"Many children do, when they're young." But that was an odd way to ask the question, not how, or when, but why.

"I knew that," he said, "but I forgot. Your life is harder than ours, isn't it?"

Gwyn thought he wanted to change the subject. "Were there no other boys to play with?"

"Cousins, but—we didn't talk, we just tried to beat one another out because—at lessons and at swords, because—we're not ever alone, you know."

"I didn't know that. You mean, not ever alone with one another? Why should that be?"

"There's always a master there, or one of the adults, to see how we're doing."

"What about the girls?" Gwyn wondered.

"Oh—the girls, they stay with the women. They embroider. Or something. I don't know what they do."

"It sounds like a large family," Gwyn said. She had climbed up the ladder and was hacking off some of the meat. He watched her.

"I could do that. Could I do that tomorrow? Can I cut it up? It's large, but we all lived in Grandfather's house."

Castle, Gwyn amended in her mind.

"Except he died."

He cut up the meat and stirred up the stew in the pot. Gwyn took a turnip from Old Megg's meager store and scraped off the tough skin, working beside him. "My Granda just died," she said. "He had the Inn before Da. We had the burning while you were there. He was almost sixty." She waited to hear about his grandfather.

"What burning?" he asked.

"Of Granda's body, on the pyre. Didn't your grandfather have one?"

"No, he was buried with our family."

"Buried?" Gwyn asked. "Is that what Lords do?" The carcasses of animals were buried, never people. If people were buried, wolves or foxes or even dogs would dig them up. "How do you keep—" she started to ask, then stopped herself. His face looked pale and carefully expressionless again. He cut the meat slowly, pulling off fat with careful fingers. His hands were pale and soft. He wore no signet.

They worked in silence. Finally, she asked him, "Is something the matter?"

"No."

"You don't have to tell me anything," she said. She guessed he must have loved his grandfather. "I only ask because—you're like a summer rain, you were talking away as if you'd talk for hours, and then suddenly you stop. That's what summer rain does, you know? But, in my experience, it's not what boys do."

He worked beside her with his slight shoulders held stiff, his whole body held stiff, looking like a grown man. Gwyn felt sorry for him, which was ridiculous because there was nothing for the people to pity the Lords.

"It's just"—She hesitated before speaking. But after all, what could happen besides him going silent on her again, as he had been all the time except this morning. "I'm sorry about whatever—is making you unhappy."

He remained silent. Gwyn sighed and got back to work on the turnip, cutting it into little chunks, then adding it and the meat to the pot, then pouring on a little water. He was sitting on the bed, watching her, when she turned around. "Do you want to go outside and work with the staffs?" she offered.

He shook his head, his face down and his hair falling around it.

Gwyn took her cloak off the hook. "I'm going to start breaking a path up around the hill. If we can get a path started, then that'll be that much less to work at when we leave. Da's vineyard is on the other side," she said, just to be saying something. "I could use your help."

"All right." He put on his own cloak and followed her outside.

Before they started up the hillside, however, they cleared the way to the privy, which leaned up against the goat pen. That job taken care of, Gwyn led him around behind the hut.

She shouldered her way through chest-high snow, clambering more than walking. The crust broke beneath the weight of her body and she crawled up until she felt her feet touch firm ground, then she stood. The path gave way unevenly under her feet and she tried to jump on the snow, to give it some packing. The Lordling struggled along behind her, stamping with his feet.

It was hard work and hot work, under the bright sun. It was cold, wet work too, and her cheeks felt numb. It was slow work, pushing uphill through the mass of snow. They spent the morning at it and had not even reached the crest of the hill when Gwyn halted. She turned around to look at their progress.

Down the hill the little hut crouched against a white background, smoke rising up in a thin line from its chimney. Only the dark roofline of the goat pen showed, and white hills undulated upwards to the far mountains. The mountains spiked up into the sky.

"From here, the mountains look like a wall, don't they?" Gwyn said. She was breathing heavily and had her cloak curled backwards over her shoulders, to let her body cool.

The Lordling looked better for the exercise. His cheeks had a faint pink color in them. He had shoved the damp strands of hair behind his ears.

"They *are* a wall," he told her. "Don't you remember the map? But my father says you don't know whether a wall walls in or walls out."

Like the walls around the cities, Gwyn thought, or even the courtyard at the Inn, which was walled on three sides by buildings. "Nobody knows what lies beyond the mountains," she said, her eyes on their peaks.

"Yes, they do."

They slid back down the long hill. This made the pathway more firm. Gwyn had thought that his mood was eased by the hard work, but when they reentered the hut to eat she saw again the sad, firm set of his mouth. He didn't even grieve like a boy.

Without any thought, she kneeled down in front of him and wrapped her arms around him. "Osh, lad," she said. He didn't push her away. He just bent his head to bury his face on her shoulder.

When he did pull away, it was to accuse her, "You said you wouldn't tell. Not ever."

"Then I won't," Gwyn answered, worried and confused. "You'd better hang up these cloaks while I serve the stew."

"I'm not hungry." He didn't move.

"Yes, you are," she snapped.

He ignored her. "When they bury someone in winter, they have to burn fires on the ground if it's been cold," he told her. "So they can dig. If the ground is frozen. Because my mother died in winter," he told her.

Gwyn went on with her hands' tasks, getting down bowls and spoons, cutting chunks of bread and cheese. She didn't turn to look at him.

"So when you drop your handful of dirt on her, it was cold and hard. It was like pebbles and I had to because everybody has to." His voice got cold and hard at her back. "Then the servants shoveled the dirt over, just shoveling, and it thunked—and the shovels scraped. Because it was cold. I didn't want them to put all that dirt, because it's too heavy—but I didn't do anything. I'm not big enough, I wasn't; as fast as I could throw it out they'd put it in all over me too."

He stopped talking. He sat down at the table. Gwyn served him his bowl and sat down with him, but she had no more appetite than he had. This would give anyone nightmares.

"How long ago did she die, my Lord," she asked, without making it much of a question.

"Last winter. She was supposed to have a baby but she died instead."

Gwyn put her spoon into the hot stew, but did not lift it out. "You dream about her."

He didn't answer.

"When somebody dies, they can't feel anything, or see, or think. Or anything," she said.

"Do you really know that?"

"How could I really know that?" she demanded. "But I've killed chickens. After you chop their heads off it's just— meat." She wished immediately that she had not said that. "I mean, everything alive is gone."

But he didn't seem bothered by the comparison. "I never killed anything."

"Not even hunting?"

"I'm not old enough."

"How old do you have to be?"

"Twelve."

"How old are you?"

"Almost eleven."

"That's about Tad's age, my brother. You've seen him. Tad wouldn't come with us when we burned Granda, he didn't want to watch."

"Has he killed chickens?" The Lordling at last picked up his spoon and took a bite.

"He's watched. I guess he thinks people are different."

"Don't you think they are?"

"Not that way, no. Because animals and people both have blood keeping them alive. Turnips are different, I think, and apples, things like that." The relief that she hadn't put terrible ideas into the Lordling's head lifted Gwyn's spirits and loosened her tongue. "People are different from chickens in other ways, and cows and horses. But not that way."

"I agree," he decided. "Do you think people are better? Than chickens? Or horses; I know more about horses."

"Oh, well then, my Lord," she answered with a quick tongue, "I'm not often pleased with people."

The look he gave her was not a boy's look. "Nor Lords either?"

Gwyn felt her face grow hot. That question she did not answer. She bent her face to her bowl and ate. When she dared to look at him again, he was grinning at her.

"I know nothing of the Lords," she told him, cross.

He just grinned away.

"Nor am I curious to know."

"That's not true," he crowed. "You're as curious as can be, that's why you ask all those questions."

"I didn't ask that many questions," Gwyn protested, but then she had to admit it. "Not all that many. And why shouldn't I be curious."

He ate on, well pleased with himself.

"You aren't dull yourself, are you my Lord," she finally gave in to him.

"It's all right, I won't tell," he promised her. "If I did, you know, I'd get in as much trouble as you."

"More, I hope."

As they ate, with good appetites, Gwyn hoped the Lordling had not noticed that they were more than halfway through the hanging meat; he could not know, she knew, that at the rate they could move through this snow, they would be caught by night long before they could reach the village. And she wondered about the burial of his mother; she wondered why the Lords would put their dead into the earth, like animals. She thought she knew why he had dreams—she had never seen such a thing, but she could picture it; a Lady—his mother —lying in a hole in the ground; and she could imagine how it would feel to look down as the face was covered with dirt. She could imagine also, she discovered, how it would feel to lie there, still and dead: The dirt would fall soft, at first, soft as rain and as light, and then it would lie heavy, pressing down —Gwyn shuddered. She was no longer hungry.

"What's the matter?" he asked her.

Gwyn tried to smile easily. "My mother tells me I have too much imagination."

"I think you're right, though, about the chickens."

This was what boys did. They thought their own thoughts and when you thought they had forgotten something they would surprise you. "What did she look like?"

"She was beautiful, she was tall and quiet. Her hair was brown, like mine, but darker. It hung down her back like silk. I can't remember much. It's been so long since I was in her care."

"What do you mean?"

"When boys turn five they go to live with the men, in the men's quarters. Only girls stay with the women." He sopped gravy with his bread. "Or sickly boys; if you're really sick then you go to the women's quarters, but I never was. But I could see her at dinners, when she was at the high table next to my father, so I know she was beautiful. You should wear your hair long that way. I don't know why you all want to look ugly."

"Long hair would get in the way. It would fall into the stew. It would be in a terrible mess every night and I'd have to spend hours combing it out when I only wanted to go to sleep. Look at your hair now from not being cared for—it's like a bird's nest. Hair like that would be nothing but trouble to me."

"The servants take care of it."

"I have no servants."

"What about Burl?"

"That's different."

"How is it different?"

She tried to tell him about Burl, whose parents had died of sickness in Hildebrand's City, when he was a boy, how the priest had brought him to one of the fairs and Da had bought him, to train him. The Lordling pelted her with questions about that, asking what would have happened if the Innkeeper hadn't wanted him, where else he might have gone, asking what would have happened if Burl had been a girl, asking why the priests hadn't brought him to the Lords to be a servant, asking if he would serve Tad when Tad inherited. His spirits certainly seemed eased, Gwyn observed to herself, patiently answering his questions.

They talked through the afternoon, sometimes with the Lordling answering Gwyn's questions about life in his Grandfather's house, sometimes with Gwyn answering his about how

Da's holdings increased. They went outside, where he insisted that she let him hide and then come to find him. She had no trouble seeing where he was, until he demanded how she knew, and she showed him the way his tracks through the snow gave him away.

Inside again, he helped her shake out the bedclothes to freshen them and they turned his mattress over. They ate cheese and bread, drank melted snow, built up the fire. He took out the long book again, and the bits of charcoal and continued talking as she sat at the table with him.

"When do you think we'll be able to leave here?" he asked her. He had taken one of the last pages for his own and was making marks on it. She watched him, envying the work of his fingers. She wished her hands had some work, even knitting, to occupy them.

"Maybe soon. Not tomorrow yet."

"We've started the last of the cheeses. Should we eat less?"

"Not yet, my Lord," she decided.

"It would be all right. I expect I can stand to be hungry." She thought that was true, and she thought he wouldn't complain about it either.

"I know that, my Lord." Firelight gave his face warmer colors, but even so, she thought, he looked less pale than before. His voice, too, when he spoke, seemed livelier.

"What about you?" His eyes caught hers.

"Me?"

"Will you marry?"

"Me?"

"You're almost too old, aren't you? What happens if you don't marry by the time, what will you do? Do you want to?"

Such questions he had no right to ask. "I don't know, my Lord."

"But you must have thought about it, Gwyn."

"Aye, I have. But my thoughts are my own business."

She should not speak that way to a Lord, however young, and she knew it.

He did not seem to notice her stiffness. "What if you

don't, what if there's nobody you want to, you could come be my servant. I'd like that. I would, wouldn't you? We'd have to cut off your hair and pretend you were a man, or a boy because you wouldn't need to shave a beard, but what if we did? If we did, when I marry then you could serve my wife." He watched her face eagerly. Gwyn didn't know whether to laugh at his tumble of ideas or pity the loneliness that made him dream up such things. "I mean it, Gwyn. We could do that. Would you like it?"

She hesitated.

"No, you wouldn't. Neither would I, if I were you," he said. "I wouldn't mind if we didn't go back for a long time. Would you?"

"No, my Lord, I wouldn't," Gwyn told him honestly. She liked this boy, this Lordling. "Except that I have so little to do," she admitted. "I'm used to having my days busy."

"We could carve wooden swords and I could show you how."

That wasn't a bad idea. "And we can continue breaking a path," Gwyn said. It was only the evening that stretched so long and empty. "I would make a terrible servant." She laughed. "I have a temper and a sharp tongue and I don't like being lazy."

"I know," he answered, not looking at her, watching his own hands where they moved on the paper. "I know you'd hate it. You'd get all sour, like green apples."

"And everybody knows how bad green apples are for you." She was enjoying his idea of her.

He laughed with her and closed the book. With the charcoal, he made marks on the wood of the table. Gwyn watched him. He was making letters, four of them, but not in a cross the way the maps made them. He wrote them in a straight line. Two she recognized.

"That's your name," he told her. She stood behind him to look at the letters. GWYN. She studied them in silence, while he wrote something else underneath. Just as she opened her mouth to see if he would name the two letters she didn't know and wondered if she dared ask him to give her a piece of charcoal to copy the shapes herself—if she would be going too far to ask that—he pointed to the long line of letters underneath her name.

"That's my name," he told her.

Gwyn could think of nothing to say. She did not look at the Lordling. Her eyes were caught like a hooked fish on the long line of letters. The first and last were the same as in her name, she noticed.

"My name's Gaderian," he said. He turned his face to look into her eyes.

Gwyn didn't know what she should say. She didn't know if she ought to say anything, or if this was something she ought to begin forgetting right away.

Oddly enough, it was the Lordling who reassured her. "You won't tell."

Gwyn shook her head. No, she never would. "Hello, Gaderian," she said.

That struck him funny. "Hello, Gwyn." He giggled.

Then she dared to ask him the name of the first letter, the round one with a tail. Then, when he answered that, the name of the middle one, the one that looked like a forked twig. He answered both questions, so she knew the names of all the letters in her name. She asked him about the letters in his own name, the tall mountain peak letter first, then the big-bellied one.

"You'd better learn the alphabet," he told her. "Sit down here," he told her. She pulled her stool over beside him. He put a piece of charcoal into her hand.

"But you have to promise, on your honor—" he said.

"On my honor," Gwyn promised.

"And I give you my word too, on my honor," Gaderian said to her.

They got to work.

~~≫≋~ Twelve

THE NEXT three days passed quickly, with too much to do in them. Gwyn and Gaderian broke more of a path each morning. The weather held clear and cold. Under each day's sunlight, the snow sank, until it was no higher than Gwyn's knees. It was heavier to push through then, but even so they could make better progress. Often Gaderian could move right along the surface, because his weight was not enough to break through the thickened snow. Then he would suddenly fall through at a soft spot and emerge with his head and cloak coated. Usually he worked patiently behind Gwyn, trampling down the path she had broken. Sometimes, she would hear his voice and turn to find herself alone: When he hid like that she would track backwards until she could see where he had gone off the rough path, then her eye would search out the marks on the snow's surface until she saw a mound suspiciously higher than the rest. Sometimes, if she had not marked carefully the direction of his voice, she could not find him. He was getting better at concealing his tracks. In the mornings, they trekked across Da's vineyard and down that hillside to the dell, where the snow was piled up deep and heavy, and up the next rise. On the third morning, Gwyn heard the distant song of a bird from among the trees ahead. They were just past halfway to the village and she told Gaderian, "I think tomorrow we can go home."

"It's not my home."

They stood side by side, with the sun high overhead. She could see distant lines of smoke rising up into the clear sky. She put her arm around his shoulder for a minute and told him, "I too will be sorry to come to the end of these days."

"Anyway we're running out of food," he consoled them both.

During the afternoons they had mock battles with the staffs and with rough wooden swords they had made out of thin slats of wood. Gaderian tried to explain to Gwyn that it was entirely different with steel at the end of your arm. The wood, he said, was too light to really give you the feel of it; steel could bend and spring, slice and jab. But Gwyn could learn to keep her free hand behind her, and how to move with the parry-thrust of the one-handed weapon. When they fought, with staff or sword, they took care not to strike one another around the face or head, but went freely for other parts of the body. Most often, they both picked up a few bruises. As they played out their matches, Gwyn learned some of Gaderian's quickness of foot, as if it were a dance, not a match. He, in turn, became more aggressive, bearing down upon her steadily when he had an advantage, as if it were a march, not a match.

When the sun slid down the sky, they went inside. They ate as little as possible and added water to the stew to make it a soup, so that it would last longer. It might always snow again. In the evenings, they worked over the letters. Gwyn learned them quickly. Although her hand formed them clumsily on the wooden tabletop, her memory could hold their shapes and their names. She learned how the letters stood together to make words. "What I'll do with this knowledge, I don't know," she often said.

"The same thing I'll do with my knowledge of how to use a staff," he answered her. "I could send you a book, if you'd like that."

"And have the Bailiff after me?" she asked, laughing. "No thank you very much, I've no wish to go to prison."

"Nobody goes to prison for something like that, Gwyn. You don't really think they do, do you? Besides, I bet I could do it secretly."

"I hope you won't even try."

"Not even maps?"

"Oh," and Gwyn hesitated. She never tired of looking at the Lord's maps, at the design the lines made; she liked understanding the bird's view of the Kingdom, and where places were in relation to one another.

"Does your father mean to map the lands beyond the Kingdom?" she asked Gaderian. It seemed to her that his father must be the King's mapmaker, and that he must be training Gaderian to his art.

"We may not leave the Kingdom," Gaderian answered her idle question. By that time, Gwyn knew better than to ask him why. He kept his secrets, and she knew no more about his own home or his proper title than she had known the first time she had heard of him.

Gwyn had no time to get back to the secret cupboard in those few days. The thought of the clothes hidden there was often in her mind, but she didn't dare risk looking at them with Gaderian so often at her shoulder. He was both curious and quick-witted, and Gwyn thought that until she was sure she knew exactly what it was she was hiding, she would give him nothing to question.

She had told him tales of Jackaroo in the same spirit that he had told her stories of knights who fought dragons and rescued princesses from dark towers. "I don't believe in dragons," she told him. "Nothing made of flesh could have fire inside it to spit out, and they must be flesh or they couldn't be slain."

"This Jackaroo is nothing but a thief, a vagabond," Gaderian had told her. "No Bailiff woud be as stupid as that, you know. If he was that stupid, he couldn't be a bailiff. The people would always be tricking him, the Lord's revenues would fall off and he'd get rid of that Bailiff and put in someone who could do the job."

"And Ladies would never wander the countryside alone, even asking for someone to save their fathers."

"No more than a King long dead would dress up like that and ride around trying to atone for his wicked life."

"But they are good stories," Gwyn said.

"I like stories," he agreed.

"You wouldn't expect to be sent off to fight a dragon, would you?" Gwyn asked Gaderian.

"No more than you would sit back and wait for Jackaroo to come rescue you from trouble," he answered her, laughing.

Gwyn almost asked him what he would make of the clothing hidden away behind the cupboard. For all that he was so much younger than she was, he had a much broader knowledge of the world. She had already opened her mouth to tell him, and show him, and ask him, when she realized how foolish that would be. Until she knew whose they were and how they had gotten there, she shouldn't put knowledge of them into the Lord's hands. Not even into Gaderian's hands.

The last days in Old Megg's hut were good days, for all that they ate sparingly and were never far from hunger. Gaderian no longer dreamed and Gwyn had put aside the question of her own future. The last days went slowly and peacefully by them.

They were both in high spirits as they closed and latched the door behind them. Gwyn carried the Lord's saddlebag over her shoulder. The long book and pieces of charcoal were safe inside it. They had tidied the house, covered the last log with ashes so that it would burn out safely, and piled fresh-cut wood beside the fireplace, should another have need of it. There was a little meat left and the last part of a cheese. The saddle and bridle were safely hidden in the loft, and Gwyn had folded the blankets from the bed to add to those that filled the secret cupboard, to preserve its secret more safely. They set off together on the white path they had made for themselves, Gaderian chattering about the surprise their arrival would be, as they climbed the hillside and crossed the vineyard.

By the time they had reached the crest overlooking the village, the sun shone high overhead. Although the first part of the journey had been easy, once they were breaking fresh paths it grew arduous. On the crest, Gwyn hesitated, looking down at the cluster of houses. Everybody was inside. Smoke rose from chimneys, but not from the forge. Paths had been shoveled between the houses and the well.

When Gaderian spoke, she realized with a start how long it had been since he had ceased his chattering. "I think you're right; I think my father must have made his way to safety, don't you think, Gwyn?"

"I think," she said.

"We could be wrong."

"Yes, my Lord, we could."

"Then I could stay with you," he explained to her. He had obviously been considering this. "Because if my father—didn't arrive safely, then neither did Burl, so there would be work and I could disguise myself. Don't you see?"

"Like a story, my Lord?" she asked him.

He didn't answer. After a while, he smiled reluctantly at her.

"I suppose some stories might be true," she teased him.

"Give me a head start and I'll bet you can't find me. I remember the way from here, I do. I can see the smoke from the Inn. Will you, Gwyn?"

"Innkeeper's daughter, my Lord," she reminded him.

His face grew solemn, but he refused to be entirely quelled. "Then I order you to do it, Innkeeper's daughter. You must count to fifty—you can count, can't you?"

"Aye, I can count, to fifty."

"And turn your back."

Gwyn turned her back. She stood dreaming over the village, seeing how the hills undulated in the background, falling down to form the little valley where the houses nestled together around the well, and how the roof that covered the well echoed the shapes of the hills. The sky above was covered by a dusting of filmy clouds. She stood, for more than the count of fifty, and then she moved on.

She followed his footprints into the trees. There, the snow lay less deep, under a thicker crust. His footprints no longer showed.

Gwyn kept her eyes open and her wits clear as she followed the way home. Nowhere could she see tracks. Nowhere could she see any movement. Nowhere did any shape look like a boy hiding himself under the snow or within a snow-shrouded bush. She half expected him to call out to her at any moment, but there was no sound in the woods but her own steps.

When she emerged on the hillside behind the Inn, Gwyn forgot all about Gaderian. Smoke rose out of all three chimneys, and her heart rose with it. There was someone in the guest quarters. It could not be the Messenger, because he would have left the Inn before the blizzard came down. The chances were, then, that it was the Lord who burned the fire that gave out smoke from the guest wing. Which meant that there was a chance that Burl was either in his own little room or caring for the animals or sitting at the kitchen table playing a melody on his pipe.

Gwyn looked down on the familiar scene. The windows were shuttered against cold. The garden lay under a blanket of snow, but the chicken coop was dark with life and paths led there, as well as out to the privy. She turned around to call behind her. "I'm here. I didn't find you. You've won, my Lord."

She turned to go down the hillside and in her eagerness called down to the Inn, cupping her hands around her mouth to make her voice carry. "Halloo! Halloo the Inn! Halloo!"

The kitchen door opened. She saw her mother standing there, her hands under an apron. Gwyn waved her arms in the air and scurried down the hillside as fast as she could, more excited than she had known. One by one they came out to meet her, stopping by the door as she rushed toward them, her mother and father, Rose, and then Tad yelling wild greetings, which she couldn't really hear. Even the Lord came out. He made his way through her family and crossed toward her as she hastened up to him. His eyes were on the hillside behind her and his hand on the hilt of his sword. He strode out long in leather boots.

Gwyn had moved past him to the circle of her family—but where was Burl?—before she heard what he was saying. She halted, and turned.

"Innkeeper's daughter."

"Here is your bag, my Lord." She dropped it at his feet since he did not reach a hand for it.

"I asked you, where is my son?" The cold voice rang, like steel on steel.

Gwyn looked back to the hillside, where the trees began, and opened her mouth to answer him. He had his sword at her throat before she could speak a word.

"I left him in your care." His cold eyes pinned her and his distant voice was icy. "We see what care you took of him. You should not have returned, Innkeeper's daughter."

Fear was at Gwyn's throat, too, as cold and sharp as steel. "No. I didn't—"

The sword pressed deeper. The swords with which she and Gaderian had played had been such toys, Gwyn thought. Fear sat stiff along her spine, like a blade. He would kill her here, without hesitation, she knew it.

"My Lord, he—"

But the sword pricked and his stony face showed her that nothing she could say would enter his mind.

"He was tied on, and the mare came back, and now you have come back. See her, Innkeeper." He spoke over her shoulder. Gwyn turned her head to see her parents standing close together. Shame was written on their faces, and their eyes would not meet hers.

"I'll have my son of you, Innkeeper's daughter."

She wondered if he meant to slaughter her there and then, as they watched. And if he did, which was what he wanted to do, Gwyn imagined his surprise when Gaderian finally decided to come out of his hiding place. It would serve the Lord right, she thought bitterly, to kill her and then have to learn his mistake when nothing could undo it. It would be no comfort to her parents either, and they deserved none if they did not know she would not do such a thing. She raised her eyes to the icy blue ones and at her expression, the sword pricked again.

"You ought to hear her speak, my Lord." That was Burl's voice, calm and unafraid. When Gwyn cautiously turned her head to see him; he was moving clumsily through the group by the kitchen door, a stick in his hand and one foot wrapped up.

"You ask too much, lad," the Lord answered, his voice cold metal.

"I ask only that you hear her," Burl said quietly. "I know her."

What the Lord would have said to this, they never found out, because just at that moment a high happy voice called down to them: "Father? Father!"

The steel fell from Gwyn's throat as he let the sword drop into the snow beside the saddlebag. Gwyn didn't wait, not even when Gaderian's voice summoned her back, then was muffled by snow as he tumbled and rolled down the hillside. He got quickly to his feet and ran to meet his father.

Gwyn went past her family. She didn't stop in the kitchen, but stormed right through and crossed the yard to the stables. She was shaking with fear and rage. Rage ran along her blood and licked like flames along her bones.

They all of them had condemned her.

She let herself into the mare's stall and buried her face against the warm brown shoulder. "Good girl," she said to the horse. She breathed in the warm, rich smell of horse hay. "You did it. Good girl."

She had never understood how alone she was. She had never understood anything.

The chestnut turned her head to nuzzle at Gwyn's shoulder. When she heard someone walk along the narrow passage she thought it must be Burl and he, at least, had known.

But it was the Lord himself who stood at the open stall, in his tunic and leather boots, his sword sheathed at his side. "It was a mistake, Innkeeper's daughter."

Gwyn faced him. "Aye, it was that, my Lord," she agreed, angry.

"I am sorry for it," he said in his distant voice.

He didn't sound sorry. The mare moved, rustling the straw. "Are you now," Gwyn answered him, not bothering to conceal her disbelief.

"How was I to know—"

"Aye, the Lords know nothing of the people—"

"—when you didn't say—"

"—and care little for what they know or do not know," Gwyn finished.

He warned her then: "You shall not speak to me so."

So Gwyn stopped speaking. She held his eyes and held her tongue. But the anger burned in her.

Burl appeared behind the Lord, who stepped back to let him through. But Burl did not want to enter and leaned on his stick, looking from one to the other of them. Nobody spoke.

At last the Lord broke their silence. "I would know how the Innkeeper got such a daughter, and such a servant," he said. "The irony of it is that now you will never trust me, and now you can trust me for anything." He left them.

Gwyn's anger choked her throat, and she could not say the words of thanks to Burl that she wanted to speak. Burl handed her the brush: "You might curry her. I've not been able to take proper care of them."

"What happened to your foot?"

"Frostbite," he answered. Gwyn ran the brush down the

mare's neck and the muscles underneath the skin rippled in pleasure. Even when Burl spoke that cold word, frostbite, his voice sounded warm. Not hot and angry, like hers, but warm and quiet, like the warm quiet of a plowed field. "I have nine toes left," he told her.

"But you were riding."

"Not always," Burl answered. "The Lord became feverish in the night and—I walked beside him. It's lucky he was too ill to protest the indignity of being carried like a sack of grain."

Gwyn grunted and moved on to brush the muscles of shoulder and leg with the rough strokes the mare enjoyed.

"You cannot be angry at them, Gwyn," Burl's voice said behind her. "They thought of what they would have done in the same situation. Later, when they had thought more, they—"

"Later would have been too late, wouldn't it?" Gwyn asked, surprising herself by her calm. "The Lords don't stand under the law."

"They are the law."

"It's their own law."

"Aye. They will not want you to have seen," he advised her.

Gwyn knew which *they* he meant. She knew also how they must be feeling now, to know they had betrayed her so: sick at heart. She was the one betrayed and she felt a death in her heart. How would they feel, being the betrayers.

"Well then," she said, "I will not have seen." What had been done could not be undone. What she had understood could not be forgotten. "It will be a small lie."

"That will not be the lie," Burl corrected her.

His rightness angered her. "I would finish this in peace," she told him, hearing without any pleasure how like Gaderian she could sound, giving the order. Burl obeyed her, however, without question. Gwyn did not watch him go. She continued currying the mare. The lie would be pretending that everything had not changed.

Part Two

Jackaroo

Thirteen

GWYN TOOK her time currying the mare. She spoke a few words of greeting to the stallion. Then she returned to the kitchen. She wore her face like a mask.

They were waiting for her. Rose hemmed a chemise with delicate stitches. Her mother peeled potatoes while Da cut smooth the legs for a new bench in the barroom. Tad sat by the fireplace, doing nothing. They hadn't changed, although they looked different to Gwyn. She had changed, she thought; everything had changed. She hung her cloak from the hook by the door.

"Now that you've greeted your precious animals, you'll come to greet us," her mother said.

"Oh, Mother," Rose said. She smiled up at Gwyn, her fingers drawing thread through the fine cotton. "It's good to have you back, and safely. After so long, we were afraid—"

"You did well, daughter," Da announced. "You'll be hungry, I expect. And thirsty too. Tad, fetch your sister a mug of cider. And how would some of your mother's apple pastry taste to you, with cheese beside it? Or would you rather start with a bowl of stew?"

Gwyn wasn't hungry at all. "No, thank you," she said. She made herself sit down at the table, but she couldn't make herself look into their eyes. They were pretending that nothing had happened.

She could see why they wanted to pretend that. If they said anything at all about that scene in the garden, they thought they might betray to her what they assumed about her—which they hoped she had not noticed.

Tad set the mug down so hard that it slopped over. He stood there, looking at the pool of brown. At last, his mother fetched him a cloth to wipe it up with.

"Where were you all that time?" Rose asked. "Who found you?"

"We were at Old Megg's, so we were safe."

Tad slammed a pastry and the cheese down in front of Gwyn. The knife clattered onto the floor, but he had returned to his seat by the fire.

"We had food enough," Gwyn said. She took a breath. "When did Burl get back?"

"That first morning," her father answered, relieved to talk about this. "The Lord was sick for three days, and your mother had to nurse him."

"And that's gold hard-earned," her mother said. She gathered up the potatoes and carried them over to the pot, to drop them in one by one. "There'll be gold for you, too, I don't doubt."

Gwyn didn't think she cared to have his gold.

"It'll make you a rich dowry," her mother said. "The men'll flock around, you'll see."

"Gwyn has a dowry," Da pointed out.

"This'll make it more," his wife answered. She scraped the peelings into a bucket for the goats and moved a low stool over by the fire, where the butter waited to be churned.

What Gwyn wanted to do was go back to the horses, to get out of the room and away from them. She made herself stay at the table and chew on a bite of pastry. She drank slowly from the mug of cider, not tasting it. She felt alone, even there in her own kitchen with the fire at her back. But it didn't feel like her own kitchen, not any more, and her family were strangers, who would have let the Lord condemn and execute her. They were wearing masks. It would hurt them if they knew she had noticed; and it wouldn't do any good for her to be angry, it couldn't change what had happened.

Gwyn didn't want to think about it, because it frightened her to realize how little she belonged here, in the one place where she belonged more than anyplace else. So she changed the subject. "Did the Messenger arrive?"

"No sooner were you out of sight than they rode up," her mother answered. "If I were a suspicious woman I could tell you what I'd think."

Gwyn had to smile at that. Her mother caught her eye and smiled back. "I'd be right, too, I'd wager on it."

"If we were ever likely to find out, I'd wager you were," Da said. They had all relaxed, as at some danger now past.

"I'm thirsty too," Tad complained.

"Then get yourself some cider," their mother snapped at him. "You're not helpless. No, you'll spill again, I'll get it for you."

"The Messenger rode to Earl Northgate from the King," Da reported. "The soldiers said there is war in the south, and I know no reason to doubt their word."

. "War among Earl Sutherland's heirs?" Gwyn asked. Thinking of what Gaderian had told her, she suspected otherwise; from what Gaderian told her, the greatest danger came when the Lords rebelled against their Earl; but she was not supposed to know anything Gaderian had told her.

"So I assume," Da said. "I think we'll hear soon that the Lords of the north are calling for soldiers. The King must settle this, I think. The Earl's sons fight to their deaths among themselves, I hear, and the southern Lords will look for profit from that. The King must name the next Earl himself, I think."

"Which will mean higher taxes this year, and the next as well," Gwyn's mother predicted.

"Aye," Da agreed. "But we can pay them."

Many, Gwyn knew, would not be able to do that. He would profit from this, and the Innkeeper's family would be fatter for the ill luck of other men. For a minute, she saw her father as others probably saw him, as Cam saw him, feeding off of the misfortunes of others. Then she saw him again as she always had—a steady man, who poured fair measures, who husbanded his holdings well. She did not know which was the true, which the false Innkeeper.

Two days later, their guests left them. The Innkeeper's family stood in the courtyard, with Burl leaning on his stick behind them, to see the two off. Gwyn had not exchanged a word with Gaderian since they had returned, and she had seen him only once or twice, looking out the window, his expression hidden, as if their time together at Old Megg's had never happened. She was not, she told herself, disappointed; she had not expected anything of him. He was, after all, a Lord.

The morning he left, Gaderian sat the mare with no sign of life from the slight body beneath the cloak. If Gwyn felt his eyes had sought her out from under the folds of his hood, she thought she was mistaken about that. Before he mounted the stallion, the Lord gave into Burl's hands a purse. Then he approached her with another. Gwyn took the soft leather into her palm, feeling its weight. To refuse it would be to raise questions.

The Lord made a little speech then, in his distant voice, about his gratitude, and how he was in debt to the family, more debt than gold could repay. They rode out of the yard, turning east to follow the King's Way back where they had come from. The snow was still packed thick under the horses' hooves, so their leaving was as swift and silent as their arrival.

Back in the kitchen, they would not leave Gwyn alone until she had counted out what she had been given. Burl escaped to his own room, but Gwyn had no such luck. Rather than quarrel, she pulled at the drawstring and poured the coins out onto the table. Tad bounced beside her, wondering if the coins would be gold, wondering how many there would be, wishing he had been the one to travel with the Lords and get the reward. Gwyn had opened her mouth to tell him that if he had been the one, there would have been a funeral not a gift-giving, when she saw a folded piece of paper slide out among the gold pieces. Her hand moved quickly to hide it, but he had seen.

"What's that? It must have been left in the purse; they must have used this purse for something else before, but what do you think it is? Do we have to take it after them?"

"I thought you were going to count the coins for me," Gwyn reminded him. "And if you don't stop pushing at me and shoving and grabbing, I won't let you."

"Do you need to speak to your brother like that?" her mother asked. "You can't blame him for being curious, can you?"

Tad's attention was now on the coins, which he stacked up before him. Gwyn opened the paper. Her eyes moved slowly over the letters. GWYNIDONOTFORGETYOUDONOT-FORGETMEGADERIAN.

He had written them out without spaces, without marks for the end or to separate, but she could read the message. She kept her face a mask, even as her heart rose.

"What have you got there?" her mother demanded.

Gwyn spread the paper down on the table, for all too see. None of them could possibly read it, she knew. "Some message, I guess," she said, trying to sound bored. Then she began to enjoy her secret. She touched the letters with her fingers. She could surprise them—what they would say if she read it to them and showed them her own name spelled out there. "They're careless with paper, aren't they. Tad, do you want to keep it for drawing?"

Inside herself she was laughing. They did not know, and she did.

Tad looked at her curiously, then shook his head, his attention going back to the coins.

"Well, then," Gwyn said, crumpling the paper up in her hands. She turned around to toss it into the fire, where it lay for a minute, round as a tiny snowball, before the flames took it. As it burned, it opened out and she saw the black letters standing out, before a sheet of flame took the whole paper and turned it to ash.

Gwyn looked at the people gathered around the table, staring at the pile of coins. "I hope it wasn't anything important," she said, pretending ignorance. "I hope they won't ride back for it."

"If it had been important they wouldn't have left it in an empty purse," Da told her. "The Lords keep important messages in the long books."

Gwyn mimed relief. She tried to think of some way to drag out the play, but there was the danger of going too far with it and giving herself away, so she let it go.

"Don't you want to know how much it is, Gwyn?" Tad asked. His bounciness had left him, but she didn't care about that, not even enough to wonder.

"How much what is?"

"The gold, stupid."

Tad's voice held hurt feelings, and jealousy too. She wondered how it was that he was still such a child, when Gaderian who was only a little older was so much more grown up. She wondered why her stocky, redheaded brother had to be the whiny, sulky one. "Well, how much? Since you've been so busy counting."

He almost told her he wasn't going to tell her, but then he saw that she didn't care what he said, so he answered, "Twelve. Twelve gold pieces."

"Oh, Gwyn," Rose said. "That's one for each day. I'm sure you deserve the luck."

Gwyn gathered the gold pieces together and dropped them back into the bag one by one.

"You'd better give it to Da to keep," her mother said.

"I'll keep it myself. I'll keep it safe." Gwyn kept her voice level. It was not as if she wished to have a quarrel, and she knew if she sounded calm they would not oppose her. They would not dare oppose her and start a quarrel in which truths might be told. If the note had not been in the bag, she knew, she would have given it to Da for his own use, she would not have taken anything from the Lord. But from Gaderian, she thought, holding the bag in her hand, she would take it gratefully.

"With twelve gold pieces," Rosie suggested, "if there were a man spoke for you who had nothing, you could bring him a holding for his own."

One of the things she would do with this gold, Gwyn thought, looking back to her sister, was to buy a wedding gift at the Spring Fair. She remembered some skeins of fine wool she had seen last fall, at a table where many Ladies gathered. The wool had been spun so delicately that it was as soft as new grass. Traders from the south had brought it up to sell, and Gwyn had stood nearby, not daring to touch it, but wondering at the fingers that could spin such softness from the hair of sheep. She would get some of that for Rose, for the babies she and Wes would have, to make blankets to wrap them in while they slept.

Her mother's voice cut across her dreaming. "With the gold, Gwyn will wed a man with his own holding to inherit, a rich holding. I don't doubt Raff will ask for you now, Gwyn, and you know how broad his father's holdings are."

Da moved impatiently to the fire, to kick at the logs with his boot.

"You know that's true, husband," Gwyn's mother said.

Gwyn took a deep breath. "I will not marry."

For a long time, nobody said anything. Their faces were frozen with surprise. She waited for the arguments to begin, and she knew already that she would not answer them. She understood herself.

"Don't be a goose, daughter. You'll marry. You'll have your choice of the men now. You don't want to live like Old Megg, do you?" her mother asked.

Gwyn shook her head. "I will not marry," she repeated. Maybe she would live out her days alone like Old Megg, but she would not throw her days away caring for the comfort of some man who asked for a bag of twelve gold pieces, never mind the girl who came with it.

"But Gwyn," Rose started to ask.

"It's foolishness and she knows it," Gwyn's mother announced. "This gold has gone to her head, I don't doubt."

For a wonder, Tad had nothing to say.

"It's just some mood she's in," Gwyn's mother continued. Rarely had Gwyn seen her mother so angry. "It's all your fault, Innkeeper; it's all because she wants that boy, the Weaver's boy, and he'll never ask. Just to get even with you. You think you're better than the rest of us," she told Gwyn, her voice vinegar. "But you'll find out where the stubbornness gets you. She doesn't mean it," she said to her husband. "You'll see. Ask her again."

Gwyn stood up, her own temper rising. "I will not marry," she told her mother. "If Da does not make the announcement, I will."

Da looked from his wife to his daughter. Gwyn was too angry to feel sorry for him.

"I'll make the announcement, if I am sure it's what she really wants," he told his wife. Then he looked at Gwyn. "If I am sure, I will make it."

That was good enough for her. She left the room. They could talk about her now, in peace and at length. She put the bag of gold under her mattress and then went out through the barroom door, to clean out the empty stalls so that they would be ready when next they were needed.

Fourteen

GWYN WENT up to the village the next day, to talk with Old Megg. She told no one she was going and no one asked her, as she took her cloak from the hook and left through the garden door, what she might be doing. At the Weaver's house, the loom was working and the shutters were open to let in the sunlight. Gwyn watched the work for a few minutes: the rising and falling of the combs, the shuttle moving through the threads like a mouse bolting for its hole, the finished cloth slowly rolling up at the end, the Weaver's bent head and her clever hands. Then Gwyn went to sit beside Old Megg, who kept to her bed alone in a darkened room. Gwyn opened the shutters to let in light.

The old woman had been dozing. She was surprised to see Gwyn. "They said you were dead. Lost in the storm," she greeted her.

"Only trapped," Gwyn answered. She built up the fire and prodded it into life. "How is your ankle?"

"I'll never mend, you know that as well as I do. And you'll live to wish you'd died, Innkeeper's daughter. When you're old and helpless and in the care of such people. They grudge me every bite of food that goes into my mouth, every minute of care."

"Osh aye," Gwyn said, pulling a small stool up to sit by the bed. "And I wonder if you know what saved me."

"Saved you for what, that's what you ought to be asking."

"It was your own house where I stayed. We ate your cheeses and your meat, we burned up your wood you have stored, we slept under your blankets." At that last, Gwyn watched the aged face closely, to see if the eyes became secretive, or the mouth fearful. But she could see no change.

"I cleaned the house out properly," Gwyn told Old Megg.

"Gwyn, listen to me. It's been a terrible life, unwed. I'd have taken anyone who asked, and I was pretty enough. I was. Nobody asks for a girl with no dowry, no holding, and her only family a brother who goes off for a soldier."

"Aired the bedclothes, and those deep cupboards too," Gwyn hinted.

"Do you want to end your days in the care of such as she?" Old Megg's eye went to the open door into the kitchen.

"You ought to be grateful, old woman," the Weaver's voice answered.

"I can't remember how long you were there," Gwyn asked. "How long were you there, Old Megg? Was I six when you left us?"

"Osh no, it's only been five years, you were starting to shoot up."

"I was wondering." Gwyn took one of the rough hands in her own, to fix the old woman's attention. "Who lived there before you."

"Lived where?"

"And you know full well, Innkeeper's daughter, just whose house that was. Before your father gobbled it up."

Gwyn didn't rise to the bait. "It was empty all those years?" she asked, putting as much surprise as she could into her voice.

"I'm not the one to go back and dream over things I can't have," the voice told her, above the clacking of the loom.

Gwyn drew the blanket up over Old Megg's hands. "I'll come again," she said.

"Bring me some ale, I'd enjoy a mug of ale," the old woman whispered.

Gwyn hesitated beside the loom. This cloth would be sold at the Spring Fair. The Weaver and her daughters worked all the year round, making cloth for the fairs. They made light cloth for the Spring Fair, then during the summer the woollen cloth for the Harvest Fair, both dyed brown.

The Weaver, she thought, would speak more freely in anger. Gwyn considered how to phrase her question.

"He's over to the Blacksmith's," the Weaver said.

"I was just thinking," Gwyn said, "that it must be bitter to leave the house your husband gave you, and the vineyard that should belong to your son."

"Your pity is not welcome here. I can see to my family myself—and better without a man to get in my way. As I've done, with no thanks to anyone, all these years."

"But the land, that had been in his family for—" Gwyn put all the pity she could find into her voice and the Weaver cut her off quickly.

"It was his father had it forced upon him by the Bailiff, because it had ruined the man before him. You think we wanted to be vineyarders? And live in that tiny hut so we could see the misery of those vines dying, all day long, day after day? You may have a fine spirit, Innkeeper's daughter— if what they say is true—but you are mightily ignorant," she concluded with satisfaction.

"That I am," Gwyn agreed. "I'll be away then."

"Aye, go run him to earth."

Gwyn didn't bother answering that last barb, but she didn't go to the forge either. Instead, she went back to the Inn, where there was work to be done. The Inn had belonged to Granda's father, and his father before him, and back out of memory. There were, she knew, cupboards and parts of the Inn cellar that nobody would have seen into the back of for maybe a hundred years.

If Old Megg knew about the secret cupboard, and its contents, she would keep her secret. The Weaver knew nothing, of that Gwyn was sure. The Weaver's tongue ran away with her in anger and she would have spoken. Besides, the Weaver would have sold the clothes if she'd found them. So Gwyn was no nearer an answer to her questions.

And the snow, she noticed, was settling, so winter was drawing to its close. Soon the barroom would be busy, especially on market days, with the men taking their winter's work to the cities to sell, so that they could pay the tithes and feed their families until the crops came in. They would have furs to sell, or stools and tables, carved boxes and shelves, or eggs, butter, and cheese. They would have day labor to offer to more fortunate farmers who needed the help to plow fields or to plant them. And the men would stop off at the Inn on their way home from Lord Hildebrand's city, or the Earl's city, to exchange news and boast of their sales, and to put off for an hour the return to their homes. The Inn would need to be ready for their custom.

Getting the Inn ready meant washing down the floor of the barroom with buckets of water heated over the fire, waxing the heavy tables, sharpening knives, and hauling up sacks of flour and casks of ale from the cellars. Because Rose and her mother were busy finishing off the sheets and blankets, the nightgowns and chemises and underskirts that Rose would take to Wes, the work of readying the Inn fell mostly to Gwyn and her father, with Tad an unwilling extra hand and Burl there whenever his chores did not keep him elsewhere. It was late in the second afternoon when, her back aching and her belly nagged by the dull pain of her monthly courses, Gwyn blew up at Tad. She had her hands in the bowl of flour, working the lard into it to make pastry dough. It had rained heavily in the night, mists rose from the hills, and the barroom would be busy. Two casks of ale had to be brought up, the barroom floor had to be washed again and the water for that job steamed over the fire. Tad sat by the fireplace, scraping with his knife at a stick of wood, letting the shavings fall onto the stones. "You'll wash the floor," Gwyn decided.

Tad didn't look up.

"Or I'll box your ears until they ring for three days," she promised him. She had no patience for his laziness, no sympathy for his youth. "It's past time for you to do your share."

He still didn't move, but his eyes were on her face and his knife was still.

"Unless you'd rather do the pastry," Gwyn said, adding nastily, "but you know what it'll taste like and Mother will be angry, even at you, if the pies prove bad." Her fingers worked as she talked, rubbing against the chunks of lard, breaking them down and mixing them in with the fine flour.

Tad shook his head.

Gwyn wiped her hands on the cloth she had tied around her waist. She would have him do one piece of honest work, and if she had to club him to do it well, she'd do that too. He knew that, and he was frightened. She knew he was frightened and that pleased her. "There's nobody to hear you if you cry so you'd better make up your mind, Tad."

"But I can't. You know that. I'll spill and burn myself. I'm not big enough and you know it and if you make me . . ." He didn't finish the threat.

"If I make you—and make no mistake I plan to—what will you do? Yell for Mother?"

"I'll burn myself. I always slop water from the bucket, because I'm not big enough."

"I was carrying those buckets when I was much younger. You're just soft."

"I can't help it," he said, his voice sulky. "It's not my fault."

He sounded like he really would wail, so Gwyn put her hands back into the pastry and tried to explain things to him. "Look. You don't fill the bucket to the top, that's one thing.

And you take off your boots and stockings, because it's the way stockings hold the heat makes a bad burn, so you work barefooted."

"But Mother—"

"Mother will know nothing about it. Honestly, Tad, anyone would think you didn't have any brains at all. Anyone would think you were just a baby."

His cheeks flamed. "Am not."

"Then why do you act like one."

"Do not."

"Do too," she told him, enjoying the quarrel, letting off her bad temper.

He jumped up and removed his boots, then peeled down his stockings. He took a jug, to ladle steaming water into the waiting bucket. Watching him, Gwyn saw that he really did think he would manage to spill boiling water on himself. How could he be so foolish? How could he think that something everybody else could do was beyond him?

Just before he bent to pick up the bucket he told her, "It'll be your fault."

"Roll up your trousers," was Gwynn's only response. She deliberately did not watch him go into the barroom. He'd yell loud enough if anything hurt him. She could count on that.

The flour coated her hands and her fingers moved in it, sifting through to find the chunks of lard, her thumb rubbing the softening fat against her fingers. The quarrel with Tad had made her feel physically better, at least. The dough was almost fine enough, she thought, digging her hands down along the sides of the bowl, lifting them up to mix the dry pastry, letting her fingers do their quick work. You had to work quickly or the fat softened too much and the pastry would not bake up as flaky as it should. She heard no howls from the next room and felt a grim satisfaction at being proved right. That boy would just grab at any excuse to get out of work.

She heard him sweeping for a while, then he came back for more water. He would cover the floor with water, then sweep the water and dirt off together, out the door to the yard. She watched him refill the bucket. This time, he picked it up without hesitation, and at his first quick step some water slipped over onto his leg. She waited. He waited. Nothing happened. The water ran down his leg. He looked quickly up at her, but she had her eyes on the flour by then. Of couse, she thought, he would not say a word, to admit he had been wrong. She heard him begin sweeping again.

Gwyn worked cold water into the dough and then let it rest while she set out the molds that she would line with pastry. The filling waited in another bowl—mixed pork and onions and potatoes, seasoned with salt and dried herbs. She took the rolling pin down from the shelf and started to roll out a handful of pastry. The texture felt just about right, she thought.

"Gwyn?"

His voice sounded panicky. What had he done now? She went to the door to see.

Tad had swept himself into a corner, the farthest corner from the door. He stood there, his pants rolled up, the bucket beside him, the square of dry floor under him. His hand held the broom upright and a film of dirty water lay over the boards. "I don't know—" he started to say.

Gwyn burst out laughing.

At first, Tad didn't want to join in, then he couldn't help himself. "But what do I do?" he asked her.

"It won't bite you if you walk through it. It's a little shallow for drowning in."

"But my feet'll get dirty."

"Nobody will know if you get your stockings on fast enough."

"But Mother'll know from my stockings."

"Maybe she will, but what can she do when it's already been done?" Gwyn asked him. "She never noticed in mine though, so I wouldn't fret about that if I were you. I'd fret about getting this dirty water out the door before Da and Burl try to bring up the ale."

He put his broom to work immediately. She watched him

for a minute, padding in the water, sweeping it toward the door. The floor looked clean enough.

And Tad looked pleased with himself. She continued her thinking as she went back to rolling out pastry dough. What was there to look pleased about in cleaning a floor, she wondered. Nothing, she answered herself, nothing at all; anyone could do it. Except Tad seemed pleased that *he* could.

No wonder, she thought, with everybody telling him he couldn't, that he would hurt himself or catch cold. He probably thought he wasn't given chores because everyone knew he couldn't do them.

Gwyn filled the pies and set them in the baking oven, built into the stones at the side of the fireplace. She was seeing her family now as if they were strangers. That wasn't surprising, since she felt like they *were* strangers—or was she a stranger? She was more critical now, no doubt of it, although, for another change, she never gave voice to her thoughts. But she could see that her mother's bitterness was never allayed, not even by Tad over whom she clucked and worried so much. She could see that Da's patience and carefulness came from a desire to soothe his wife, and she could wish Da would govern his wife more. But why should her mother be so bitter? And why should Da be reluctant to govern her?

Gwyn felt as if she could see through the masks people put on, and she didn't much care for what she saw underneath.

In the barroom at day's end, too, serving mugs of ale and plates of pastry to the men, she wondered why—in this hungry time—they spent any of their precious coins at the Inn, while their wives and children waited. Their talk was conducted in angry tones, but she could see the fear behind it. Rumors flew, as thick in the warm air as the smells of the room, wood smoke and ale, the tallow from burning candles. The Lords were raising the taxes to half of what a holding would earn, to three-quarters, the men grumbled. The Lords were going to be short of pay for the soldiers, so they were going to seize the holdings from men who couldn't pay taxes; these would be given to the soldiers instead of pay. Any day now, Messengers would ride into the villages to announce the new taxes, which must be paid before the Spring Fair.

"What I'll do," the men said, one to the other, "I don't know."

"I'll not plant a crop for another man to harvest."

"Let the soldiers kill one another off, and the Lords too; I won't weep a tear."

They talked with their heads close together, worrying over the rumors like a dog worrying at a bone. Their voices grew loud and angry.

"What do the Lords care, as long as they can live fat."

"It's our bones, and the bones of our children, that their houses are built of. We're the meat they grow fat on."

"No wonder there's no way for a man to approach a Lord with his complaint—how many Lords would be alive at the end of a day, think you? If a man could get close to them."

Some of the rumors gave them satisfaction. "If the battles in the south rage long enough, that's where I'll take my crops to market. Starving people pay higher prices, now, don't they?"

"There's a highwayman coming to be journeyed here. As I hear it, he'll be hanged in the north."

"A man can choose where he's to make his last stop, if he's journeyed."

"I'd have myself hanged right outside Hildebrand's door then, and let him see what he's done."

"And do you think he'd even notice you, man?"

"It's been a long time since I've seen a good hanging. Aye, I'll thank the man for a holiday, if he chooses a spot near enough that I can go watch."

Occasionally, someone tried to draw Gwyn out, but she refused to answer their questions about how much gold was in the sack, how much of it she would keep for dowry. She did not respond to their teasing. They were speaking to make one another laugh and not for her pleasure; behind their eyes a secret greed shone as bright as a star, and she knew that if she were to answer any one of the unmarried men seriously then he would ask for her. The widowers had the same gleam, but they sat back, waiting. She didn't blame them, not really, any more than she blamed the bitterness of the women in the Doling Rooms; there was land to hold and families to feed and if gold was not good for that, what was its use?

So she held her tongue. Da would make the announcement, because he had said he would. He was probably waiting because she might change her mind. Mother was at her day and night to do that, and even Rose—but Rose could imagine no greater happiness than being a wife.

The snow was melting now, under rains and warmer air, until the hillsides were washed almost clean of it. Brown patches of ground showed, and the woods held only hidden pockets of snow. It was not spring yet, no little green leaves showed; but spring was coming. The days lasted longer, now, and every day melted more of the snow. Gwyn felt caged in. When Old Megg died, Gwyn welcomed the chance to go to the burning, just to see different faces. She felt ashamed of that thought, true though it was. But she felt like a horse kept too long in its winter stall, and even while she admired Rose's miniature stitching along a hem, she longed to kick with her legs and kick herself free.

☙ Fifteen

O N THE DAY when the village bell rang out to summon
them, people gathered quickly. Only Da and Gwyn
went from the Inn. They were fairly sure they knew why they
had been called so there was no need for everybody to go.
There were more than fifty people gathered around the well
when the Lord read the announcement, sitting high on his
horse with four soldiers close behind him. He was Hildebrand
himself, the people murmured, but Gwyn didn't think this was
so, because Hildebrand would be a man of full years and this
Lord was too young, and he kept close to the soldiers as if he
was unsure what would happen were he to ride alone. Hildebrand would not have been unsure, Gwyn thought.

The Lord, whoever he was, unrolled the paper and read
out the news: The taxes for that year would be a quarter of
a holding's crops and earnings. Then he added something unexpected: Lord Hildebrand was offering one gold coin for every
unmarried man who would become his soldier. The coin

would be paid to the man's family. Men who wished to take advantage of this could report to the Steward at the Doling Rooms, or to the Bailiff when he came to gather the taxes.

When he had rolled the paper up again, he turned his horse and rode away, with the soldiers close behind him. Nobody spoke until the sound of hoofbeats had faded entirely away.

"Osh aye, and I didn't know where the tenth was coming from," one farmer said.

"At least you've got three sons," the Weaver answered him.

"Osh aye, and what if they had taken a half?"

The people agreed that a quarter wasn't as bad as it might have been.

Hearing that, Gwyn turned away. If she were a Lord, she would have put that very rumor about, just so that the people could take some comfort when the taxes were not as great as rumor had numbered them. She suspected that the Lords had done just that, to keep the people quiet.

That night in the barroom, several men took Da aside, leaving Burl to fill the mugs and take the coins. Gwyn watched these conversations. Once the Innkeeper nodded his head and shook the hand offered to him. The other times he shook his head and the man went back to his table to bury his face in his ale. The Innkeeper's holdings would increase this year, Gwyn thought.

Most of the men had left by the time the Fiddler entered. The Fiddler was an old man, as thin and bent as his own bow, who played for the dancers at the fairs and eked out the coins that fell into his cap to keep himself in his little house through the rest of the year. His clothes, shirt and trousers, were so patched that even the patches were worn threadbare. He was a timid man who avoided company except when he was among them to play. But when he put his fiddle under his chin and drew his bow across it, the music danced out bold and glad.

Out of charity, Da gave him a mug of ale and told Gwyn to serve him a slab of pie. The Fiddler didn't even sit down at one of the tables, but stood at the bar to drink and eat. Then he spoke his reason for the unexpected visit. "It's the taxes. A half, as I've heard, Innkeeper."

"Only a quarter," Da told him.

"That's as much trouble to me as a half. And I was wondering." He did not have the voice to continue the question.

Da shook his head. "I've no use for your house, man."

"It's only one silver coin I need. Even the Bailiff knows how little my value is."

Da shook his head. Gwyn held her tongue—there were twenty silver coins in a gold one. It was not much the man asked.

"If not the holding, then—I could write a dance for Rose's wedding. I could do that, and it would be a song people would remember. It would be a fine gift for a man to give his daughter, on her wedding."

"What man would pay coins for a song," Da said.

"As I've heard, the Lords do." The Fiddler spoke in a low voice.

"I'm not a Lord, man." Da's voice carried through the room. The few men still drinking there looked up at him then quickly down, as if they did not wish their thoughts to be seen.

"Then I'll have to pledge you my fiddle. It's all I have."

"How would you keep yourself without your fiddle?" Gwyn asked him.

"I can't keep myself with it, now can I, Innkeeper's daughter?" he asked her, his voice cracking with the shame.

Da didn't need to say anything. The Fiddler knew his request had been denied. But he stood helplessly there, his hands opening and closing. Gwyn felt sick at heart.

"Your brother wouldn't have denied me. Win wouldn't have said me no," the Fiddler muttered.

Da's anger flowed out of him, like fire leaping up. "Win would have long ago been begging himself, Fiddler. As you well know. And I've kept the Inn and made it prosper, while he would have wasted it. As you well know."

The white, lined face collapsed. "Aye, aye, I know it. All

the same," and he smiled as if his eyes were looking at something nobody else could see, "he was a grand fighter. A grand lad."

"A grand fighter," Da agreed.

Gwyn left the Inn the next morning early. Her mother's voice followed her out the door. "What's got into you? Where are you going? Answer me, miss—or are you too proud now to speak to your own mother? And I want to know who's going to—" But Gwyn never heard what chore would fall onto somebody else's shoulders. Let Rose come down from sewing on her pretties for a time. Let Tad try his hand at it, whatever it was. And why didn't Mother do it herself? But she did not answer and she did not turn back.

She skirted the village, leaving it behind her. She went on to the vineyard, where the stumpy vines still waited in their winter death. She crossed the vineyard and slid down the muddy hillside to Old Megg's house. She did not go in immediately, but lingered outside, looking around her at the empty goat pens and the empty hillsides and the distant line of silent mountains. When she had looked her fill, she entered the house.

She kept her cloak on against the chill, but she opened the shuttered window and left the door open behind her, for light and fresh air. Although it was not in her plan, she took a piece of charred wood from the fire and wrote her name down on the tabletop, where she and Gaderian had worked, so many evenings ago. She wrote her name first; and then she wrote all the letters of the alphabet in a line.

That satisfied her, and she rubbed them all out, leaving a smear of charcoal on the wood. Then she went to the cupboard.

It was all there, just as she had guessed. She spread the clothing out on Old Megg's bed. The sheathed sword she put on the table. She touched everything with curious fingers. The wide brim of the hat was wrinkled from being jammed into a corner, and its white plume hung down dejectedly. The white shirt was softer than any shirt Gwyn had ever touched, with a silk ribbon to tie it at the neck and buttons at the ends of the full sleeves. The scarlet cape had been folded so carefully it wasn't wrinkled at all and lay bright as blood on the blankets.

There were trousers, too, and a braided silk belt to hold them up. The tunic was blue, as the stories told, but they did not tell the way silver threads had been woven into the fabric, making it glimmer in the light. The clasps, six of them, going down the front of the armless tunic, were of heavy silver, plainly wrought. The boots reached up over Gwyn's hips when she stood them beside her, but the tops were made to fall over in a cuff. The mask Jackaroo wore was red silk, not black, with tiny stitches to hold the hem around the eyeholes. Gwen tied it around her head. It covered her hair like a cap and hung down almost to her collarbone. She could see out of it easily.

She stripped off her own clothes and put on the shirt, tucking it into the trousers, which she hoisted up high then allowed to fall over the belt when she had tied that tightly around her waist. The tunic was long, reaching halfway down her thighs, and for for all its richness the fabric was light to carry. She slung the cloak over her shoulders then pulled on the long boots. Everything was large, made for a man, but as she looked down at herself she saw that she looked like a man. Her breasts and the curve of her hips were all concealed under the straight tunic. Her hair was covered by the mask. She put the hat on, but it caught on the coils over her ears and wobbled. Impatiently, she removed it and untied the mask, then pulled the bone pins out of her braids. She piled them on top of her head, and pinned them in place. She tied the mask on again and replaced the hat. Now it felt right.

Gwyn laughed at herself, and she was afraid. She didn't want to think what she was dreaming of, and she did not know how to stop herself from imagining. At last, she picked up the sword in its scabbard. She buckled the broad belt across her hips.

Alone in the small room, she strode back and forth, getting used to the feel of boots on her skirtless legs. She was swaggering, she thought, laughing aloud now. It would never do to swagger so. She tried to remember how the Lord had walked long across the garden and she stepped out boldly in imitation of his memory.

Twelve paces across the room, turn, twelve paces back. The boots were too big for her feet, and her ankles wobbled in them, but you could stuff them with straw to make them fit. The sword hung heavy at her side, clumsy. She put her hand on the hilt as she had seen the soldiers do, and it rode easily then.

Gwyn strode out the door, out and away from the house. Her whole chest felt as if it were quivering—with excitement, with joy, with fear. The empty hills around her could not see, could not speak. She was safe, safe enough. She pulled the sword from the scabbard and held it out in front of her. It was heavier than the wooden swords she and Gaderian had matched with, but it had a balance that made it easy at the end of her arm. Her hand fitted well within the metal cuff of the hilt.

Her feet planted wide apart, she raised the sword to the sky. "Jackaroo," she said, her voice a whisper. The name reverberated inside her head, as if it were the note of a single horn singing across the hills, calling up to the mountains—Jackaroo.

$\smile\!\!\!\mathcal{D}$ Sixteen

PRING SPREAD its broad cloak over the countryside. The first little green buds appeared on the trees, as the sap rose up into their branches. Patches of moss and ferns appeared in the woods, and a few fragile flowers came up, yellow crocuses, blue periwinkles. The wombs of the goats swelled out with young and the kitchen garden lay brown and empty, its seeds growing secretly underground. Farmers planted their fields with turnips, potatoes, oats, onions. There was fish to be bought at market.

Gwyn welcomed the first sudden days of spring, when every morning carried an armful of surprises—the surprising brightness of sunlight or gentleness of spring rain; the surprising softness of air all around and ground underfoot; the surprise of birdsong. It was on one such morning that Da surprised her when he found her alone in the barroom. Gwyn had sent Tad out to look for weeds in the garden and break up the ground after a rain. Burl was cleaning the barn stalls. Mother and Rose were upstairs, making preparations.

"This wedding," Da said, standing at the doorway to the guest rooms, which he was getting ready against the Bailiff's stay, "it's only a fortnight away. You'd think a demon drove your mother."

Gwyn swept warm water over the boards, sweeping out the dirt of the last evening's business. "Mother wants to do Rose proud."

"Aye and she will that. Your mother's a fine, proud woman."

Gwyn didn't say anything. She wondered if Da was going to ask her about marriage. Mother had been after her, and Rose too, in a gentler way. She hoped Da wouldn't say anything. It was not that she wanted to change her mind. Far from it, although she understood her own reasons for that no better than she understood the reasons for the many other changes she felt taking place within herself. A few years earlier, when her body had so suddenly changed, she had felt awkward and uneasy, unsure; she recognized that same feeling now, but it was not her body that caused it, it was her self. Everybody seemed a stranger to her now, even the Innkeeper's daughter, Gwyn, herself. She swept the wet floor and waited to hear what Da would speak of.

"I saw you, daughter, when the Fiddler came to ask—"

Gwyn grunted, to show she had heard and understood.

"I want you to know—because I know how rumors are, and how little truth there is in them, and I wouldn't have you think ill of me. The rumors exaggerate."

"Exaggerate what, Da?" Gwyn asked. She leaned on the broom. "Exaggerate the troubles in the south? Exaggerate the hunger here? The dangers on the roads?"

"That too, but I'm speaking of myself. They exaggerate my position."

"I know." Gwyn resumed her work, the brown water flowing before her.

"Do you?"

"Da, of course. Your holdings are the vineyard and two small farms to the west of the village, and both of the farms are kept by the men you bought them from. I know it's not the wealth of a Lord that you have."

He smiled at her, then. "I have also given dowries to two daughters in as many years."

"While keeping the holdings for the Inn's welfare," Gwyn agreed.

"It's not that I didn't want to help the man, daughter. It's that I cannot. If I were to help one, then all would come to stand in line before me, their hands out. I'd run out of coins soon enough. And where would we be then, come the Autumn Fair and the Bailiff's next visit, were summer to scorch the crops, or the war in the south spread north and—"

"They'd resent it more, anyway," Gwyn told him. "It would be like the Doling Rooms."

Da sighed and agreed. "I just wanted you to know, daughter."

"I know," Gwyn answered, her arms busy.

"Do you know also what it is you have chosen? What it will mean to you?"

Gwyn stopped work again. She looked at her father. He was, she reminded herself, concerned for her well-being. That was what prompted his question. "No," she said. "How can I know that? How can anyone know that?"

He let the questions go. "We'll have Messengers and soldiers soon, and the Bailiff."

"We'll be ready." The Bailiff collected the taxes before the fair, probably because any man with money near his hand on the day of the fair would spend or gamble it away. The Lords made sure they got their taxes before the mechants and mountebanks put hands into peoples' pockets.

"I would like to help the Fiddler," Da said. "If I had only myself to think of, I'd have gvien him the coin."

"Aye, I know," Gwyn reassured her father. She thought, perhaps he would have. But the fact was that he had not.

She swept the shallow tide of water out onto the stones

of the Innyard. Burl was crossing it with two buckets of water in his hands. His foot had healed and he walked without any trace of a limp. He greeted her without stopping. Gwyn stood with the mild sun on her face and the air sweet at her nose. "It's a nice day, isn't it," she said.

Burl set his buckets down then. "Aye," he said. "It happens every year. Every year I begin to think that there is nothing worth hope in this world, and then every year spring comes—like music."

Before she could answer him, he had picked up the buckets and moved on. Gwyn stared after him. His shoulders, under the rough shirt, were broad and strong. He worked with steady energy, without complaint. He spoke seldom, and then always in the same tone. But he played his pipe and she wondered whether Burl too wore a mask. He moved into the dark barns and she went back to the house. Everybody else did, so why not Burl as well?

No reason, Gwyn thought later, striding through the woods. How could she know the reasons for anything when she didn't even understand the reasons for which she was where she was, dressed as she was, and for what purpose. The high boots shielded her legs from snapping branches, the mask hung close over her face and the short red cape swung with her shoulders. Her heart sang.

She carried the hat in one hand and held the sword steady with the other. The gold coin she had put into a cloth bag, tied at her waist. Her legs felt long without skirts to wrap them around, and her stride was free.

The Fiddler's hut had been built beside a little stream, to the west of the Inn. In summer, the water was choked by watercress, but in early spring it chuckled freely along south-ward, to join the river. Gwyn stood among the willows crowd-ing close to the stream's edge and studied the tiny house across the way.

A thin trickle of smoke rose from the chimney leaning against one end. The door was opened and so were the shutters of the window. Except for a breeze that rippled the surface of the water, nothing moved in the quiet glade. Watery spring sunlight poured down over the scene.

The house sat at the edge of a narrow clearing, with the trees and undergrowth of the woods close up behind it. Now that she was there and dressed and ready to act, Gwyn realized that she did not know how to do what she wanted to do. She leaned against the trunk of a willow, hidden by its flowing branches where yellowy-green leaves sprouted, and considered the situation.

It was easier if you were on horseback. If you were on horseback, you could announce your arrival with a thundering of hooves. That would get people out and waiting. No explanations would be necessary. But Gwyn was not on horseback.

She looked at the hut and its placement. She took the piece of gold out of the little purse and wrapped it around with her fingers. Then she placed the hat on her head, took a breath, and stepped into the shallow stream.

Reminding herself of who she was—Jackaroo—she stepped out long across the little clearing. She did not knock on the door. Without any hesitation, because to hesitate would mean to doubt and to doubt might give her away—she thrust the door wide. It banged against the wall inside.

The Fiddler was sitting beside his fire, his head in his hands. His fiddle lay on the bed, as if it were a baby, sleeping safely. He turned to see Gwyn, and his eyes grew wide.

"What do you want," he whispered, afraid.

Gwyn stood in the doorway with her feet apart.

"Who are you." Fear muted his voice. He backed up against the wall of his house. His eyes flew to his fiddle and he almost moved to take it in his arms.

Gwyn pitched her voice low and tried to remember the cadence of Gaderian's speech as she answered the Fiddler. "You have nothing to fear."

He didn't know whether to believe her or not.

Without waiting any longer, without explaining, Gwyn

opened her hand and let the gold coin fall out of it onto the dirt floor. "This is small reward for your songs, Fiddler, but it is yours."

He didn't move. She turned abruptly and walked around the house, into the woods.

"Wait." She heard his airy voice behind her. She hesitated, turning.

"Jackaroo?" he asked. Even with his white hair, he sounded like a child, asking the question.

Gwyn swept the hat off and made him a low bow. Then she turned abruptly and entered the woods. With her head high, knowing how the plume must wave in the bright air, she entered among the trees. She wanted to make as little noise as possible, to somehow give the illusion of great strength. She pictured the way Jackaroo would look, walking through the woods as if they were a grassy meadow, and she stepped out. A root caught her foot and pulled it out behind her. She stumbled, tumbled, and crashed flat on her face onto a scrubby bush.

Gwyn lay still, humiliated and alarmed. She didn't dare move, lest the Fiddler hear her and come to her aid and find her. She could hear him moving about in his house. Until she heard the glad voice of his fiddle, she remained where she was.

When he had started playing, she knew she was safe again. On her hands and knees she moved as quietly as she could through the underbrush. When she had reached a safe distance from the hut, she stood up, brushed off the dried twigs and wet dirt, and recrossed the stream.

Once across the stream and hurrying back to Old Megg's house, Gwyn allowed the laughter that had been building up to go free. She laughed aloud. The laughter flowed out into the trees and rose up into the blue sky, like a song.

During the next days, as spring spread over the hills and up toward the mountains, leaving in its wake a trail of blooms and green shoots, the Inn concerned itself with preparations for Rose's wedding. The sheets and pillows were packed into the trunk Rose would take to Wes, along with the skirts and shirts, chemises and drawers. Custom was busy at the Inn, with soldiers on the move through the countryside, sent to chase out the bands of outlaws who had emerged from the hills and forests to prey on travelers along the King's Way. Troops of soldiers moved east along the Way toward camp at the High City, where it was rumored that the King was gathering an army. The Bailiff spent several days at the Inn with his guard, as he collected the taxes from villages and holdings. Gwyn was kept occupied by day and by night, cleaning, baking, serving. Tad worked with Burl, to care for the animals and maintain the garden Mother was too busy to weed and hoe. Perhaps working with Burl was good for Tad—certainly he worked now with a better spirit without Mother's voice to argue his tiredness.

Rumors crowded the barroom: the troubles in the south, where the Lords had risen up against the Earl's sons or against one another or even, so one rumor reported, against the King himself. The King's Way was crowded, with people carrying goods to market and with soldiers, with Messengers whose horses arrived in a lather, to be walked cool by Burl, or Gwyn, or even once when everybody else was busy, Tad. Blithe came to visit, but was no help at all—she sat listlessly by the fire. Sometimes she could be persuaded to churn the butter. Sometimes she simply sat, with tears oozing out of her eyes, until Da sent her back to her husband. "We need hands to help, not a mouth to feed, daughter," he told her.

In the midst of this, Gwyn heard one evening—the first evening no fire was lit in the barroom—a rumor that Jackaroo was riding. She listened eagerly. The Fiddler told the story himself, a tale of despair and the unexpected gift, of how Jackaroo had appeared out of nowhere, and then disappeared into the woods, like a spirit. "Aye, he was there and then—gone. Faster than the blink of an eye," the Fiddler told his listeners. "Aye, he spoke to me too, believe me or not. Where else would I get the money for taxes such as these?"

"You can steal as well as the next man," somebody suggested.

"Who is there to steal from?" the Fiddler answered. "I'm telling the truth, whether you doubt me or not. He spoke to me, just as I'm saying. 'This gold is to pay your taxes, Fiddler.' That's what he said to me, and no farther from me than the Innkeeper stands now. 'But your songs are worth more than gold can pay.' He said that too, said it to me. That's how it happened, just as I said. I never thought I'd see the day."

Gwyn listened with no expression on her face, but her heart laughed.

Seventeen

THE MORNING of the Fair the sun rose into a gray sky. Burl and Gwyn carried Rose's trunk through the woods, to the village, so they were at the tail of the crowd going to Earl Northgate's city along the King's Way. The Fair was held outside of the walls, and it spread over fields and through woods. As they climbed up the last hill, they heard the gatehouse bell toll out. Gwyn increased her pace. She wore her best shirt, with embroidery at the neck and wrists, and a fresh skirt. But Mother had carried her shoes for her. They weren't fit for walking, so Gwyn would lace them on when she got there. The notes of the bell rolled over the hill to greet them. Burl, who had no best clothes to change into, looked as always and refused to hurry. Gwyn left him behind.

At the crest of the hill, she looked down. The field was spread with tents, within which merchants offered their wares. From the woods, where paths wound, rose the fires from camps, where merchants and entertainers had slept the night.

Up against the tall walls of the city, tables of food and drink were set out, and meat roasted in deep pits. Over all of this scene, gray clouds floated.

Gwyn hurried down the hill, her skirt wrapping itself around her knees and slowing her down. She found her family gathered with all of the families of the couples to be wed. Quickly, she changed her shoes, leaving her boots with the pile of belongings they would pick up at the end of the fair. The red leather shoes, with their elevated heels and narrow toes, pinched her feet but made her feel different, lighthearted and fickle, as if she could dance all night and never tire.

At her waist, Gwyn had a purse holding the twenty silver coins Da had given her in exchange for one gold coin. She had on her feet the shoes that she wore for dancing. All around her, people moved, talking and laughing. The fair had begun.

For the first hour, while the marriages were performed and toasts were drunk, the people had the fairgrounds to themselves. Then the Lords would arrive, the men in bright tunics, the women with their silken dresses and their long hair flowing. For most of the afternoon, the fair would belong to them, as they moved among the booths and entertainments. After they had left, the field would be cleared for dancing, and the fiddles would come out.

For now, it was the dozen brides who were the object of all eyes. Rose waited quietly among them, her hair loose down her back, the prettiest of them all. Gradually the crowd surrounded them, keeping a space between. Then the priest arrived from within the city walls. The grooms stepped forward and the couples arranged themselves. The priest began the ceremony.

Gwyn stood with her parents and Tad, her eyes taking in the scene. Despite the gray clouds and the plain brown of clothing, despite the priest's black robe and the weighty words he spoke, despite the gray stone wall climbing up behind the priest, there was light all around. The couples stood, with hands intertwined at the ends of crossed arms. The girls' hair gave color—yellow and brown and black waves, flowing down their backs for this one day. Gwyn's eyes looked at the scene and then traveled up the walls to where the clouds were at last breaking up, separating under a high wind.

She caught her breath. There, at the top of the wall, a body hung from a scaffold, its head down, turning in the wind. Its hands were bound behind it, and it looked, at the distance, like a broken doll or a scarecrow.

The couples below had eyes only for one another. The watchers had eyes only for the ceremony. When a bar of sunlight broke through, to illuminate the small scene, a happy sigh went up from the crowd. Only Gwyn saw how the hanged man dangled there from his own neck, at the edge of the picture.

It made Gwyn uneasy. Why would the Earl leave him up there, on this day? It was as if the hanged man were on display there, to warn, to cause fear. Who had he been? What had he done?

She forced her attention back to the ceremony, where the priest now moved along the couples, placing his hand over each set of joined hands, to say the words that bound them. The crowd watched this silently, as if it were one body. At last, the priest came to the end. He moved on, through the crowd and away, his work done. The couples turned to face the crowd, standing hand in hand for a long minute, and then the scene erupted as families and friends stepped forward, to celebrate.

"Have you seen Blithe?" Rose asked Gwyn quietly, while Wes's family and the Innkeeper's family greeted one another formally, and they all moved off to the tables for a mug of ale and toasts. "I hoped she'd come."

Gwyn just shook her head. Blithe would stay stubborn in her grief and would be sitting by the dead fire at her home, even now. The press of people pushed Gwyn away from her family, where Mother held Tad by a firm hand to keep him from going off and disappearing. Gwyn let herself be carried away. She let her eyes go back up to the troubling figure at the gallows before she turned to move with the crowds again, toward the tables. "They say he struck one of the Earl's soldiers." It was Burl, speaking from behind her. She knew his voice.

"He was a hot-tempered man," the voice told her quietly. "That's what rumor says."

Gwyn stopped again and turned her head to see Burl's face. "Why would he strike a soldier?"

"The soldier struck him first."

"Why would a soldier strike him?"

"The barroom was crowded. This man had a seat and the soldier did not."

"And the soldier? What's happened to him?" Gwyn asked.

"A soldier answers only to his captain."

A shower of sunlight washed over them, and another, as the sun fought its way through the clouds. But Gwyn felt cold.

"How do you know all this?" Gwyn demanded.

He shrugged.

"And why do you tell me."

His dark eyes held hers. "I thought you would ask," he told her.

He was right, Gwyn knew, and her eyes fell before his. Her feet were already hurting, and she felt suddenly impatient, almost cross. But when she lifted her face again to snap at Burl, he had melted into the crowd. Once more she looked to the figure dangling from the gallows.

Well, everybody knew there were hangings. There always had been, there always would be. She moved off to join her family.

When the Lords and Ladies arrived in a long procession, with servants behind them, the whole fair brightened at the colors they wore. Merchants uncovered their wares and the people hung back, speaking in quiet voices, staring. Gwyn took Tad with her, and they wandered away from the bargaining, following a path into the trees.

Tad's cheeks were pink with excitement and his eyes went

everywhere, trying to see everything at once. He had already untucked his shirt from his trousers, so it hung loose. The red curls on his head moved like sunlight on a brook. He grabbed at her arm and pointed, "Gwyn, look." And then again, two steps later, "Look, Gwyn!"

Gwyn looked around her, at the people before and beside them. She saw faces and bodies, men and women of all ages, and children running among them. She saw the same eagerness that filled Tad in their faces. But, as with the hanged man off atop the walls, her eye was caught that day by a crippled hand, its fingers stiff and unnaturally bent where bones had been broken; by the face of a girl her own age with a scar like a brand running from forehead to jaw, a scar that pulled her mouth up permanently into an unnatural smile; by a lame child, who stumbled far in the rear of the other children, his stiff leg dragging like an anchor; by men whose shoulders could no longer be held straight and women who could move their stiff joints only with the aid of walking sticks. There were more beggars that year, Gwyn thought, and if their eyes were anything to go by, more people who would be eating and drinking with their eyes only. There were more soldiers, too, swaggering around in groups.

"Gwyn, look!" Tad pulled on her arm. They joined the circle of people around a juggler's camp. Three men in red and green striped leggings were juggling red balls. Their hands flew as they kept three, four, and then five wooden balls circling in the air. At one end of the circle of watchers stood a few Lords and Ladies, who applauded with gloved hands as the jugglers gathered in the balls and took their bows. After the applause, one of the men stepped forward to announce that the next, and final, trick was one never before seen in the whole Kingdom. "If the Ladies," he bowed toward the Lords, "are delicate, they might turn their backs. The dangers of the act may frighten them. They surely frighten me, and I should know." He held up both of his hands, where three fingers were no longer than one knuckle. The crowd oo'ed sympathetically. Then he unfolded the fingers he had doubled down and the crowd laughed, applauded, called out to him. He bowed and took into his hands three knives. He held the knives up, that all might see.

"You're thinking now that these are dulled blades. I know your suspicious minds. But look you—" He held one knife up and approached a girl among the people. Gwyn knew her, it was Liss, from the farm northwards. Her brothers were with her, and they stepped in around her as the juggler approached. "I ask only a lock of your lovely hair," the juggler said to her. He was a man no longer young, his face brown and his smile easy. Liss laughed, covering her mouth with her hand, happy to be singled out for attention. The juggler reached out and took into his fingers one of the curls that had escaped the coiled braids. He held it straight out for a second and then, his hand swifter than a bird's wing, he cut it.

"Aaah," the people sighed in satisfaction. The juggler held the dark curl high above his head in one hand, with the knife held high in the other, and paraded around the inside of the circle. Back at the center, he asked Liss, "Would your young man like to have his treasure?"

"I have no young man," Liss answered, while her brothers tried to shush her. Gwyn was smiling.

"No young man?" The juggled seemed amazed. "What fools they are, then. Think you?" he asked the crowd.

Everybody agreed noisily, and one or two voices offered to remedy that situation if Liss was willing. Her brothers looked sternly around to find out the speakers.

The juggler stood at the center of the circle, before the fire, and held the three knives aloft, until he had everyone's attention again.

"He'll never do that now, will he?" women asked.

"He'd better, after all this fanfare," men answered.

So he did, sending the knives up into the air so that their metal blades caught at the sunlight. Slowly at first, then faster, the knives circled from his hands. The crowd watched, silently.

He juggled the knives around his back, then under a raised leg, without any hesitation as the blades rose and fell, and his hands caught at them and held them briefly before sending them aloft again. When he gathered them together in one hand and took his bow, the crowd stamped and clapped. "If we have pleased you," the juggler said, "as I seem to think we may have, do not hold back in showing your gratitude. If it's a lean year for farmers, think of how hard it is for jugglers."

His two assistants passed among the crowd, carrying shallow baskets, going first to the Lords and Ladies. When the basket came to Gwyn, she saw two silver coins and four pennies. She caught the eye of the young man holding the basket. "What the Lords leave will barely keep a juggler from one fair to the next," he told her.

Tad put in two of the pennies Da had given him, when Gwyn promised to pay him back for one, later, when her coins had been changed. Many people, she saw, had moved quickly away as the young man approached, their faces ashamed.

"Osh aye," the young man said, watching them melt away into the passersby. He spoke with the slow vowels of the southern kingdom. "I'd not begrudge them a free show."

"Aye," Gwyn answered, "but they might have stayed to pay their thanks."

They moved on, she and Tad, stopping to greet Liss, whose excitement matched Tad's, and then to watch a puppet show where a wooden knight fought a wooden giant to win a painted wooden princess. They passed the fortune-tellers, and a dancer who moved to the music of her own tambourine, lifting her bright skirts high while the audience, all men, hooted and cheered. Tad wanted to see the sword-swallower, whom he remembered from last fall.

There, the crowd was large and impatient for the performer to begin. When he stepped out of the tent hung from a rope behind the campfire, there was a burst of eager clapping. He was a large man, the top of his head bald, his beard trimmed short. He wore black trousers and had no shirt on under his leather tunic. He paraded twice around the circle, bowing to the Lords and Ladies at the side before beginning.

His performance was short, but the more dramatic for all that. Speaking never a word, he lifted the blades high over his head, arcing them to show that there was no trickery behind it. One after the other, he proved the blades, and then, his body drawn up tall, his head thrown back, his mouth opened wide, he started to swallow them. Gwyn watched, as breathless as she had been each time she had seen this man perform. His throat rose and fell, like a snake eating a mouse, as the blade went down it. Her own throat wanted to gag, watching his. The hand that held the blade above his open mouth lowered slowly, slowly and then, with painful slowness, lifted.

The blades grew longer, until it was a blade as long as Gwyn's forearm he lifted out. The watchers whistled, stamped, clapped their hands. Tad turned to Gwyn. "He's going to do it now, isn't he?" Gwyn nodded. She had caught sight of a woman's face peering out of the tent briefly and smiling at the sword-swallower. The smile revealed dark gaps where teeth were missing. The woman's skin was pale, her cheeks hollow.

The sword-swallower lit a torch. Its handle was wooden and the cloths that made up its head had been soaked in oil. It flared up with a muffled roar. He swept it around at the people circling close to him. They drew back before it. Then he opened his mouth and swallowed fire.

Gwyn had seen this before but it still caught her. Like everyone else, she waited without breathing. He pulled the torch from his mouth and the torch was smoking.

"Did you see that, did you see that?" Tad was jumping up and down and pulling on her arm. "Did you see?"

"Aye, I saw."

The sword-swallower moved into the crowd. One of the Lords spoke to him, and he bowed his head slightly. He would be asked to the castle, where he could hope for good pay, Gwyn knew. But he didn't say a word to the Lord or to anyone else as he moved among the crowd, his eyes proud. Tad put coins into the basket, but he moved behind Gwyn's skirt when the man came near. Gwyn saw the sword-swallower's eyes flick contemptuously over Tad.

When they walked on, Gwyn started to lecture Tad. "You mustn't do that, you're too old to hide now."

He did not ask her what she meant. "That's easy for you. You're brave."

"Aye, tell yourself that," Gwyn snapped back at him. "You might as well be wearing skirts."

"Who are you to talk? You act like a man anyway. Why do you think no one wants to wed you?"

Gwyn's temper flared to meet his. "What did you say?"

He moved back, out of reach. "You're not a proper girl at all. You might as well be wearing trousers and a beard."

"Get off, before I clout you all the way to tomorrow," Gwyn told him. "Run back to Mother. You'll be safe there," she called after him.

But his words had cut her like a knife. She knew it, and she felt how different she was from—everybody else. She didn't fit into this world, and even at home, at the Inn, she didn't fit in any longer the way she was supposed to. She no longer suited their lives, and it worried Mother and it worried Da, and it worried Gwyn and made her cross.

She worked her way along the path that wound through the trees, not seeing anything. All the people around irritated her. She could feel their glances, as if they had actually touched her, the way you might reach out a hand to touch something strange, or dangerous, that you had in a cage.

It wasn't as if she cared. It wasn't as if, she thought bleakly, even if she cared she could do anything to change herself. That was a bitter thought. But it took Tad to tell her to her face. She might as well have a scar like the one she'd seen on that girl, since everybody saw it anyway. Whatever it was.

Near the edge of the trees, under an oak that spread broad overhead, a man played a lute and a girl sang, and the crowd moved on unheeding. The girl's face was as hollow with hunger as her body was swollen with child. The two played and sang listlessly, without hope. Gwyn stopped to stare at them. The girl's thin voice recited the words to an old song and the lute stumbled behind her. The basket lay at her feet. The unheeding crowds, the despairing music, all seemed more than Gwyn could tolerate just then. She moved closer, on her tight shoes, just then noticing how much her feet hurt. Aye, that would pass; it always did; and she would bear it. Seeing Gwyn, the girl looked up and her smile became fawning, eager to please, like a whipped dog.

It was terrible, Gwyn thought, as her throat closed against her rising heart. Terrible hope and terrible disappointment and the terrible promise of life growing in her belly. Gwyn fumbled at the purse at her waist and took out one of her coins. She stepped forward and dropped it into the basket, then turned quickly to leave them there. Terrible music too, she thought.

She was stepping into the open field before her brain registered what she had seen lying at the bottom of the woven basket—a single golden coin.

She knew who had passed that way before her. Burl. She knew those coins; she had ten left under her mattress. She smiled to herself at the picture of Burl, slipping the coin into their basket, and they would never suspect him of it. She thought she knew why he had done it—it would have been because of their music. And because of the world.

Gwyn raised her head and looked over the field, where the stage waited for the play that would be the last event of the afternoon, before the Lords left and the dancing began. In front of her, groups of people milled about, the Lords and Ladies moving within some invisible shield, as the people drew back from them. The Lords and Ladies did not even look at the crowds around them. Their interest was on the amusements and the wares. The people might as well have been blades of grass.

Overlooking the field, Gwyn realized that much as she might long to fit in, she was also glad she did not. Tad had said it to hurt her, but it was the truth just the same. Gwyn turned her head to look back into the trees, at the crowds flowing out, and then to the city walls. She fit into this world like the hanged man did, she thought. She could not see him from where she stood, but he dangled at the edge of the fair, and she did not forget that. Let others forget.

ᘒ Eighteen

GWYN STOOD back from the booth while the Ladies
considered the merchant's goods. There were three
Ladies. Their servants waited behind them while they held
up the skeins of wool, talking of the colors in low voices.
Jewels shone on their hands. Their gowns flowed down like
water from bodice to hem, pale yellow, blue, and green, each
with lace at the throat. The long hair flowed down over the
colors of the dresses, dark brown, light brown, and gray. Each
Lady had tied her hair back with a band that matched the
color of her dress. They were a long time over the wool, and
Gwyn waited impatiently. One had a useless nose, not much
bigger than a button. Another was as plump as a hen fat for
the spit and strained the seams of her gown. The third talked
constantly in a bitter voice about the quality of the merchant's
wares, how carelessly wares were made, now, that in the time
of her youth had been patiently worked to perfection. Her long
fingers picked at a knot in the wool.

The merchant said nothing, just nodded and smiled, his hands clasped in front of him. The servants said nothing, but stood waiting with baskets on their arms. Meanwhile, the Ladies stood deciding, talking about who the color would suit or the stitches for embroidery, talking about the troubles in the south and how they affected the wares at the fair, talking of marriages in the making and the behavior of children. At last, the complaining Lady selected a small skein of red and motioned to the servant behind her. The servant made the purchase and put it into her basket.

Gwyn could have laughed at the expression on the merchant's face. But she didn't. She moved up before the stall and looked over the skeins for the kind of wool she had seen last fall. When she saw it, she reached out to take it up in her fingers, but the merchant's voice stopped her. "Get away, girl, you're costing me custom. Move on—did you hear me?"

Gwyn looked up to meet a pair of piggy eyes under heavy eyebrows. His gray beard was trimmed to a point. "But I—"

"Was only looking," he finished for her. "You can stop looking and move on. Or I'll call a soldier to chase you away."

Balanced between anger and laughter, Gwyn made her eyes wide. "Yes, Wool Merchant," she said, with exaggerated respect. If he only knew, she had a purse full of coins that were hers to spend. "You will excuse my impertinence." He would be sorry, if he knew.

She saw to it that he did know. She moved to the next booth but one, checking to be sure he watched as she looked over the wares on that wool merchant's table. She made a great show of her selection, even though she knew as soon as she saw it that the skeins of white wool, white as snow—no, white and soft as clouds—were what she would buy. When she was certain the first merchant could see her, she took out her purse and let the money flow out into her hand. Then taking one coin, she turned it in her fingers before paying, with a smile back over her shoulder to the merchant who had refused her custom.

Gwyn moved on by the booths and tables, her eyes studying the displays. There were soft leather gloves and broad leather belts, daggers with carved hilts, and long books, bound in leather, as well as smaller books enclosed by rough slabs of wood. A fletcher displayed arrows of different lengths to two young Lords. Bolts of cloth and piles of pewter bowls caught her eye. The sunlight sparkled on little glass bottles of perfumes, from the lands beyond the Kingdom. Voices swirled around Gwyn, people pushed at her, then apologized, laughing; and her feet hurt. When a hand held her arm, she turned quickly to shake it off.

"Nay, Innkeeper's daughter," the young man said.

It took Gwyn a minute to recognize Raff. "Good day to you," she greeted him, sorry to see him if he was here—as her mother suggested he might be—to speak for her. Then she wondered if she should make some excuse for wandering about on her own.

"You've been hard to find," he said.

"Yes, it's time I returned," she agreed.

They stood together for an uncomfortable moment. Over the winter, Raff's beard had changed from a boy's to a man's.

"I would speak with you, Innkeeper's daughter," he said. "Your father said I should find you." Then he apparently changed his mind about what he wanted to say. "That's a pretty wool," he said.

"For Rose."

"Fine wool," he said. He took a breath and looked at the ground at his feet. "It's time I was wed, Innkeeper's daughter."

Gwyn's heart rose into her throat, then fell to her pinched feet. She liked Raff. He was a blunt, hardworking man, with a good holding to offer any girl. "Think you?" she asked him.

"I think," he said. He still did not meet her eyes.

"Then," Gwyn spoke hurriedly, "I'm glad you told me, because I have a bride for you."

At that his eyes did meet hers. "You've been in my mind this winter, Raff," she teased him. "A man like you, with a good holding, needs a wife who can work hard." She didn't wait for him to agree with her. "I have a bride for you who will do that, and with a light spirit, and be pretty into the bargain. What do you say to that?"

He didn't say anything.

"But Gwyn—"

"Her name is Liss," Gwyn cut him off. It shamed a man to be said no to, and she had no desire to shame Raff. "You'll have to prove to her brothers that you'll take good care of her."

"Liss is a child," Raff said.

"Think you? Then you'd better go seek her out, because it's not a child I've seen today. And I'd better find Da." She left Raff standing, in her haste to find her father. It was time the announcement was made. She did not know why he had delayed so long.

Gwyn met her family at a table of ribbons. Wes was selecting a ribbon for Rose, to tie around her hair on this day and to pretty her neck on later occasions. Rose hung from Wes's arm and their eyes were locked together as if there were nobody else in the world.

At the sight of the two of them, so happy, a wave of sadness washed over Gwyn, and she tasted bitterness briefly in her mouth. Mother stood among women, with Tad at her skirts. Da was talking to a young man with a thick beard, whom Gwyn recognized as a cobbler from Lord Hildebrand's city. By Da's expression, she knew what they were speaking of and wished she could interrupt. The young man broke off the conversation and started to approach Gwyn. She interrupted Rose's and Wes's soft talk, to thrust the wool into Rose's arms. "It's a wedding gift," she said.

Rose held the wool in her fingers. "I've never seen anything so soft. Wes?"

Wes held two ribbons in his hand and a penny lay on the table before him. "Very nice," he said. He dropped the ribbons back onto the table and covered the penny with his broad hand. Gwyn could have bitten out her tongue. She had hurt him, by giving a gift more than he could buy for Rose. She had given the wool at the wrong time, in the wrong way.

"It's not for Rose, though," she said.

"But I thought—" Rose protested.

"It is for your first child," Gwyn said, "and for all those that follow."

Wes's mind took that information in slowly, and then a smile spread over his face and he reached out to touch the soft wool. "Is it now?" he asked.

"Aye, as I've said."

"You're in a mighty hurry for a baby, sister," he said. Gwyn didn't answer. "Did you get some of this fine wool for yourself as well?" he teased her.

"No," Gwyn said. "And what would I want with it?"

For answer, he indicated Da, in conversation with a man Gwyn had never seen before. Gwyn sighed. Wes would not understand. Even Rose could not. Da and Mother, they did not. And Gwyn herself, she recognized, was not sure of her own thoughts.

It would be good to have her marriage day in the fall, to let her hair loose down her back and stand as Rose was, with her arm held close under a man's. She let her gaze rove over the people standing about and saw whose eyes lowered before her own. Then she saw the black figure above the battlements, twisting slowly, and the birds gathering around his head to take his eyes.

This had been a living man, just last night. She wondered if he had left behind a widow and children, and how they would live. If a man was hanged for his quick temper—if that was to be the law, now—there would be many of the people hanged along with him.

Nobody else saw him, nobody else looked to him. Only Gwyn. And who would want such a girl for his wife, if he knew what she saw.

If, Gwyn thought, there were one of these young men who also saw the hanged man, then that one she might take. But if they saw, they did not speak of it, as if by not speaking they could make it disappear; and such men Gwyn would not marry.

She went to her father, pulling him away from the men

around him. "Your mother is angry at you," he said. "You left Tad."

"I'll make peace with her," Gwyn promised. "But you must make the announcement."

"Daughter," he asked her, "how can you be so sure?"

Gwyn made herself smile into his worried face. "Aye, I am, Father."

"Your mother says—"

"You gave me your word. Would you have all these young men go unwed because your wife is unwilling to have an unmarried daughter?"

"Your tongue is too sharp."

"And would you wish that on some poor youth?"

He sighed. "As you will."

"Thank you, Da."

"I hope so," he answered.

If you knew what to look for, you could see the whisper spreading through the people and the speculations among the women. The Lords and Ladies knew nothing of it, of course; they sailed through the crowd of people like clouds through the air. Relief at knowing the announcement was made lifted Gwyn's spirits. She took Tad by the hand and dragged him off to buy him a fairing. "A ribbon for your wife?" she offered.

"You're teasing," he protested.

"It's never too soon to begin saving up gifts, a fine lad like you and will be the Innkeeper's heir. You'll have your choice, and you'll want a pretty to give her."

Tad's face grew red with embarrassment. She pulled him toward a booth where ribbons were displayed. "Gwyn!"

"Then perhaps a scarf, to tie around your neck when you go dancing and courting?" She pulled him in another direction.

"A scarf? What would I do with a scarf? You've gone mad, Gwyn."

"You could cover your ugly face," she teased, pulling at his hair.

"Then you'll be getting one for yourself, as well."

They laughed together and went to look at a booth where daggers lay out in rows, their wooden handles polished until they shone. "Gwyn," Tad said, as they looked them over, "I'm sorry. I am. I shouldn't have said—"

"Perhaps not," Gwyn agreed. "But there's truth in it, isn't there?"

"But it was unkind. And besides, I like you, the way you are," he told her. "I do, you know." He sounded surprised and that amused her.

"And so do I. Now, make your choice before I fall asleep standing here waiting."

Tad stuck his new dagger into his belt. "You'll have to take orders from me," he warned her. "When . . . you know."

"Then they'd better be sensible orders," Gwyn warned him.

They spent the afternoon together, joining occasionally with other people. They sat with Liss and her brothers to watch the play performed. The people sat on a grassy hillside, behind the benches on which the Lords and Ladies sat. The play told the story of the farmer's wife who scolded the devil and then chased him out of her kitchen with a rolling pin. The actors wore paint on their faces and shoes with built-up heels, so that they seemed not real. They spoke like the people, but they moved clumsily across the wooden stage and their words were often stupid. Gwyn did not enjoy the performance as much as she had in previous years, and despite her fine shoes she felt ill at ease. Liss chattered away, while her brothers made ominous remarks about anyone who might ask to dance with her. Gwyn answered Liss's remarks with only half of her mind. They required no better attention. With the rest of her thoughts she considered Tad, and the man he might become, and she wondered if the players felt as safely hidden within their costumes as she had when she walked into the Fiddler's house, and she wished Blithe had come to see Rose wed, giving up her stubborn grief; she decided she would get some sweets for herself and Tad, and she thought she might speak a word of comfort to Burl, on Rose's wedding day.

The play ended without her noticing it, and the actors bowed briefly, passing their baskets among the audience. They would be hurrying into the city for the night's performance before the Lords. Gwyn wondered what play they would do there. Most likely something with princesses and dragons, like the tales Gaderian told.

The people moved about the fairgrounds again, making their last purchases when prices could be bargained lowest. Gwyn sent Tad on ahead to find the sweet vendor, giving him four pennies to spend. She had seen a booth where the Steward had stood earlier and Bailiffs gathered. It was run by a wizened man with a withered arm. But when she went looking for the books spread out over the table, it was empty. The man stood alone.

He was suspicious of Gwyn, at first, but she told him about how she liked to draw pictures. "If you take the charred wood from a fire—but you must wait until it has cooled down," she added.

An expression of disgust at her stupidity washed over his face.

"It will make lines. But it's only wood I have to draw on. And my Da gave me coins. He said I could have whatever I wanted with them. He said I was too old for such foolishness as drawing pictures, because I should be wed. But he said I could have what I wanted—" She looked as sad as she knew how. "But I don't have very many coins, I don't know—is a book, just a little book, so very dear?" She fumbled in her purse and drew out a piece of silver. He had been ignoring her until his eye was caught by the coin. "That's all I have and I don't think it's very much. But have you anything? I don't care how small it is. Have you anything this coin will buy?"

His eyes shifted to the booths nearby, but nobody saw him.

"Aye," he said. He reached into a sack behind him and pulled out a small book, its leaves of paper held between two clumsy slabs of wood, which were joined by rough leather hinges. The thing was worth nothing near the value of the coin. Gwyn knew that.

"Is this enough?" She pushed the silver coin across the table at him. "I'm sorry I don't have any more, but—"

"It's not enough, but you've a pretty face," he told her, taking the coin quickly.

"Oh sir," Gwyn said, her voice like honey off a spoon. "Oh sir."

She took up the book and hid it in the folds of her skirt until she could turn her back on the crowds and fit it inside of her shirt, where the waist of her skirt would hold it safe. The sharp corners of wood cut into her stomach, but that didn't bother her. This, she thought to herself, was a present to herself. And was there any reason why she shouldn't buy herself a present? A non-wedding present, that's what it would be.

In the late afternoon, the fiddlers gathered in the field, pitchers of ale on a low table behind them, tuning their strings into harmony. It was the young who would dance the sun down, while the rest watched and listened and remembered and talked. Gwyn wondered if she should stand out, but thought that this last time she would dance with the rest.

She found a place beside Liss in the circle of girls. "Isn't this fun?" Liss asked. "Isn't it fun to be away from my brothers?"

"They're still watching you," Gwyn warned her.

"I know, but they can't hear what I'm saying. I do love dancing, Gwyn, don't you? I always feel so—pretty," she said.

"I feel as if my feet hurt." Gwyn laughed.

"Is that Raff talking with my brothers, think you?"

Gwyn thought so.

"He looks a man grown."

"Aye, and he is. Just as dull and serious as Da."

"He's serious, but not dull," Liss answered quickly. "I think it's better if a man is serious, don't you?"

The music started so Gwyn didn't have to answer. She had already heard what she was listening for.

They danced the circle dance, a circle of girls inside a circle of men. Their feet moved lightly under the music. The two circles turned, one inside the other, and then stopped so that couples might dance a round. At the end of the round, each partner moved back to his original place. Gwyn danced one round with Cam, whose eyes mocked her. "Is it true, then, what I hear?"

She could think of no response.

"And what of my broken heart?" he asked, as they held hands to spin one another around. "You might have given me a chance."

"A chance to what?" Gwyn laughed. "Break *my* heart?"

"You have no heart to break, Innkeeper's daughter." His face looked serious and his eyes held hers. "Or didn't you know I was thinking to ask you?"

Aye, he said that now, now when she must say no, Gwyn thought, because he was a false man. Their round ended, and she danced back to the circle of girls, smiling to Cam as she left him.

When the face of the sun touched the horizon, Gwyn left the dancers and moved back to join the watchers. She had found little joy in the dance. She slipped her feet out of her shoes and felt the soft grass against her soles. When a short, round man with a wheaten beard that grew wild over his face stepped up to her, she almost put her feet back into the shoes, for decency's sake. Then she decided not to: In this one thing, at least, she would entirely please herself.

"It's been a good fair," the man said. His name was Am, and he had a holding to the north of Blithe's home, north of Hildebrand's City, where he kept pigs. He was a round man, with a round head, round eyes, and a round belly underneath his shirt. "Have you enjoyed the day, Innkeeper's daughter?"

"Aye, I have," she answered him.

"And have you heard the rumors?" He stood beside her and they both watched the dancers. He was a widower, she knew, with three young children in his house.

"I hear nothing but rumors," she answered cautiously.

He continued as if she hadn't spoken. "There's not one of Earl Sutherland's sons left alive. Of all the six, not one. These are dangerous times."

Gwyn nodded.

"The King has taken an army into the south. Will the trouble spread north, think you?"

"I hope not," Gwyn said.

"But it could," he told her. "Even if we don't have the battles, we'll have the soldiers, and the thieves. I have a good number of pigs, even after the winter."

"Do you?"

"Aye, and I'll be taking my meat to the south to sell, if not this year the next. With the extra gold I'll increase my herd."

The sky above Earl Northgate's City flamed red as the sun sank. The walls were outlined in red; they stood like black mountains. The figure of the hanged man was not visible from the field where they danced.

Am repeated, "Dangerous times. A woman needs a man's protection."

Gwyn didn't respond.

Am's round cheeks were pink and a little sweat beaded his round forehead. "As I hear, there will be no journeying after all, for the highwayman. Because the King cannot spare the soldiers. It would be better if they journeyed him—it's fear of hanging keeps the people honest."

"Think you?" Gwyn wondered.

"Aye, and in such times as these. I heard a rumor I was glad to hear." His plump hands clutched one another. "They say you're not to wed."

"Some rumors carry truth," Gwyn said. She wished she could leave the conversation, but that would insult Am. She was afraid of what he wanted to say to her.

"I have three children."

"You are fortunate."

"Osh aye, I am—they're good children and two healthy.

It's much for a man to do his own work and a woman's too. The pigs, and the taxes and the meals. They want a woman's hand."

Gwyn couldn't think of anything to say.

"With the levies so high this year."

Gwyn nodded, although what the taxes had to do with a woman's hand for children, she did not know. She felt sorry for him.

"We've not much, but nobody's gone hungry at my holding."

"That's good luck."

"So—if you'd think to come to us—to me—"

"But I cannot leave the Inn." Gwyn made herself look at his face as the quick excuse tumbled out of her mouth. "Not in times like these."

"Aye—no—I thought not," he mumbled.

She saw then that his trousers were frayed and his shirt worn thin. He had come to her in need. It would give him no cheer to know that she pitied him.

"Not such as I," he said, moving backwards. "But I just wanted to ask. To tell you. That if you ever—" He stumbled away from her.

Gwyn rubbed her hands over her face, her fingers working at her eyes, because she could have wept for him. He had tried so hard to be dignified, so that he would not seem to be begging. He had bragged falsely of his means, but she could not blame him. She watched three children come to crowd around him and pull down on his round arms: the oldest was a girl, her yellow hair in clumsy braids and her skirt out at the hem. Two ragged little boys hung onto his legs, one thin and weak. Without looking back, the family left the field. They would have a long walk home, longest for the man who moved with bent shoulders, as if his burdens were too heavy for him to carry.

Gwyn moved to the safety of her family, overhearing snips of conversation as she moved among the watchers. She had left her shoes behind, standing side by side in the grass like a girl and her bridegroom.

"—even here then? It would be dangerous to him here," a voice whispered near her. She could not tell if it was a man or a woman, the voice was so low.

"Aye, as I hear, and left a gold coin with a poor singer. They never saw him."

"He's not seen unless he wants to be," the first voice answered.

Mother would not speak with Gwyn, for anger. The anger would burn itself out, Gwyn thought, and she was feeling too strangely glad and bitter mixed together to try to jolly her mother. She picked out Rose among the dancers, moving lightly, her hair washed with the red of the setting sun, flowing like a branch of flowers, with a bright ribbon tied into it.

"I would see you among the dancers, Innkeeper's daughter." Burl spoke beside her.

His face was in shadows, so Gwyn didn't know if he was asking her to dance with him.

"It isn't seemly," she said.

"No," he agreed.

He didn't have to agree with her, Gwyn thought crossly. The music made her feet want to move. She felt the grass under her feet. "Besides, I don't have any shoes on. Can you imagine what my Mother would say."

He chuckled. "Aye, I can imagine. No, it would be most unseemly. Even so—"

"I wondered if they might be here, the Lord and his son," Gwyn asked.

"So did I. But if the rumors are correct, every armed man has gone to the south. Even a mapmaker might be needed."

"Rumors are never correct. You know that as well as I do, Burl."

He neither agreed nor disagreed, and in the failing light she could not read his face.

"You'd have made a good husband to Rose," she said to him, giving him her sympathy.

"Aye, I think so." He looked toward the dancers. "But I wonder if Rose would have made a good wife to me. Think you?"

"I never thought of that." Odd, she thought, too, that she didn't feel sorry for Burl and never had. He was a proud man, in his way. Aye, and he'd a right to be, she thought.

Gwyn left the fair when her family did. The dancers would start home later, when stars had filled the sky.

~⧉⧇⧇~ Nineteen

SHORTLY AFTER the fair, as the trees were coming into full leaf, soldiers came to the Inn, where they were quartered. The soldiers and their captain, a tall man with deep creases on his face, all wore the emblem of the bear, Earl Northgate's sign. Their duty was to ride guard along the King's Way between the Inn and Earl Northgate's City. They were also to keep the district peaceful, because their presence would discourage thieves and other outlaws from preying on the people. They would eventually accompany the highwayman on the last part of his journey, which had even now begun in the south. All along the King's Ways, in the north and the south, such troops of soldiers had been sent by the King's orders. Every Inn, in the cities and the country, had such troops quartered upon it, as did many of the villages scattered across the countryside.

There was nothing Da could do about it. The Captain

was given room in the barn, and the cows put to pasture in the lower field. The soldiers set up tents under the trees near the King's Way. Some of their horses were stabled at the Inn, some kept near to the camp. Those goats that had been living in the barn were given into the care of the farmer on one of Da's holdings.

The Inn was kept busy from early morning to late at night. The soldiers and their Captain must be fed, their horses cared for. In the evenings, the barroom filled early, as men— hopeful for the summer's crops and the herds' numbers; not mindful of high taxes in the fall—found the pennies for ale. In the evenings the barroom and courtyard were busy. Messengers came frequently and left rumors behind, rumors that spread like water into every corner of the Inn. There were battles in the south and the King's forces were winning and the King's forces were losing. One of Earl Sutherland's sons had been sent out of the Kingdom in disgrace, years ago; he would return to claim the title. There was only a baby left out of the entire family and he hidden away somewhere, and nobody knew where; the King was seeking him, to give him the title. Only a daughter was left, and she of marriageable age; one of the southern Lords had taken her, had locked her away in a tower until she would marry his son. The armies stole from the people of the south, trampled the fields and vineyards, slaughtered the herds. The Ways across the southern King-dom were so perilous that there had been no Spring Fair. More soldiers were needed. The flames of war were moving northward.

At the end of the day, the Innkeeper's family sat around the table and talked over the rumors. Da argued that they must be exaggerated. "The journeying is still going on. If the King didn't hold rule in the south, the journeying would not go on."

"They say it won't be long until the highwayman comes by here," Tad said.

"They say the man walks slowly," Mother said, "as if he carried a great burden. I wonder what he did."

"He was a highwayman," Tad told her. "I want to see him, when he comes here. I've never seen a highwayman."

"You'll go to the village," Mother said. "You'll stay with Rose."

"Da?" Tad asked. "Do I have to?"

Da studied his hands. "The boy will stay with us and see this man, wife."

"But, husband—"

"And the hanging?" Tad pressed his advantage.

"Not the hanging," Mother declared. "You'll stay home on that day. I've never seen a hanging and neither will you, as long as I live. I've no desire to watch a man die, as if it were a play upon a stage."

"But I can see him journey," Tad said.

"Your father has said so," Mother answered bitterly.

Gwyn watched this conversation with interest. With Rose gone, more work had fallen to Tad. Of necessity, Tad had served in the barroom and cared for the animals. He seemed to have taken over the kitchen garden as well, with Mother kept busy at the ovens and at the washing tubs. Tad made mistakes enough, but he was learning. It was that learning that emboldened him to cross Mother's wishes about the highwayman.

Gwyn had little time to herself those days. For a few minutes at the end of each day, alone now in the room she had shared for so many years with Rose, she wrote letters in the book she had bought at the fair. At first she could not remember words. But that soon came back to her as she scratched on paper with a bit of charcoal until her eyes were too tired to focus on the marks she made. She practiced the shapes of the letters, and some words too, just to see how they would look. DA and MOTHER, RAMS HED INN, and TAD. When she figured out how to write Tad's name, she was so pleased she wanted to go into his room and show him, even though she knew she could not. JACKAROO, she wrote, liking the look of that better than JACARU or JAKUREW.

However tired she was, she always hid the book carefully at the back of her cupboard before going to sleep.

It was many days after the fair before Gwyn got away to do what she had decided at the dancing that she would do. She watched for her chance. That chance came when a Messenger and his two guards arrived unexpectedly. Their horses had been ridden hard, all the way from the High City. Gwyn said that she would take the job of walking the horses cool. It was almost midday by the time she led the three horses behind the village and then, climbing onto one and holding the reins of the other two in her hands, took them at a faster pace up to Old Megg's. There, she shut them into the empty goat pen and changed quickly into boots, trousers, tunic, cloak, and mask. She did not want to risk wearing the hat on horseback, but she also dared not risk appearing without it. For the same reason, she belted the sword around her waist.

She found the mare's saddle where they had left it, up in the loft. She tossed it down to the floor. She had decided which horse was the quietest, and when she buckled the girth around its belly, she spoke cheerfully to it, so that it would get used to her voice. The horse seemed docile enough. Gwyn pictured in her memory the way the soldiers mounted, then put one foot into the stirrup and swung the other leg across the horse's back. It was harder than she had thought it would be to mount that way. She turned the horse's head to the east.

Am's holding lay, she knew, over toward Lord Hildebrand's city, little more than an hour's walk beyond Blithe and Guy. The house was, if Blithe spoke truly of it, little better than the pen where his pigs wintered. The holding, Gwyn remembered, lay upon a rocky hillside, up to the north from Blithe's house. She would head for Guy's holding, which she knew well enough. Then she would follow the little trail northward. A number of small holdings dotted those low hills, but she would trust to luck to find the right one.

Riding along, with the horse at a trot and the leather

creaking under her, Gwyn grinned to herself. If she couldn't find it then she would stop for directions. It might be that luck would ride with her. If not, as Jackaroo she could ask a question and no one the wiser. But she could not lose too much time, she thought, urging the horse to a faster pace. The horse broke into a canter and for a minute Gwyn stiffened in alarm. But the motion merely rocked her. She thought she could stay on.

The countryside flowed past her at an alarming rate. Spring rains had been gentle and the sunshine generous. Green shoots grew up in neat rows on the plowed fields. Flowering bushes looked like low fountains of color, white, yellow, and many shades of red. Newborn kids suckled at their mothers.

Gwyn had never ridden on a saddle before, nor in trousers, and she found it comfortable, as comfortable and easy as the smooth gait. In a short time, she could look down over Guy's holding, the low stone house where he and Blithe lived with his family, the farmyard and fields where men bent in labor. Gwyn turned the horse northward, following a narrow path toward the mountains, the lower slopes of which showed green.

When there was cover, Gwyn kept within it. When she emerged from sparse trees into open land, where sheep grazed and distant houses nestled in folds of earth, she circled the dwellings closely enough so that she could see if it was squalid enough to match Blithe's description. These dwellings were far from one another, and Gwyn followed the smoke from kitchen fires to find them. At the fourth holding, she reined in her horse and looked down. Sunlight poured over her shoulders, where the red cape hung. Gwyn shifted her seat and put a hand on the hilt, to keep the sword from striking the horse's side.

The house below was windowless. Its chimney leaned weakly against the wall, as if a strong wind would blow it over. Nothing moved, except for a child playing at the open door. Another child came out to join the first, a girl whose fair braids caught the sunlight and shone gold.

Gwyn rode down the steep hillside, leaning backwards while the horse picked its careful way. The two children watched her approach, backing toward the open door as she came close. Gwyn sat the horse with her shoulders squared and reined it to a halt directly in front of them. There were two little boys now, one hiding behind the skirts of his sister. Their round eyes stared up at Gwyn.

"You are the children of Am, the pigman?" Gwyn asked gruffly.

They nodded.

"Where is your father?"

They said nothing, just stared up at her. Gwyn knew that she must frighten them, that the horse frightened them. She ought to dismount, she thought, but she knew that if she did she would have to mount again, and she could not do that as easily as the soldiers did. Even such children might notice her awkwardness and she could not risk that.

"Where is your father?" she repeated sternly.

The girl pointed with her finger off to the north. "Trading a shoat." Her voice was small with fright.

"When will he return?"

"Suppertime."

"Are you in charge?"

The girl nodded. Her eyes were fixed to the mask covering Gwyn's face.

Gwyn reached with one hand under her tunic and took out the bag. She leaned down to put the coins into the girl's grubby hand. "Give these to your Da when he returns."

The girl nodded.

"Do you know who I am?" Gwyn asked her.

The girl nodded, her face solemn.

"Who?" Gwyn asked.

A smile broke over the child's face, like the sun breaking through clouds. "Jackaroo," she said.

"That's good," Gwyn told her. "Goodbye. Don't forget."

"I won't forget," the girl promised.

Gwyn turned the horse around and rode away, up the

stony hillside, at a walk. At the crest, she turned to look back. The three children still stood together in front of the house. Gwyn lifted her hat and waved it in the air. They waved back at her.

Gwyn's heart was light as she kicked the horse into a gentle canter. She could feel her body riding easily, and how strong her legs were to grip the horse's sides. She could see the hills rising and falling before her. The two pieces of gold would solve so many of Am's problems, and that made her glad. She was glad to have been the one to do that deed and especially glad that it was for her that the smile had come to that child's face. It would be, she thought, remembering back to that midwinter day, like the granny's memory of Jackaroo— the child would grow up to a woman, and she would remember this golden morning as if it were a dream.

Gwyn was, she realized, more at ease when she wandered about the countryside as Jackaroo than at any other time. It was odd that dressed up as Jackaroo she felt much more like herself. Odd, and pleasant. She liked herself. And in the disguise, she was free to do what she really wanted to do, much freer than was Gwyn, the Innkeeper's daughter. She wondered if she would hear, someday, a rumor about Jackaroo and the pigman's child. She thought about how the rumor would exaggerate, misrepresenting what had actually happened, just as the rumor of Jackaroo's presence at the Spring Fair had spread falsehood.

Gwyn had never been so pleased with her life. She guided the horse between the hillsides and savored her pleasure, as a hungry man savors a meal. It might even grow into a story, telling how Jackaroo had brought two gold coins to a widower, to feed his children.

It was clouds of smoke that caught her eye, rising up over the crest of a hill. The smoke billowed upward, thick and round. A fire.

Among these isolated holdings there would be no village bell to ring the alarm. Gwyn turned the horse to climb up the hill, staying in the open so that they could move more quickly.

The smoke rose from trees in a hollow at the base of three hills. Gwyn thought she heard a cry, like a woman screaming, but the sound ceased. She urged the horse downhill, not bothering to keep to the shelter of the few trees, toward the smoke.

A hut burned, and two figures dragged something toward the flames. Gwyn's horse faltered at the sight and sound of flames, hesitated, then dug its four feet into the ground, refusing to go on.

A third figure held ropes around the necks of two goats. The little animals bleated and tried to pull away from the clearing. Smoke billowed up.

Gwyn never knew how she knew so immediately what she was seeing. But she knew surely that the three men had attacked the house. Her mind raced as fast as her heart while she sat for seconds that ran slow as hours, trying to think of what to do. She was alone and did not know how to use the only weapon she had to hand. She was a girl and there were three of them, three men.

They had not seen her yet. Gwyn unsheathed the sword and opened her mouth to cry: "Stop." But the sound that came out of her mouth was a wild cry, bearing no resemblance to any word.

Three faces turned to her, hairy and amazed.

Gwyn dug her heels into the horse's side and urged the animal toward the clearing. She held her sword high against them.

The two men dropped their burden at the door of the flaming hut. They ran. One of them moved with a queer dragging gait. The man holding the goats had disappeared into the trees without waiting. The other two disappeared after him, as fast as they could. Gwyn chased them to the edge of the clearing and then jumped down. She could hear them crashing away through the trees. They wouldn't return, she thought, looping the reins around a branch. She hurried back to the burning house. She knew she had seen those faces, and that crippled gait too.

The heat of the fire burned out at her. She dropped the

clumsy sword. Just beyond the door she stopped, feeling as if the skin of her hands was being singed. Heat pushed against the mask covering her face.

What they had been dragging was the body of a woman, whose skirt lay over the lintel, her feet—in felt shoes with big holes in the soles—lay out from the fire, pointing in opposite directions. Her hair had already caught fire. Flames danced around her face and crawled along the floor to her blood-stained chest. Inside, the body of a man burned, as black as a log. One of the walls crashed in, obliterating the man.

Gwyn stumbed backwards. There was a pain like a knife in her belly.

The fire roared in front of her.

Gwyn gulped for air, as if it were drink, but her lungs heaved it out before she could swallow it, and her shoulders were rising and falling. She needed to throw up.

She turned to the trees and bent down, heaving until her stomach was empty. But her chest still heaved and the hand that held up the long mask was wet—with her own tears, because her face was as wet as if she had been standing in a thunderstorm. When she straightened up her legs shook.

She wanted to ride away and never to have seen what she had seen.

She wanted to ride those men down and put her sword through them. Or tie ropes around their necks and drag them to Hildebrand for hanging. Or burning, over a slow fire that gave little smoke so that it should be flames licking up over their legs that would kill them slowly, while they screamed.

Bad enough that the Lords should treat the people as they did, but that the people should so—slaughter one another was—horrible. As if hunger and poverty were not enough as enemies, so the people turned upon one another.

And here she had been, riding along as if it were a game or play, dispensing a gold coin here and there, careless as a Lord.

Gwyn watched the fire, diminishing now. There was little to fuel it. It was like a funeral pyre, and she the only mourner.

That was how it would be too, she knew. No one would know what had happened here today, not until the Bailiff came out for the fall taxes. He would be irritated at the loss of coins, no more. He would see charred ruins and be cross at having come so far for nothing. He would make a note that the holding could be sold now.

At last, Gwyn bent to pick up her sword, replacing it in its sheath. There was an anger burning along her bones, licking now like the little flames from the ruined hut. It was anger at herself for being blind to so much: She knew as well as anyone that until the crops came in and the berries ripened on bushes and trees, hunger would rule. The air might be soft and gentle, but that was only spring, which dressed itself out in its pretties but brought nothing that people might eat. She was angry at the world in which such cruel death could come for a man and his wife. She was angry at the outlaws—

But she knew them now, she had recognized them. They were the three men from her winter journey, whom the Lord had sent to sleep with their goats.

She would have those men. Somehow. She knew that limping gait, and she had seen the scarred face among the three that fled from Jackaroo riding down on them. They would pay. Somehow.

Gwyn approached the horse, which waited uneasily, tied so close to the trees that it could barely move its head. "Osh, aye, I'm sorry," she spoke quietly to it. Her voice sounded thick to her ears, thick with tears and anger. She loosened the reins.

Within the trees, she heard a wailing cry. A child, it sounded like a child, a child too young to speak any words.

Gwyn left the reins and followed the sound to where a bundle of cloths lay hidden under a bush. The cloths moved.

It was a baby, too young even to crawl. When she had uncovered it, its arms waved in the air and its voice wailed. Thin silky hair bushed out over its head, and its eyes were closed with its crying. There were no teeth in its gums. The cloths around it were wet.

Gwyn changed the baby into dry cloths. It was a boy child. His mother must have run to hide him here, to save him. She must have been mad with fear not to know that this would only save him for a slower death. It was such a slim chance that Gwyn had been riding by, and had frightened off the men, and had heard the baby's cries. It was no chance, and the woman must have known that. But she would have clutched at that slender golden thread of false hope.

Gwyn knew what she would do. She wrapped the boy around with his knitted blanket and held him against her chest. He turned his face to her tunic, as if he would suckle, got one of the silver buckles into his eager mouth, then spat it out, crying furiously.

Gwyn mounted even more clumsily than before, with one arm holding the baby. She rode the horse away from the clearing and back up the hillside she had descended. This much she could do, and she would do. For that poor woman, dead now. For this child, and whatever his hard life would bring to him. For the world, that it should not be entirely cruel.

She took him to Guy's holding, riding hard across the hills, not bothering to conceal herself. When she thought back to that ride, Gwyn could only count her luck that nobody had seen her, because she took no trouble to be secretive. When she dismounted before the door to the house, she was not Gwyn, the Innkeeper's daughter. She was Jackaroo, riding the land.

Blithe sat hunched on a stool beside the fire. If there was anybody else in the room, Gwyn did not see them.

Blithe turned to see who had thrown the door open. Gwyn strode to the table and lay the baby down upon it. Her voice still thick with anger and weeping, she spoke to her sister. "Woman, you will raise this child."

Blithe stood up to back away. She shook her head. She put her hands behind her back in refusal.

"No," Blithe said stubbornly. "I will have none but my own son."

"You will take this child and he will be your son."

Blithe shook her head.

"He has need of you, woman," Gwyn said. She moved away from the table. The baby opened his mouth to wail, now a weak and helpless sound. Before she could help herself, Blithe had moved to touch him and then pick him up.

Gwyn left the room as abruptly as she had entered it. There would be no question now. Blithe's stubbornness would see to that. She put a foot into the stirrup and hauled herself back on the horse.

The horse's head hung with fatigue by the time she got back to Old Megg's, and Gwyn herself felt exhausted. But she changed back into her skirt and shirt and felt shoes, then walked the three horses back to the Inn yard. The sun hung low in the sky as she stabled the animals, and Burl looked questioningly at her, but she did not care to make any excuses.

Da required an answer, however, so she told him that one animal had gotten away and she had spent the afternoon chasing it. He knew what would happen if they lost an animal in their care, so he didn't scold her. "Your mother wanted your help," he said.

Gwyn shrugged. There was nothing she could do about that now. There was nothing she cared to do about it, either. Let her mother have her bad temper. They had lived so long with good luck at the Inn that they had grown soft. They had forgotten how hard the world really was, just as the Lords had forgotten.

A terrible thought came to her as she stood nodding her head at her father: She had forgotten to remove the saddle. She left her father and rushed into the yard.

Burl was walking the horse, whose head hung low and tired. "It ran away," Gwyn repeated her lie.

"There's a saddle needs cleaning," Burl answered. She knew then that he didn't believe her, but she didn't care about that, either.

The memory of that burned hut and those two burned bodies rose before her eyes, and she thought she would weep again, and she thought the smell of it was in her clothing.

"Gwyn?" Burl asked her, quietly.

She answered him, letting anger speak, not sorrow. "There is no reason for good luck or ill luck. There is no deserving."

"No," he agreed.

"But people—they act so—as if—"

"Aye," he said, letting the horse stand while he spoke with her. "When my parents had the fever, and my brother and sisters, nobody would come to our house. Not even to bring us water and leave it outside. They thought it might be plague. I would have liked a bucket of water left at the door."

He did not sound angry. But how could he know that and not be angry? Gwyn turned from him to clean the saddle she had used and hide it away among the others. She wiped the leather dry, then rubbed it with oil, turning it over to clean the underside as well. At the inside of the flap of leather that hung down beside the stirrups she saw, burned into the leather, the shape of a bird. Bending to look closely at it, she recognized the falcon.

Twenty

E RIDES: the word spread like flames through a dry field. Rumor moved through groups of men hunched over mugs of ale in the crowded barroom. Gwyn watched the secret faces, and the way conversation changed when soldiers joined a party of men. The soldiers came to drink among them now, as spies. Even Cam came back to drink at the Inn. "Now that the Innkeeper knows that his daughters are safe from me."

Little was said, more than those two words, *he rides*, but there was wariness on all faces. It was not safe to speak too freely, just as it was not safe to go about alone. In spring, it was the city that felt the bite of hunger sharpest. Men and women traveled to market days in packs, their numbers protecting them from the thieves they might meet as they brought their wares in or took their coins home. In the streets of the cities, rumor said, each new day discovered new dead. The Lords kept themselves safe behind thick walls with their servants and soldiers to guard them, but there was no one to protect the people. Bands of soldiers fled from the south, rumor said, lived in dark city corners, roamed the countryside. Rumor said that the Lords of the south had defeated the King and were even now marching on the High City. The Messengers, with a double guard, rode back and forth on the King's Ways. Troops of soldiers marched eastward. The air was filled with the sound of horses' hooves and marching feet.

But the Inn was quiet enough, with its troop of soldiers camped nearby, and many of the villages, too, were protected. The men in isolated holdings sent their families to relatives in the villages if they could, so rumor said.

Gwyn listened and watched and did her chores. Da believed little of what he heard. "Rumors exaggerate," he said. "Aye, wife, and do you know one house in the village that has extra folk in it? Have you heard any man you can believe say he's seen this Jackaroo?" He reassured them all: "If they halt the journeying of this highwayman, then I'll be worried. Until that happens, we can sleep sound. Although, I'm not happy to hang my hopes on the back of a man walking to his death."

Gwyn listened, but said nothing. Often, in those days, she felt like an actor masquerading as the Innkeeper's daughter. Gwyn felt as if she were two people. The outside one, the Innkeeper's daughter, curried the horses in the stable and gave them exercise; she served the trays of ale; she snapped back quick responses to Cam's teasing. He never let up teasing her now, never let her pass without a mocking remark. Perhaps that was because he sat among the soldiers. "It was fear of me that kept her from marrying," he said. The soldiers urged him on.

"Fear of you?" Gwyn answered. "Aye, as I fear a kitten." The soldiers laughed.

Cam didn't like being laughed at. "Maybe there's more to me than you see," he told her. "Maybe if you knew all there is to know, you'd know—more."

"And what might that be, Weaver's son?" a soldier asked, his voice thick with drink but his eyes alert.

"And would I tell anything to the Lords' men?" Cam mocked.

"Would he have anything to tell," another soldier said. "He's naught but wind."

Cam answered that only with a secret smile. Gwyn wondered at his foolishness, but moved away without comment. "Innkeeper's daughter," a voice called across the room, and a hand held up an empty mug upside down. She answered the call.

But inside she burned with anger. Inside, it was Jackaroo paced up and down, making his plans. The rumors and the hopes for a good crop this year did not move him. He was not deterred from his business. Inside of her head, Gwyn saw constantly the smoking ruins of the hut, and those three men fleeing into the woods. Nothing mattered except delivering justice upon those three.

There was no law for the people, only the Lord's law over them. If she knew where to find Gaderian and could even then find a way to speak to him; then . . . but even then, what could a Lordling do? The Lords only concerned themselves with taxes and troops. If she even knew who Gaderian was, she might risk a letter, somehow. But the High City was two day's hard ride away, and no doubt crowded with Lordlings.

If she were a man she might find the three out and hang them herself. But she could not fight them herself, not with the surety of winning.

At last, the only possible plan came to her. It had no certainty, and it might easily result in Jackaroo's capture, but she did not care about any of that. She cared only for the terrible deed that had been done upon that helpless couple, and taking their vengeance.

At the next Doling day, Gwyn rose from her bed in the deep of night. She dressed and put her knife at the waist of her skirt, but wore no shoes. She crept down to the kitchen and took Da's long cape from its peg by the door. Her bare feet made no sound as she crept into the tackroom to take a bridle and Gaderian's saddle. Burl would not wake: he was exhausted by the work of the Inn. They all went exhausted to bed these days, Gwyn like everyone else. But she was not tired that night—anger gave her energy and made her restless.

Gwyn tied rags around the four hooves of the horse in the stall farthest from the Inn. This was the only time when she might be stopped, she thought. She opened the gate between stall and Innyard and led the horse out. Its muffled footsteps sounded loud in her ears.

She walked close to the horse's head, holding its reins. Once beyond the Inn, she removed the cloths and saddled it as best she could in the starry light. Then she walked it northward, circling the village widely, moving slowly through the dark massed shapes of woods and bushes, the broad, flat darkness of fields. She skirted the edge of the vineyard and tied the horse to the fence of Old Megg's goat pen. She changed her clothes then settled down to wait for first light. She had needed the darkness and the hour to make good her escape. Now she needed light to make her journey.

Gwyn tied the horse among the woods that grew up close to the walls of Earl Northgate's City. The plume of her hat made it impossible to pull the hood of Da's cloak down over her masked face, so she pulled the feather out of the band and dropped it on the ground. Da's cloak dragged around her boots. The hood fell down over her face. Her knife she had stuck into the cord holding the trousers up—if she should fail, then she would use it on herself and leave the Lords with a mystery. Should she fail, she thought the mystery would turn into rumors, the rumors into stories, and Jackaroo would not die. Only the Innkeeper's daughter would die, with no explanation made. Jackaroo would be safe.

Gwyn joined the city women in the Doling Room. They were gaunt with hunger, and each kept herself away from her neighbors. Fear and hunger isolated them. As Gwyn had thought, the Steward kept them waiting.

When the room was as full as she thought it would get,

Gwyn pushed her way to the front of the twenty-odd women. They watched her listlessly, until she threw back the hood of her cloak. Then they huddled together like cows under a storm, not even daring to whisper to one another, their eyes fixed on her masked face.

Gwyn took out of her purse the silver coins she had exchanged at the Inn. She had enough, and more than enough. In a rough voice, she told the women what she wanted. "You know me," she said. "I have two silver coins for each of you, to do as I ask."

They listened with full attention.

"I would have you take the coins and go back to your houses. I would have you say nothing until the day is over."

Still they stood silent. A few tongues licked nervously over lips. Their greedy eyes calculated what two silver coins might buy. They would do it, Gwyn saw. She caught a sidling glimpse from a pair of ferrety eyes. "You will know which of you are not to be trusted."

Heads nodded. They were like cattle, Gwyn thought. Not one of them dared to ask her any question.

"Those women I ask you to keep beside you. I will trust you. And I will tell you a story, which is true.

"Between this Doling Day and the last, three men crept out from their hovel beneath the mountains. They slipped through the woods like wolves until they came to a lonely holding. In that holding lived a man and his wife and their one child, a baby not yet crawling. The man had two goats. The three from beneath the mountains wanted those goats. They came out of the dark woods with knives. They killed the man. While he tried to fight them, his wife took the baby and hid it in the woods. The three came after her and caught her and killed her. They burned the house, leaving the bodies inside, and slipped back into the dark trees, taking the goats. The baby was left in the woods."

A sound, half growl and half moan, ran through the herd of women.

"I have come for those men who did this," Gwyn said, her rough voice low in the listening silence of the room. "Go away home now."

The women melted away through the door, some holding firm the arms of others, each with two coins in her hand. She thought that the two coins and the tale would keep Jackaroo safe from any reward the Lords had offered.

Gwyn wrapped Da's cloak around herself again and stood waiting in a far corner of the long room. She stared at the empty table. When the Steward entered, through the door at the front, he didn't see her at first. He stood at the table with two soldiers behind him. Gwyn moved forward a little, to catch his eye.

Just a little light came into the room. The Steward, having seen that someone was there, sat down without looking at her. He opened his long book and turned the pages. The soldiers, their short cloaks loose around their shoulders, lounged at the far side of the fireplace, talking quietly. The Steward raised an impatient face. "Then come up, woman."

Gwyn hunched her shoulders and shuffled the length of the room to stand before him. The table gleamed between them. He had his head bent over the book, his pen poised to write her takings. His scalp showed pink beneath his blond hair, and the gold signet ring shone on his finger.

In one smooth gesture, Gwyn threw back her cloak and unsheathed the sword. Before the soldiers had understood what the sounds meant, she had the sword's point at the Steward's throat.

She held in her imagination the way the Lord had looked when he had threatened her in the same fashion. She wondered if she herself had looked as frightened as this Steward did.

"You won't get away with it," he warned her.

"Tell your soldiers to disarm themselves."

He did as she asked. She moved slightly, to watch the short swords fall to the ground. "And now yourself."

The Steward moved carefully to take the dagger from his belt and drop it onto the dirt floor.

"Send one of your men to order the servants back to the castle with the food. Should he try to get help, nothing will save your life. I care not for my own," she told him.

She had in her voice the ice she had heard in the Lord's voice, and the Steward believed her. He gave the order.

While they waited for the soldier to return, Gwyn spoke not a word. The Steward's pale face stared up at her, sweat breaking out on his forehead. He moistened his lips. He swallowed. Gwyn felt the movement of his throat run along the steel and into her hand. He could try to disarm her, but any movement she made, however involuntary, would drive the steel into his throat.

She meant what she had said: She did not, at that moment, care for her own life. She didn't even feel any fear. She was entirely Jackaroo. The mask hanging down over her face concealed the face of Jackaroo.

When the soldier returned and went to join his fellow at the opposite corner of the room, Gwyn gave her next order. "Disrobe."

The Steward's eyes quickly met hers.

"Not you, them."

The soldiers obeyed. One naked man carried the pile of all their clothes over to lay them on the table. Gwyn did not look at him, or away from him, any more than Jackaroo would have.

When the Steward had gathered up the armful of clothing, she told the soldiers to stay where they were and wait for the Steward's return.

"Do as he says," the Steward echoed her.

Gwyn held the sword unsheathed but concealed under the folds of Da's cloak. With her free hand, she pulled the hood up over her hat, to conceal her masked face. "Bring the long book," she told the Steward.

He obeyed her without any question, even though his burden was awkward.

"We'll go out through the other door," she told him. "Move along now. Don't try any tricks."

The Steward's blond head nodded.

Gwyn could have laughed at the sight of the richly clothed man she followed. She walked a pace behind, as would any cloaked woman. He held his armload awkwardly and carried the long book jammed in under one of his laden arms. He looked like a man setting out to the washing tubs.

Speaking softly from behind him, she directed him away from the city walls and down into the woods, where the thick trunks and shade would conceal them. Her horse was tied a short distance from the clearing where she allowed the Steward to drop his burdens. She could hear the jingle of the reins as the animal bent his head to graze.

They were alone in the woods, the two of them. No human voice spoke. The Steward watched her, the heap of clothes at his feet. Fear made him plead. "I'm an honest man. I've never cheated the people. I've never cheated the Earl. You have the wrong man if—"

"Quiet," Gwyn silenced him. "Sit down." He sank to the ground as if his legs had collapsed. She threw back the cloak again and held the sword out between them.

"I have no wish to harm you," she said. Relief washed over his face, and a little rush of air came squeaking out of his mouth. She let him enjoy that feeling briefly, then added, "I would not hesitate to do so."

He nodded, not so worried now. "What is it you want of me?"

Distant birds sang to one another and her horse moved quietly. "I want you to bring three men to justice. I know that they are thieves and murderers, and they may be much else besides."

"Are they soldiers?"

"Three of the people."

"But I can't do that. The law doesn't—unless—did they attack a Messenger?"

"No, they attacked a holding."

"But you know as well as I do that—"

"You will have these men taken, and you will hang them for their crimes."

"I can't. I really can't. You have to see that. There is no law for that."

Gwyn's temper rose. "Steward, you will do this."

He shook his head slowly.

"And why not?" The heat was in her voice.

"Because I serve the Earl only as his Steward. I have no power to—"

Gwyn hadn't thought of that. "Who has the power?" She cut him off.

"The Earl, if he wanted. I'm afraid what you ask is impossible for me to do."

"The people are hungry and afraid. They fear famine and the Lords' taxes, they fear the soldiers and the rumors of war. Now they fear one another. Does the Earl not know what men filled with fear and with little to lose might do?"

Of course the Earl knew this. Why else did he guard his own with so many soldiers?

The Steward's light eyes assessed her masked face. "Yes, he knows."

"Then, Steward, you will have to convince him. The people will remain quiet under a Lord who protects them."

He couldn't argue the truth of that.

"Will you convince him?" Gwyn asked.

"I will try. I give you my word."

Gwyn didn't care to rely on his word. Cold again, and scornful of his cowardice—he feared her, he feared his master, who did he not fear?—she made a suggestion. "The Earl will be grateful to the man who put into his hands such a means of quieting the unrest in his land."

His face showed how he was calculating that. "Yes," he finally agreed, "and especially if that man sought no fame for himself in the deed." He considered the whole thing, and then nodded his head, once again himself, Steward to Earl Northgate. "You have proof?"

"The proof of my eyes."

"I doubt somehow that you will be allowed an audience with the Earl."

Gwyn didn't care for his sarcasm. She didn't respond, but stared icily down at the man sitting cross-legged in his finery on the ground, until the Steward remembered his own situation.

"Then, sir, can you give me a description of the men?" he asked her.

"One has a gimpy leg, and one has a scar like a crescent on his cheek. The third—has no such mark on him. All are unshorn, unkempt, filthy. They live together half a day's journey to the west from the waterfall that begins the river that runs to the west of the High City. Their hut has no fireplace and no bed. There is a shed nearby, a three-sided shed. The holding sits on the eastern side of a rocky hill."

The Steward opened his long book and wrote in it with charcoal. Gwyn looked down on him, watching his hands move. She held the sword steady.

"And if they say they are innocent? Which is what they will most probably say."

"Put the book before me," she said. He placed it open at her feet. She crouched down, shifting the sword to her left hand. He dragged himself back several paces, to show that he would not try to attack her. And no wonder, Gwyn thought; if he could gain favor with the Earl, that would be worth more to him than capturing Jackaroo.

She turned to a fresh page. "THESE ARE THE MEN," she wrote. Underneath, she wrote her name, JACKAROO.

She stood up, and he crept over to read what she had written. "It's not—"

"Men have been hanged for less," she told him. "The birds have had their eyes while the people danced below."

That silenced him.

"My word is good," she said.

He shrugged.

"Now, I will have your ring," she said.

"But—"

"Give it to me." She spaced the words well apart, so that his heart would fail. He slipped the Earl's signet off his finger. She leaned down to take it from him.

"This will come back to you when the three have been taken," she promised him. "You will know by that that you have taken the guilty men. The Earl would not want to hang innocent men." The Earl, as Gwyn well knew, cared little about hanging innocent men, and neither did his Steward. This was the only safeguard Gwyn could think of, and she hoped that it would make the Steward careful to take the right men. It would be all too easy for a troop of soldiers to ride out of the city gates and take up the first three men they saw and hang them. But if the Steward had lost his master's ring, he would be eager to get it back before the loss was noticed. Eager enough, Gwyn hoped, to see that the job was done properly, and quickly too.

The interview was over. She planted her feet apart and held the sword out straight at him, its hilt in both her hands. "You may go."

He scrambled up. He gathered into his arms the soldiers' clothing and his long book. He stared hard at her. "I will know you again, sir," he said, bold enough now.

Gwyn did not respond. She waited where she was until his footsteps had faded and then turned quickly to mount her horse and ride off. One of the first things the Steward would do, if she read the man correctly, was return to this place with a troop of soldiers.

With Da's cloak flung over the front of the saddle, she rode for open fields, skirting the edge of the woods. She dared not take the King's Way. It was too crowded in those days.

Gwyn scarcely recognized the field she rode beside until she turned her head to the left and saw the log house there, its chimney smoking only a little on the warm day, and the three figures outside in the sunlight. Hap leaned his back against the side of the house and Granny walked slowly, bent over, to pour out a bowl of dirty water. The goat was grazing peacefully.

The goat lifted her little head at the sound of hoofbeats. Granny saw it and looked up. Gwyn reined in the horse. She lifted her hat from her masked head and waved it in the air. The old woman's hand rose in answer. Gwyn rode off.

There was a smile on her face as she rode on east, but it soon faded. As the horse cantered along underneath her, she wondered where the gladness had gone.

But she knew the answer: because ride as she might, all the days and nights of her life, she could never do all that might be done. The Kingdom was too large. It needed more than Jackaroo to safeguard the people.

The Steward's ring hung heavy on her thumb, rolling loosely around. It was cast of gold, with the bear cut deeply into it. As Gwyn walked back from Old Megg's, leading the horse, she held the ring heavy in her hand. She would hide it with her few remaining coins. How she would return it to the Steward, she had not thought. If Jackaroo rode in to give it back, they would be waiting for him.

First, she would see those three men brought in, then she would worry about the ring. In the meantime, there was her father to be answered.

It was not only Da, but Mother and Tad as well, in the kitchen when she entered. She hung Da's cloak back up where it belonged. Burl had taken the horse from her without a word and told her they wanted her inside. He had no question for her.

Mother started in while Gwyn's back was still to the room. "Well, Gwyn. And what do you have to say? Aye, don't try to make excuses. I don't know what you've been up to, where you've gone—who you've met with. Leaving your day's work for other people is bad enough. And the worry—Just look at her, husband, walking in here just as if she—as if butter wouldn't melt in her mouth. It's a thrashing she needs, and I say so to her face."

Tad's eyes danced. Gwyn thought she'd like to clip him one, just to take the smugness off his face.

"Have you nothing to say for yourself?" Mother continued. "Where have you been?"

Gwyn didn't speak.

"She's no better than she ought to be, I'll tell you that," Mother warned Da.

"Was it a man?" Da asked.

Gwyn didn't answer. It would be better if they thought she had been meeting a man.

"It'll be that Cam, I'll wager," Mother muttered. "She's just about that much sense. Well, you can try to talk to her. I've no interest in her. I've sheets to hang out and no time to waste on a girl who doesn't care how her family worries, or what people say. You should have made her marry, husband, and I told you so at the time. If the fancy strikes you, daughter," she said bitterly, "you might make some pastry. Tad—you come with me."

"But, Mother," Tad protested.

"You heard me. Don't you start giving me trouble too. You see how it is, husband?"

When they were alone, Da told Gwyn to sit down. She obeyed, holding her hands folded together in her lap, to conceal the ring she wore on her thumb.

"Well, daughter?" Da asked. He stood by the fire, looking down at her. Gwyn met his eyes, but said nothing.

Da looked unhappy, and she was sorry for that. But there was nothing she could do about it.

"Were you with a man?"

Gwyn did not answer.

Da sighed and sat down facing her. His neat beard was redder than his head, which dimmed as he grew older. His eyes studied Gwyn's face. "Is it that you are regretting your choice?" he asked gently. "Because if you are, I would say you had changed your mind. Let people talk; I would say that for you."

His gentleness almost undid Gwyn. "You know you can't do that," she reminded him.

"Aye, and I don't. I know that nobody has done it." He was angry. "I know also that I would want you to have a husband, to govern you. It's almost my birthday."

Gwyn didn't know why he should mention that.

"I'll be naming my heir. I would name you my heir."

He had utterly surprised her. She opened her mouth, but could find no words to put into it.

"It would be better if you had a husband."

Gwyn had never thought she would be named the heir. Not when he had a son to inherit. She didn't know he thought so well of her, or so little of Tad. She was pleased and she was sorry, and she didn't know what she might say to him. "Aye, perhaps it would. But it is too late for that now."

He shook his head impatiently. "I would say you had persuaded me against my better judgment. Let people talk—they could do nothing."

Gwyn shook her head. If she had known he was thinking of this, there *were* perhaps men . . . If, if, again if. She remembered her thought on the day of the fair: If there were a man who also saw the body hanging above the walls, then that man she might make her life with. But there was no such man and now it was too late. The announcement had been made.

"You might take a widower," Da suggested.

"No," Gwyn said. She had made her choice and she would abide by it. She had put Jackaroo's mask on and worn his clothes. She had become him and he had become her. There was no going back now.

"Then I will name you even without a man."

"Da, you must let me think." She could be the Innkeeper, and she would husband the holdings and take care of her family; she would do it well, she knew that, and she could do it easily. "You must say nothing until I think," she told him. There was steel in her voice.

Da recognized it, and she knew she had routed him just as much as she had routed her mother. There was no one but herself, now, that she would follow. Others might try to impose their ways on her, but they could not now move her, any more than the winds **could** move the mountains. She felt sorry for Da, though, and glad of his faith in her. "You think too little of Tad," she said.

"Think you?" he asked, without real interest. "Perhaps there is only so much second best that a man will take for his fair measure."

That puzzled Gwyn and she could not answer it, so she held her tongue.

"You've changed, daughter."

She didn't deny it.

"I think I should never have sent you north with the Lords. Did something happen, while you were away—?"

She couldn't tell him that what had happened had happened when she returned, and that it was he himself who had done it. There would be no profit to telling him that. So she smiled at him, her face a bright mask, and said no, nothing happened. "But something will happen if I don't start the pastry." She laughed.

"Aye," he said, giving up, giving way. "We've had word that the highwayman will journey by here in two days, so there'll be an extra lot of baking to be done." He left her then.

Gwyn hid the ring away in her purse with the remaining five gold pieces. Before she set out to work measuring flour and lard, she went into the stables to see if Burl needed help with the horse she had ridden. She found him currying the animal. "Have you time for this?" she asked.

"Osh, aye, I do," he answered quietly. "But we must be more careful with these beasts. Too many get away when they are in our care."

"Did the Captain ask for it?"

"Aye, and he'll be pleased to learn that you have caught it."

So now Gwyn knew what to answer should anyone question her.

"Gwyn, are you content?"

What an odd question, of all the questions he might have asked. Gwyn thought for a bit before she answered. Burl asked questions even as the land grew grass, as if he would wait easily for the answer. She was, she thought, happy enough, and proud, yes, that; she was fearful, and with some reason. "I'm content," she told him. The question was so like Burl, it was so like him to think to ask that question, that her spirits eased a little. "Are you?" she asked.

Burl had a slow, easy smile. "Content enough, if you are."

Whatever that might mean. "Da wants to name me his heir." Gwyn surprised herself by saying that aloud. She thought she had learned to govern her tongue.

"Will he do that, now," Burl wondered.

"I don't know. I don't know if he should."

"Until it is decided, I don't think you should tell anyone else," he advised her.

"How stupid do you think I am?" she snapped at him, turning abruptly on her heels and leaving him behind. But she heard him laughing quietly behind her as she strode across the yard with her head high.

~~✦~~ Twenty-one

THEY KNEW, almost to the hour, when the highwayman and his escort of soldiers would journey along the King's Way. By early afternoon the Inn was crowded with those who had come from the fields and hills. The day shone with early summer sunlight, and the people were merry, as if it were a fair. Gwyn served cider to the women, who waited in the Inn yard with the children. Tad helped Da inside, among the men. When the time was right, they all went to take their places alongside the King's Way, basking in afternoon sunlight and holiday conversation.

The Innkeeper and his family, Rose and Wes with them, stood in a little group together. No hint of a wind moved the sign under which they stood. Burl waited nearby, his pipe playing quietly until he took it from his mouth at the sound of hoofs.

Two soldiers on horseback came first, their green capes bright and their faces tanned. Behind walked two more soldiers, high boots dusty and short swords at their sides. Between them walked the third man.

The highwayman's clothes were brown and torn, stained with dirt and sweat. Two ropes circled his neck before leading like reins, one to each of the soldiers walking guard. His hands were tied behind his bent back. His feet, the soles of the felt shoes flapping, dragged with exhaustion. As he came up to the pathway to the Inn, he lifted his face and squared his shoulders. He looked about him.

The people stared at him, even the children silent. His faded hair hung lank and uncut down to his shoulders; his beard hung gray and greasy over his chest. His eyes scanned the watching people without interest.

The little procession halted, so that the people could look their fill.

His face was lean and pale. His nose jutted out. His eyes moved listlessly over the faces and then toward the land beyond them, where the Inn stood invisible. He breathed in, as a thirsty man drinks water. Gwyn could not look at him and turned her eyes to the dirt at her feet; but she could still see him—a tall, thin, exhausted figure, with the ropes leading off as if he were a dangerous animal.

She heard her mother draw in a hissing breath. When she looked to see what was wrong, she saw that her mother stared at the highwayman with a stony face.

"Innkeeper"—the highwayman broke the silence—"I could swallow a glass of ale." His voice was cracked and ragged, but still bold.

Da answered slowly. "Highwayman, it is not permitted."

The highwayman shrugged thin shoulders and then smiled right at Da. His teeth were rough and yellow, where they were not black with rot. When he smiled he looked like a wolf.

"Come on, you," one of the soldiers said. The procession moved along, took the turning to the village, and headed north. Some of the people followed, joining others who walked along behind; others turned back to the Inn while the rest returned home. There was an air of excitement. "Aye, he'll not hang easy." "He's been kept hungry, and whipped too I don't doubt, in the cells." "Osh, if that's all they've done to him he'll count himself lucky."

Da had an arm around Mother's shoulder and she walked close up next to him. He told Burl to serve with Tad in the barroom and went with his wife into the kitchen, sitting down beside her at the table. Their shoulders touched, as they sat there, but they did not speak to one another. Both stared unseeing at the table.

Gwyn waited for several minutes before she opened her mouth to ask them what was the matter. But she never got to ask the question, because Blithe marched into the kitchen at that moment, her black hair shining and her shoulders high. In her arms, she carried a baby, wrapped around with a soft blanket. She sat down facing her parents, her expression defiant, the baby held close to her chest.

Da and Mother looked at one another, but Blithe was already talking.

"Guy has gone to see the man at the village. We were late leaving the holding, but I wanted to visit with you. How have you been keeping, Mother?"

This was the old Blithe, her lips biting back a smile, her chin stubborn as she waited to hear what her mother would ask about the child.

But Mother was slow to speak, so Da said, "We have been well. We have soldiers quartered here."

"Soldiers are quartered everywhere, in all the nearby villages," Blithe said. "So I hear. Aye, and there's need of them. One of our neighbors, Am, the pigman, was attacked in his own house. Beaten and robbed."

"Am robbed?" Mother asked. "But what could he have to take?"

"Nothing now, but he had two gold coins. He'd been boasting about what he'd do with them; he'd talked carelessly —he said Jackaroo—"

"He always was a fool," Mother snapped. She seemed to have regained her spirit, Gwyn noticed.

"Still, it would be hard," Da tried to make peace.

"And what is that baby doing?" Mother demanded.

Blithe unwrapped the blanket to display the sleeping child. "What do you think?" she asked. "Isn't he handsome?"

"He's not yours," Mother announced.

"Aye, he is."

Mother snorted.

"He was given to me to raise. His parents were killed."

"Who were his parents?"

"That, I don't know," Blithe said. "I've named him Joss."

Mother stood up abruptly. "You've given him the name of your own son?"

"Aye, he is my own son now, Mother," Blithe said.

"Is Guy letting you take in some—foundling—and who knows who his parents were?"

"Aye, he is," Blithe answered.

"That somebody dropped into your cowshed at night, I don't doubt," Mother said.

"No. He was brought to me and I will raise him. He'll be your grandson, Mother," Blithe insisted.

Gwyn kept her face like a mask. She had thought Blithe would prove stubborn.

Mother was doubtful. "Brought to you, and by who then?"

"Jackaroo," Blithe told her.

There was a moment's silence.

"You know better than to believe those old tales," Mother scolded, her voice scornful. "Or to expect me to believe them." Then she burst into tears and fled from the room.

Gwyn didn't have to pretend surprise. They all listened to the sound of Mother running up the stairs.

"You shouldn't vex your mother," Da told Blithe. "And I wouldn't quarrel with her myself, daughter, but you look as you should, with the child in your arms, I'll not deny it."

"It's true, Da. It's really true. Guy's mother was there, she saw. He came into the house, just the way he does in the stories. Just the way we used to talk about it, Gwyn. He was there, suddenly in the room, and tall and—Lordly. Da? He didn't say anything, except about raising Joss, but I could see— He had high boots and silver buckles, and his voice rang out. I couldn't say no, Da."

Lordly? Gwyn felt her cheeks burning. And tall? People saw what they wanted to see. She could keep herself from smiling but she knew her eyes were shining. Just like in the stories, Blithe said, and Lordly.

Da had eyes only for his eldest daughter. "Take the boy up to your mother, Blithe, and sit with her. She—remembers the past too clearly, sometimes, and she loved your Joss."

"So did I," Blithe answered. "As I love my Joss here."

"She will too," Da promised. "You know your mother."

It was Tad, Gwyn realized, reminded by Mother's sudden tears, who was most like Mother. She hadn't realized before how like the two were.

She did realize, however, that something was troubling Da, who had sat down to his own thoughts before Blithe had even left the room. "Are you worried about Mother?"

"A man can expect his fair measure of worry," Da answered her, telling her nothing.

"Da—he shouldn't have asked you for a drink. Why did he ask you? Did you know him?"

"Aye, I knew him once, long ago," Da said. "I'll hear no more questions, daughter. Have you nothing to do?"

If Gwyn had stopped to think, she would not have said what she did. But she did not stop to think. "If I am to be your heir," she said, "then I should have the truth of it."

Da looked tired, worn down, and sad. "Aye, perhaps. You might find the truth not welcome though. The truth is, that man is my brother."

"Your *brother*? I didn't know you had a brother."

"Aye, you did know. It's Win."

"But he's dead."

"No, daughter. Not yet."

Gwyn thought. "And you refused him a drink."

"It isn't permitted, you know that. As he knew, too."

"Oh, Da, I'm sorry," Gwyn said, although precisely what for she could not have said. She sat down with her father. "He doesn't look at all the way I imagined Uncle Win."

"And how would you look, do you think, after a winter in Sutherland's cells and that long journey through every village for the people to stare at and the hangman's noose all that awaited you at the end."

They heard the tolling of the bell from the village, calling people to hear the highwayman do what he must. Gwyn sat silent with her father, hearing not the sounds nearby—the voices from the barroom and the Inn yard—but what she could not hear: The worn voice of the highwayman, inviting all who stood gawping at him to come to his hanging, that they might see what waited for such men as he.

After a while, she said, "They'll hang him at Northgate's City."

Da didn't answer.

"I wonder what turned him to it," Gwyn said. And why, she asked herself angrily, had they all been told that he was dead.

"He turned himself to it," Da answered.

"It's not every man hanged who is guilty," Gwyn answered.

"They do not journey a man unless they know what he is," Da reminded her. His voice was low and ashamed.

"Do they hang women?" Gwyn wondered.

"If it suits them, I think they must. We will all go to this hanging then, think you, daughter? I would not have him die alone."

"Aye, Da," Gwyn agreed. But, she promised herself, he would not die at all if she could manage it. Highwayman or no, he was her father's brother, and her own blood. Surely the long winter in Sutherland's dungeons was punishment enough for whatever robbing he had done. "I'll weed the garden, since Tad is busy," she told her father. She wanted to pull up the little green weeds and to think. Because what did she mean making herself such promises? Who did she think she was?

"See that all is well in the barroom first, if you will," Da asked her. "I would—sit here awhile yet."

Only Tad served in the barroom, and the men were leaving to go back to their holdings and their work. They had a hanging holiday ahead, so they stepped lightly back to their labors. Tad stood by the door, to wish them a fair journey home, his eyes going often to the few remaining men, ready to answer their calls should they need more. Gwyn saw Am sitting alone near the empty fireplace, his round head held low, his face bruised, and his mouth split by a deep cut. He held one arm painfully still in his lap while the other curled around his mug of ale. She went to him.

"I am sorry to hear of your trouble."

"Trouble," he mumbled. "It's not just a trouble, it's my downfall. It was two gold pieces they took, and with the one I could have paid the next year's taxes as well as this, and with the other I could have offered a woman a home and now—" His round eyes filled with tears as he looked up at her. "What will become of me now?"

Gwyn had no pity for him. It was his own loose tongue that had done this to him, and he felt only pity for himself. The man was spineless. The two coins had been wasted on him.

"Aye, well," she murmured, turning away.

His hand grabbed at her skirt. "Innkeeper's daughter, could you not take my girl to work at the Inn here?"

"She's too young. Don't you need her to take care of the boys? What are you thinking of?"

"What is there for me to think of but trouble and more trouble. There were so many of them, seven of them and trained fighters; how could I fight them off? How can such a man as I am take care of his own? Aye, you have no idea."

Gwyn had an idea that there were no more seven thieves than there were no thieves. Am was telling the story his own way, to wallow in his own bad luck.

"I'll take the children to the Hiring Fair, then," he said.

"Though it's hard. The priests will find places for them. The girl is pretty enough, she might be taken into a Lord's service, think you?"

"You should find a woman," Gwyn told him, her voice cold.

"You're cruel, Innkeeper's daughter."

Gwyn thought perhaps she was, but nonetheless she turned away from him. It was little use to give him gold. If she could find a fine, strong-tongued woman to drive him, that might be of use to him. She went back through the kitchen, where Da did not hear or see her, and out to the garden. There, she bent to the weeds.

Her strong fingers worked in the soil, pulling up the little shoots, and the sun poured down over her back. Was she then to put into Am's hands another pair of coins? All he would do would be to lose them, somehow. There were too many like Am among the people, too many who gave up the fight. But what could you expect, when all of life was so hard and hopeless? How could someone fight and know he never would win? And who was the enemy? Could a man fight off a long winter or a dry summer? No more than he could fight against the Lords. Aye, the people could not manage without the Lords, they were children unable to take care of themselves.

Why should Jackaroo take such risks, for such people, Gwyn asked herself. But even as she asked she knew that she would try to give the coins back to Am. If it was right to do so once, then it was right to do so again. He might even have learned his lesson. He might even hold his tongue and guard his holding this time. Aye, she had no choice in the matter any more.

Having decided that, she crawled down the rows of young plants, pulling up weeds that would grow to choke them if left alone, and considered the problem of the highwayman, Uncle Win.

～ⓔ Twenty-two

THE LATE SUMMER sunset shone over the hills as Gwyn approached the village. Under one arm she carried a small cask of Da's best wine. Over her shoulder she had slung a piece of salted pork. The salted meat would give them a good thirst and the wine would give them a good sleep.

The four soldiers sat around a fire by the last small house. Its inhabitants must have been ordered to sleep elsewhere, Gwyn thought, approaching the seated men. The prisoner was, she knew, inside. Not because they wanted him to have the comfort of a roof and bed, but because he could not then escape. The shutters on the house were latched, and the door was barred across with a thick piece of wood.

She had no intention of trying to get inside the house. She walked up to the soldiers.

"What's this?" one asked her.

The other houses were closed and silent. Buckets of water

had been brought to the soldiers for drink and washing, but the villagers did not want to be near them.

"My father, who keeps the Inn, thought you would want food and drink," Gwyn said.

They stood up and around her, to take the cask and meat from her. "Tell your father we are glad to have them," the oldest said to her. He was a small man, with graying hair. The others were all young men. One of those, whose blue eyes were boldly studying her, asked if she would stay to sup with them. The rest laughed and nudged one another with their elbows at his daring.

"Da said I was to come right back." Gwyn made herself smile at them all, as if she would have stayed with them, given her own choice.

"Does Da have spies around, that you cannot join us for a drink of the wine?" the blue-eyed soldier asked.

Gwyn pretended confusion.

"A pretty girl always sweetens the wine," he continued.

"Oh," Gwyn said. "Oh but . . ." She let her sentence dribble off.

"Aye, Miss, and we could tell you some stories you'd not hear elsewhere."

"Oh," she told them, wide-eyed. "I think you could. Why, I was thinking about just that, and even today you've come farther than I'll ever get to go, in my whole life."

"This day? This duty is nothing. He's not much of a man; there's no fight in him. Now, when I was in the south, we had some trouble there. That was the kind of danger a man likes."

"Were you in the south?" Gwyn asked, awe in her voice. "Are you bored with this journeying?" She let questions tumble out. "I wouldn't be. Have you been with him all the way, from the start? Don't you feel sorry for him? I do. Will you give him some of this food?"

They laughed. "Waste this good food on him? Why, he'll barely live long enough to swallow it."

"Aye," another joked, "but it might make the hanging easier, give him more weight to pull against the rope."

"Then that's another reason not to feed him. It's only two days more until he hangs, and he won't complain if his hanging take a little longer. I like this part of the world—the girls are awfully pretty, much prettier than in the south, think you? So we'll get ourselves a little extra time here—"

"And a little extra food for our bellies into the bargain—"

"And we might even spend another night at the Inn, on our way back, into the bargain—"

"To see the Innkeeper's daughter again. Would she like that, think you?"

"Oh," Gwyn said again. "Oh." Beneath her pretending, she wondered if there was any girl so foolish as to believe this kind of flattery.

They crowded around her. "Stay for just one drink with us. Don't despise the poor soldier, and he far from home," they said.

"Aye, Gwyn," Burl spoke from behind her. "It's time we returned," he said, his voice as calm as always, but speaking as a servant to his mistress.

The soldiers fell back, not unfriendly. Gwyn turned, relieved to see Burl, but trying not to show that.

"I told you to wait," she said haughtily. She didn't know what he was doing there, and she was afraid he would make the soldiers suspicious.

"The paths aren't safe. Your father gave the order," he said humbly.

"Gwyn, is it?" the black-eyed soldier asked. "Your name's as pretty as you are. We'll meet again, maybe? Keep her safe, lad," he said to Burl.

Burl bent his head humbly.

"Or you'll have me to answer to." The soldier smiled at Gwyn.

"Oh," Gwyn said. Her heart was beating fast, but not from pleasure. She did not know what Burl was doing there, or how much he had overheard.

As soon as they were out of earshot, she turned on him. "What are you doing following me about?"

He answered her with a quiet question. "What are you doing creeping out with meat from the pantry and a cask of your father's wine, Innkeeper's daughter?"

"I don't have to answer that," she told him.

"Aye, no, you don't," he agreed.

They walked through the leafy woods, its air dim in twilight. Burl carried a staff, and she wondered if he had expected trouble. She hoped he didn't think that the soldiers could have given her any trouble, and she had opened her mouth to tell him just that, when he told her, "I came to see you safely home."

Immediately a new fear caught at her. "Did Da send you?"

"No." He sounded as if he were amused. What was there funny?

"Mother?"

"No. I came to see you safely home," he repeated.

Gwyn lay down on her bed, but she did not undress and she did not sleep. When night was heavy around her, and all the Inn slept, she once again took a horse from the stable. She took only the bridle from the hook by its stall this time. Win would have to ride bareback. She was sorry for Da, who would have to take the blame and make the loss good, but since it would be assumed that the highwayman had stolen the beast, that would be the worst of it on somebody's else's shoulders, not Da's. Her purse, and her knife, were at her waist. The moon was on the wane so darkness cloaked her around.

When she had changed and tied the horse to a low fruit tree set back from the village, she crept around the side of the highwayman's prison. Dark as it was, she had little need of her mask. Probably she hadn't even needed to ride as Jackaroo, but she had done so just in case the plan failed in any way. She had brought no food for Win, but she planned to give him gold pieces, the three she had no need for. Gold and a horse should see him safely away.

The soldiers lay sprawled around the fire, which was burning out. The ripe smell of wine lingered over them, and they snored heavily. Gwyn lifted the bar from the door and set it silently onto the ground. Quietly, she tried the hinges. They did not squeak as she stepped into the little room.

A candle burned on the wooden table. The highwayman lay stretched out on the bed, his eyes open. In the flickering light, he looked weaker and more wolfish than in daylight. Gwyn eased the door closed behind her.

For a minute he said nothing. His eyes stared out at her from his bony face. He didn't even move a hand. She had about decided that he was so weak she would have to drag him ouside to freedom, when he began to laugh.

His laughter was quiet, but it rolled over his whole body and pulled him erect on the bed. He laughed into his hands, his shoulders shaking. When at last he lifted his face, she saw tears of laughter streaming down his cheeks and into the matted hair of his moustache.

"Come," she said in a horse whisper, as urgent as she could make it.

He threw back his head and laughed.

She moved to stand before him. "They're asleep, drunk. Get up."

He shook his head: no.

She pulled out her purse, to take out the coins so that he could know he had hope, but he finally spoke.

"I thought I had laughed my last," he said, his voice as soft as hers. "Oh, but life always holds one more joke. I thank you, whoever you are."

Gwyn fell still, puzzled. She did not understand.

She reminded herself of her purpose here. "Don't be a fool."

"Oh, no, my friend, it's you the fool. Maybe you don't know it yet," and now he was entirely serious, all traces of laughter gone. "But if you don't move out of here fast, your Jackaroo days will be even shorter than mine were."

"Highwayman, I would lengthen your days."

"Then you'd do me no favor, Jackaroo," he answered. "Do you think I want to live any longer than I have to? No, I'm finished with it; it's more than I've the strength for. I've spent years living like an animal—aye, and the Lords are just, I've cut throats for a piece of bread and not cared whose throat I cut so long as the bread went into my own mouth. I am done with myself."

They had broken his spirit, Gwyn thought. First she had to get him away, then she would deal with this new problem. "Talk can come later," she said.

"No and it can't. I've learned at least that much hard wisdom. I didn't have any wisdom about me when I put on your mask."

"You put on my mask?" Gwyn had forgotten that she wore one, so closely did it fit her now.

"Maybe not that very same one. As you know."

But Gwyn knew nothing.

"I put it on for a game—there was no need, and I rode out the once, all for the pride of it, for the joke . . . and came so close to getting caught it was years before I slept a night through."

"I don't understand."

He grinned up at her. "No, my friend, you don't. You know no more than I did. And I'd not be you, not for the world. I say that, and today I saw that the girl I should have stayed home to marry has married my brother, and the children I should have had were his, and the Inn that was mine had prospered under his hand. All because I put on that mask. Did you know what it meant when you put on the mask?"

Gwyn shook her head, no.

"Aye, you'll find it out. Maybe, if we knew, we'd never dare to put it on, and maybe that's why nobody tells that hard truth. Think you?" He looked up at her, curious.

Gwyn had nothing to say.

"Except there is need now. That much, at least, is in your favor. You ride in need. It'll make no difference in the end. Things will turn out the same."

"Tell me," Gwyn asked.

"Tell you? And take away the joke? I'd not do that.

What kind of thanks would have I given you then? For you've sent me smiling to the gallows and I would thank you."

Gwyn felt a fool, and she felt angry, and she felt entirely confused. The highwayman lay back on the bed, his arms folded behind his head, his face happy.

"I will give you one piece of advice, though; if you live. If you want to live. If, if—what's the use of if's. I'll give you advice, because you've given me laughter when I'd given it up. You should leave the Kingdom if you've a chance. That's the only way. What will happen then, I don't know. I didn't have the wits, or the courage, to take my chance when I could have. I wanted to stay in my own land. And by the time I knew how I must stay, the only way I could stay—it was too late."

"Too late?" She was standing there stupidly repeating his words.

"Aye, because what changes putting on the mask had begun, I had myself finished. So farewell to you, Jackaroo. I pity you, with all that's left of my heart—but that's not much."

"You'll not come away? I've a horse—"

"Will you understand? I wouldn't escape if the King himself came to lead me out. If—well, he's settled the southern Lords now, he might have nothing better to do. That's a picture anyway, isn't it? King and highwayman together. No, you can escape, tonight, if you will. But come and see me hanged. I'd like to think you were there and watching. You'll see that I'm smiling, and you can know that I'm grateful. I'm out of the trap that held me, and it's that same trap you're snared in. Jackaroo," he said, and chuckled. He closed his eyes.

Gwyn left the hut, barring the door behind her. She felt as if someone had hit her over the head with a heavy staff, and although she walked out steadily, she felt as if she were reeling from the blow. She had not even called him by name, she realized, untying the horse. She hesitated in the dark air, wondering if that would bring him out. But she couldn't call him by name because that would give her identity away. She didn't know if she could trust him to keep her secret. So she had no choice to claim her Uncle Win.

Gwyn pulled herself up onto the horse, but she didn't go back to Old Megg's. The night air was cool and the sword rode heavy on her leg. She had no desire to sleep.

He had been telling the truth, she understood that, turning the horse to the north. Sorrow sat next to her heart, wrapping her heart around with its cold arms, and she knew Win had spoken the truth. By all the proud and painful deeds she had done, she had lost the Inn.

Knowing herself, she knew she could not go to Old Megg's and hide the masquerade away forever. She would ride as she was riding now, without any joy, to Am's. She would ride as she was riding now, in darkness, because she was an outlaw. Jackaroo rode outside of the law, and that was why the Lords wanted to take him. The law couldn't hold Jackaroo. He would do what he wanted and that made him an outlaw. Gwyn would never have chosen to be an outlaw. She hadn't chosen that, she had only chosen to do what good she could, for the people. It was just as Mother said, she had too much imagination, too soft a heart. She had not known what she was choosing. But even if she had known, Gwyn knew that she would have chosen the same. This knowledge was not sweet, not joyful.

She rode through the dark night, never any faster than a trot. She didn't want the horse to stumble or injure itself. She didn't want to fall off. At Am's house, she slid down and stormed through the door. She said never a word, because she had only angry words to utter. It was almost, she thought, climbing back onto the horse and turning it toward home, as if the very heat of her anger had filled that little room and kept silent the four figures who sat up terrified in their beds as she strode in, threw the coins onto the table, and strode out. Well, maybe that would make Am cautious. Maybe fear of Jackaroo would force him to discretion, and the coins would then not be wasted.

Before the first dawn showed at the rim of the sky, Gwyn was back in her own room with nobody—except her—the wiser.

Twenty-three

ON HANGING DAY, the sky overhead was a cloudless blue that went on forever. The air was as motionless as the stones of Earl Northgate's walls. The group from the Inn arrived early. They walked the long Way through cool morning air, to be sure to stand at the front of the crowd, where they might be seen. A tall wooden gallows stood between the gatehouse and the Doling Room, empty, waiting for midday. Da and Mother, Gwyn, Tad, and Burl had come together to the hanging.

Tad, Gwyn thought, was finding that it was not always a pleasure to get what he wanted. He had insisted that he wanted to see the hanging, but now he was here, and waiting, he seemed restless and uneasy. He wandered off whenever Mother's eye was not on him. He walked around the Doling Room, he walked around other groups of people as they drifted in; but he did not walk around the gallows as the other little boys did.

Mother scolded him half-heartedly when he came back, but as soon as her eye was off him he disappeared again. Finally Gwyn protested. "Leave him be," she asked her mother, because her father was saying nothing, just standing with his eyes fixed on the long-legged gallows with its steep stairway up.

"We should not have let him come," Mother said, turning the force of her anger on Gwyn.

Gwyn could match that force with her own, and overmatch it. "It's time he faced up to things," she said. She didn't think Tad knew who the highwayman was; she suspected that her mother didn't know that Gwyn knew. "It's not good for you to baby him so," she told her mother.

"Aye, and what do you know?"

Gwyn couldn't answer that. She knew more than was good for her. She knew nothing.

"You'd feel differently if you had children of your own," her mother said to her.

"No," Gwyn answered, "I wouldn't. And if I did, I'd be wrong. And if I did, I hope I'd remember that I'm wrong."

"Hush now, daughter," Da said, not turning his head. Gwyn obeyed him. Besides, she had remembered to feel pity for her mother. If she had understood him correctly, Win had planned to marry Mother, so that Mother must have said yes to him. But she had married his brother instead, when Win was lost to her. Da, too, she pitied, because this must have been what he meant by second best. Second best to his wife, and second best to his father, who had named his oldest son heir, before Da.

"I'll find Tad," she said to her parents, by way of apology.

A large crowd had gathered. People approached from the city gates and from the King's Way. Everybody wore fair clothing and bright ribbons were tied around the women's necks. The hanging was scheduled for midday, to give all, even those from distant holdings, time to get there. The people waited patiently, talking among themselves. As Gwyn made her way through and among them, she overheard scraps of conversation. There were rumors from the south, of peace, of burned fields, of soldiers who hid in the thick forest to sweep out and attack enemy camps when they were least expected. The King had fallen in battle, she heard. The King had named a new Earl for the south, one of his own sons, she heard. The King had abandoned the southern lands to their own misery and retreated into the High City. The crops in the north, men said, were growing well, tall shoots coming up to promise a rich harvest. The goats and sheep, cows and pigs gave birth in record numbers. They had hope for a good year.

Gwyn made her way among the people, staring around her, at bent bodies and straight bodies, at familiar faces and strange faces, at the marks of long hunger now fading under the land's summer bounty, at eyes that were bitter or eager, curious or thoughtful. For all the differences between them, they were the same: the men bearded and the women with their long braids coiled over their ears, their interest only in the rumors and the crops. They had come to visit, to gossip, to holiday; that a man would die meant little to them.

She found Tad hidden at the back of the crowd, leaning against the closed door of the Doling Room. His felt shoes scuffed at the dirt. His hair shone like little flames, and his mouth drooped. "It's time," she told him. "Mother wants you."

He shook his head.

"Aye, Tad," she said, "I'd rather be home myself. But if you were to be hanged so, would you want to be alone?"

"It's nothing to me," Tad argued.

"No, but it is something to this man. Think you?" He had to agree. "So you must take your courage in both your hands and stand to watch."

He shook his head.

"No, you know better." Gwyn waited in front of him, watching his face.

"I can't," he whispered, at last.

"Aye, and you can, and you will."

His eyes at last met hers. "I wish you'd get married and leave me alone. Mother says it's because you want the Inn."

He was trying to make her angry, so that she would walk

away and leave him. Instead, she answered him honestly: "I want the Inn, yes, but I won't have it. You'll have it. Now, come do what you must."

She turned away then, knowing he would follow.

A dozen soldiers escorted the highwayman out from the city. They formed a line with their backs to the people. The highwayman waited in front of them, facing the crowd. The people fell silent.

A line of Lords and Ladies came to stand then at the high tops of the walls, their hair shining in sunlight, their clothing bright with many colors.

The highwayman's eyes scanned the crowd, never resting, not even when they saw Mother and Da. Win would keep his secrets, Gwyn thought. Behind him, wooden steps led to a high wooden platform. The tall gallows had been built at the center of the platform, and the rope hung down from that. The highwayman had his back to it, and his head held high.

Everybody waited. The line of soldiers stood with their feet slightly apart, not speaking, watching the highwayman. Their blue capes hung over their backs, their hands rested on the hilts of short swords, ready.

"Do they fear a rescue?" someone whispered behind Gwyn.

"Or do they fear Jackaroo?" someone muttered.

"Aye, they always have," was the low answer.

Jackaroo had tried his rescue, Gwyn thought, and the man himself had refused it, if they only knew. The man himself had ridden out as Jackaroo, if they only knew, and had lost his whole life for it.

She made her eyes stay on the thin, straight figure, on the expressionless face. She did not move her hand, as she wanted to, to protect the purse hung concealed inside her skirt. There would be thieves in this crowd, probably worse men than the man to be hung. Her protection from them was her ordinariness. The Steward's ring hung heavy at the bottom of the purse, because she had forgotten it was there when she took up her three remaining gold pieces. After a hanging, the Steward would offer the body of the man for sale. If his family dared to claim him, they could have him for a gold piece. If nobody took him for his own burning, he would hang upon the gallows until the birds had picked him clean—as a warning to all who would harm the Lords.

Gwyn thought that she would step up to claim the body. Certainly, she had no reputation left to lose. She was the Innkeeper's unmarried daughter, willful and difficult. Da could not claim his brother because then questions would be asked and rumors would start. But if the Innkeeper's unmarried daughter claimed the body of a highwayman, the rumors begun would be so far from the truth that nobody would stand in any danger.

When the Steward emerged from the gatehouse, the black-hooded executioner at his side, the crowd stirred. From that moment, things moved quickly. There was no naming of the man's crimes: The people could think what they would, as long as they knew the surety of the Lord's punishment. The highwayman was given no chance to speak.

His hands bound behind him, the highwayman walked without hesitation up the stairway. The executioner mounted behind him. When the highwayman stood beneath the circle of rope, facing out over the crowd, the executioner lowered the noose around his neck and pulled it tight with practiced hands.

The people watched.

Win's eyes found out the little group from the Ram's Head and stayed there for the endless time it took for his executioner to kneel down and find the catch that held the trapdoor closed. Then he looked over the heads of all, to the hills and mountains that rose beyond, closed his eyes, and thought his own private thoughts. These thoughts seemed to amuse him.

The executioner slid the bolt open. The trapdoor fell away. The body plummeted down and hung. In the silence, the thunk of the weight of the body reaching the end of the rope seemed loud. The head lolled sideways, the feet kicked, and then the body rotated gently at the end of the rope.

The crowd let out a long, sighing breath.

This was a skillful executioner, whose knots would break a man's neck rather than leaving him to choke for many long minutes. Gwyn looked away from the hanged man and noticed that Tad had fixed both of his hands into her arm with a grip so tight she would probably have bruises. But Tad did not turn his head away.

They waited out the long minutes, while the Steward made sure that the man was dead. The highwayman hung now below the level of the platform, his feet only inches above the ground, down at the level of the people. The crowd murmured.

At last, the Steward stepped forward. Gwyn reached inside her skirt to put her fingers into her purse. She looked over at her parents, who stood like stone people, with expressionless stone faces.

"Who owns this man?" the Steward called out over the crowd.

Unclaimed, the body would be hoisted up high again, until his head almost touched the pulley over which the thick hanging rope ran, so that all might see him.

"Does any man claim the body?" the Steward called. Gwyn took a breath and clutched at a coin in her purse.

"I will, if it pleases you," Burl spoke, stepping forward from behind her. He moved calmly forward to stand before the Steward.

The soldiers parted to let him through.

"Have you the coin?" the Steward asked.

Burl produced it, and the Steward held out a gloved hand to accept it. Gwyn was willing to wager that he slept with his gloves on, these days.

"Who are you?" the Steward asked.

"My name is Burl. I was born in Lord Hildebrand's City." Burl answered the questions in his usual calm voice.

"What is this man to you?" the Steward asked.

"He is nothing to me," Burl answered. "I have no family, parents, brothers, sisters, wife, or child."

The Steward did not like this answer, but there was truth in Burl's voice. Gwyn waited nervously to see if the Steward would now release the body to Burl. If he were to ask where Burl lived, or how he kept himself, or even where he had gotten the coin, he might come dangerously near to the truth.

"Then why do you want him?" the Steward asked, suspicious.

"He's a man alone, as I am," Burl said. "I claim him, as I hope someone will claim me when I die."

The Steward answered him quickly. "Will you, too, die at the end of a rope?"

"Aye and I hope not," Burl said, laughter in his voice. "I am an honest man, Steward."

"That he is." A few voices spoke from the crowd. "We know him." The Steward looked around to see who had spoken, but he could not catch them out. Reluctantly, he gave the signal for the body to be lowered. A man came forward with a wheelbarrow and helped Burl fold the body into it. Win's arms and legs hung out. Burl took the handles of the wheelbarrow into his hands and rolled his burden away, through the crowd. Burl looked at no one as he passed through.

"Come," Da said. The crowd broke up into groups of people talking. The Weaver reached out a hand to catch Mother's sleeve. "Did you know him then?" she hissed.

Mother tried to shake off the hand, but she did not answer the question. Gwyn looked up to find Cam's eyes on her, mocking. Did he know the truth? Probably many did know, or at least suspected. But the Lords did not, which would keep the Inn safe from their notice. Gwyn smiled boldly back at Cam, letting him think what he would.

It was the gatehouse bell ringing that turned the crowd back and caused it to close in again. Gwyn found herself at the front of a crowd that kept pushing her forward, with Cam beside her and Tad holding onto her hand on the other side. "What is it, Gwyn?" he asked her. "I thought it was all over."

She shook her head. She had no idea. She would have liked to follow Burl away from the city, but the thick crowd pushed her forward.

"Gwyn?" Tad pulled on her hand. She looked down into his big eyes. "I'm scared."

"And so am I," she told him. He looked surprised at that. Then he squared his shoulders and nodded his head at her. He let go of her hand, but stuck close beside her.

The Lords and Ladies at the battlement were looking off to the north of the gallows. Gwyn moved, to put Tad between herself and Cam. They were at the front of the crowd, which might prove dangerous. "He's the one we'll look to, if we have to." She spoke over Tad's head to Cam.

"I'll be all right," Tad said.

Cam spoke at the same time. "Is he now?" His eyes mocked her. Then his face grew serious: "If you'd only waited, I would have asked, Innkeeper's daughter. Father or no father."

Gwyn's temper rose. He looked, for once, as if he meant exactly what he said. She didn't know how to answer him, how to spare his feelings as she acknowledged that she would have said no.

"For I've need of gold," he said, and laughed aloud.

Gwyn didn't speak the words burning on her tongue, because at that moment a single soldier led three men across the front of the crowd. The soldier's cape was travel stained, and his boots covered with mud. The three men he led were tied together along a single length of rope. They were filthy, hairy, and defeated. They moved slowly, their pace held back by the third man, who dragged his lame leg painfully behind him, trying to keep up.

Gwyn knew them, although she masked her recognition. The Lords and Ladies leaning over the battlement watched the motley parade with interest. The Steward stepped forward to greet the lone soldier, while those who had formed the highwayman's guard arranged themselves now around the three prisoners.

Whispers spread around behind Gwyn, voices trying to

identify the men, wondering what the Steward was up to, commenting humorously on the fact that one soldier had captured and brought in all three. The three stood huddled together, eyes glaring at the soldiers, at the Steward, at the crowd, at one another.

The Steward turned to claim the crowd's attention. He held up his gloved hands for silence. When he spoke, his voice was round and solemn, like a Priest at the marriages.

"These three have raided and burned your holdings. They have killed men—and women too—in their thieving." The crowd uttered low angry noises. The three men huddled closer to the soldiers. Their leader raised his scarred face and spat in the direction of the crowd. The people rumbled.

"Hearing of this," the Steward continued, his voice carrying strong up to the battlements, "Earl Northgate sent to find out and take these men, who preyed upon his people."

He lifted one arm and held it out toward the Lords and Ladies above. One man stood forward, his white shirt gleaming under a blue tunic, his silver hair gleaming on his head, his head ringed by a golden coronet. The people behind Gwyn broke into cheers of approval and thanks. Voices rang out. "Aye, and that's a Lord who will care for his people."

When the cheering was done, and the Earl had left the battlements, the crowd turned its attention back to the prisoners. "Will they be hanged, Steward?" a man called out.

The Steward's head turned to find out who it was, but he was too slow to see.

"Hanged they will be. The Earl has put his law on them."

"Hanging's too quick," a woman cried.

"Osh, aye, hush now. The Earl will see to it," someone answered her.

Gwyn's first fierce rush of joy had given way to the worry she now faced. She had given her word, Jackaroo had given his word, that the ring would be returned. The Steward and his soldiers lingered, but paid little attention to the prisoners. It was as if they were waiting for something. The crowd sensed that and waited with them. They were waiting for

Jackaroo to ride in, Gwyn thought. Aye, and that was canny of them, and they were prepared for him.

She had no choice, and at that moment she didn't much care. At that moment, her only thought was to return the ring to the Steward. She could take it up boldly herself and lie, saying she had found it on the roadside. She could lie more convincingly and say she had it from Jackaroo himself, who had sought her out and given her instructions. She could lie and say she had it from a strange man, and she could pretend to search the crowd for him. But all of those lies would bring questions upon her, and once more the Inn would be dangerously close to the Steward's attention.

Gwyn took the ring from her purse and closed her fingers around it. The crowd was beginning to break apart. She would have to do something quickly, if she were going to do anything now. Perhaps she wouldn't bother—surely the Earl would be so pleased with the Steward that he wouldn't question the loss of a ring.

Except that Jackaroo had given his word.

Without any more thought, Gwyn pulled her arm free at her side and tossed the ring up, into the air. It soared in a high arc, glistening in the sunlight, before it hit the Steward on his chest and fell in the dirt at his feet.

He had been looking over the heads of the crowd to the King's Way, expecting a rider from the east, so he was slow to recognize the ring. His face was momentarily puzzled, and then his eyes found it lying at his feet and he bent swiftly to pick it up. By then, many of the crowd had seen it and those standing at the front were close enough to identify what it was.

A rustling sound, of voices spreading backwards and muffled laughter, sounded behind Gwyn where she stood. She made her face blank and dull, and she turned her eyes as if trying to hear what was being said behind her.

With anger in his face, the Steward peeled off his glove and put the ring back on his right hand. He could not be secret about it. His eyes slewed over the faces of the people.

Gwyn felt them come to her face, and she tried to wrinkle her brows in confusion. The eyes moved on, to Cam, where they rested: Cam had burst out into loud laughter, which he quickly smothered. But he could not conceal the mocking humor on his face and he did not try to. The Steward stared at him for a long minute before he turned abruptly away from the crowd and strode back through the gatehouses into the City. Gwyn finally heard Tad's urgent voice: "Come *on*, we've got to get *home*—please, Gwyn, quickly."

He was pulling at her hand again and there was fear on his face as he pushed their way through the milling crowd, with Gwyn following. He moved urgently, as if trouble might be on his heels.

Da, Mother, and Burl waited for them at the top of the first hill. They stood with the wheelbarrow and its load. They stood with their backs to the King's Way, not to see the people moving along it. Those who passed by averted their eyes from the people of the Ram's Head.

Tad led Gwyn up the hill, constantly at her to hurry. She obeyed him mechanically. Mother didn't give him a chance to speak. "So there you are. I don't know why you had to disappear like that. You're young, but I'd think Gwyn would have had enough sense to stay with us. I don't know, I just don't know—I've tried to teach you to be responsible—" She pulled Tad into a close embrace, and glared at Gwyn over his head.

Gwyn barely registered her mother's anger. She couldn't think, and she needed to sit down.

"It's all your fault, Innkeeper, for making us come to see—"

Da looked like Gwyn felt, dazed and unhappy.

"And who knows what mischief's happened at the Inn, and us all gone from it," Mother insisted. Then she burst into sudden tears and turned abruptly away, holding onto Tad's hand, dragging him along at her side. Da hurried off after her. Tad turned back and saw that Gwyn still stood there, with Burl. But he could do nothing against Mother's insistence.

Gwyn's legs collapsed underneath her and she sat down. Her head felt dizzy, so she buried her face in the dark skirt over her knees. She heard the voices of the people walking along the King's Way. The voices grew quiet as they saw the wheelbarrow, then mounted again as they moved past and away. After a while, there were fewer voices passing, and she heard the music of Burl's pipe. She did not raise her head, although the sun was hot on her neck and back and she was no longer dizzy.

It was almost as if she had wished the Steward to know who she was, she thought, or else why should she return the ring to him in such a way. She had acted without any thought at all. She had acted dangerously.

Ever since that conversation with Win, her thoughts had been closing in on her, like a circling fire. She had beaten the thoughts back, held them off, as she would beat out a fire with blankets. But then she had tossed the ring to the Steward just as if she were throwing herself into the fire, tired of waiting for it to slowly creep up on her and take her.

It would have been easy to ride up to Hap's old woman, as Jackaroo, and put the ring into her hands, to be returned to the Steward at the next Doling Day. But she hadn't even thought of that. The sheer stupidity of what she had so boldly done frightened her.

And Cam, laughing into the Steward's face as if he wished to claim the deed for his own—didn't he know what would happen if the Steward decided that Cam was the man? The music played around her ears, quietly. She had not known how deep Cam's vanity ran. Da was right about Cam: He could never be trusted with anything of value.

That thought lifted Gwyn's face from her knees. She had been lucky. If Cam had asked for her, at any time before—up until this winter—she knew how she would have answered him. After that time, she was not sure. She could not be sure of anything about herself, after that time. But if he had asked her she would have wed a man not to be trusted. Gwyn felt her face flame with shame—she had not known how foolish she could be. She did not like remembering how she had longed for those mocking, empty eyes to look with approval on her.

Gwyn shook her head and started to rise from the long grass. The music ceased and Burl asked her, "Are you ready to go home?"

At the word, Gwyn almost laughed aloud, but she was so frightened by the impulse that the laughter froze in her throat. "Aye, thank you."

They walked slowly, with the clumsy wheelbarrow, which had to be held back from rolling too swiftly down hills and had to be pushed laboriously up hills. All around them fields flowed over the hills, the crops growing tall. In some places you could look to the side and see how the fields melted into the forests, where the forest lay like a massed cloud of green lying close over the land's surface. Overhead, the sky shone blue. In her imagination, Gwyn's eye moved ahead and afield, tracing the land's slow rise upwards into the mountains. It was so beautiful, this country, the rich valleys and the steep hillsides where gray rocks cropped out. The tall wall of mountains: They were beautiful the mountains, in all their seasons, but especially in the fall when shivering gold aspen leaves striped the mountain sides.

If she had understood him correctly, Win—dead now, now a body whose head lolled against the wooden sides of the barrow—had meant to tell her that she would inevitably be stopped. That Jackaroo must cease to ride. She would not have believed him had she not seen her own arm toss the ring into the air at such needless risk. For the first time, Gwyn did not know what she would do with her life. No, that wasn't true. She didn't know, for the first time, what she *could* do.

The King's Way curled ahead of her and behind her, its fence flowing beside. The land spread out all around her, with the beauties she could see and those only her imagination remembered. Gwyn sighed, as her feet moved slowly along.

"There were three men?" Burl asked her.

"Aye. The three from that hut, in the winter. Do you remember them?"

"I do."

"The Steward said," Gwyn told him carefully, "that they had been robbers and murderers, that they robbed the people."

"I'm not surprised," Burl said. "Are you?"

"No," Gwyn said.

"But what made the Earl concern himself with crimes done to the people," Burl wondered.

Gwyn shrugged.

"Well, whatever, it might be a good thing." The wheelbarrow creaked as he shouldered it up a steep rise.

"How did you know?" Gwyn suddenly wondered.

"I heard the talk, as people walked along the Way. They said the Steward's ring—"

"No, about him." Gwyn pointed to the body in the wheelbarrow.

Burl halted at the crest, to catch his breath and to look down into her face. "I didn't know anything. I guessed that might be Win, your father's brother, when he looked around him—like a man who is measuring changes in something familiar. I could think of no other reason why he should ask for a drink. I thought that—if he was Win—I owe your father much, and this was something I could do for him, without putting him at risk. I thought that if I was wrong, it would do no harm to take the man for burning. Whoever he was, he died bravely."

Burl's beard grew dark and thick, concealing much of his face. His dark eyes studied hers without any question in them. He was only a little taller than she was, but he felt as sturdy and deeply rooted as a tree.

"It was Win," she told him. "Da will thank you."

"Osh, and I don't look for thanks," Burl said. He picked up the handles and moved on again. "I am in his debt."

In his debt when Burl's work at the Inn occupied every hour of every one of his days?

Burl answered the question she didn't ask. "A boy alone—the priests don't care who takes boys, as long as he is off their hands and they have his price in their purses. Your father makes a good master, and I am lucky to be serving him."

Gwyn was disappointed in Burl. "Is there any reason," she asked, "why any one man should serve another?"

At that Burl laughed. "No reason I can think of. Only we do, each one of us."

"Except the King," Gwyn said.

"Aye, even the King. I'd wager if you could ask him, he'd say he served the land."

"And the land serves the people." Gwyn smiled reluctantly. "It's like a child's rhyme, Burl. The land serves the people, the people serve the Lords, the Lords serve the Earls, the Earls serve the King, and the King serves the land."

"Aye, like a child's rhyme."

Even Jackaroo, Gwyn thought to herself, fit into that circle. He served the people. He served them outside of the law, but within the turning of the wheel.

Twenty-four

THEY SET WIN'S BODY on the pyre early the next morning. It was only those from the Inn who stood watching as the flames licked upwards. None from the village came to grieve with them. Even Rose stayed away, as now she must because she was the wife of the Blacksmith's heir.

At some time during the long journey home, or the long night's watching over the body they had washed and clothed, Tad had been told the truth. As they waited for the last flames to burn down to embers, Gwyn noted the pale, uneasy face and his firm, resolute mouth. This last day had made him years older, she thought. She could see the beginnings of the man he would grow into, now.

She held Da back as the silent group returned to the Inn. When the others had moved ahead into the thickly grown woods, she told him, "I think you can name Tad your heir."

Da shook his head slowly. "Aye, daughter, and he cannot do the work."

Gwyn knew he would say that. He had been so wrapped up in work and sorrow that he had seen no changes in his son. "If you had died a young man, who would have run the Inn for your children?" she asked him.

He smiled. "Your mother, as you know. She's often told me she could do it by herself. When she's angry, she says she could do it better." The smile did not leave his face. "And she's not entirely wrong."

"He's like her, Tad is."

"Think you?"

"Aye, and if you watch, you'll see it. But you must find him someone strong and steady to marry, someone who can govern him when he needs it."

She watched Da think over her words, and what her words had not said directly. She saw that she had pleased him, which was her intention. "And you'll help him," Da finally said.

"As much as I can," she answered. That was true as far as it went. Only Gwyn knew that she could not promise how far it would go. A covey of grouse whirred in the bushes and flew upwards into the trees. She and Da stopped to watch them.

It rained that day, and all the next, a warm summer rain that fell straight from the sky and soaked into the ground. The men who came to the barroom for the evenings wrapped winter coverings over themselves to keep dry. But their spirits were not dampened by the rain. It was a gentle rain and the land welcomed it.

All the news was good. There was peace in the south, rumor said, and all else was false rumors. There would be good market for their crops and goods in the south, so they had hope for paying the high fall taxes. The new Earl had been named and anointed by the King in the High City and now, rumor said, he was traveling with his train to introduce himself to the Lords of the North and would stay for feasting with Earl Northgate. Who he was, nobody knew for sure.

Some said he was one of the southern Lords, who had remained loyal to the King. Others that he was a younger son of the old Earl, who had been out of the kingdom when the rebellions broke out. Others had heard that the King had known for years in advance that trouble was coming to the south, that he had tried to warn the old Earl who, in his pride, would take no heed. All agreed that they were glad to be northerners, under the care of an Earl who would hang any man who preyed upon his people.

There were quieter rumors, spoken of in low voices, about the Steward and his ring. It was Jackaroo who had taken it from the Steward, they said. Why and how they did not know, except that it had been returned before the people and the Lords, so that all might know Jackaroo's power. Some said that the Steward had given it to a girl of rare beauty, who wanted none of his attentions and had turned to Jackaroo for help. Others said that it had been hurled back to the Steward in disgust by a landowner who had profited from the taxes buying up the holdings of poor men, and that he had returned it in that public fashion in order to shame the Steward before the Earl, who had known nothing of the secret dealings that lined the landowner's pockets and the Steward's. But that rumor Gwyn barely caught a whisper of as she moved among the tables. That rumor they did not speak of openly at the Inn.

It was five days after the highwayman's death, a hot full summer morning, that horses' hooves clattered into the Inn yard at midday. Gwyn saw soldiers, their faces red and sweating after the fast ride, as she stood cutting meat for stew in the kitchen. In this weather, with the fires in the kitchen high for cooking, they kept all doors and windows open. The soldiers' shirts were stained with sweat, and someone was calling for drinks, lots of it, and food, and more drink. She dried her hands and went out into the yard.

Burl was hauling up buckets of water for the seven horses. "It's the Steward," he said, his face red with effort and his dark hair matted on his face and neck. "Your father wants you in the barroom."

Six soldiers hunched over six servings of pastry at a long table. They were eating in a great hurry, Gwyn thought. They drank thirstily. One of them thumped an empty mug down on the table, banging it like a drum. "More ale—where's that man?"

Gwyn hurried to take his mug. Da joined her behind the counter, returning from the guest parlor. "There's to be a tithe for the crops," he told her quietly. "We all have to go hear what it is. Steward's orders. Find your mother and Tad, will you?"

Gwyn nodded. The tithe would be used, she thought, to refill the storehouses emptied by the Doling Rooms. It would be wise to have them full again, even if the crops promised well for full larders through the winter. She took up the mug and leaned over the soldier's shoulder to put it near his hand. He was too hungry and thirsty and full of his business to notice who served him.

"—the fame of being the ones to make such a capture," he was saying.

"And is that the kind of fame you'd like? To be the man that brought Jackaroo to hanging?"

Gwyn froze where she was.

"It's not Jackaroo, you clot; it's some villlage boy— Steward knows him."

"Steward's eager to hang anyone, just so's the Earl's questions are answered."

Gwyn turned and fled from the room.

He would have spent the days asking questions and listening to the answers, she thought. She found Burl in the yard and gave him the order to find Mother and Tad. She looked around her, but the only horses in the Inn were those seven. She could not take one of those.

"Gwyn, what's wrong?" Burl asked.

"Nothing, nothing's wrong. Oh—they're going to announce a tithe on the crops—and—" She had no time to make further excuses. She ran into the kitchen and through it. Burl moved more slowly into the barroom, where the soldiers called out for more drink and continued their argument.

It was all her doing, Gwyn knew. But she would have thought that the Steward could have found a lie to satisfy the Earl. Instead, he had asked questions and heard how the Weaver's son mocked and boasted. She should have found another way to return his ring, she thought, running up through the woods. The Steward was a Lord, after all, and the Lords did not let you shame them.

Her breathing was ragged as she stood in Old Megg's empty hut, and her hands shook as she stripped off her own clothing to change into Jackaroo's trousers, shirt, tunic, boots, and cape. Cam should have known better. She was tempted to leave him to his fate, but she could not do that.

It wasn't even, she realized, that she cared what his fate might be. But since it was her responsibility, she had to do something about it.

What that something would be, she had as yet no idea. That realization was like a splash of cold water over the panic that burned at her. She undid her braids and piled them on top of her head calmly. Her mind at last was working. As she tied the mask over her face, belted the long sword at her side, and picked up the soft hat, she worked at the difficulties.

Although she heard the bell summoning people, she did not run back to the village. There would be time, time for the people to gather, time for the Steward to make his announcement. Now that her mind worked coolly, she knew what she had to do. If Jackaroo stood up before the people and the soldiers, the Steward could not arrest Cam. But she must have a horse, to ride away on; and they must not have their horses to pursue her.

Gwyn approached the village from a hill opposite to her usual path. As she descended, she could see people gathered in the central green, while a soldier stood by the well, ringing the bell insistently. Some men hurried down a hillside to the west, and Da led Mother and Tad out of the woods. She watched them hurry along between the houses, to join the crowd at the well.

Gwyn crept down behind the Blacksmith's house, where the horses were tethered. She untied them, wrapping the long reins tightly around their saddles so that they would not catch their feet as they ran. One horse she brought to the back door to the Blacksmith's shop, looping the reins through the latch. He whinnied gently, his head turned back towards the others. Gwyn left the door open and slipped into the shop. The fire burned at the forge; the bellows and hammer lay where they had been dropped. She crept to the front door and took off her hat.

Standing unseen behind the doorway, she heard the Steward's voice explaining to the people that the tithe was the Earl's way of husbanding supplies against the need of the Doling Room during the winter, explaining that this was yet another way the Earl looked out for the welfare of the people. Hearing the man's smooth and convincing words, Gwyn wondered why he was frightened of the Earl. Surely the Earl knew his Steward's value.

It was not fear of the Earl, she suddenly knew as surely as if she had been there to hear their conversation about the ring. It was not fear that drove the Steward. It was his own desire for revenge. The rumors of the Earl's anger were only rumors and perhaps started by the Steward himself. Maybe, she thought hopefully, this story of an arrest was also only soldier's rumors. Gwyn stood in the protection of the forge doorway, looking out around at the scene before her.

The Steward stopped talking, and the air waited quiet around him. Gwyn watched, where his hair lay pale and flat over his scalp. His voice carried easily across the village cupped between the hills, for all who stood facing him to hear. Gwyn watched the people's faces as they listened attentively to the Steward.

"There is a man," he said, speaking out again, "who has been preying upon the Lords, as other men have been preying upon the people." He let his meaning sink in. "There is a man who has taken from the Bailiff taxes the people have paid out of their own hardships. He has urged discontent upon the people, leading them to wish to act against their Lords."

Few men gathered there were innocent of complaints against the Lords and guilty eyes fell before the Steward's glance.

"He has dared to come even into the Doling Room— taking food from the hungry," the Steward's voice announced. Gwyn moved back into the shadows and put on the hat, settling it firm on her head. That it was lies did not matter, if the people believed the Steward. She stepped into the shadow of the doorway.

"I have come today to take that man, who has made the people doubt the Lords and the Lords doubt their people." He pointed with a finger and gave the order, "Take him!"

Gwyn watched through the doorway. She would wait for her moment in silence and then she would step out, to announce herself. *You have the wrong man*, she would say, low and bold. As soon as they had all seen her, she would turn and run.

Da stood with one arm around Mother and the other around Tad. Rose had worry and fear on her face, where she stood next to Wes. Everybody's eyes followed the soldiers, who marched in formation to pluck Cam out. The people near him stepped back.

Cam tried to pull free from their hands, shaking his head, his eyes wide with terror. He looked around, searching out the faces of the people. "But I didn't," he said, "I never did. I never would." The Weaver cried aloud and held one of the soldiers by the arm. The people were stiff with fear and surprise. "You all know me," Cam wailed.

The soldiers dragged him before the Steward and pushed him roughly onto his knees. The Steward smiled down at Cam. Gwyn watched, motionless.

"You've got the wrong man. My Lord, I never did those

things; you've got to believe me. Ask anyone." He grabbed at the Steward's hand, clutching it in his own. "Somebody tell him!" He turned to look at the people. Nobody spoke.

"You will recall that ring," the Steward said. He was enjoying this.

"But I didn't do it," Cam wailed, dropping the hand and covering his eyes with his own hands, to hide his tears. "It's not right to hang me; I never did. It's not fair." He cowered on the grass at the Steward's feet.

"What a man is this, people," the Steward called over Cam's bent head. "Is this your Jackaroo, then?" His questions were greeted by a shamed silence.

The soldiers stood near to Cam, three on each side.

Gwyn stepped out from the doorway. Nobody saw her. She took air into her lungs.

"Look!" Cam cried. Still on his knees, he pointed with his arm off to the path leading from the woods.

Gwyn's head swung around.

There at the edge of the trees stood Jackaroo, his feet wide apart, his face hidden by a black mask that fell down over his chin, a bright red feather in his wide hat. He held a thick staff in gloved hands, and he stood there in dappled sunlight, as straight and strong as the staff he held.

"I think you are looking for me?" he asked. "I don't think you want to take the wrong man." His voice rang out, as rich and warm as the hills swelling under sunlight.

Gwyn stepped back into the shelter of the Blacksmith's shop, although there was little danger that anyone would notice her. Everyone in the square stood motionless, except Cam. He scrambled to his feet and slid back into the crowd, wiping his face with his sleeve, already grinning.

Gwyn didn't know what to do. She would have to disappear, and quickly.

"If you will take any man, Steward, it must be me," Jackaroo called down. His voice rolled over the quiet scene, calm as the land itself.

Burl's voice.

What was Burl up to? Gwyn thought angrily. What did he think he was doing, dressing up as Jackaroo and standing there, so close, just asking for trouble.

"Take him, you fools," the Steward finally found his voice. "I don't care if you take him alive, as long as you take him."

Gwyn didn't wait to watch what the soldiers would do. She wheeled around and ran to the back door. She mounted the horse, who stepped back nervously at her haste. "Hwyya!" she cried, riding among the four horses who still lingered. They trotted away from her, heading up over the hillside. Their own stables were in Earl Northgate's City and that was where she hoped they would go.

Two soldiers appeared around the Blacksmith's house as she turned her horse's head to ride away. They did not pay any attention to her, in their pelting race to capture their own mounts.

Two gone meant four would be after Burl, Gwyn thought. She entered the woods, her mount slowed to a walk, her ears listening. She heard voices calling, and the sound of men breaking through underbrush. She followed the sounds, bent low over the horse's neck. The last thing she needed at that time was to be dismounted by a low branch.

A voice called out in recognition, and others answered it. Gwyn urged the horse on.

The soldiers had caught up with him in a shallow dell near the far edge of the woods, not far from the Inn. He had turned to face them there, his staff held in both hands. Three of the soldiers were closing a broad circle around him, while the fourth lay cursing and clutching his ankle where he had fallen. The soldiers had their short swords out and spoke to one another. "He's only got the staff. Move in now, easy. He'll surrender soon enough. We'll even take him alive."

Gwyn walked her horse onto the path behind them and unsheathed her sword. At the sound of ringing metal, their faces turned to her. She spoke over their heads to Burl: "My Lord, you had better find your own horse and be off. I can hold them here."

His masked eyes met hers, but he didn't move. It was the soldiers who moved, joining closer together, conferring. They were in the middle, between the two Jackaroos, at the hollow at the base of the dell. "Go now," Gwyn ordered Burl.

"As you wish, my Lord," he answered her.

He turned up the hillside, into the trees, and Gwyn gave her attention to the soldiers, who did not quite dare to move to follow him. They were muttering to one another, two blades held toward her, one towards Burl's retreating figure. There was no one to give them orders, and they were not used to that. All she had to do, Gwyn told herself, was keep them occupied long enough for Burl to make the safety of the Inn. Once there, he could hide in any of a dozen places where they would never find him.

The soldiers seemed to realize this, belatedly. One of them broke away from his fellows to follow Burl. Gwyn rode right at the three, then, forcing her reluctant horse. She hoped that their instinctive fear of being trampled would override their skill with the swords. She rode right at one soldier, who threw himself into the bushes to avoid her.

Once beyond the three, she turned again, trying to hold the horse in control. The soldiers muttered together, their eyes fixed on her. The fourth soldier called out: "If you lose this one, there'll be the devil to pay."

"It's the devil playing against us now, I don't wonder," panted the man Gwyn had driven into the bushes. "There's no sword made to kill a man already dead."

"Do you not see that it's two different men, you superstitious fool?"

"I see what he wants me to see," the soldier muttered. "There's never a soldier sent out has taken him. And many sent out that never returned, these hundred years."

"I see one man in two places," another said.

"Circle him round," the fourth advised.

"Aye, if he's living we can take him," one of the three said boldly. This rallied them.

The three soldiers split apart, one staying in front of Gwyn the other two circling to her sides. Their faces were grim. Gwyn watched their movements, her sword out and ready. She didn't know what she should do. She didn't even know how to use a sword in battle. She understood then exactly how ill-prepared she was for the role she was playing.

Her horse backed nervously beneath her. For a second, she thought she would lose her balance, then she clamped her legs tighter. The horse must do as she willed. And, if they had her, they would pay for the capture, she promised herself. But they wouldn't take her if she could help it. She had the horse, and they had none. She had the long sword and their own fear.

Gwyn slashed with her sword at the man on her left. He backed off and she turned quickly to the man at her right. It was his arm she hit—for a brief time the sword felt thick and heavy in her hand, before she pulled it free. She did not hear his cry, but looked to the front, where the third soldier reached out to grab at the horse's bridle.

Without thinking, Gwyn dug her heels into the horse's sides. The horse leaped forward. She saw the soldier's face close as she went past him, and she felt his lunge at the leg she thrust out to kick him off. Her horse shied to the side. Swaying, Gwyn grabbed for his mane with both hands. She dropped her sword.

There was nothing else for it now, so she bent low over the animal's neck and urged him on, into the woods, away from the path. Burl had his head start and that was all she could do. She must make her own escape now. Jackaroo could not be captured. Riding low over his neck, she slapped at the horse with her hand, forcing his pace.

She kept to the woods until she was beyond the village, then she headed across open land, down hill and up. She had no idea where the soldiers were. She was coming up on the vineyard before she realized that she stayed in the saddle only by her hands wrapped into the horse's mane, that her body bounced helplessly. Only one leg gripped at his sides, and that was no good. She looked curiously down at her left leg.

Blood streamed out from the split leather. It ran down

over the shoe, thick and red. Gwyn's head swam at the sight, and at the recognition that it was pain she felt, spreading outward from a numbness at her leg. The horse threw her off.

Gwyn landed with a blow that knocked the breath from her body and knocked her hat off. She had no time to think. She was just below the vineyard, so she grabbed at the hat and forced her legs under her. She stumbled up between the rows of vines and fell down onto her knees again concealed.

The sun poured down on her back and her ears rang. She could hear nothing but a curious whimpering breeze and her own heartbeat. Beside her, the twisting vines rose, each one covered with broad leaves and heavy with purple grapes. Gwyn's mouth was dry and painful, and she wished the grapes were ripe. She would have liked to put a grape into her mouth and feel it burst there with sweet liquid.

The whimpering came from her own mouth, and she clamped her teeth shut over it, to silence it. There was no sound of pursuit, but she thought there would be pursuit. She knew now how the hares felt, when the dogs were after them. Like the hares, she was too frightened to move. But she would like, she thought, to have just one grape and to burst it with her teeth.

And she would have liked, she thought dizzily, to know what Burl was doing dressed up as Jackaroo, although she began to believe she had imagined all that. She was no longer quite sure how she had come to be crawling here in Da's vineyard, with one leg uselessly dragging behind her, and the soil soft and clinging underneath her. She remembered that she must not be found as she was, although she didn't know what was wrong with the way she was.

Gwyn dragged herself across the dirt of the vineyard between the tall rows of vines. Insects buzzed all around her. She did not know why it was so important to keep her hold on the hat she clutched, which slowed her down terribly and was, anyway, too bent and dirty ever to be worn again.

She emerged at the crest of the hill on her knees and looked down the long distance to the hut and shed. That steep distance, she rolled down, which seemed—curiously—to take no time at all. The first thing she did, when she came to a stop against the goat pen and pulled herself up once again onto her knees, was vomit.

Gwyn slid under the fence, pulling with her arms because her legs were of no use to her, and dragged her stubborn left leg behind her as she made her wormlike way across the pen to the open gate. What luck that the gate was open, she thought, crawling up to the house. The door to the house was open too, and sh pulled her body inside.

Gwyn took off the mask she wore. But why should she wear a mask? She proceeded with her three-limbed crawl across the dirt floor to the open cupboard. It took some time to remember how the clasps of her tunic worked, but she knew she was undressing as fast as she could. As fast as she could was too slow, and although she did not know why she should hurry, she knew that she must.

The boots were hard to remove, especially the left boot with a gaping hole just below her knee. It was a pity that someone had slashed such fine leather, she thought, bending over to pull the boot down, wondering why it should be so painful to do that, as if her flesh too were slashed open. The boot was ruined, and that was a great waste.

She had shoved all the clothes up into the cupboard, but with the nagging sensation that she had not done things right, when her strength gave out. Gwyn thought she would lie on the bed until she felt better, except that the bed was far away and a girl had left her skirt out on it. Gwyn hoped the girl wouldn't be frightened to find her here, in her home. She hoped the girl would have something to drink, too.

Gwyn pulled herself up onto her one good leg, her hands on a wooden table, to see if the girl was on the bed. She tumbled forward onto her face. At least, the strange thought drifted across the cloudy blackness of her mind, Burl was safe. The black clouds closed in around her.

Twenty-five

GWYN SWAM through fire—someone, at the back of her mind, asked if this was burning and were the dead then not meat at all. She turned to ask someone how the news could be carried back to the living, but nobody stood there. The fire was water, and she let it drown her.

Gwyn toiled along the mountain's stony face. The stones burned underfoot and against her palms. They burned where they touched her leg. She had to find the eastern pass the Lord had spoken of, but she lacked a leg so her progress was slow. Sweat poured down over her naked body. She stood under the waterfall then and opened her mouth to take in the sweet cold water. When her foot slipped on the rock, she had no strength to grasp at the stones, so she let the waterfall carry her down, laughing aloud as she tumbled along the foam.

Jackaroo rode by her, in the night. He reined in in front of her and took off his mask. He was Win, with his wolfish features and his sad laughter. He took off his mask. He was a girl, her hair the color of maple leaves in autumn, riding high and proud. He took off his mask. He was a Prince, just a boy . . . No, a young man and angered, and the dark figure on the horse took off his mask. He was dead, long dead, his eyes blind sockets and his fleshless jaw hanging down. He rode his horse over her. The iron hooves pounded on her leg. Then Jackaroo's bones crumbled and the heavy tunic fell down upon her. He wanted to smother her.

Gwyn opened her eyes. Heavy bedclothes lay over her. It was a dream. She was alone. She slid into sleep.

It was dark when she awoke again. A sound in the darkness had roused her. She could not turn her head. Light came —a candle. She remembered how to turn her head and saw a dark figure seated with its back to her, its head low so that all she could see was the dark shape of shoulders.

This was Old Megg's hut she lay in, but she was too tired by the effort of moving her head to be surprised. Hazily, she remembered Gaderian. He must build a fire, or they would freeze.

The figure at the table turned around, but it was Burl. "I knew you were," she said.

"Are you awake then," he asked her.

Gwyn shut her eyes.

She heard him bring a stool over, near to her head.

"If you would eat," he asked her.

She opened her eyes. "I'm not hungry."

"Aye, Gwyn, and you are." It was easier to agree than to argue. He had soft pieces of bread, which he soaked with wine before dropping them into her mouth. She swallowed as many as she could before raising her hand to push his hand away.

In the candlelight his eyes were shadowed. She fell asleep.

Light lay in the room when she awoke again. The window over the bed was open, as was the door. Burl was still there. There was pain in her left leg, which throbbed and burned. She pulled herself up in the bed, but had no strength. He fed her again, cold broth into which he dipped pieces of bread.

"What happened?" she asked him.

At that, he laughed aloud, putting the bowl back on the table and bringing a bucket of water to her bedside. "I must change the bandage on your leg."

"I remember *that*," Gwyn said angrily, dismayed at how weak her anger sounded. "But what happened since then. That's what I want to know."

He didn't answer her, and she lacked the courage to look down at her leg. She felt him unwrapping, then the cool water, and then a dry, tight bandage. She should have had the courage to look, she thought.

"In the cupboard, Burl," she remembered.

"No, I've buried them," he soothed her. "You've had a fever—the wound inflamed. It's been five days. The sword cut almost down to the bone, and then—it was filthy. I had salt for it. Aye, Gwyn, you didn't like that. But it's healing now."

"Next time I'll look at it," she promised. "But Burl—" She tried to sit up.

"Nay, rest, I'll tell you." He sat down on the stool. She fixed her eyes on him and waited.

"You look tired," she finally broke his silence.

"Aye and you look yourself like death. I made it safely back. I thought you would come later, but you didn't. I didn't know what to do and Tad—he thought you might come here. So we came here and found you."

"Thank you," Gwyn said. "Tad?" she asked him.

He shrugged.

"How did you know?"

"I watched where they held Win, that night. I didn't know what you were thinking of, why you had brought food and wine to the soldiers, what you might try. I saw you go into the prison house."

"But I was—"

"Osh, and you think I don't know how you walk? And didn't you recognize me?"

"But how did you?"

"You've been in a fever these five days. I have come, when

I could. Tad too, but they keep him close. They say," and his eyes stayed quiet on her face, "that the Weaver's son has gone to be a soldier."

Gwyn didn't know why he told her that as if it mattered.

"They say that the Innkeeper's daughter ran off to be with him. It's certain that she hasn't been seen nor heard of since that day. She has taken her gold with her, they say."

Gwyn swallowed that information. Then she sputtered with weak laughter. "There's not much gold left. Aye, Mother'll not be pleased. Does Da—?"

"They say it serves him right. They say it's time he had some bad luck to bring him even with others, after he spoiled the girl so."

"He doesn't know?"

Burl shook his head. "If you had died," he explained, "it would have made no difference. I don't know now what you want him to know."

"I would not have him think I ran off with Cam."

"He's sent for the men to pick the grapes," Burl told her.

"Then I have to get out of here." Alarm gave her energy.

"We have a day or two yet. You should sleep again now. I have to return before I'm missed."

She didn't argue. Besides, she was exhausted, and sleep was welcome.

Someone who was not Burl entered the hut, waking her, late in the afternoon, stepping out of golden sunlight. Gwyn felt her helplessness sharply.

"It's only me," Tad said. "How are you?" He too carried a bowl. He too pulled the stool over to her bedside, as if he were accustomed to do so.

Surprise opened Gwyn's mouth, and he put in a piece of bread, soaked in lukewarm broth, into it. She chewed and swallowed impatiently. "I can feed myself," she told him.

Tad grinned at her. "Burl said you were much better. Aye, you frightened me, Gwyn. And why did you do that, anyway," he asked, switching to anger.

"I don't know what you mean," she mumbled.

"I saw you throw that ring. I'm not as stupid as you think."

Gwyn ate with her fingers and considered her little brother. "I've never thought you stupid," she told him at last. "It's good to see you, Tad."

"And you, Gwyn. It's good to see you. I thought—we were afraid—"

"That I'd run off with Cam? Well, I can understand why you would," she finished his sentence for him.

"No, I knew you wouldn't do that. Da only thinks so because Mother wants him to."

"She dotes on you."

"Aye, she does. Well, that needn't ruin my life, think you?"

"No."

"What we thought was that you'd die."

"Without you, I might have, as I understand it. But I didn't, did I? What I'll do now, since I haven't died, I don't know—except I think I need to go to the privy."

"Oh good," Tad said, then he blushed red. "No, I mean, you've been so sick, and we couldn't stay with you. They'd know, if I left the Inn at night. Burl's making you a crutch to walk with, he'll bring it here tonight. Use my shoulder," he offered.

They hobbled together down to the privy, and then back again. Gwyn's forehead was cold with sweat when she finally lay back on the bed. "Are you all right?" Tad asked.

"Weak. I didn't know I'd be so weak. Tad—" Her hands flew to her ears and then to the rest of her head, where there were no braids. "Where's my hair?"

"We had to cut it off. You were twisting and it was hot, you said."

Gwyn's fingers found where her hair stopped, just below her ears.

"I'm sorry, Gwyn. We had to."

"That's all right. It just felt so strange for a minute. How do I look?"

"Pretty terrible," Tad told her. "Burl will think of something," he promised her.

Gwyn was asleep again, before she could answer that.

Gwyn's strength came back rapidly, with food. Burl brought her an awkward crutch. They talked about what she might do, where she might go, as she made slow progress around the little room, her skirt clumsy around her leg. "Don't tire yourself," he warned her.

"There'll be an empty holding I know of, north of Hildebrand's City, but the house is burned," Gwyn said. "Or that one we went to in the winter, where the three men—"

"Aye, Gwyn, you cannot stay nearby."

"But that's not near, and I don't ever need to . . ." she started to argue. But he was right. It was only what Win had told her. "Then I'll go to the mountains," she said. She would live high in the mountains, in a cave the first winter, but she should be able to build some kind of shelter, later. She would live high and solitary in the mountains. The idea pleased her.

"That's foolishness," Burl told her. "How could you live there?"

"There will be a way."

Burl shook his head. "No, you can't do that."

A house of stone, a little house, and when the aspen shivered gold in the fall she would stand among them. She didn't bother to answer Burl.

"You will not do that," he told her.

Who was he to tell her what to do? As if she were his servant.

"You're not a foolish girl, Gwyn; you've got a good head, better than most. Use it."

She wouldn't answer him, when he spoke to her so.

"If you go to the mountains you'll only die. What would you eat? Where would you shelter? You know nothing of how to trap animals, if there are any about. You know nothing of how to protect yourself there, or how to build a house."

Just because he was right didn't mean she wouldn't do as she wished.

"We'll have to think of something else, Innkeeper's daughter."

"Do you think I haven't tried?" she demanded.

"Aye, that's just what I do think," he told her calmly.

Well, he was right. But she would have liked to live among mountains. It would have suited her.

"South, then—and—I know the work of an inn, there'll be inns to the south. Or if I could find entertainers from the fair? Do you think they would ever take someone in to work for them?" Her shoulders sagged, and the rough crutch, which forced her to bend over painfully, bit into her armpit. But it was no good regretting. "Or the Lords, our Lords from the winter, I could find them out to go into service." That would at least keep her fed. She was not sure, otherwise, how she might keep herself fed. She had never understood before how much it was to be sure of your roof or your dinner.

"They came from the south," Burl said thoughtfully. "There was the falcon on their saddles," he explained.

"I saw it."

"We don't know how they will have fared during the war."

Gwyn had never thought about that. She hoped that both of them had come through it alive. "He was with the King," she said. That at least was hopeful.

"Aye, he was the King's man, first."

Gwyn sat on the bed, the strain of moving having used up her strength. "I couldn't travel far, as I am."

"No, you'll come with me tomorrow," Burl told her. "I will tell them I bought you from the priests in Hildebrand's City. Until you're strong again," he said to her astounded expression. "Aye, Gwyn, we have no choice," he apologized, as weak tears slid down her cheeks. "The pickers will arrive, and you can't be seen. I can think of no other way."

He didn't know at all why she was weeping, and neither did she, really, except at the wonder of having such a friend.

"It won't be for long, I promise you," he comforted her.

. . .

They were making their slow way down to the Inn, avoiding all the hills they could, Gwyn bent over the crutch, hidden beneath Burl's long winter cloak, when they heard the bell summon the people to the village. The notes of the bell rang out, calling them where they stood, just within the woods that separated the village from the Inn.

Gwyn felt the same alarm she saw on Burl's face. "You go ahead, I'll catch up."

"No, we must be seen together." She had learned better than to question him. They retraced their path until they stood at the edge of the village, next to the house where Win had been held.

It was Jackaroo who rang the bell, standing tall in his stirrups to pull on the rope. The villagers had gathered back near the Blacksmith's house—Gwyn saw Rose where she stood within Wes's arms. A few men hurried down from the fields. Still the tall figure on horseback, his face hidden by a red silk mask, his long boots folded down to his knees, rang the bell.

It was not until Da and Mother, with Tad behind them, hurried down the path into the village that he ceased his clamorous call and sat easily back on the saddle, keeping the horse motionless with one gloved hand on the reins.

Gwyn was transfixed at the sight of him. He sat the horse as if he had been born to it. He was a man of purpose and authority, with or without a mask. He was Jackaroo himself. His silence, waiting for the Innkeeper's family to approach, had the patient certainty of mountains.

Had she ever appeared so to those who saw her? She could not believe that was true, but she knew it was. Because that was true, it was all worth it, whatever else might happen in her life.

"Innkeeper," Jackaroo called Da forward. Da stepped out alone. He looked worn, but not frightened as he stood before the mounted man.

"Innkeeper, would you be a Lord among the people?" Jackaroo asked, in a voice as cold and distant as the winds from the high mountains.

Da stepped back, as if Jackaroo had struck him. Then he shook his head slowly, no. He did not seem surprised at the question, Gwyn thought, her hand clenched tightly around the crutch.

"Then your holdings must go back to the men who first owned them. Will you do that, Innkeeper?"

Gwyn knew that voice, knew its cold authority. It was Gaderian's father.

"Hush, lass," Burl said softly.

"You needn't warn me," she whispered back. But she had not thought that the Lords, too, would go outside their own laws to ride as Jackaroo.

Da answered, "Aye, I will do that." He spoke plain and clear, for all to hear.

Jackaroo reached under his cape to draw out, not a knife as Gwyn had unreasonably feared, but a rolled sheet of paper, tied around with a red silk ribbon. His clear voice spoke so that all might hear. "In four days time, Earl Sutherland will ride from Northgate's City on this way to the High City. You will give him this, Innkeeper, for me. It asks that each Lord— each of the six Lords, each of the two Earls—set a day in every season when he will hear from the people themselves. It suggests that one man of the people take before his Lord the needs and requests of the people and any of their quarrels that the Lord must settle. It asks that the Innkeeper from the Ram's Head be the man for Hildebrand, and that all the men chosen be men of the Innkeeper's fair measure and men of substance who will understand the Lord's feeling for his land."

He reached down the paper to Da, whose hand rose to take it.

"Will you deliver this to Earl Sutherland?"

"Aye, I will," Da promised.

He had lost much and gained much, Gwyn thought. There was fair measure in that, too.

But if Win was right, what had Gaderian's father given up to ride as Jackaroo? Unless it was only the Lords who could ride outside of the law safely, and that was why any of the people who did must pay—for their high dreams, for taking a Lord's high place.

One among the villagers did not like what she had heard. The Weaver shoved her way out to the front, although she did not approach Jackaroo closely. "You give *him* honor," she cried out bitterly. "But I won't let him take it. The vineyard must stay with him, let him remember. He's taken everything from me—everything—so he must keep it, and I hope it will be bitter to him. He's taken the vineyard—aye, years ago, and he must keep it, for he'll not force me take it back and nor can you. And now his daughter has taken off my son, my only son, with her twelve gold pieces to tempt him—"

"Osh and hush your face," voices told her. "Thoughtless woman." "This is *good* news." She looked around at them and then stomped away, entering her own house and pulling the door closed behind her.

Jackaroo waited until her little surge of bitterness had died down, before he spoke again. "If you will do this, Innkeeper, you may tell the Earl one thing for me. Tell him that if the Lords will be advised by me in this, then I will sleep once again in the old stories."

Without waiting for any reply, he reined his horse sharply around and rode off at a gallop to the north, leaving behind him only the cold sound of his voice and the warning to anyone else who might think to ride as Jackaroo.

Gwyn looked to Burl's thoughtful face, but for a wonder could think of nothing to say.

⁓⊚ Twenty-six

I T WAS NOON of the fourth day that Tad, who had been watching along the King's Way, came running into the Innyard, calling out to his father and mother that the Earl was on his way. Gwyn hid herself by the sheltering door to the stables. The sky overhead was gray, promising rain by evening. Rain or sunshine were the same to Gwyn. She saw neither, kept away in Burl's little box of a room. She had stood that first afternoon beneath Mother's bitter words, her exhausted body held up by the crutch, the cloak covering her face and her cropped head. Why Burl needed to bring such a useless creature to them, nothing but another mouth to feed, when he had gold pieces for someone strong. What had he intended, doing such a thing without first asking his master's permission? Whether he didn't intend some disservice to the Inn, and how could he be trusted now, she had wondered.

"Aye, wife, a man should have a woman."

"It's not this one who will bear him children—look at

her," Mother said. Then she had turned away saying, "I don't know what our world is coming to," with such confused unhappiness in her voice that Gwyn couldn't blame her cruel words.

Gwyn had fallen onto the pile of straw that served Burl for a bed, too worn out to even think over the events of the day. All the next day she lay there alone in the windowless room, without even the spirit to get up. The next day, however, and the day after, she had walked the tiny room, to make herself stronger. By the third day she no longer needed the crutch, and she could see by the thick clotted crust on her wound that it was healing and that the scar it would make would be a broad white slash down her calf forever.

Burl brought her food, and some few times Tad came to sit and talk with her. Burl slept in the empty stable, when he slept. They told her, between them, all the news of the day. "But where did you get Jackaroo's clothes," she finally asked Burl, when she realized he wouldn't volunteer that information.

"They were hidden under a floorboard in your Grandda's room," Burl told her. "When I found them, I left them there, when I was clearing the room. But I thought that day—when it was Cam they were after—that you'd want something to save him."

They sat by the light of a single candle. Gwyn was on the straw, with her back against the warm stones of the chimney. The crutch she no longer needed leaned by the door, near to where Burl sat facing her. If he had stretched out his legs, as she had hers stretched out, their feet would have touched.

"That's true," she said. She didn't have any interest in continuing that subject, however. "Are there many then, hidden away under floors and behind cupboards?"

"So I think. There must be some truth behind it all, to begin all the stories."

"And in castles too," she added, trying to fit that into her understanding of what could go on in the world.

"Aye, so it seems," he answered.

On the third night, Tad brought Da into the room. He sat with Gwyn for a long time, but said almost nothing. Later he returned with Mother, who was almost speechless, with her tears and her clasping of Gwyn. She brought Gwyn a bundle of clothing tied into a blanket, scolding at her for her pig-headedness, telling Da his family must have bad blood in it, wondering if it wouldn't have been better if Gwyn had run off with Cam after all, telling Gwyn over and over again that she was sorry. She had thought of everything, even the soft cloths for Gwyn's time of the month, as a mother will. "What will you do?" they both asked her.

Gwyn could not answer that. "I won't turn to thieving," she said. "But what did Win do?"

Her parents looked at one another, then Mother answered her. "He came riding up to my parents' door, in all the finery, and he gave me a flower. A stem of quince blossoms it was. It was such foolishness . . ."

Gwyn wasn't about to argue with that.

"Did you recognize him?" she asked.

"How could I?" Mother asked. "It wasn't until later that I heard about what happened to him. But Gwyn, what will you do, where will you go?"

"I'll be well," Gwyn said.

"But how?" Mother asked.

Gwyn was worrying that same question as she stood by the doorway watching the double line of horsemen ride into the Innyard. They wore green tunics and short green capes. The first four carried high flags that rippled in the wind, the golden falcon on a green field with his wings spread out. Da came out and heard the order for wine and food, for the Earl who rode just behind them, and for his retinue who were thirsty and hungry.

Everyone who had come to wait at the Inn this fourth day had gathered outside the wide barroom door as the two horses, riding a little ahead of a dozen others, walked over the stones. The two were a man and a boy, both splendid in long green capes and soft green velvet hats, edged with white fur. Burl stood in front of Gwyn at the stable door, so that she might see without being noticed. She looked around his broad shoulder— and smiled.

Gaderian rode beside his father as a prince must ride, straight and solemn. His eyes, however, were not still. They searched the family and then went around to the windows and doors. As they came near Burl, Gwyn drew back.

"My Lord," Da sounded surprised.

"As you see me, Innkeeper," the Lord answered, his voice high and light and pleasant. "I remember your wine and your wife's pastry."

Da's mouth flapped. If Gwyn had been there, her mouth would have been flapping too. *So*, she thought. She looked over Burl's shoulder and saw the two dismounting, to be escorted inside for refreshments.

"Burl," she whispered. "I can go south with them. He said, the boy—" But that wasn't the first step. "You have to talk with them."

"I won't be able to get near them," Burl said. Gwyn knew he was right.

"I can follow them and catch them up," she said.

"They're mounted," Burl pointed out.

"Go find out what's happening," Gwyn ordered. Then she heard her voice and said, "Please, Burl, it's a chance."

He turned his face to her. "I'll be going with you," he told her quietly, and left before she could answer that.

Gwyn went back to the little room and stood in front of the table. A candle burned on it. If she had her paper, she thought—but she could not go up to her room to get it, and now Burl had gone it was too late to send him. If she had only thought. If she could only get some message to Gaderian, she thought. There was no charcoal in that room, to make marks on a piece of wood. Her knuckles rapped on the tabletop as she thought frantically. She stared into the candle's flame, as if the answer might lie there where wax melted down into a tiny pool before running over the sides to harden. The flame danced before her eyes. The Innkeeper's daughter was days gone from the Inn. She could not suddenly reappear, to hang off the Earl's stirrup and ask for shelter. There would be too many questions asked.

He had said, she remembered from a long time ago, that she could now trust him for anything. She hoped he spoke true, because she must trust him now.

The tiny pool of yellow wax rolled over the edges and slid down the candle's length, making a design like the icicles they had seen near the frozen waterfall.

And that was the way. Or, rather, it was a chance when she could think of no other.

Gwyn took the candle up in her hand and tipped it sideways in its stand, letting the melted wax form a pool as broad as her palm on the tabletop. When it was thick enough, she set the candle down and, with a piece of straw, started the letter G in the soft wax. The straw broke. She took another and doubled it over on itself, digging out the shape of the letter.

The wax cooled quickly. She levered it gently up from the wood and—holding it gently in her hand—took up the parcel of clothing in her other hand. She returned to the stable door. She waited for the Earl and his son to reappear. If Burl could get the wax into Gaderian's hand, if he would understand it, if his father would give him his way . . . If, if, again, she thought. So much depended on chance.

She held her crutch at her side as she waited. Burl hurried across the Innyard, to tell her that they were rising from their lunch, and two men went to bring forward the Earl's horses from where they grazed beyond the Innyard.

She put the wax into Burl's hand. "You have to give this to him, to the Lordling," she told him.

"Aye, Gwyn." He started to protest, but she saw the two men returning, mounted and leading the riderless horses forward.

"Burl, just do it, please," she asked.

"What is it?" He looked at the disk flat in his hand.

"It's a G. A letter, the first letter of my name."

"You know letters?"

She nodded impatiently.

"All of them? Do you know—"

"Burl."

"Could you teach me?"

"Yes." She would have promised Burl anything to get him moving before it was too late. "Just give it to him, to the Lordling."

"You're a terrible woman when you've got your mind made up," he told her. She had no time to wonder at the laughter in his voice. She just shoved him out of the doorway.

The Earl mounted high on his horse. His son mounted beside him, his face masked into a formal expression as he gathered the reins into his gloved hands. His eyes no longer searched the Inn yard.

"I will read this, as you ask," the Earl said to Da, holding the rolled paper that he had, himself, given Da a few days ago. Gwyn smothered laughter. There was so much masking and masquerading going on, it was a wonder the world didn't just crumble apart, like an overdone pastry. But she didn't mind. It made a fine joke.

That was, she thought, what Win had meant, perhaps. The joke had been enough for him, and it might be enough for her; since she had given up everything else. She relaxed for a minute, to enjoy the Earl's performance.

"And I will report what the man told you to the King," the Earl said.

"Thank you, my Lord."

"But I am sorry to hear that your daughter is gone," the Earl went on.

"As are we," Da agreed, meaning more than the Earl could understand.

Meanwhile, Burl had slipped around the horses toward Gaderian. When one of the Earl's men tried to stop him, he called out, "My Lord?"

The Earl recognized him. "Yes, lad, what can I do for you?"

"I have a gift for your son," Burl said. He passed the wax disk to Gaderian, who took it with a puzzled expression. He looked first to his father for permission and then down at his hand. A mask seemed to fall over his face and his hand folded around the disk, crushing it.

Gwyn's heart fell.

Burl waited. The minutes stretched out as the Earl hesitated, politely, to see why Burl still stood before him. Burl said nothing.

Gwyn could have kicked him into speech, and her hands were clenched into fists under the silence forced upon her.

At last Burl risked speaking. "My Lord, I would go with you."

Gwyn let her breath out.

The Earl frowned. He looked at the Innkeeper and the frown didn't leave his face. "I don't think—"

"But Father," Gaderian interrupted. "We are in his debt."

The two Lords looked into one another's faces. Gwyn could have cried aloud with the waiting. However, these two had never spoken much with words, so perhaps this was their way. Her way had to be this helpless waiting.

"All right then," the Earl agreed at last. "If the Innkeeper will permit."

Da looked as surprised as everybody else. "I will," he said.

"My Lord. . . ." Burl's voice, calm as a summer afternoon, made another request. "I have a woman with me now."

Gwyn saw Gaderian's swift reaction to that, and how he held his eyes from searching the Innyard again. She leaned on her crutch, ready to step out. She would take nothing more than the parcel of clothing with her, and that was right. The Inn was Tad's, and the three gold coins in the purse under her pillow. He would never know, but they would pay him for the goat. So he would have fair measure of her.

"I will trust anyone who travels with you, lad," the Earl told Burl.

Burl waved a hand to Gwyn and she hobbled out into the yard. She saw the disappointment in Gaderian's face before her eyes returned to the ground. In her mind's eye, she held the image of the old woman, hobbling along beside her up the snowy Way, and she swung her head back and forth as the old woman had done and imagined the weakness in her bent legs as she stood hunched over her crutch among the horses at the center of the Innyard. Her appearance had shocked them, she could feel it. They ignored her, as people will when they do not like to see.

"You'll need to ride in one of the wagons, lad," the Earl said. "I'll find work for you, in my service."

"Thank you, my Lord," Burl said. Like everyone else, he ignored Gwyn. "I have everything that I need."

"Then we will go on."

Gwyn could see no higher than the Earl's legs, so she studied the stones at her feet as she listened.

"Innkeeper, I thank you for being a good master. And you, mistress."

"Aye, Burl," Da's voice answered slowly. "I'm sorry you must want to go. I had thought to leave my house a man who could serve it well and loyally."

Burl accepted the rebuke. "Such servants come to houses that merit them," he answered.

They were talking with masks on their words.

"I had thought, lad," the Earl spoke sternly, "that you would keep your master's daughter from mischance."

"That was my hope, too, my Lord." Burl's voice was quiet, untroubled. That would puzzle the Earl, Gwyn thought, but it would comfort her parents.

"Maybe you'll come back." That was Tad's voice.

"Maybe," Burl answered. "But if I do, it will mean that I've failed."

"I don't care," Tad said stoutly. If she had not been so carefully acting her part, Gwyn would have smiled. The way was made, now, for Burl's return to the Inn. Everything was done.

The horses turned to go. She followed Burl's legs, losing distance at every step. She left the Innyard with her back bent over the crutch, her feet weak on the stones, the parcel dragging on the ground. She could not even turn her face to take a last look at her home, and that was hard, but it was how she must go.

◢◣◥ Twenty-seven

WEEKS LATER, Gwyn stood beside a broad river. The water ran with the colors of sunset. Thick forest crowded up to the bank opposite. The purple sky was wide overhead here, because of the cleared land behind her. Long feathered clouds stretched across it, their edges burning gold. Soon it would be autumn, although in the south, Gaderian had told her, autumn came later and the winters were not so severe.

She had traveled the entire Kingdom now, had even seen something of the High City, where the King's castle stood on a tall bluff looking over the joining of two rivers. She had crossed the southern lands, where fields rolled gently. She had followed the King's Way where it ran straight beside this broad river that flowed on now before her, heading south, into forests that spread for miles all around her. She was hungry, but her eyes were caught by the moving water and her ears by its steady chuckling conversation, so she did not turn back.

So much lay behind her now. Even in these recent weeks, starting from the evening Gaderian had burst into their tent, at the first dark. He had rushed through the entry and then stopped dead at the sight of her sitting cross-legged by a candle. "It's you!" he had cried, delighted. Then his dignity had fallen over his shoulders.

"Aye, my Lord," she said with a laugh.

He had become the boy again and crowded down next to her on the ground. "It's all right, Father knows where I am," he reassured Burl. "But what happened?" They had answered him with lies, as they must. He didn't question them carefully, because he had his own story to tell. At the end he told Gwyn: "Father knows."

"Knows what?" Was she in danger again?

"I told him about—how you took care of me and—how we talked and—and everything."

"Everything?"

"The letters too," he said. "But I don't think he's angry at you."

Gwyn considered this. "Is he angry at you?"

Gaderian looked uncomfortable. "Not very. He said it was a difficulty I had made for myself and would have to deal with myself. Because I'll be Earl too," he explained, as if she hadn't already figured that out for herself. But she could see what the Earl meant. It would be difficult to be a Lord and not despise the people. It would be more difficult to rule over people than cattle.

There was nothing she could say to Gaderian about this; she knew too little of what it was to be a Lord. So she answered the boy. "You'll make a fine Earl."

"I don't know. It's not easy, being an Earl," he told her. She knew enough to suspect just how hard it would be.

Once away from Hildebrand's City, Gwyn could uncover her head. No one would know her. The Earl's servants avoided her, except for occasional pitying glances, and his retinue never noticed her. To anyone else, she and Burl were just a part of the new Earl Sutherland's entourage, which made its stately way to the cities of his own lands, where he accepted the fealty of his Lords.

They had only themselves for company, she and Burl, but even so they did not speak much. The cart driver's ears could hear, or those sleeping close by. Burl played his pipe as the slow days passed, some bringing sunshine, some rain. They saw young crops in the southern fields, and burned holdings, and whole farms where a battle had turned the soil to mud. They saw men and women scarred by famine and battle, and children too. For all that, the people who came out to cheer the Earl seemed glad, with peace upon them.

The last city was walled, like Earl Northgate's City, a border fortification. As they had waited for the Lords' feasting within to come to a close, so that the Earl would return to his camp outside the city walls, Gwyn had known it was time to tell Burl that he might leave her now. Burl had his gold pieces. The land was at peace. He would be able to make a safe journey back to the Inn. She did not like to think of how much she would miss his company. However, only the forest waited beyond these walls, and beyond that the unknown kingdoms to the south where her own destination lay.

"It's time you turned back," she had told him. She still leaned on her crutch, even though they were alone by the broad river, which sparkled under moonlight.

"Aye and I think not," Burl answered.

"But Burl—you said it would not be long," she reminded him. "You said it would not be for long."

He wasn't looking at her. His eyes studied the surface of the running water. "Did you ever think, Innkeeper's daughter, how very short life is?"

"You're not answering me," she pointed out.

He didn't respond.

The next day, instead of heading back east to his own

city, the Earl led them into the forest, taking only Gaderian and two of his retainers. That day Gwyn walked upright, having discarded her crutch at the Earl's bidding. The wound had healed to angry red skin that was not even sensitive to the touch anymore. It felt good to walk free again. They slept out that night under trees. This was an old forest, filled with life of its own, where the wind whispered through heavy branches. They traveled for a second day, but on the morning of the third, the Earl and Gaderian told Burl and Gwyn to mount up behind them, and they left even those two retainers behind.

The path they followed led up to cleared fields, neglected and overgrown with brambles. A two-story stone house, with stone barns behind it, faced across a low meadow to the river. The forest wrapped the holding around.

The Earl led them through the house, with Gaderian running ahead, from room to room. The house had two bedrooms above and four rooms below, and a privy inside on the ground floor, next to the largest bedroom. The smallest room downstairs was lined with open cupboards in which books stood and flat maps were kept. Gwyn tried not to look too greedily at that room, and she tried not to wonder at the Earl's reasons for showing them over this abandoned house. The kitchen hearthstone was cold, and the big room beyond that filthy with dust and cobwebs. The barns held stalls and hay for animals to eat. It was curious, Gwyn thought—the holding was not so much abandoned as neglected, as if it had once been kept ready for visitors who had long since ceased to arrive.

"These are borderlands," the Earl said to Gwyn as they all stood again in front of the empty house. "This is a hunting lodge that belongs to me. It's been empty for—" He looked at his son.

"Years and years, since I was a boy," Gaderian answered.

"I would have you live here, as lodgekeepers," the Earl announced in his distant voice.

"But Father, I *told* you," Gaderian started to say, then

stopped himself at the expression on his father's face. Gwyn herself would have stopped speaking at that glance. This was the man, she reminded herself, who had fled the intrigues of his father's court to put himself under the protection of the King, letting his brothers slaughter one another in their greed. Now he gathered up their inheritance for his own. He was also the man, she reminded herself, who had ridden as Jackaroo, for the sake of the people. He was a man to respect and fear and trust.

"I would have lodgekeepers such as you," the Earl said. "I would have people I can trust at the borders of my lands."

Gwyn thought she could manage the house and a garden and some animals to feed herself. Service to the Lords would be her lot then, and it could have been a harder lot, she knew. It was Burl who wanted to refuse.

"Merchants travel the river, and our trade with the kingdoms to the south will increase. An Inn here will prosper, in time."

"Aye, it might that," Burl agreed, with doubt in his voice.

Gaderian subsided, with a grin at Gwyn.

"Earl Northgate told me a story," Gaderian's father said, looking at Burl, not Gwyn, "of his Steward, and Jackeroo. He had to force the tale from the Steward, but he finally got it all out of the man. When I heard it, I thought of the Innkeeper's daughter. Who had saved my son."

Gwyn didn't dare to look at the Earl or to speak. She couldn't be sure if the Earl was threatening Burl, or explaining himself. "As you wish, my Lord," Burl said.

"I will send you supplies, food, drink, seeds, and animals."

"But won't people ask questions if you do?" Gwyn protested.

"The people do not question the Lords," he reminded her.

And the Lords cared nothing for what people might say, Gwyn knew. Well, neither did she. "I thank you," she said.

"I would pay you for these, my Lord," Burl said. The Earl drew himself up, displeased. "Aye, it will be your own gold I pay you with," Burl reminded him. "The house is gift enough."

"But Burl," Gwyn started to say.

The Earl cut her off. "All right then, lad. And I will marry you before we leave you."

"But you can't," Gwyn said quickly. "I can't." She must not force Burl, who had been so good a friend, to be exiled from his own land. What kind of thanks would that be to him?

"Aye, Gwyn, you can," Burl spoke at her side. "My Lord, if we could step aside?"

He pulled Gwyn after him around a corner of the house where they could not be overheard.

"You know Da made the announcement." She turned on him angrily with the only excuse she could think of.

"When I thought you were lost in the blizzard," Burl told her, "it seemed a long time left that I must live. A long time, and the season would always be winter." His dark eyes held hers.

Gwyn was dumbfounded. "Why do you tell me that?" she said stupidly.

"I thought you would ask."

He had said exactly that to her, once before, she remembered, hearing in his calm voice the echo of his earlier words. At the fair it was, when he told her how the man had come to hang above the battlements. And Gwyn herself had thought that day, that if one man had seen the hanging body, as she had, then that man she might marry; but she had not even noticed at the time that Burl was that man. Well then, she must keep her word, she thought. What good fortune that she could keep her word so gladly.

"But my hair is so ugly," she said.

"Would you have your hair keep us from our years together?" he asked her, his voice—for once—not calm.

She shook her head, feeling oddly shy with him.

"Then will you have me, Innkeeper's daughter?"

She nodded her head, her eyes on the ground, her cheeks

warm, her heart rising up in gladness and gratitude. It was . . . more than she hoped for of her life, that such a man as Burl would ask for her.

She did not know how to tell Burl this. "Will we be southerners then?" she asked him.

"Outlanders, more likely."

"Yes. Well, that's fine," she said, not recognizing the sound of her own voice.

Burl led her back to the Earl, who said the words over them and then mounted his horse.

"My Lord," Burl said, calm again, to the mounted man. "I would not have my children be servants, unless they choose."

"Well, Gaderian?" the Earl asked his son, in that cold and distant voice.

"There's land to be cleared," Gaderian answered quickly. "Holdings could be made from the land, and a village. Empty forest earns no tithes," he reminded his father. "We'll come back, sometime," Gaderian promised. "For the hunting."

"I'll welcome you," Gwyn answered him.

"She's as good as you deserve, lad," the Earl said to Burl. "I have often thought how much I heard myself talking during those cold hours. I waited for rumors to reach me, but those rumors I never heard. I have wondered how to pay my debt to you."

So Burl had known all along. After the two Lords had ridden off, she had turned to Burl crossly. "You might have told me."

"Aye, I might have," he agreed.

Gwyn had laughed aloud then, at his answer, and she laughed again, but softly, remembering it. The river ran singing before her, and she thought they would make a boat, and she thought there would always be fish in the water if she could learn to catch them. She thought how much there was to do and how the work would suit her, and how the holding with its deep hearthstone would suit her, house, fields, forest, and river; and the man, too; the man especially. She thought it was past time to return to the house behind her, the Inn, and she wondered what they would call it. The Falcon's Wing, she thought; if Burl agreed, that name would do.

Burl appeared beside her. "Aye, Gwyn," he greeted her.

"Aye, Burl," she answered, having no words to tell her heart.

While the light held, they stood there together. Then they turned to go back. "But there will be no more Jackarooing about for you, lass," he told her, as they crossed the long grass of the meadow.

"What makes you think I would want to?"

He didn't bother to answer that.

"I know my luck," she spoke seriously.

"Sometimes I think we make our own luck. Think you? But you will tell me about all that happened, won't you? I'd like you to tell me. Before you forget the time."

"I won't forget the time," Gwyn told him. But even as she said that, she could hear in her imagination how she would tell the tales to Burl, and how they would change in the telling.

About This Point Signature Author

CYNTHIA VOIGT is the award-winning author of twenty novels for preteens and young adults, including *Homecoming;* Edgar Allan Poe award-winner *The Callender Papers;* 1984 Newbery Honor Book *A Solitary Blue;* and *Dicey's Song,* winner of the 1983 Newbery Medal.

Among Cynthia Voigt's other popular novels are *David and Jonathan, The Runner, Building Blocks,* and the Point Signature paperback *Orfe.* Her most recent Kingdom book, *The Wings of a Falcon,* will soon be available as a Point Signature paperback. The author's newest work is *When She Hollers,* published by Scholastic Hardcover.

Mrs. Voigt lives in Maine with her husband and the younger of her two children.